T0276926

THE
GUEST
HOUSE
BY THE
SEA

ALSO BY FAITH HOGAN

My Husband's Wives
Secrets We Keep
The Girl I Used to Know
What Happened to Us?
The Place We Call Home
The Ladies' Midnight Swimming Club
The Gin Sisters' Promise
On the First Day of Christmas

Faith Hogan

THE GUEST HOUSE BY THE SEA

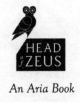

HEAD
of ZEUS

An Aria Book

First published in the UK in 2023 by Head of Zeus
This paperback edition first published in 2024 by Head of Zeus,
part of Bloomsbury Publishing Plc

9 7 5 3 1 2 4 6 8

A catalogue record for this book is available from the British Library.

ISBN (PB): 9781803282558
ISBN (E): 9781803282527

Cover design: Leah Jacobs-Gordon

Printed and bound in Great Britain by
CPI Group (UK) Ltd, Croydon CR0 4YY

Head of Zeus
5–8 Hardwick Street
London EC1R 4RG

WWW.HEADOFZEUS.COM

For James xx

June

Monday: The first day of the season

I

Esme

It was nonsense, complete and utter nonsense. It would take more than some fancy doctor telling Esme Goldthorpe she was going blind to stop her running the Willows. It had been in her family for almost two hundred years, run by the women of generations before her. Strong women, just like her own mother, who had died right here, just as she had been about to book in a party of five. And Esme had long since decided she would be no different; she would keep this place open, right up to the end. It would take more than a leaking roof or a notion of frailty to make her stop running the guest house. Sell out to the Fenlons indeed! That would be the day, over her dead body. She'd show them; there were years ahead of her yet and she intended to live every single one of them just as she pleased.

Now, where did she leave the guest book? She was quite sure that their first guest, Joel Lawson, was due to book in tomorrow.

Of course, Esme could ask Marta to help her find that book, but she wasn't completely helpless – regardless of what those eye tests showed. It had to be here somewhere; after all, she'd had her hands on it only a day ago. If only she could remember what she'd done with it or maybe, more accurately, where Marta had tidied it away. Marta had obviously been polishing again, the sour tartness of vinegar and lemon juice still lingered on the air. Esme wrinkled her nose as she searched everywhere she could think of. If right was right, it should be left on the Victorian desk that doubled as the guest reception. The last place she could imagine anyone wanting to store it was up here on this high shelf, but with Marta flying through the place armed with a duster in one hand and what smelled like a demonising array of cleaning products, well, the devil himself couldn't predict where anything would land. The strong, energetic woman from the Basque Country who had lived with Esme for over a decade cleaned more thoroughly than a dose of her grandmother's salts.

Only a few years earlier, Esme would have reached this shelf easily if she stood on her tippy toes – well, almost reached it. Esme dragged the low coffee table across the rug towards the sideboard and felt her way along until she knew she was at roughly the right spot. The table was sturdy, as robust as she'd need to balance safely; she was only a tiny woman, small and birdlike, where once she had been young and tough. It wasn't heavy; she edged it gently against the wall before her with her shin. Position was everything. She arranged it right at the centre of the old sideboard. It was all about reaching and patting her way along the uppermost shelves.

The table wasn't even a foot off the ground and wide enough for both of Esme's slippers; it was only a step, really.

It wasn't all that long ago since she'd scaled the rickety winding staircase in the nearby church without a second thought to sing with the village choir every Sunday. One deep breath and she was up. She felt her way along the shelf, her hands splayed, reaching deliberately as deeply as possible towards the back. Dust. She could feel it under her fingertips, soft and yet grainy. Damn, she should have tucked a cloth in her waistband; honestly, she thought, was there no beginning or end to getting this place in shape for the season?

She used the cuff of her sleeve to dust off the empty shelf. It was no good. The remains of what she assumed was a dead fly stuck stubbornly. She wet her thumb with a little spit, rubbed vigorously and perhaps it was this careless movement that unsettled her balance, because just as she was moving her cuff towards the spot again, she felt a disturbing wobble. Was the table about to go from beneath her? No, she knew as she drifted, swaying for what seemed like an age, over and back, over and back, it wasn't the table. She was suddenly light-headed. And then, as the room rose up around her, like an incoming, unstoppable tide, she was falling.

The thud when she hit the ground seemed inconsequential for a woman of her age. She lay there for a moment and began to laugh. Shock. It was ludicrous; she couldn't be lying on the floor of the main hall. She had far too much to do. She tried to pull herself up, but it was no good. Bruising against her thigh, she felt her mobile phone. She eased it out of her pocket, only mildly aware of the film of sweat beginning to pulse from her pores. She'd have to ring Marta to help her, which would result in a good-natured but stern lecture, rolled eyes and one of Marta's frowns, which filled her voice with even more worry, regardless of how much she believed Esme could not see. Perhaps, if she just rested, for a little while, the light-headedness would settle and nobody need know how silly she had been – falling off a coffee table indeed!

She held the phone in her hand for a moment. Suddenly, her head felt much too heavy to hold up and she was bleakly aware of a creeping wooziness. She was drowning in fatigue. Just in time, she hit the contacts button. At the very top, Marta had saved an emergency number with a line of capital 'A's. Esme smiled, remembering those days they spent trying to figure out how to use the mobile.

Then, she felt it; the most unbearable, crippling spasm – invading her system like venom, creeping slowly along her left calf. It was a radiating, chilling agony that briefly absorbed every thought, ominous in both its ferocity and stealth. *Who was she kidding? She was just a silly old woman and it was all too much for her.* Oh God. She hit the As, but her grip had deserted her and the phone fell from her hand.

'Marta,' she shouted, but it was little more than a murmur. She tried to gather up all her strength – 'Marta' – and by some miracle within seconds Marta appeared with her calm assuring voice, briskly moving about her. Assessing the damage done and then, vaguely, Esme was aware of her gently moving her wrist, feeling for a pulse, taking her cardigan from around her own shoulders and placing it over Esme.

For the most part, Marta's words drifted past her, she was vaguely aware of that familiar accented voice, 'Oh, Esme, what have you done?' Esme scrunched closed her eyes, tensed her whole body as if the pain might pass, but it didn't.

'... *fall, maybe unconscious, or perhaps a fracture, oh God,*' Marta was saying into the phone, but darkness fell then as the pain finally engulfed what remained of Esme's awareness.

A month before the
season begins...

2

Cora

Up until the first dance, everything had been perfect. It was such a beautiful wedding, all that Connor and Lydia had hoped for and more. Everything had gone off with hardly as much as a hiccup; the best man's speech had been funny and just the right side of tasteful. There were no embarrassing stories or bad language to upset the parish priest, who could at times be a bit of a dry stick. And even Father O'Sullivan himself had managed to give a sermon that was both sincere and entertaining, which might have been a first. The guests had arrived from all over, with a fair contingent from London who looked as if they'd never been further than the last stop of the Tube line before this. Connor and Lydia had more friends, it seemed, than Cora could count.

The women turned up in hats – when had hats come back into fashion? Cora had worn a feathery affair perched jauntily on her newly done hair, just to keep Lydia happy, but then she was the mother of the groom, and she had even persuaded Michael into a morning suit. Cora had admired him in his steely grey waistcoat, of course she hadn't said anything as she'd straightened his cravat, they'd long since stopped mentioning what the other looked like much beyond an undone button or a stain that hadn't shifted in the wash.

It really was the perfect wedding.

Cora enjoyed every second of it, until that moment.

She wasn't even sure what it was about seeing her son and his new bride dancing to a song that was such a hackneyed wedding tune it shouldn't have stirred anything more in her than admiration and joy for the lovely couple. Maybe she did know what it was and she just wasn't brave enough to put the words on it. She felt huge, hot tears well at the back of her throat – a mixture of joy and loneliness churned up in her after such an emotional day.

She was standing, an insignificant part of the large circle that swayed around the newlyweds, the band belting out the well-loved chorus. Even Connor rubbed his eyes and she knew he too was overwhelmed. He was filled with love for this girl who had stolen his heart four years earlier when they were both post-grad students in university.

The guests around Cora were heaving closer to the floor. Lydia's sister Lenore and the best man had taken up position to join the bride and groom for the first dance. Next it would be the turn of the parents. Lydia's parents were older than Cora and Michael, but she watched them take to the floor with a confidence that spoke as much about their ease with each other as their ability to dance together.

Michael was not a dancer, but he'd promised Lydia he would do one circuit, just one, and then he was off the hook for the rest of the evening. Connor nodded towards them now, it was their turn to join the dancing and Cora turned to Michael next to her. He placed one hand firmly on her hip; with the other he grabbed her hand. For a moment, she wondered if perhaps he'd been awake on some of those evenings she'd been engrossed in *Strictly Come Dancing*. They shuffled awkwardly about the floor. There was no conversation and she wondered about saying something, but honestly, she wasn't sure what to say to him.

Cora looked up into her husband's face and that was the moment she realised Michael was not really there any more. Well, that's to say, he was standing right in front of her, but he might as well have been sitting on the moon, because, suddenly, she was completely alone. In that split second it felt as if her very core shifted, as if the whole dance floor had been tipped at the slightest angle and her happy equilibrium sloshed over the side and so there was a discharging gap within her. She could almost feel her natural ease spill away from her. It was a strange sensation of being emptied of something vital, when she should have been brimming with nothing more than complete and utter joy.

Cora's mind began to race. When was the last time Michael had put his arm around her? She couldn't even remember the last time they'd held hands. It was strange, she could recall very clearly the *first* time they held hands. She was nineteen, he was twenty-three, and they were walking back from the local night club. His hand had been big and strong and, when she closed her eyes now, she could still remember how it felt when it enveloped her own. Her heart had missed a beat, in the way it does when you're young and it feels as if the simple things are absolutely momentous.

Surely they should be sharing this moment, and they were,

but somehow they weren't. In the important ways, they were a million miles apart from each other. Even though he was holding her tightly in his arms, there might as well have been the Suez Canal running between them, because they were in different worlds, never mind different continents.

How had this happened? How on earth had they become strangers while living in the same house and sleeping in the same bed for the last thirty years? Cora thought the music would never end; she felt like a fraud. No. She felt let down, cheated in some way by the happiness that seemed to be all around her and at the same time she was suffocating in its scarcity.

When the band finally milked the last chorus from the song – God how many times could they play the same string of lines over and over? – Cora stepped away from Michael. And then, without waiting another second, she raced from the reception. She needed to breathe, to make sense of the feelings that had completely overtaken her. She stepped outside into the cool night air. The sky was filled with stars, a few smokers standing about chatting beneath an awning at the side of the hotel. She walked, as steadily as her kitten heels allowed, towards the car park. She had no real destination in mind; she just needed to escape. She rounded the car park, which was far too brightly lit, and panic rose up in her. What was she doing here? How had things turned out like this? How could she go on living with Michael when it felt as if there was nothing left between them any more? Tears rolled down her cheeks and Cora cried as if her heart was broken, because, maybe, suddenly, she realised it just might be.

One week before the

season begins...

3

Phyllis

Phyllis wasn't sure when it had started, exactly, but she knew precisely where it would finish, even if she didn't want to admit that to herself, and she certainly wasn't ready to offer up her thoughts to anyone else at this point. It was early days. Wasn't that what people said in order to make things seem better? Maybe it worked for slow-growing roses that didn't take off in their first year. But this was different. Alzheimer's and dementia didn't get any better with time, they got worse. This much she knew from the bitter experience of watching her father-in-law slowly drift away from the people he loved.

Today, with the sun shining and the garden almost bursting with summer colour, it was easier to convince herself that it was all in her imagination. She watched Kurt push the mower in straight lines up and down the lawn. There had always been a precision to him and it was still there today. She remembered so clearly the first time she saw him. He had rented the ground-floor flat in the tall Edwardian house where she and Esme had taken over the first floor shared before them by their aunts.

Phyllis smiled now, thinking of those first days, when she'd watched him come and go about his business, always making her heart skip. It had been love at first sight for her. Now, Phyllis stood a little back from the window and took a deep satisfied breath. Today was a good day. Everything was going to be fine today.

Well, hopefully. She caught a glimpse of her own reflection, hair uncombed, still in her dressing gown, although she'd been up since before five, making Kurt breakfast, talking him out of putting on a suit and commuting to the job he'd retired from years earlier. She looked worn out. She rubbed her eyes, knowing her hair was standing on top of her head, and sighed. Her temples throbbed from lack of sleep, she was overtired and grimy. She needed to have a shower and brush her teeth, but still, she was reluctant to take her eyes off him just yet.

This morning had been hard. Another deep breath. She could admit that now. She smiled automatically as he turned the mower and worked his way back towards the kitchen window, waving at her and pointing towards the hedge where he had perhaps spotted a flower or bird worth noticing.

He's fine, a little voice inside her urged. Just five minutes, in and out of the shower, it'll take him that at least to finish the lawn. And he would finish it. She was pretty sure of that, habit would surely win out over anything else.

She moved quickly upstairs towards the bedroom. She had a five-minute shower down to such a fine art; if there was an Olympic medal, she would surely be gold standard at this point.

The warm water blasting on her face and shoulders was such a relief, wakening her and caressing her skin as if to soothe her nerves and ease away her tension. The noise of it was a blessed balm from trying to tune into the mower outside. Hair dripping, feet still slippery on the tiles, she pulled open the bedroom door to hear the lawnmower still humming along. She imagined Kurt doing his best to get as near to the verge as possible and manoeuvre around the flower beds and the narrow crazy paving that ran beneath the clothes line.

The sound of the lawnmower was like a pacifier and Phyllis lingered long enough to dry herself properly – a rare indulgence – wash her teeth and dab a few fingers of moisturiser on her face. It was amazing, she almost felt human.

It was only as she drifted downstairs, wrapped in a gentle reverie of temporary well-being, that something about the sound outside jarred in her awareness.

The lawnmower was not moving.

There was a whining sound coming from it, as if the motor was stuck, perhaps with something caught in the blades.

Dear God. No.

She raced to the back door, flung it open. She was standing on the lawn before realising she wasn't wearing any shoes and the grass still damp from the dewy morning mist seeped in icy coldness through her from the ground up.

'Kurt.' She shouted his name, over and over. It was not a big garden, but she spurted to the end, digging through the mature shrubs that had been planted over their almost forty years living here.

The lawnmower was left abandoned on a pile of cut grass.

She sent up a prayer of thanks, because part of her had feared the worst, that Kurt might be knotted in the blades. Had she really thought she might find him torn to ribbons? She was shaking now, but she tried to calm herself with the uneasy thought that there couldn't be much worse than that.

At the back of the garden, through the thick hedging, the railway track ran along, silent now, but too often busy with morning and evening trains ferrying people in and out of the city. She tried to stay calm, checking for gaps in the perimeter of the garden; although she couldn't see any, still she didn't quite trust herself at this point. The rail people checked along these fences regularly. They couldn't risk a child getting through.

'Phyllis.' She heard her name called from the other end of the garden. 'Phyllie, are you back yet?'

Kurt was standing at the back door. His shirt undone, his vest covered over in what looked like mud, but as she made her way closer, she realised it was coffee. It smelled strong and, when she laid her hands on it, it was still warm.

'Oh, Kurt. What have you done?' She shepherded him back into the house, she would have to wash everything and pray he hadn't managed to scald himself with the hot liquid.

'I thought we'd have coffee, in the garden, but I couldn't find you and I tried…' He looked towards the front door which was wide open now, their next-door neighbour standing on the doorstep.

'Is he all right?' Their neighbour, Prisha, filled the doorway wearing a look of concerned embarrassment; it stretched her lips into a joyless smile. She lingered on the threshold, unsure if she should come in or not. 'I found him on the street; he seemed to be confused…'

'I'm fine.' Kurt was always a little abrupt after one of these episodes. 'Honestly, can a man not go out and prune his roses without all this nonsense.' He stomped up the stairs, pushing past Prisha and almost knocking her over.

'He's fine,' Phyllis said wearily. 'Thanks for making sure he got in safely, sorry about…'

'Don't worry, I just hope you're both going to be okay?' Prisha looked up the stairs and back towards Phyllis again. And there it was, the one thing Phyllis didn't ever want to see, a mixture of concern and pity in people's eyes.

'We're grand. Really.' Phyllis tried to sound reassuring as she closed out the door firmly behind Prisha.

Suddenly, she was exhausted, washed out with the uncertainty and responsibility of it all. She couldn't bear to think of their son Rob having to shoulder this too. He had enough to worry about, a single dad with not a lot to look forward to in life as it was.

She slid to the second step on the stairs, sat there for a while, trying to pull herself together, and then she heard it. The hushed keening noise of her husband; crying softly so as not to upset anyone else. She padded up the stairs to him and seeing him there, sitting on the bed, his face drenched with tears, his clothes stained with coffee, her heart began to break all over again.

'Oh, Phyllis, I'm so sorry. It happened again, I didn't mean it to happen, I just…'

'What happened?' she asked in her steadiest voice, although beneath the surface, if he'd looked into her eyes, he'd see how weak she really felt, because it was all so hard to understand and they were still at that stage where she hoped, maybe, if she understood she could do something about it.

'I don't know what happened, but...' He shuddered with what she supposed was anguish or, worse, maybe fear. He was losing *himself* and she had to constantly remind herself that it was probably a lot worse than losing your husband.

'It wasn't too bad. Just a little coffee spilled, that's all.'

'But it's not about the coffee, though, is it? We both know where this goes. I don't want to be a burden; you won't let me down, when the time comes, will you? I don't want to be like my father, I don't want you to have to live like my mother.'

'Don't be daft.' She hugged him close to her. She even managed to sound carefree. 'We're not your parents, you're just forgetting yourself occasionally, it was something very different for your father.' She pulled him even closer, but there was no ignoring the fact that he felt different, somehow, less like her Kurt with every passing day than before.

'We made a promise, I still remember that.' He pulled away from her, pinned her with those familiar eyes. 'You know what I want you to do, when the time comes.'

'Of course, but we don't even know that there's anything wrong yet.' It was a lie. Just because a doctor hadn't confirmed it, didn't mean she didn't know. Kurt knew too, he knew at times like this, and it was breaking her heart that his worst fears were coming home to roost.

'All we need is a little holiday, both of us, we haven't been anywhere for ages,' she said brightly and it was true. Maybe that's all they needed, a little holiday away from it all. It might do them both the world of good. And instantly, she knew, there was only one place she could go. She would ring her oldest friend Esme, nothing could possibly happen to Kurt at the Willows in Ballycove, could it?

Friday: Three days before the season begins

4

Cora

Cora pulled her rain jacket tight up around her shoulders. Someone needed to tell the weather makers that it was the last day of the school term and time to dig the sunshine out. She stood for a moment, surveying the car park beyond the school gates, while a group of second-year girls giggled over a selfie to mark the end of another year. She smiled. It was hard not to be infected by their excitement. Twelve whole school-free weeks. Let's hope the weather picked up.

'Okay, Megan and Clara – you can run out now; I see your mum is waiting for you at the gate.' She waved at Debbie Donegan, who looked as if she'd give anything to make the school holidays just a few weeks shorter. Suddenly, Cora envied Debbie. From the corridor behind her, there was a tight squeeze, like toothpaste pinched from the tube as more kids pushed their way out into the driving rain. It didn't take long for the hallway to empty and, with a final cheery wave, Cora pulled in the door and headed back to tidy up the classroom after the day's work.

'Friday feeling!' one of the younger teachers squealed as Cora passed by her door.

Cora nodded, as if she too couldn't wait for the holidays to begin. Twelve weeks. It caught her breath for a second. It'll be fine, she kept telling herself. She had been trying to shake off an encroaching sense of doom since Connor's wedding. On days when she was busy it was easier, but there was no getting away from the fact that since her son got married the house had felt filled with a sort of silence that threatened to drown Cora. Michael was oblivious of course, but then, one day was the same as the next to him, he probably wouldn't even take holidays this year.

'Yes, Friday feeling,' Cora trilled and decided that a bottle of Pinot Noir was in order tonight. She'd pick one up in the supermarket on the way home from work. That was all they needed – she and Michael would be just fine. She took a deep breath. She'd make his favourite Friday dinner, they'd have a glass of wine and this evening would be the first evening in a new chapter of their lives together. Maybe, they could get back to those days when they used to chat for hours – she'd loved those times. Maybe, they'd even rekindle some of that passion that had ebbed away over the last decade or more.

'God, it's a mess,' Vera said when she arrived back from having her cigarette break at the back of the school.

'Ah, it's not too bad.'

The girls were supposed to take all their belongings home with them and, as the classroom assistant, it had become Cora's job to check and double-check. She grabbed the bin and did one last round to save the cleaners any extra work.

'How on earth, after the term from hell, can you possibly

still be so chipper?' As far as Vera was concerned, every school term was hellish. 'Praise be, it's the holidays.' She set about packing up her own bag, dropping in her glasses and the scarf she wore for yard duties. 'Any plans yet? What is it this year, skydiving or waterboarding?'

'Stop it, you know well what waterboarding is!' Cora laughed. Vera was planning on doing the Camino Way with her partner Brendan. She wasn't particularly religious, but she was glad to be seeing the back of school and rain and children. She had asked Cora if she and Michael would like to come along, knowing there wasn't anything to tie them down for the next few weeks. When they'd chatted about it over coffee break months earlier, it really felt like something she could look forward to and Cora had even saved enough to pay for the holiday with plenty of spending money left over if she could talk Michael into staying on a little longer. In hindsight, it was the height of wishful thinking. Michael had nearly choked on his boiled egg when she mentioned it, so that was that.

'And you know what I mean…' Vera smiled and Cora knew exactly what she meant. Over the last few years, Cora had taken on a summer project, just something to fill the weeks off, so last year she'd volunteered with the local cemetery clean-up group.

'Actually, no, I haven't made any plans yet.' Cora scrubbed at a stain on the desk that was no longer there. These days it felt as if all she did was fill up the empty space time had become for her. She was either cleaning or volunteering; well, she had to do something or she felt as if she'd go mad with boredom. She was too young to just stop and watch television. She was only just gone fifty. That was the problem with marrying your first love. Love, marriage, family, it was all over in the blink of an eye. Not that she was complaining, marrying Michael Doyle had been the best thing she'd ever done. She loved him, she really did, and perhaps if she held onto that, then sanity would prevail, and everything would be fine.

Cora got into her car that afternoon, resolved that she would buy that decent bottle of wine, shake off this feeling of foreboding and make the most of the holidays. She would start with candles on the kitchen table, make a bit of an effort for a change. Upstairs, somewhere in the attic, she was fairly sure the old record player was still working; she could take it down and root about for some of the albums they hadn't listened to in years. Michael had always liked the Eagles.

In the supermarket, it seemed she knew every second customer and, with time to spare, Cora stood and chatted as she picked up the few provisions she'd need to make dinner. She'd love to do something different, like beef bourguignon, but Friday meant shepherd's pie, so it was mince and onions, and she had everything else at home. She dawdled over the fruit stand and pulled out a bag of cooking apples. She'd make a tart and they could have it with ice-cream after dinner. She shouldn't really, but Michael had a terrible sweet tooth. Who was she kidding? She'd manage to make her way through a third of it over the weekend with hardly a thought. A cup of coffee here, a mug of tea there and, by Monday, she'd be ready to bake all over again. The truth was, Cora loved baking. Well, she loved being busy and, over the years, she'd managed to build up a list of sweet treats that were always popular.

'Summer holidays, lucky you,' Gina on the till said, completely oblivious to the rain drumming against the windows at her back. 'Going anywhere nice?'

'No. No, I don't think so.' They hadn't gone anywhere in years, not since Connor was young and she'd persuaded Michael to go to the seaside one gloriously hot summer. For a second she thought about that little guest house by the sea – it'd be lovely to go back there again.

'Still, it's nice to be off, isn't it?'

'Yes, I suppose it is.'

Oddly, by the time Cora got home, she actually felt deflated, as if there had been a build-up to some great event and then, suddenly, it had been cancelled. It was ridiculous, because holidays were holidays, weren't they? They were what you made of them. But as she stood before the calendar, looking at the three months stretching ahead of her, with the wedding over and Connor back in London again, the only thing she had to look forward to was a visit to the dental hygienist in August. She sighed. Enough of this. She shook herself off and made dinner and an apple tart with 'Good Vibes' worked out in block pastry letters across the top.

As usual, everything was ready for dinner at six o'clock when Cora heard Michael make his way in through the garage doors. Was it boring that she knew he would have taken off his dirty boots, shaken the sawdust from his clothes and hung up the old jacket he wore to keep warm if he was working on a roof or decking? Would some women consider that a comfortable shorthand in their relationship of knowing someone so well? Cora felt her heart plummet, as if the delicate balance of emotion she'd been trying to load in favour of optimism was in danger of crashing down.

'Hi,' she called a little too brightly, so to her own ears she sounded more like a demented parrot than the mature, calm woman she so wanted to be right now.

'How do?' he said, easing his feet into the slippers he'd left at the back door that morning.

'All ready to go,' Cora said, nodding towards the oven. She'd set the kitchen table. And he glanced at it, then back at her, as if she was playing some sort of trick on him. 'What?'

'Nothing,' he grumbled. 'I'll be down in a minute.'

And, she knew, he'd peel off his work clothes and drop them on the bathroom floor then slip into the shower for less than four minutes, just enough to wash the sawdust off. He'd pad across the bedroom, leaving damp footprints on the carpet, then pull on tracksuit bottoms and an old T-shirt from the wardrobe to lounge in for the rest of the evening. The predictability of it all made her feel nauseous.

Thinking like this wasn't doing her any good. She had to stop it. She had to either do something or walk away. Oh, God, *walk away*? Was that what this was coming to?

'So, how was your day?' she asked as she scooped vegetables onto their plates.

'Grand, grand. The usual, you know…'

'Oh.' She handed him his plate and watched as he trooped past her towards the sitting room, bypassing the kitchen table. In fairness, she hadn't been able to find matches, so she hadn't actually lit the candles. 'I thought we might eat out here tonight?' she said.

'Really?' He looked at her as if she'd suggested something crazy, like adopting a pandemonium of parakeets. 'Why?'

'Well, just, you know, for a change.'

'Ah Cora, can't we just sit like we usually do?' He was hovering between the kitchen and the hall.

'I fancy a change.' She moved her lips into a tight smile.

'Well, I don't, so I'll just pop in here and I'll give you the headlines when you've finished.' He winked at her and headed for the sitting room.

She turned and placed her dinner plate on the kitchen table, took a large gulp of her wine and sat for a moment. This was no good, if anything it was worse than the two of them staring mindlessly at the telly all night. She picked up her plate and followed him through.

'You win,' she said, flopping down in her usual chair.

'Huh?' Michael looked at her almost guiltily with his forkful of pie held before his chin. 'Sure, we might as well be comfortable?' he said before scanning the room to find the remote. Was it wrong of her to hide it down the side of the sofa?

'Did you manage to get that gable end finished?' She heard the desperation in her own voice, as if she was almost nagging in an effort to make normal conversation.

'Eh?' He raised his eyebrows and looked across at her. 'Where's that telly remote gone to?' he asked as if he hadn't even heard the question. Then he popped his plate on the coffee table and found it beneath the cushion where she thought he'd never look. 'Ah, blast, we've missed the headlines now,' he said, digging into his dinner with his eyes glued to the TV screen.

Cora felt as if she would choke if she ate another bite. Was this it? Forever and ever? What would happen when she retired and she didn't have work to look forward to? She could see it now, both of them, shuffling about this house into old age. Surrounded by the furniture of a lifetime together with nothing more in common than memories they never talked about and a son who only rang occasionally. She was going to be sick. She flew to the bathroom, retched over the toilet for as long as it took to know that there was nothing more to come and then she stood up and inspected her unhappy reflection in the mirror.

She couldn't go on like this forever, could she? She gripped the sides of the sink to steady herself. She felt weak now, as if she'd been wiped out with the certainty that life as she'd once believed it to be had suddenly been pulled from under her.

5

Niamh

Over the years, Niamh had managed to convince herself more and more that perhaps children not being on her to-do list was okay. After all, it didn't seem to bother her three best friends, and, from what she could see, the women she worked with spent more time sitting in doctor's and dentist's offices or at football games or swimming galas most weekends than they did anything else. Sometimes, when she thought about it, she wondered how on earth they managed to fit work in around the heavy social calendars of their children. Perhaps she'd never been particularly maternal to begin with or maybe it was the knowing that it would never be on the agenda with Jeremy that had helped her to switch off, but somehow she'd managed it.

She was almost forty years old and she had no regrets, but sometimes, over the last few years, she'd convinced herself there was still time. There had been an occasional Friday night, on her own in the flat, when she'd wondered if in some parallel universe she might have been just a little more fulfilled, a smidgen more content, if she'd settled down with some nice man and had her two point three children, instead of spending her weekends watching TV alone with a glass of white wine in a flat that was maybe just a little too pristine.

None of these things mattered now. Because against all that was meant to be, last Saturday, the unthinkable happened. She'd missed her period. Not something to be immediately alarmed about. She couldn't be pregnant because she was on the pill. It had never failed and she hadn't given it a second thought in years. Niamh hadn't remembered about her missed period again until Thursday morning, when she got up, about to sip her first taste of coffee, only to feel as if she was sicker than she'd ever felt before. After fifteen minutes' retching in the bathroom, she stood before the vanity mirror. She looked like a ghost, pale, eyes hollowed out and a shadow of herself. She knew then, as she stood there shivering with her hand placed gently on her stomach – she was pregnant. She didn't need a test, she just knew it.

All the same, she convinced herself – maybe not. She was at that age, wasn't she? You know, more and more women hitting early menopause, she could just be going through the change. It had happened to Annie. She'd been just thirty-five and her gynaecologist told her she should think about either getting pregnant quickly or having her eggs frozen. Annie had laughed and booked a week in Mexico, thrown away her contraceptive pills and gotten a prescription for HRT instead. She'd never looked back.

But Niamh Brophy wasn't living in San Francisco, she was living in Ireland and she was working for the civil service. And if it was just *the change*, that was one thing, but if she was pregnant that was a whole other ballgame. She would get rid of it, of course. She wouldn't be the first Courtney woman to have a termination. Her mother had made the same decision when she found herself pregnant years earlier, just as they realised that her father had been diagnosed with pancreatic cancer. They had never looked back or wondered what if; it had been the right thing to do at the time. Of course, back then, it had been a trip to England and a disgrace if anyone found out.

Thankfully, the country had got sense and moved on.

Even so, Niamh believed, children need two parents or, at the very least, one who knew something about babies. Without even mentioning it to Jeremy, the one thing she felt certain of now was that she would be on her own if she had this baby. And whatever she felt about rearing a child on her own, which was never going to happen, if she factored in the certainty that she would also lose Jeremy, well, it just didn't feel as if there was a choice to be made.

It took only twenty seconds for a thin cyan line to confirm what she already knew. She sat in her flat with the pregnancy test kit in her hand for hours afterwards, overflowing with a mixture of shock and disbelief. It was terrible news, and yet, she imagined the baby inside growing and moving about and one day having long red hair like hers and deep brown eyes like Jeremy. It was late when she finally roused herself from the sofa and stumbled to bed, only to toss and turn, falling in and out of dreams and nightmares about babies and terminations and losing Jeremy. When she woke in the morning, it felt as if she hadn't slept at all, except she had that hollow feeling where the raging emotions of her dreams had emptied her out.

She rang in to work, claimed a headache and worked from home instead. Her recent promotion meant sickness was a luxury she couldn't afford. If she didn't turn up, the tasks just stacked higher on her desk. Her recent promotion was just another tick on the list of things that weren't compatible with a small baby.

It took until lunchtime before the morning sickness subsided. As soon as she felt well enough to speak, she dialled a clinic and made an appointment for the following week. She would book some time off work, take herself to a little guest house she'd found on Tripadvisor. It looked peaceful, the sort of place where she could rest and relax before returning to Dublin and getting her life back to normal.

'Are you all right darling?' her mother asked when she rang later that day. She'd already tried the office only to be told that Niamh was on leave.

'I'm fine, I think it's hay fever. I woke with a stuffy head and groggy and you know the way people are about you turning up to work with anything that looks remotely contagious.' She heard her own tinkling laugh and it felt completely alien to her. She was holding her stomach. It seemed her hand rested there automatically since that little blue stripe had thrown everything up in the air. This would be her mother's first grandchild, and her only shot at it – Niamh was her only child, there was no one else to take up the baton. Absolutely *no regrets*, but a wave of panic rushed through her, making her want to retch again.

'Ah, I had thought I might bring you for early dinner this evening, I'm having to pop into town and I'd have been passing near your building.'

'Bad timing.' Niamh was genuinely disappointed, but she couldn't see her mother looking like this. Her mother would instantly know she was pregnant. She seemed to have an infallible radar for it; she'd always been able to pick out baby news before anyone else. She wouldn't judge her, but somehow, Niamh wanted to hold this news to herself, for as long as it was something real – until it wasn't any more.

'Well, maybe next week?'

'Yes, maybe.' Except, Niamh couldn't think about next week, she sighed. She was being ridiculous; it would be all over by then. Everything would be back to normal. Yes, there was no way she could be in a worse state than she was now. She was a grown woman, she would take care of this, no point in worrying her mother. 'How's Dad?' she asked to send the conversation on a different route.

'Oh, the usual, when he isn't gardening, he's looking up new shrubs he can try out or wanting to drag me to some old country house to snag cuttings from some plant he's eager to set.' Her mother paused, because they both knew that her father had been looking forward to retirement for almost twenty years and, these days, he was living the dream.

'Anyway, I've taken up bridge, so I better get going, I have a game in half an hour,' her mother said brightly and Niamh felt a little lighter inside; at least her parents were making the most of things.

'Oh, Mum.' Niamh closed her eyes, she hated lying to anyone, but most of all to her parents. 'I just remembered, I have to go on a conference next weekend. I'll be gone from Wednesday morning, it's all booked, I...'

'Don't worry darling, it'll do you good to get away, I hope they're sending you somewhere nice?'

'Oh, the usual, a think-in in some out-of-the-way hotel in the middle of nowhere.' She laughed, she could almost convince herself that life was so simple, that she might just as easily be going to work next Wednesday and not visiting a clinic on the South Circular Road before disappearing to the other side of the country to pull herself together again.

*

She *almost* convinced herself that it felt as if everything was normal by the time she saw Jeremy. Busy week, he'd been in Brussels and London with the minister he was advising and only just managed to catch an earlier flight which gave him the night at her place. He would lie to his wife, of course, tell her he was still in London, in some anonymous hotel, and he'd be home the following day. Niamh had spent so long pretending she didn't care about this that it didn't bother her any more, well hardly. She threw herself into his arms when he walked into the flat.

'Oh, Jeremy, I'm so happy to see you.' Suddenly, all of the emotion she'd been sitting on boiled over and the more she clung onto him the more it spilled out of her. Suddenly, she was sobbing and blubbering and giddy with nervous exhaustion.

'Woah, what's all this?' he asked, holding her at arm's length and searching her eyes for some of the details she hadn't actually managed to put into words yet. Everything came tumbling out in the space of five sentences and if Niamh felt much better in the sharing of her news, it didn't take long to register the fact that Jeremy looked as if his world had come crashing to an end at the same time.

'You'll get rid of it, obviously.' His voice was emotionless, as if the man she loved had taken temporary leave of himself. His normally sallow skin had faded and suddenly she noticed creases about his forehead and lines along his mouth that hadn't been there before.

'Well of course,' she said quietly, dropping onto the sofa, aware that if she didn't sit she might fall over. It felt as if her blood pressure had plummeted along with all of the bubbling excitement she hadn't realised she'd been feeling until this very moment when it was stolen from her. 'Obviously, I mean, what other options have I?' She heard her voice and it sounded as if it was coming from the next room.

'There are no other options. I mean, are you even sure you're pregnant?' He dropped down onto the sofa next to her.

'I'm sure.' When Niamh looked at him, a cold shiver ran over her.

'But you're on the pill... You have been taking it, haven't you?'

'Of course I've been taking it, what do you think I am? Do you really think I did this on purpose? Everyone knows, even the pill isn't one hundred per cent reliable.'

It was her own stupid fault, she'd realised when she'd got her positive result and done the maths. Food poisoning after a work do, dodgy caterers and shellfish. It was enough to put her off lobster for life. She wasn't going to say that now. She moved away from him, stood at the window looking out onto the small yard at the back of her building. It wasn't much of a view, but she'd sacrificed that for a decent postcode when she bought the place, which as it happened had doubled in market value, and in the meantime, she'd made do with good art on the walls to compensate for a vista that was better with the blinds pulled down.

'Oh, come on, it's not the end of the world,' he said eventually and put his arms around her, but somehow, it felt as if everything had changed.

*

The following morning, Niamh confirmed the appointment to pick up the tablet that would flush away this problem between them and immediately afterwards she put the call through to confirm her booking in Ballycove. It felt like going to the Willows was the right thing to do now.

She texted Jeremy the details of the appointment. She didn't ask him to attend and she knew she'd be waiting until time's end if she expected him to offer to come along with her. They'd managed to keep their relationship completely under wraps for this long; there was no way he'd take that sort of risk now. There had been many times over the years when she'd felt angry and jealous of Jeremy's wife and family; today, strangely, she just felt lonely. She could plead with him to come with her. Although, the sensible part of her knew, if he'd wanted to come, he'd have offered. And so, she couldn't ask, because that was the first rule of being a mistress – make no demands.

Monday: The first day of the season

6

Cora

It was Monday morning before the reality of what really lay ahead of her hit Cora once more. She sat in the kitchen, having washed the breakfast dishes and tidied the sitting room, with nothing more to do and a full day stretching out ahead of her. It was depressing, three decades spent here raising her family and suddenly it was just her. Nothing had changed here and yet everything had changed. It was clean as a new pin, but shabby and dated. Every corner wore an air of neglect in spite of being regularly wiped down – the paint, once a vibrant yellow, had faded to a sickly lemon. Even her wedding ring had grown dull and now, it felt like everything else around her had too – like a weight she wasn't sure she had the will to carry any longer.

But it wasn't just these things that were the problem. After all, she knew that, next door, Tanya Farrelly had boxes of shiny trinkets and her house was a show house, really, like Tanya: small but perfectly presented. But it was desolate in a way no Jo Malone diffuser could cover over. Tanya had a string of lovers who seemed to come and go without any great consequence, but the house never managed to feel as if it was a real home to anyone. Cora got up from the kitchen table, walked out to the hall, into the sitting room. It was the same here, faded, stale, tired – but, a little voice niggled at her, it was homely.

The fact was, she'd given up asking Michael to redecorate it years ago. Instead, she'd learned to live with yellow paint she hated and a green-velvet three-piece suite that had seen better days. She'd added things, of course, over the years: a cream throw from Corrigan's mills and a collection of paintings and prints from local artists that she could see now only added to the clutter. In the middle of them all was the framed photograph from her wedding day all those years ago. She couldn't help it. She was drawn to it now, like a pin to a magnet, and there was no fighting it. She moved closer and studied the picture, in a way she had never really looked at it before. She had been so young. Michael had been her first real boyfriend. They'd been crazy about each other back then, there had been no doubt in her mind but she wanted to marry him. Other girls had taken on jobs or gone to college, but all Cora had wanted was Michael Doyle.

And then it came back to her, that day, six months before they'd walked down the aisle. She'd been sitting in that same church and it was packed to the gills. She and her mother, staring wordlessly across at a coffin she could hardly believe contained her father. Michael had walked to the top of the church that day and sympathised. He was just back from England and he'd come directly to the funeral when he'd heard about her dad.

'I'm so sorry for your loss,' he'd said to her mother and

FAITH HOGAN

then he'd moved on to sympathise with Cora. There were no words, but he took her hands in his and, suddenly, it felt as if she wasn't quite so alone.

'Ahem.' Father Gilmurray cleared his throat, he was about to begin the funeral mass.

'Sit here,' her mother had whispered and Michael had ended up sitting in the front pew next to Cora. Somehow, in that surreal moment, having him there felt just right, as if her father had sent him especially to look after her.

'Uncle Jimmy has hurt his back,' her mother whispered to her, nodding meaningfully across at Michael. 'Do you think your young man would mind helping out?'

'Of course I don't mind.' Michael had overheard and stepped out of the pew when the time came for the pallbearers to carry her father's coffin from the church. Cora followed the coffin with a mixture of emotion that she knew her father would enjoy. For that short time, she imagined him up there smiling down on them all. Her young man. Michael Doyle – her young man, yes, he would have a good old laugh about that.

Now, looking at the photograph on the wall, she recalled that the day of her wedding had been happy, but she could see the underlying grief in her eyes too. She would have given just about anything to have her father walk her up the aisle that day, but instead, it was Uncle Jimmy whose bad back had miraculously recovered enough for the job.

The whole memory was so vivid, it might have happened five minutes ago. Cora stepped back from the photograph. Was she losing all perspective? Surely those thirty-odd years counted for far more than a niggling feeling that had come from looking at the spark between Connor and Lydia.

And then she started to cry, huge tears running down her cheeks, there was no stopping them, she didn't want to stop them, she wanted to feel every ounce of sadness drain from her, she might feel better then. Maybe that was all she needed, a good cry and everything would be grand. But at the end, nothing had changed; there was nothing to look forward to, nothing to do, nothing she could see of value to this world that she had spent her life working towards. It had all come to an end, like a neat short story. She felt as useful and interesting as the faded wallpaper that she'd hung halfway up the walls along the stairs years earlier.

Cora was relieved when the phone rang.

'It's our one-month anniversary.' Lydia sounded so happy it brought a lump to Cora's throat.

'Already? I can't believe it's a month,' Cora said.

'Yes, officially, in about an hour's time, I will have been Mrs Connor Doyle for a full month.'

'Well, happy anniversary.' God, had Cora been feeling this awful emptiness for a full month? On the other end of the line, Lydia was chatting away about the arrival of the wedding album, but Cora had just tuned out. It was the realisation that she had spent a full month completely absorbed in this weighty misery.

If she was completely honest with herself, it had been much longer than just this last month. It had been there, like a shadow, while Lydia had been planning the wedding, only Cora had been far too busy to examine the reality of her own life while so immersed in getting the arrangements in place for Connor and Lydia's future.

'So, that's a date?' Lydia was asking her.

'Sorry, I must have missed that,' Cora said.

'I just said, when we come home next, we'd like to take you and Michael out for dinner just to say thank you.'

'Oh, Lydia, that's so sweet, but there's really no need.'

'There's every need, Cora, you saved my life about a hundred times over the last year with getting the wedding organised. I couldn't have done it from over here, we both know that. Dinner is the very least we can do.'

'Do you want me to book somewhere?' Cora asked, but she was actually half wondering if Michael would even go out for dinner with them. Would he insist on bringing the remote control? She smiled in spite of herself. 'You two should just go together, it is your celebration after all.'

'I won't hear of it. Everything is organised. I've booked a table for four at the Railway Hotel for eight o'clock; all you have to do is put on a nice dress and get into a taxi. I'm planning on making a late night of it and, if it's the only thing I do for the weekend, I'm going to make sure you have a late night of it too!'

The Railway Hotel was the swankiest hotel around. It was also where they'd gotten married just four weeks earlier. When she was giving the final numbers, Cora had managed to talk the owner into throwing in a complimentary weekend stay for the happy couple afterwards; since they had such a huge contingent of guests filling the hotel for the full weekend before the season had properly begun.

Maybe this dinner would do her and Michael the world of

good – wasn't it exactly what she'd been craving: something to look forward to, something they could do together?

*

Michael was later than usual that evening. 'Just making hay while the sun shines.' He seemed tired and Cora felt a stab of guilt for the thoughts she'd been having all day when she looked at him. He had always worked so hard to look after his family, maybe that was half the problem.

'Lydia rang today,' she said as she ladled carrots onto his plate. She'd have quite fancied salad this evening for a change, but Michael was strictly a meat, potatoes and two veg man. It was just another thing to get on her nerves, wasn't it? The predictability of their dinners – *stop it*, she told herself, *just stop it*.

'Hmm.' He didn't lift his eyes from the newspaper in his hands.

'Yes, she's pregnant, with twins, and they're moving to Mars.' She followed Michael into the sitting room.

'That's nice.' He nodded, but he obviously wasn't listening to her at all. She sat on the chair opposite and lowered the volume on the TV, to which he responded with a startled look, as if she'd broken some unwritten commandment.

'They've invited us out for a meal,' she said and actually, the more she thought about it, the more excited she felt about eating something she hadn't cooked and didn't have to wash up after.

'What did they go doing that for? I hope you told them that we wouldn't be going,' he said as he sawed into his chops.

'No, it's very nice of them to invite us.'

'But didn't you tell them that we're not keen on meals out and all that nonsense?'

'Since when were *we* not keen on all that nonsense?' Cora left down her fork slowly, deliberately.

'Well, we've never been the kind of people who go gallivanting when there is a perfectly good dinner to be had at home.' He lifted his head slowly, as if alerted to the fact that there was more at stake here than just a meal out with his son and daughter-in-law.

'That's the thing, Michael, I'm not sure what kind of people *we* are any more?'

'What sort of silly talk is that?' he asked between mouthfuls.

'Is it silly talk?' she whispered, feeling a well of emotion at the back of her throat. 'Don't you feel it too? As if we're missing something? As if there should be something more to us? To this life?'

'Huh?' He looked at her wide-eyed as if ambushed unexpectedly. He put down his knife and fork, sat back in his chair and looked at her. Silence wedged between them like a truculent child. This was Cora's chance to get things out in the open.

'I mean, look at us, we're still young, there has to be more to life than this…' How could she put it into words? She felt completely invisible, just trundling along, living alongside someone who hardly noticed her, hardly spoke to her, and this was meant to be for the rest of her life.

'Ara, come on now, Cora, you know well, we have a perfectly good life. We have a lovely home with all the mod cons anyone would want, you have a reliable car under you and a little job for pocket money. Our future is well provided for, I've seen to that.'

It had been his refrain for over twenty years – the notion that he had to save every penny to pay off the mortgage and put enough aside for the rainy day they were still waiting to see.

'I can't do this any more.' She got up and took her hardly touched dinner plate towards the kitchen.

'Is it that job? It's too bloody much for you, I said it from the beginning, racing about after other people's children, it only catches up with a person when they stop for a break.'

He really hadn't a clue.

'It's not the bloody job… If you want to know the truth, my job is the only thing I have that's worth getting out of bed for in the morning,' she screamed, spinning around to face him. 'This is about us, Michael, it's about our marriage and…'

She lowered her voice this time; some small part of her didn't want Tanya next door hearing every single word of this row, if that was what they were having.

'It's meant to be my holidays, a time when other couples have a week away, or even just a few days. Tanya went to Egypt last year and what did I do? I went down to the graveyard and spent weeks on end mowing grass and pulling weeds.'

'No one said you had to,' Michael grumbled.

'That's not the point, the point is, there was nothing else to do. You never want to do anything with me or go anywhere as a couple.'

'Ah, come on now, we're just after having a great time at Connor's wedding, how much more do you want out of the year?'

'Seriously?' It felt as if the blood was draining from the top of her head. 'Can you really not understand this?'

'Look, love, it's been a very big year for you. Connor getting married and these last few months you've never been busier, what with all the preparations for the wedding. It's only natural to be on a bit of a downer now that it's all done. Connor is *really* gone now. It's empty nest, isn't that it? They're always on about it in the women's pages. That and the *change*, sure how could you be feeling right?'

'This is NOT empty nest syndrome, Michael, and… and…it's not the bloody menopause either.' She was livid, shaking with rage. How bloody dare he try to psychoanalyse her with babble from the women's pages of a trashy red-top newspaper, how bloody dare he?

'I know, it might seem like something else, but…' He was so calm. He actually scooped up another forkful of peas, popped them into his mouth and began to chew. She watched him and realised: he was completely and utterly oblivious to everything apart from the hamster wheel he was currently trudging on.

'Michael.' She took a deep breath. She would not be a hysterical woman for this conversation, even if her heart was hammering in her chest and she felt her stomach plummet towards her knees. 'I can't go on like this.'

'Well, maybe you should go and see the doctor, have you thought about that?'

'It's not about me going to see a doctor – or a counsellor,

before you suggest that either – it's about us. Things are not right between us, they haven't been for a very long time, can't you see it?'

She was looking into his eyes and trying hard to find something in his expression to make her want to hang onto things as they were, or maybe just a glimmer that things could change. Instead, Michael shook his head, looked down at his plate. This was an occasion when it wasn't good to be a man of few words.

'Ara, Cora, I only sat down to eat my dinner… can't you leave a man alone until he has his dinner eaten?' He sighed and that was when she knew. There wouldn't be any changing things. There wouldn't be any moving forward or making things better. There was just this, hanging about for all eternity, and it was truly stifling her with every minute that passed between them.

'I can't stay here tonight,' she said. She took a long deep breath; she wasn't sure if she was relieved or ready to curl up in a corner and cry for Ireland.

'Why, just because I said I wanted to eat my dinner in peace?'

'No, but if it's any consolation to you, I'll be giving you plenty of peace from here on in, Michael. I'm done.'

'What do you mean, you're done?' A shadow of something unfamiliar unfixed his features and, for a moment, Cora wondered if it might be panic, but he left his cutlery down so carefully, she suspected he was trying to make sense of what she was saying.

'Seriously, Michael, do I have to spell it out for you? I'm done with this, with all of it, with hanging about until you get home. I'm sick of the silence between us, of sitting in front of the telly every night while you fall asleep. I'm done with feeling lonely, even when we're lying next to each other in bed. Do you know how long it is since we…'

Did she have to put it into words?

'Oh, come on, Cora, no one our age has sex any more.'

'NO ONE OUR AGE HAS SEX ANY MORE?'

'Will you stop shouting; do you want to tell the whole place that we're having a row?'

'But we're not having a row, are we?'

'Well, what are we having then?' He shook his head as if he'd realised there was no reasoning with her and that just made Cora even more livid.

'I think it's too late for fighting now, Michael. I mean, if it's too late for sex, then it must be too late for everything else, mustn't it?'

And with that, she turned on her heels, stormed upstairs and packed a bag with a random selection of bits and pieces. She couldn't think beyond getting out of there, much less count in knickers and bras and gather up moisturisers or sandals. She was in shock. Maybe she knew it as she raced around the bedroom, flinging odd bits and pieces into Connor's old kit bag, but whatever it was, she knew, it would take a tornado to turn her back now.

*

It was only as Cora stood outside her own front door, with a bag in her hand and knowing that she couldn't face going back, that she realised she had nowhere to go. She had left her husband. She had finally snapped. The emptiness had won in the end and it felt as if it had cracked her heart into fragments too tiny to ever reassemble again. She had left her dinner plate on the draining board and Michael fretting over his cold chops and peas.

She hadn't even driven out of Cherrywood Crescent when it began to hit her. She was shaking, quivering from the top of her head right down to her feet so the whole car juddered with her as her limbs lost constancy with the basic skill of driving her car. It was a strange physical event passing over her, her whole body caught up in a rhapsody of jangling nerves.

She pulled the car into a lay-by near the playground. She couldn't steady her foot on the accelerator. Her hands were trembling; a small muscle at the side of her cheek was gnawing at her. It felt as if it was jerking one side of her face completely out of line, but when she glanced in the rear-view mirror, she looked exactly like she always did: wishy-washy, hair tied up on top of her head – the only giveaway was that her eyes were red from crying. When had she cried? She didn't remember crying, but perhaps when she'd been flinging things into her bag… oh God, it was all such a mess. Words floated back to her, Michael's words, parts of sentences, and she had a feeling they would carousel about in her brain for a very long time.

He probably thought she was crazy, that she'd be back in a few hours, slip into the bed beside him, or maybe, if she was trying to make a point, sleep in the spare room for a night or two and then everything would go back to the way it was. But she knew, if he thought that, he was very much mistaken.

She clenched her hands around the steering wheel now; they were still shaking. She felt awful but, at the same time, she knew she couldn't go back there.

Then, a thousand other thoughts floated up in her mind. Like telling everyone – wouldn't it just be easier to go back right away rather than upset everyone, just when Connor and Lydia were happy? Where would she live if she didn't live in Cherrywood Crescent? It had been her home for most of her life, hadn't she thought it would always be home? How would she manage on her own? She had never lived alone before. She had moved from the little terraced house next to her father's shop into a tiny flat when she married Michael. Then, when Cherrywood Crescent was finished and came up for sale, they'd gotten a mortgage and moved in. It was chock-full of memories and little knick-knacks that she'd picked up along the way. It was, truly, the story of her life, contained within those four walls. She had never wanted to live anywhere else. She had never wanted to live alone.

Then, suddenly, the terrible trembling that had taken over her body stopped and she was filled with some new certainty. It felt like a wave of ice washing over her and it took a moment to put a name on it; a shiver ran along her spine and Cora knew exactly what it was: stone cold fear.

She sat there for ages, until some kids walked across the road in front of her car. The engine growled under her foot, making her jump. She must have depressed the accelerator; how long had she been sitting here with the car running? She looked at the clock on the dash, too long. She had nowhere to go. And then she remembered that guest house over in

Ballycove. She could book in there, just for a few days – actually if they had a room free, she could probably book in for the whole summer. She still had all those savings that she'd been hoping to spend on the Camino Way, if Michael had only agreed to come.

She checked the time. She could be there in just under forty-five minutes. Without another thought, she pulled her phone from her bag and found a number for the place online.

'Hello? It eez the Willows.' The woman's voice was foreign and harried.

'Hi, hello, yes, I wondered if I can book in with you for tonight?'

'Tonight? Oh, tonight is...' It sounded as if the place was being pulled apart by an army of big men behind her. 'I am sorry, it's just we weren't going to open until tomorrow and now I have to go to the hospital with Esme and...'

'Oh no.' Cora couldn't keep the despair from her voice.

'So, you see, there won't be anyone here and...'

'I could let myself in, I really wouldn't mind, it's just...' God, she couldn't go telling a perfect stranger that she'd just left her husband. As things stood, she couldn't imagine telling Connor, let alone anyone else. 'I had so hoped to stay there.'

'Well, I suppose you *could* let yourself in. We have rooms, there aren't even guests here until tomorrow, we weren't going to start our season until... but then Esme fell and...'

'That's fine. Absolutely, I can let myself in, just leave a key somewhere, I'll be no trouble, I promise. I don't even need breakfast, I can...'

'Oh, Esme would never forgive me if you didn't have...'

Marta laughed and suddenly it felt as if there was some warmth back in the world again. 'It's okay, I will leave a key in the porch...'

'Oh, thank you, thank you so much.' Cora wiped the tears that had been streaming down her cheeks and pulled the car out into the road. She was going to the guest house in Ballycove and, even if her heart was breaking, she was going somewhere she had been so happy once. Maybe it would be the perfect place to figure out what she should do next.

7

Esme

Esme was in an ambulance. She knew that much. They were speeding along, probably through Ballycove, over to the hospital in the next town. Next to her, she could hear machines and a voice, now and again, checking that she was comfortable, checking that she was conscious.

They'd given her something, or she presumed that was what was making her head woozy so her thoughts seemed to swim somewhere over the road they were travelling on. She imagined looking back at the Willows. She didn't want to leave; if she was going to die, they'd better bloody bring her back to die in her own bed. She tried to say this, but no one was listening to her, her voice too low over the noise of the ambulance.

And then, her eyes closed and she was lost to her memories once more.

The truth was, Esme could remember every shingle and slate on the guest house as clearly as she'd seen it in years. Although it was only hours since she'd fallen off that damned table, there was enough time to let her mind drift over days and weeks and years. The only thing that seemed to anchor her in the present was thinking of the Willows, walking through each room in her head, setting things straight for the season to come. But even in her mind's eye or maybe especially in her mind's eye, Esme knew she had been fooling herself, she was not a young woman any more. She was well into her ninth decade; it was time to face up to the fact that she couldn't go on forever. She shuddered, there were tears in her eyes, but she was only dimly aware of them as she cruised between half sleep and half awareness – it seemed the only place to find refuge was in her memories.

That terrible winter, when her life had changed forever, it had been bucketing down in torrents for days. Esme hadn't left the little flat in Dublin since she'd come home from the hospital over three weeks earlier.

In those days, miscarriages weren't talked about; they were another taboo subject that somehow the church and the state had colluded in making more shameful than tragic. But Esme was destroyed by it all. The loss of not only the baby she'd been so looking forward to, but also any hope of having another one in the future, and it was her own fault. She was convinced of it; no matter what Phyllis said, no matter how much she wanted to blame the doctors or the nurses or God above, she knew she'd done a terrible thing only two years ago and this was the price she had to pay for it.

Abortion. No matter what way she framed it, even if she'd wanted the child, it would have destroyed her mother. Phyllis had set it all up, she understood exactly.

Phyllis was the only one who'd come to visit after the

miscarriage, she sat next to Esme's bed, not saying anything, maybe feeling every bit as guilty as Esme did.

They sent her home after a week. Hours and days had vanished when she hadn't been able to so much as lift her head from the pillow; such was the weight of desperation that raged within her.

'Baby blues,' the doctor, a young, brisk woman who'd been sent out from the nearby practice, had diagnosed from the end of the bed. She wrinkled her nose at the smell of a sick room that hadn't been aired in almost three weeks, a room where dinners had been brought and returned uneaten, a room where the future had died and, with it, all hope.

'But she didn't have the baby, it was…' Colm was lost, truly, at this stage; he was as lost as Esme, but in a completely different way.

'She needs time. She needs to get out of this flat. Can you go somewhere for a while, just to give her a break, somewhere she can recover?'

'Well, we're hardly millionaires. You know I have to work and…' Then he stopped. 'I could take her to Ballycove, her mother is there; she runs a guest house. I'm sure she wouldn't mind…' He was thinking out loud. 'Maybe we could stay for a night or two…'

'Excellent, Ballycove sounds ideal.' The doctor clapped her hands together as if she'd sorted everything out and Esme was already on the road to recovery.

*

Esme had closed her eyes for most of the journey with Colm back to Ballycove. Not that she had slept, because at that stage she'd been too exhausted to expect anything more than breathing in the dark, feeling the emptiness of her body taking each betraying breath when all she wanted was to be with her baby.

When they arrived, Esme felt her jaw drop: the whole backdrop was spectacular and dramatic compared to the dreary streets of Dublin. The familiar village she'd grown up in felt as if it had transformed into a vibrant stage just to take her breath away. Purple heather and white bog cotton dotted the jade and russet of the land. The bare trees created a lacy patchwork against the leaded sky overhead. The ocean, normally a perfect blue, rolled silver and pewter waves crashing into the shining rocks from the inky depths beyond. The village was blanketed in cloud, as if the sea had thrown off a too-large overcoat of mist and it was determined to hang about the shoulders of the houses.

'Oh, dear, dear, dear.' Meredith cloaked Esme in a firm hug, as if she was returning from years spent on the far side of the world, and she held onto her in a way that reminded Esme she was never alone here at the Willows.

'Oh, Mammy, I don't know what to do.'

'You'll do nothing at all, the house is empty for the rest of the winter and all you'll have to think about is getting your strength back.'

Then she guided Esme to one of the best rooms that would be hers, not just for a week or two as planned, but for over sixty years.

'Come on now, get yourselves unpacked and then I'll make tea and we can watch the trawlers coming in with their day's catch from the veranda.' Meredith moved briskly, didn't waste words, but nor did she fritter away any opportunity to be kind if she could manage it.

Esme never forgot that enveloping generosity, nor did she forget those first few days when she and Colm went for walks on the beach and she felt the sea breeze begin to blow away some of the staleness of the previous weeks. It would take much more than a walk on the beach and the compassion of loved ones to set her right, but Esme knew that in Ballycove and the Willows, she had been fortified with something to help her take the first steps back to a new life.

*

On the Sunday afternoon, Meredith knocked on their bedroom door just as they were packing up their bags for the return to their little flat in Dublin.

'I just wondered if Esme would like to stay on. I mean, you know you'd be more than welcome, I'd love to have you here.' She reached out and took Esme's hand and then looked to Colm for permission of some sort.

'Oh, I don't know, I mean, staying here on your own, Esme… No, no, that wouldn't do at all,' Colm fretted. He'd seen how low she'd been for the last few weeks. He didn't dare risk leaving her alone for five more minutes than he needed to be at work for the day.

'I'd love to,' Esme heard herself say and maybe it was because it still rankled that other people made so many decisions for her. Doctors, priests and politicians had decided what was to be done about the child she'd lost and the child she couldn't carry. But mostly it was because, even in her darkest moments here, it felt as if the place was restoring her, putting her back together one small piece at a time. 'The fact is, I can't bear the thought of going back to the flat just yet.' She turned towards Colm. She was pleading with him, not complaining.

'Well, I know it's not the Ritz, but…' Despite trying to smile, his voice was unsure.

'It's not that, you know I love our flat, but these last few weeks, I've been like a prisoner there and what do I have there anyway…' This was true. She had friends, unmarried girls who still worked in jobs that had brought them to the city to begin, but the marriage bar had meant that as soon as she'd walked down the aisle, Esme had to give up her civil service post. She'd needed the baby to fill up her empty hours – and what did that say about the life they'd made in Dublin? 'Just another few days?'

'Of course, if you feel it's doing you good, why on earth wouldn't you?' His complexion had turned grey over the past few weeks and Esme could see in that moment he was so worried about her he'd have let her off to the moon if it made her feel better. 'I have to get back though; you know what John Steward is like.' He shook his head, because of course Esme knew exactly what he meant. It was unfortunate that her husband worked for a tight-fisted bully doing work that he didn't enjoy, whereas Esme had had to throw up the job she loved as soon as they were married. 'I'll come back down for you next weekend and we'll travel back together, how does that sound?'

'Oh, that sounds just perfect.' And it did, because it was a whole seven days before she had to see the inside of that flat again.

It was only as she walked along the beach later that evening that she began to examine how she felt about Dublin now. It was funny, but there was a time, not all that long ago, when all she'd wanted was to go and live in the big smoke. A part of her still loved the city, especially at Christmas time when they turned on the street lights and the shop windows were filled with Christmas trees and holly and mistletoe and it seemed like every door leaked the smell of rich Christmas cake onto the pavements.

No, she still loved the city. It was the connection it had to such recent misery that filled her with dread at the idea of going back. She'd spent three weeks in her darkened bedroom, much of it so hopeless she could barely lift her head from the pillow.

Regardless of how she felt, she'd have to go back in a week's time, but for now, as she walked along the beach with the waves roaring and crashing against the shore, she would only think of putting one foot in front of the other and she would try to claw her way back to some sort of new life.

*

Now, some sixty-plus years later, as Esme lay in her hospital bed, she knew *that* weekend had changed her life for the better. Maybe it was why, when she'd had time to think and couldn't run away from her memories, she had begun to cry. The tears streamed down her cheeks silently, a mixture of loneliness for the people she had lost along the way, first the baby, then her darling husband Colm and, later, Meredith, who had passed away almost in spite of herself, so busy was she right up to the very end.

The sound of the ambulance door being opened and a whoosh of cold air sweeping in from the hospital car park roused Esme from her memories. Then, she felt a familiar hand on her arm.

'You are okay, Esme?' Marta was next to her – had she been here all this time?

'I'm fine, just remembering.'

'I thought you were dreaming.' Marta's voice had grown softer than Esme had ever heard it before. It reminded Esme, she must keep on as even a keel as possible. Marta would worry about her; perhaps think her unfit to carry on in the big old guest house. She knew these were good complaints to have. There were so many people in here who didn't have someone like Marta who would drop everything to make sure she was all right. Dear Marta, what on earth would she ever do without her?

8

Cora

The rain had finally cleared over and now Cora squinted against sharp sun, intent on gaining ground against the heavy clouds before dusk. Light sparkled like glass smithereens off the wet road before her. Darkness would soon be unfolding above the ocean. Cora remembered the view from the front veranda of the Willows was spectacular.

Without warning, a raging emptiness cut through her as she thought of all those times when she'd hoped Michael would whisk her away to stay overnight somewhere like that, so they could hold hands, drink wine and watch the sun go down together. But the truth was, Michael was a creature of habit. She could imagine him saying, *There's nowhere like my own bed*. If he'd said it once over the years, he'd said it a thousand times. In some ways, Cora had always been grateful for it. God knew, enough of her friends were married to men who found comfort in someone else's bed. What on earth had she just done? She should be thanking her lucky stars. She was blessed to have a husband like him. Michael was a true blue. He'd be sleeping in that same bed until the day he died, if he had a choice. So why did she feel this heavy weight of emptiness instead, as if her marriage was some black hole and she was in danger of falling in and suffocating while life went on without her? Perhaps being out here in Ballycove would do *her* good, give her some perspective on things.

A huge cormorant flying high across her path made Cora slow down. He was majestic, black and hooded, carrying his catch back to a nest probably high up in trees and filled with hungry babies. Connor had been fascinated by those birds as a child. He would watch them wide-eyed as they stood on rocks along the river bank drying their outstretched wings. He would stare open-mouthed, eyes like saucers as they took flight along the length of the river that ran at the back of Cherrywood Crescent.

She switched off the radio and wound down the window of the car. In spite of the fact she was in bits, she knew, if right was right, it was pleasant here. The smells of summer growth, heightened by the rain earlier, reminded her of being a child, of summer holidays that always seemed to end much too soon.

Apart from a few evening walkers, clad in Lycra or dragging dogs behind them, the village was quiet in the evenings, it was just before the tourist season got into full swing. At the centre, the little supermarket was closing up for the night, the owner pulling down shutters; he turned to wave at her as she drove by. Something in the way he stood reminded her of her own father. Ferdia Conroy had died much too young. And even now, all these years later, Cora felt that familiar well of sadness bubble up inside her. She had been the apple of her father's eye, not that she hadn't loved her mother, not that her mother hadn't adored her too, but there had been a bond, a very special bond, with her father than neither time nor his death could diminish.

She looked back in the rear-view mirror. The shopkeeper was bending down now, gathering up the produce that lay in boxed racks outside his shop. Her father had been a shopkeeper too. He had owned a small corner shop and their little family of just the three of them had lived in the tiny terraced house next door. God, it was still all so real, she could almost feel him next to her in the car. Death, or unexpected death, was cruel like that, yanking away the person you loved so brutally that it seemed as if they were forever stranded between two worlds. She could never quite let him go and yet, she knew he wasn't really here any more. Cora took a deep breath to steady herself and then switched on the indicator, although there wasn't another car on the road, probably for miles, she'd bet, and she pulled into the drive towards the Willows.

It was all uphill. Cora jammed the gear stick into second gear. She winced when it screeched; thankfully, Michael wasn't here to hear it, she could imagine him rolling his eyes and shaking his head. He'd given up complaining about her driving years ago, but that didn't mean she didn't know exactly what he was thinking. He always insisted on taking the wheel on those rare occasions they travelled together these days.

Cora was pleasantly surprised. From the outside, the guest house had hardly changed at all. Well, perhaps it was a little shabbier, but it was all the more welcoming for that. She remembered so clearly, years earlier, walking up the steep drive with weary legs after a day spent careering in and out of the waves and building sandcastles on the beach.

This evening, the sinking copper sun made the tall Victorian house blush as if it were a great old schoolgirl, still easily swayed by the gentle flattery of the elements around it. It was an assemblage of assorted windows pointing out at odd angles with blue bangor slates falling like a heavy poncho down through several ravines and more windows jutting from the roof. At the very top, a line of soaring chimneypots rose to attention, like old generals, unwilling to stand down regardless of their futility in a time when the whole country wanted nothing less than carbon-neutral this and eco-friendly that. The window glass caught glints of light from the waves beneath, spiking occasional flashes of gold and silver that meant the house was forever catching your eye, even though the view beneath was breathtaking.

The woman called Marta had left a key for the front door on a plant stand in the veranda. It turned easily in the lock and Cora slipped it into her pocket as she pushed the door in. She felt along the wall for switches and soon the hall was bathed in sparkling yellow light from an overhead chandelier that she vaguely remembered liking years earlier. She walked beneath it, admiring the pendants; it was impossible to know how many of them there were in total. When her phone rang, it startled her out of her thoughts.

'Where in the name of all that's holy are you?' Michael sounded irritated with her, as if it was somehow her fault that he had slept too long before the TV.

'I'm not coming home tonight.'

'But where are you going to stay…?' His voice sounded odd and slightly far away, as if he'd lost some of the usual vitality from behind it.

'I've booked into a guest house.'

'*A guest house?*' She could hear the TV blaring in the background. 'Ah, Cora, sure that's just silly, come home and get into your own bed for the night. Whatever has upset you will look much better after a decent night's sleep.'

'I've been sleeping on it for weeks, Michael, and it seems to me, it never changes. It's never going to change. Maybe we just need some time apart so I can figure out what I need to do for the best in the long run.'

She wanted to cry, but instead, she bit her lip; she needed to be strong.

'So, this was all planned?'

'No. Of course it wasn't planned.'

'Oh Cora, can't you just stop this nonsense and come home?'

'I can't,' she said simply.

'Well, will I go and collect you?' He just wasn't getting it.

'No Michael. I can't go home, because I don't want to be in the same house as you any more. I'm staying here and as soon as my plans change, I'll let you know.'

'Oh.' It was a murmur more than anything else. The sound so small and defeated felt like a stab to Cora's heart. She didn't want to hurt him, truly she didn't, but she couldn't go on with the way things were. Even thinking about spending another day in the silence of her marriage made her stomach clench with the sort of dread only the nuns had reared up in her as a child.

'I rang up that guest house we came to when Connor was small, do you remember it? Over in Ballycove. I'll be here until I get my thoughts together.' If only they could have come back here together, if only things had turned out differently.

'I see.' But of course, he didn't.

'I think we need some space from each other.'

'What do you mean we need space? Haven't we a whole house here, empty apart from ourselves?'

'Yes, Michael, and that's half the problem.'

'So, I was right, you're just feeling a little off kilter after the wedding and everything... Come on home now and less of this silly talk about needing space, when all we need to do is knuckle down and get on with things.'

'You're not listening.' She sighed, because maybe he hadn't listened to her in years, or maybe she just wasn't explaining things properly. 'It's not enough any more, Michael. You and me, without anything in between, we're not enough, and I'm afraid it's too late to go doing anything to get things back to where they need to be if we're not going to spend the rest of our days just getting on.'

'But, we're happy.'

'No, Michael, you might be quite content, but I'm bloody miserable and I have been for a long time. Organising the wedding meant I could hide it from myself, but there's no running away from it now.'

For a long moment, only silence drew out the awkwardness between them. It was the first time she'd really told him how she felt.

'Well, maybe a night or two away in that old mausoleum

is just what you need so,' he said before banging down the phone and she wondered if he realised exactly what was happening between them at all, because it sounded very much as if he really thought she'd be back in Cherrywood Crescent with her tail between her legs for dinnertime tomorrow evening.

It felt strange, being here in someone else's house when there was no one but herself about; at the same time, the place felt homely, even if it looked nothing like Cherrywood Crescent. When they married first, she and Michael would often travel about to newly built estates and gaze through the windows of the vacant houses. If there was a door open or a gap yet to be sealed, they would let themselves in and wander about, mostly getting ideas for their own home when they could finally afford to buy it. She had loved those days, just her and Michael together, before Connor came along and they changed from being a couple to becoming these strangers they'd turned into.

The entrance hall was huge, big enough to fit a whole apartment into, if it was in the city. A rouge royal marble fireplace sat, empty but surrounded by a selection of dome chairs, as if waiting for Agatha Christie herself to book into Bertram's Hotel. Cora dropped into one, sinking into the deep velvety sumptuousness of it, feeling cocooned in its wings and beneath its dome. From there, she decided to explore the rest of the house. The whole place had a feeling of having been recently swept through. All the rooms were aired, the beds made up and the cupboards were stocked to get arriving guests through quite a few days.

'*Everything you need to know is written in the guest*

book,' Marta had said and Cora went back down to the entrance hall in search of it now. '*I will leave it on the table in the hall.*'

It was a huge book, leather-bound. Cora leafed through the pages, lines and lines of neat writing; it was a journal of entries, of comings and goings, shopping and cleaning lists and recipes and notes. At the start of each day, someone had written a short quote – as if to remind themselves of something that might otherwise be forgotten in the busy weeks ahead. Cora smiled when she read aloud the line at the top of the page, letting each word settle on her lips as she said them. *Keep walking through the snow, spring will come and everything will get easier.* Beneath this was filled in the names of guests arriving for the week and their room allocations.

Cora found herself wondering at the dedication involved in filling in everything from possible shopping lists to tick lists for when the piano tuner was last here two years earlier. She flicked through to open the page for that day. It was completely empty apart from a quote written out by a careful hand at the very top of the page. *Home is where the heart is.* Cora found herself tracing the words along with her finger, suddenly overwhelmed by everything that had happened that day. How on earth could a hackneyed expression make her feel as if her reserves had finally emptied out? She needed to go to bed and sleep until she could sleep no more. She was just dragging herself up to one of the more modest rooms at the top of the house when she heard the phone ring on the funny little table that acted as a reception desk. She dithered for a second or two on the stairs, but then, realising it could be Marta ringing up to tell her something important, she raced back down and lifted the receiver.

'Hello…' she said a little uncertainly, then added in her best voice, using a tone she hadn't used on the phone in twenty years, 'the Willows Guest House?'

'Ah, good, it's Joel Lawson here, I just thought I'd better let you know that I'm going to be arriving tonight, rather than tomorrow. I hope that's all right?' He hardly waited a beat before going on. 'I'll be there in half an hour, okay?'

'I… am… yes, I'll am…' Cora held the phone away from her and looked at it a little stupidly, not entirely sure what she should say. But by then the voice on the other end had hung up and so she was left standing there still trying to catch up. Had she just booked in a guest for the night? Oh, God.

She picked up the guest book again. And there he was, Joel Lawson. Well, the least she could do was let him in and show him to the room that Marta had allocated to him. How odd that, only an hour ago, she'd been a woman in need of a plan and so suddenly it felt as if here she was, thrown into a completely different life.

The sound of the wisteria rubbing against the window at the top of the staircase roused Cora from these musings. She closed the guest book. She had all she needed from it. Joel Lawson was due to arrive sometime after eleven the next morning. Marta or someone with a rather shaky hand had put a note against his name. *Rhett Butler*. What on earth was that all about? Cora squinted at the words. Could they have been written by the old lady who had been here the last time she'd visited? She must be ancient now, far too old to be booking in guests, but still, Cora had a feeling that so little had changed in the Willows, it was unlikely to have changed hands. Certainly, she could see no evidence of a new broom or any sweeping clean with any great modernising changes in the place. Maybe the old girl still owned the place, but she was a little dottier than she realised. Hopefully the trip to the hospital wasn't for anything too serious – for a moment, Cora forgot about her own worries, compared to what other people had to contend with; perhaps hers were not so bad.

Cora smiled; she already had a mental image of Joel Lawson in her mind. He was to stay in room six; a double bedroom at the front of the house, facing out onto the sea and with its own bathroom. It was, she would discover, one of the best rooms in the house, with an Edwardian four-poster bed, a cast-iron fireplace and a huge French armoire that filled one side of the wall next to the chimney breast.

Cora raced upstairs to double-check that the room was ready to go. She pulled back curtains as she went. Everything looked perfect to her admittedly unpractised eyes. Still, she threw open the windows, first the long narrow staircase window, which had only a slit opening at its base. This stained-glass window looked as if it had been in the house since it was built. In the morning, because it faced east, it cast a glorious array of colour across the landing, down the stairs and into the main entrance hallway. She remembered it from last time she was here; of course, there hadn't been a lot of time to admire it then, with a little boy to entertain and sunshine to tempt them to the beach from first thing in the morning to last thing at night. She stood admiring it now – the stained glass had a vibrancy that lifted her spirits against all that was reasonable.

The only other thing she could think of was perhaps some flowers from the garden to add a fresh scent. Last time she stayed here there was an abundance of fresh flowers in every room, Cora remembered that so clearly. She looked at her watch, plenty of time yet.

She found scissors in the kitchen and grabbed a huge vase that sat beneath the hall table. Outside, in her bare feet, the grass was still damp and it sent a deliciously cool shiver through her. The garden was ablaze with colour, it was magical really compared to the plain lawn of Cherrywood Crescent that was bordered with hardy annuals, never giving much more than shade and sparse muted colour in hesitant splurges.

Walking along the perimeter of the garden, her senses were assailed, not just by the unexpected cool bite of wet grass beneath her feet, but also the sound of the ocean, lapping against the rocks far below, and the heady scent of dewy roses, wallflowers and thick lavender. She cut bundles of them, dropping them into the vase. It didn't take long at all, in fact, she was a little disappointed when she'd filled the vase and it was time to go back inside.

At the far end of the village, she heard the church clock call out the half hour. She stood, enjoying the tranquillity of it, capturing this perfect moment for just an instant in her memory. She wondered then, as she looked out over the Atlantic Ocean, what Connor and Lydia were doing at this moment. She felt that familiar sense of loneliness rise up in her. She missed them so much sometimes, it was a physical pain. High up in the pines, crows shuffled to startle her and push back her thoughts for another time. It would do her no good to ruminate over things that couldn't be changed. There was no turning back time. What was it that she was always hearing? *Happiness is in the moment.* It felt too much like an ante-room to Cora, as if she'd moved from one phase and was standing on the doorstep, except there wasn't a familiar door to open, just an endless corridor with no signs to point the way.

She hurried back up to the house, filled the vase with water before setting it on the table that stood at the top of the stairs. Already, the scent of the flowers was beginning to waft around her and somehow it calmed her in a way she hadn't felt for a long time.

It was too nice to sit inside and wait for Joel Lawson to arrive, so she made a cup of tea and brought it and a couple of crackers she'd found in the larder out to the front of the guest house again. She stood for a moment in the veranda, listening to the sounds of the trees creak and swipe around her, the ocean in the distance crackling as it pulled away from the rocks on the shore, and the breeze winding through the chimes at the side of the house. It was glorious, magical and, for a short while, it felt as if anything was possible.

A sleek Mercedes pulling onto the drive drew Cora from her tangled thoughts.

'Hello.' Joel Lawson had a deep voice and raffish good looks that could only mean trouble for any woman who fell for him. 'Esme?' He looked at her oddly, as if she wasn't at all what he was expecting.

'No, I'm Cora. I spoke to you on the phone earlier. You made good time.'

'I did, it's always hard to gauge it on these country roads, but the scenery! I could have driven for another hour and not complained.' He was full of charm.

'It *is* beautiful here.' Cora nodded towards the front of the house. 'Come with me and I'll show you to your room.'

She felt conscious of him behind her, as if his eyes were on her all the time, but of course, he was probably just as bowled over by the guest house as she had been only a short while earlier. By the time she reached the bedroom door, she could smell his cologne, woody, musky, male. If she were to put a word on the scent, it would be as deep as his voice. Was he like Rhett Butler? Well, he was certainly tall, broad-shouldered and in great shape. No, on looks alone, she decided he was more of a Colin Firth than a Rhett Butler, but maybe that was just the fall of his hair, the clip in his accent – it was hard to determine exactly where he was from originally.

'Are you sure it's okay, me being here this early?' He kept his voice down, perhaps believing that there might be other guests to disturb.

'Absolutely.' She turned to look at him now. And no, there was no moustache; his hair was fair, more salt than pepper, wavy in a way that was distracting. But he had piercing blue eyes that disarmed her when he spoke and, for a moment, she thought, yes, maybe he is a little Rhett Butler. There was something about him, apart from being insanely handsome. It was something else, a sort of cool reserve that made it hard to pin him down. There was no wedding ring, Cora hadn't checked exactly, but she'd noticed.

'So, you're here for a few weeks over the summer, right?' She was trying to make small talk, because it's what people expected in guest houses, isn't it? That personal touch.

'That's right. I'm an engineer. My company is advising on the refurbishment of the church roof,' he said and he walked to the window at the end of the corridor which looked south towards the village.

'Good. Well, then, I think Marta has put you in one of the nicest rooms.' She was babbling on, but those piercing blue eyes were bloody unnerving. Honestly, it felt as if he could see right through her, not that there was anything to see. Of course, it probably had a lot more to do with her fragile state than the fact that Cora had always been an open book. Life was simpler that way and she wasn't sure she'd have the energy or indeed the patience for anything else. 'So, that's your room, I think you have everything you need there.' Well, as far as she'd been able to see, at least.

'Perfect.' He was standing inside the door, it felt as if he was waiting for her to leave, but her legs refused to move; she was stuck.

'So?' She tried smiling, but it seemed as if he was looking over her head. Of course, he probably assumed she was some woman, in from the village to help out at odd hours.

'So,' he smiled at her and she was sure there was something one of them should say, but neither of them knew exactly what.

'Right, well, I'd better leave you to it.' She backed away

awkwardly from the room. Definitely nerves, she was completely out of sorts. Suddenly being here felt unreal. She should be at home, with Michael, turning off the telly, heading for bed. Oh, God, don't cry now, she willed herself.

'Breakfast?' He was smiling at her now, his voice light, as if he might laugh at any moment and oddly, even if he was laughing at her strange tongue-tied awkwardness, she felt as if she too was in on the joke and it was almost a relief to have something to smile about.

'Ah, I'm not sure.'

'You're not sure?' And, when she explained that she was a guest too and she'd just let herself in with a key left in the porch, they both laughed. 'I'm sorry, I just assumed...'

When Cora made it to the bottom of the stairs, she felt like kicking herself. What was she? A lovestruck teenager? Fair enough, it was a long time since she'd actually come face to face with anyone male over the age of forty-five who didn't have a beer belly or a balding head – but that was to be expected when you lived in Cherrywood Crescent and all your neighbours were similar to yourself. Everyone she knew, or nearly everyone she knew, had spent the last twenty to thirty years rearing families, getting on with life, not jetting about the place in their luxury Mercedes booking into picturesque guest houses. Neither Michael nor any of his mates had managed to keep a waistband that was as narrow as their hips; few of them had managed to hold onto their hair, unless of course it was on their monobrows or growing in tufts in places other than the tops of their heads. Enough of the nonsense, she told herself as she rinsed out her teacup. It was late and she needed to call time on this strange day.

There were three bedrooms in the attic, small and cramped but with unspoiled views out across the sea to the rocky islands that dotted the bay in the distance. She pushed open the door to the smallest of the rooms, a narrow single, squeezed between two doubles, with a sink in the corner and an old-fashioned pink counterpane on the bed. She guessed it was the last room Marta gave out every year, but the small round window had been left open and it smelled fresh and felt cosy. It wasn't home, but it would do for now. She lay on top of the bed, closed her eyes and cried until the room grew dark and then the only punctuation was the periodic beam of the lighthouse in the distance.

In spite of the insomnia that usually kept her awake for half the night, she must have slept, because at some point the gannets and gulls cawing outside woke her. It was before five and she had a feeling they had been roused by the local fishermen heading out to sea in their trawlers for the day. Her phone, on the pillow next to her, had died during the night. She wondered if Michael might have rung again or even texted, although she very much doubted it.

She padded down the stairs, feeling as if she'd been emptied out overnight. It was probably only natural, feeling anything vaguely close to normal would have been a miracle. The house was silent, too early to go looking for breakfast and probably too late to bump into Joel Lawson. A walk on the beach would blow away some of the cobwebs hopefully and then, maybe she could stop and have a coffee if that little coffee shack she'd spotted the previous evening was open for business. At least she had a plan, Cora thought as she pulled the front door closed behind her.

Tuesday

9

Esme

When Esme woke it took a little while to figure out exactly where she was. She had been dreaming or remembering, all night apparently, because now a whole day and night had disappeared and she was still not back in Ballycove. Apart from being groggy as a hung-over jilted sailor, the sounds threw her off balance, a soft medley of rattles, echoes, squeaks and beeps. She opened her eyes slowly; it was no good of course, her eyesight had been fading gradually over the last decade so now, almost everything around the edges was eaten up by the black savagery of near blindness. She was lucky she still had any vision left at all, even if it did feel as if she was peering out at the world through a straw.

'Oh, you are awake?' Marta touched her hand gently and then withdrew as quickly. She was not a woman too keen on showing emotion in public. Or probably in private, too, if it came to it, but then, Esme knew, there were, as her own mother would have said, *Currants for cakes and raisons for everything*. Marta had good reason to be wary of any sort of physical closeness.

'I… what happened? How did I…'

'You fell. All your own fault, silly woman, climbing up on coffee tables…' Marta was bristling, but again, they'd known each other for so long, Esme understood, it was her way of handling the unease that something worse might have happened.

'Well I survived it, didn't I?' Esme said drily, although her head was pounding and she had a feeling that at some point, she must have blacked out; the previous day was little more than short clips of time, before and very little after she stood on that coffee table.

'Humph. Fractured ankle. Weeks probably here and then… poof, who knows…'

'Oh for goodness sake Marta, a little cracked ankle? Is that all? I broke my whole bloody leg when I was a child, I still managed to hobble about the place within a few days and it's never held me back.' Inwardly, Esme felt a chasm open – falls and breaks at her age were enough to finish a person off, she'd seen it often enough over the years. Not everyone was as lucky as her mother.

'Well, you're not a child any more.' Marta sniffed. Oh, my God, had she been crying?

'Marta, for heaven's sake, it's only my ankle,' she bristled with the force of a woman needing to believe it herself more than convince anyone else. 'And, the rest of me is perfectly fine. People my age, well, we break bones all the time. I'm only lucky I have bones to break; think about so many people we know – Linda Tremble has hardly any bones left at this stage, she's had so many new bits stuck in.'

She wasn't the best example, to be fair, Linda had replaced

just about everything – she had even taken to wearing wigs in her thirties, no one knew exactly what was beneath all that make-up she still plastered on. The woman was nearing ninety, for heaven's sake.

'I don't think replacing an ankle is possible, it's not the same thing as a hip or a knee.' Marta was matter-of-fact about these things. She didn't even wear lipstick, but then, there was probably a reason for that too.

'I'll be fine, just get me out of here.' Esme was drained, that was all; she'd be hobbling about the place again in no time. She sighed loudly, but she had a feeling she couldn't wheedle her way out of here until they were ready to let her go, and soon the purring machines around her soothed her back into a deep sleep once more. It was filled with dreams from her youth, from when she could see and race about and all the people she had loved were still around her. When she woke again, there were tears in her eyes and she wiped them away and sniffed and muttered something about the disinfectant making her eyes water.

'Esme? Would you like some tea or coffee?' Marta, sitting next to her bed, pulled her from her thoughts.

'Tea would be lovely.' Even though she suspected it would be as weak as water and would slop everywhere but into the cup. 'I'll need to...' she groaned; some part of her lower leg was caught up in the sheets and she couldn't be sure, but with each time she tried to pull herself up in the bed, she thought she heard an ominous rip of thick cotton beneath her.

'I am not sure if I should move you...' Marta stood, perhaps considering Esme's predicament for the moment.

Handing her a cup of tea while she was stretched out flat was akin to handing a saucer to the stork. 'Oh, you are all tied up here, no wonder you cannot move,' she said, lifting the blankets gently from around her plastered leg. She gently raised Esme's leg, freeing it from the sheets in which it had become knotted. 'You must pull yourself up, while I hold your leg.' With four almighty heaves Esme managed to pull herself almost into a sitting position. Marta fiddled with a control, eventually figuring out the shoulder rest so Esme had some support at her back.

'Indeed, that's not much better,' Esme grumbled. Her whole body ached, it felt as if she'd been lying in the same position for a week.

'Now, your tea.' Marta ignored her complaining and moved the tray in front of Esme, touching her hand to the edge of the saucer, then produced a thin bar of chocolate and handed it to her. 'I had this in my bag, just in case.' Marta was ever resourceful.

'I can't eat chocolate at this hour of the day.'

'Don't be silly, of course you can.' Marta laughed then. 'If you don't it will only make *me* fat anyway.' Sometimes, Esme couldn't be sure if Marta's generosity made her want to smile or to cry.

'So?' Esme said, feeling a little better once she'd drunk her tea and eaten the chocolate. 'What has the doctor said? When can I go home?' She'd been here since yesterday; surely someone had come to a decision about throwing her out.

'I haven't spoken to the doctor, but you'll go home when you're good and ready. You won't be missing very much in Ballycove, nothing ever changes there, only the sea eating away at the land, but it'll see us both out, if that's what you're worried about.'

'Hah!' Esme said. Marta hated the idea of the erosion – even in her decade in the village it had managed to cut out sections of overhanging cliffs over the sea. 'It's the start of the season, we were meant to be booking in that engineer today, weren't we?'

'It's all taken care of.' She had the brusqueness of the Basque, it was ingrained in her. 'You know, I will look after everything until you are fit to come home.'

'There's something you're not telling me.'

'It's nothing.' Marta stopped, but her silence was too weighted for either of them to pretend that something hadn't happened. 'It's not important, just this morning, Fenlon came calling.'

'Urgh.' Esme made a face. Paschal Fenlon had the charm of a boa constrictor and he was after her guest house. He was quick to point out that she needed a new roof. After grumbling about the state of the electrics, the plumbing and the price of keeping up an old property, he'd made her an eye-watering offer. Esme had to be firm, but Fenlon didn't seem to understand that some things were just not for sale. That was less than a week ago. That day, he could have been as persistent as he liked but, Esme told him in no uncertain terms, he wouldn't be having it. But now, today, lying here in a hospital bed, it suddenly felt as if it was all too much for her. She hadn't the money to replace the roof, never mind get plumbers or electricians in to do over the whole house.

What was she thinking? The Willows was her home

– perhaps it was the drugs they'd given her for pain relief. She closed her eyes, flinching at the pain that had begun to radiate up her leg once more. Esme had made up her mind. She couldn't have the likes of Fenlon stomping his size eleven boots all over her memories. She could pick out a happy memory in every single room in the Willows – well, she'd spent most of her life there. Some sad ones too. She had returned to it at her lowest ebb and even through the worst of times something in the fabric of the place had sustained her. It was at the Willows she'd come to terms with the fact that her marriage would never be blessed with children. It was sitting on the veranda that she'd finally managed to forgive herself for the abortion that she realised now had nothing to do with her miscarriages, but was absolutely the best choice she could have made at the time. It was there, with the tide below her gently sucking out to sea, that she had found peace in her mind and in her heart. She had a lifetime of memories there, not all of them happy, it was also there that her darling Colm had died in her arms in the double bed they'd shared for too many years to count.

'Well, you did ask.' Marta shifted on her seat and the movement created a shadow across the narrow light that was Esme's ration. 'Louis and the choir were asking for you too when I popped in for some milk this morning. They'd spotted the ambulance driving through the village to the guest house, I think they were planning to visit, but I told them you'd be home before they organised themselves.'

'Thank you,' Esme said, because the idea of having half the village descend on her here in the hospital when she couldn't be sure if the buttons on her nightie were properly done up or if her hair was sitting or standing was too much to bear. Being here was so far beyond her comfort zone, she'd rather die than have them see her so vulnerable. Marta knew it without ever having to put it into words.

*

Once Esme heard the worst – a fracture that they predicted would keep her off her feet for the summer – her next thought was of course the Willows. They had already booked in guests, not as many as they might have years ago, but still, people were looking forward to their holidays in Ballycove – she couldn't just let them down. She stuck her chin out with determination. Goodness knew there were enough challenges to keeping the place running at this stage, she couldn't let a fall from a wobbly coffee table be the straw that broke the camel's back. She needed to get out of hospital and get back home.

'Now, Mrs Goldthorp, how are we this evening?'

Esme opened her eyes and realised that she was surrounded by a wall of white coats. She peered around them, trying to figure out which was the consultant, but they were all shadows.

'So—' one of them cleared his throat and she looked in the general direction of a small figure who seemed to command the largest space about him. 'How are we feeling today, Mrs Goldthorp?

'I'm just dandy.' She tried to smile. 'And how are you?'

'Esme is intent on going home,' the matron chimed in from the other side of the bed. God, there was no discretion here, she'd only mentioned it a couple of times to nurses who passed near enough her bed to ask if there was anything she needed.

'I see, well, you do realise that your leg won't be weight-bearing for quite some time?' the consultant rhymed off, as if it was something he said to every other patient.

'Ah now, surely once I get back to my own corner?' Esme hoped she might bargain him down.

'It's a serious break, you must be sensible, otherwise...' he said flatly. 'And you'll need to keep the foot raised, so it's either bed rest or, if you're intent on being up and about, a comfortable chair with leg elevation at all times.'

'But I can't just...' Esme heard her own voice.

'There's no two ways about it, you've had a nasty fracture, you'll be in the plaster you're currently wearing for another two weeks and we'll hold onto you for that, but then...'

'So, I can't go home for two weeks?' She studied the cotton coverlet on her bed, concentrating hard so her eyebrows drew tightly together, willing herself not to cry.

'I'm afraid it will be a lot longer than that. You won't be climbing any stairs; you won't even be able to transfer yourself from bed to chair, unless you're good at hopping about on one leg.' He was trying to make light of things, perhaps to be kind, but Esme just felt her heart drift down in her as if it might reach that damned hard plaster on her leg.

'I can look after her,' Marta said quietly from somewhere beyond them on Esme's right.

'And you are?' The matron looked at Marta because they'd obviously established that she was not Esme's next of kin in any traditional sense.

'I am Marta, I help out at the guest house. I live with Esme, I look after her anyway.'

'Excuse me,' Esme started, but then she stopped, because this was not the time to talk them out of the fact that she would let Marta look after her. Still, it annoyed her to think she would need anyone minding her as if she was some sort of invalid. 'You see, I have help.' Surely once she got home and into her own familiar surroundings it would not be as bad as they seemed to be intent on painting things.

'We're not talking about help, Mrs Goldthorp, we're talking about full-time care, all day, every day for weeks ahead. Is that the sort of burden you really want to put on… Marta?' the matron said sternly. 'I have a bed set aside for you in the nursing home here in town. It's not Ballycove, and it may not be the Savoy, but it's the perfect solution to ensure you don't do yourself a further injury just because you're intent on digging your heels in.'

'Well, you better hold onto your nursing home bed for someone who's going to need it, hadn't you?' Esme pursed her lips stubbornly.

'Ahem.' The consultant bent lower to block out where the matron stood. 'It's good to hear you're determined to get up and running, Mrs Goldthorp, but it's quite a road ahead and we're just a little concerned that, well…'

'Of course, I understand, but you need to realise too, that I *am* going home, even if I have to belly flop my way out of here. I'm going back to run my guest house and there isn't a thing any of you can do to stop me.'

She felt Marta's hand on her shoulder, strong and cool.

'It will be fine, Esme. I will take care of you, just as I

always have and…' Then Marta turned her words towards the wall of doctors and the implacable matron. 'I will make sure she rests and does whatever exercises she needs to do when the time comes.'

Esme closed her eyes, thanking her lucky stars that Marta had come to stay with her all those years before.

10

Niamh

Niamh Brophy wasn't sure why she'd chosen Ballycove to run away to. Well, that wasn't strictly true, Ballycove and this guest house in particular seemed like they had called to her from not just her happy memories but with some sort of promise of peace of mind, which was all she wanted now.

She had the best memories of staying in a similar place on the east coast as a child with her grandparents. They'd visited one summer that seemed gloriously long but probably only lasted a week. Sometimes, it felt as if all her best summer memories were from playing on that little deserted beach.

But the fact was, her childhood had been happy, her life, many would say, had been charmed.

If anyone had asked her a decade ago what she hoped her life would turn into, she'd probably have said that she was on track for promotion in the Department of Foreign Affairs. She'd climbed her way up through the administrative rankings and was a middle-grade civil servant working directly in the area of the Irish Diplomatic Service. What she wouldn't have said were those million and one things everyone just assumes are written in the stars. You know, the husband, the children, the house in the suburbs, two cars and family holidays to places that have kids' clubs and all-you-want breakfasts and sun loungers that you need to place your towel on if you want to keep an eye on the pool in case those kids aren't strong swimmers even after all the lessons.

She certainly wouldn't have factored in Jeremy Standish and the fact that he would end up taking up such a huge part of her life. She'd fallen for Jeremy even though she knew he was married and she knew he'd never leave his wife. In fairness, while she was madly in love with him, she wasn't sure she could live with the guilt she'd surely feel if he did leave his wife, so it was always going to be a lose–lose situation.

In reality, her life had actually been going really well. She'd been happy to concentrate on her job, happy to have time to herself, and those moments she had with Jeremy were all the more precious for their rarity. Unlike so many of her friends, whose home lives were much more full-on, Niamh had always relished returning to her lovely flat each evening, it was an oasis of calm. She had liked the fact that the cup she'd left on the draining board that morning would still be there, untouched, when she pushed through the door after her day's work.

She liked the fact too that she could go away for a long weekend without having to check that it suited anyone else. And she still had Lorna, Debs and Annie, three friends from secondary school who had somehow ended up being as free as she was, even if they were flung to the far corners of the world. They went on holidays together every year, always somewhere exotic, always somewhere worth looking forward to.

The doctor had been nice, young and businesslike. Niamh was one of a hundred women she saw every week looking for the same answer to a problem they hadn't bargained on. She explained what would happen when the tablet was taken and how there was no going back after that. Niamh folded the script up neatly and slipped it into the lining pocket of her oversized bag. Suddenly, she wanted to be away from the city, she craved the sand between her toes and the wind blowing in her face. She remembered that childhood holiday with her grandparents that she'd never wanted to end – those carefree days by the sea that had been blessed with many good memories. She wanted to go back immediately, why wait until tomorrow; couldn't she just as easily take the tablet there as here?

She rang the Willows on her way back to the flat. The last thing she wanted was to be there if Jeremy decided to call with an empty gesture of flowers and a concerned smile on his face that she knew for certain to be false now.

'I can be there early on Wednesday, if that's okay with you?'

'Of course, your room is ready.' A heavily accented woman promised they would have coffee and warm scones ready to greet her when she arrived.

'God, I think I'd love to stay for the whole summer,' Niamh groaned, but she had to be back at work again, and she would be, of course, looking her usual professional self. It seemed that, on the turn of a pin, she'd booked two weeks off work, but she could take more, they owed her more days than she'd ever take in holiday time. Already, Niamh knew she was doing the right thing; spending time at the Willows would give her time to think, to get things straight in her mind.

Wednesday

11

Esme

It was funny, but being away from the Willows, everything smelled somehow different on her return. Fresh flowers? How lovely, Marta had thought of everything.

'You will have to move downstairs, I have set up one of the guest bedrooms,' Marta said, and her voice brooked no argument. To be fair, the last thing Esme wanted was to be any more of a burden than she already was. Travelling back to Ballycove, being transferred by ambulance, she'd felt acutely her newly acquired dependency on others; it was numbing in its substantiality. 'Now, we will set you up here, if you are not sleepy…'

'Here?' Esme repeated, because Marta had pulled up to an abrupt halt in the middle of the hall.

'Yes. It is either here or in the bedroom and we both know that you won't be able to stay out of things for very long, no matter what you promised that doctor.' She aligned the wheelchair next to the fireplace.

'I'm not sitting here in a wheelchair all day long, people will think they've walked into some sort of care home.'

'Fine.' Marta angled the wheelchair against one of the dome chairs that had been sent back from India well over a hundred years earlier. 'In you go.' She bent down and hoisted Esme effortlessly from the chair, lifting her light frame and depositing her smoothly so she sank comfortably into the worn velvet.

'These are bloody cold.' Esme pulled her cardigan up around her and shivered. The hall was fine for walking through, but it was chilly if she was going to be sitting here for any length of time.

'You want me to light a fire?' Marta eyed the grate.

'No, no, there's no need.' Esme couldn't remember the last time they'd had a fire here. Well, maybe she could. Colm had kept this fire going every winter for as long as they'd been running the guest house together. Over thirty years. In those days, they didn't close for winter and this hallway, with its fire blazing, was as welcoming as a mother's embrace when the wind howled and the sea crashed into the cliff face just beyond.

'Don't worry, it will be a novelty. I'm sure the guests will love it too,' Marta said while pulling across the ottoman and resting Esme's leg on it carefully.

'Marta, you simply can't spend your day running around after guests and putting on fires and looking after me, I won't allow it. Get me a blanket and I'll be just fine.'

'I certainly will not. You'll have a fire and you'll be happy to sit there,' she said in that way that signalled arguing with her would be a waste of time, it was already as good as done.

'Of course, we'll just have to get some outside help,' Esme said an hour later, as she listened to Marta stacking firewood in the basket near the grate. There were two local women who could be relied upon each summer, but they'd both been in touch already to say they wouldn't be able to help out this year. Well, they were both well beyond retirement age and Esme knew that even if Lena or Connie had enjoyed the pin money, neither of them were keen on the early mornings or the three flights of stairs that had to be climbed when the house was full and beds needed to be changed from the top down. Even if they'd been up for taking on the guest house, they certainly wouldn't be fit enough to care for an old invalid who couldn't do the most basic things without a strong shoulder to lean on, much less be of any help in the busy house.

'I will ask in the village, there will be plenty of the local schoolgirls who would surely like to come in and help out for a summer job,' Marta said. Certainly, there never seemed to be shortage of bright and enthusiastic youngsters in the local grocery shop. Louis had perhaps cornered the market there, in terms of collaring the youngsters into covering shifts that his family no longer wanted. Esme could just pick up the phone and ask him. 'Now, I will go and get some lunch for us and you can sit there and keep an eye on things.' Marta stopped, perhaps realising what she'd said, but she was much too direct to let it hold her up.

'You mean you're going to leave me here all day long, just... here...?'

'Here.' Marta placed the guest book on her knees. 'You can do what you do better than anyone else, meet the guests and keep everyone happy.' She opened the guest book on today's page and ran her fingers down along the names it contained. 'We have Joel Lawson, he is the engineer you booked in; we have that woman who rang when we were on our way to the hospital – Cora Doyle – and we have Mrs Blackman and her daughter Diana, who have just booked in this morning.'

And then she was gone, rustling up lunch, getting fuel for the fire that they shouldn't be lighting in summer and organising a ground-floor bedroom for Esme.

*

The sound of the fire crackling beside her and the familiar rattles and creaks of the house soon settled around Esme as she sat in the empty hall. It seemed to her that the whole house echoed with memories. They came crowding in on her as if they'd been lurking, waiting until she was alone. Perhaps it was because of her absence from it – the family ghosts had missed her. She thought about her grandmother – the gutsy Nancy Shine who had married far above her station into the wealthy Fitzgerald family. The village still remembered Nancy, who had saved many a man from the Black and Tans by hiding him in the attics above her father-in-law's bed. Esme's mother always believed that Nancy still roamed the hallways, gathering up dust and cobwebs with the old handkerchief she'd always had to hand. Nancy had loved this house and maybe it was one of those traits that she'd passed on to her daughter and her granddaughter, or maybe it just eased into them from the fabric of the place.

Esme must have nodded off, because the next thing she heard were voices from the hallway behind her chair and they startled her into alertness. It wasn't that she was eavesdropping, but you couldn't help but overhear an argument. She recognised them, mother and daughter. Esme listened to their voices; although it was a few years since they'd stayed here, their voices were still familiar. From here she guessed they were sitting in the club chairs looking out the front window with a view along the beach which raced off into the distance. It was a long time since Esme had walked down the beach, but when she could do so independently, she sat on the veranda most days and drank in the fresh breezes from the ocean and the heavy perfume of the garden. Even in winter, maybe especially in winter, when she and Marta had the house to themselves, Esme loved to sit at the front, bundled up in her warmest clothes, and close her eyes, listening to the sound of gentle rain on the plants and the ocean in the distance.

'Well, you must change it back,' the daughter was saying and Esme imagined her, chin out, cheeky and stubborn. They were arguing about who would be named on her mother's bank account. 'I'm your only daughter after all, it's not right.'

'And Peter is my only son,' the mother countered in a voice that had grown, to Esme's ears, heartbreakingly frail.

'Peter is not to be trusted, you know that, you haven't forgotten the time he gambled the telephone bill on the horses.'

'He didn't gamble the telephone bill on the horses... that was a different thing altogether.' The mother was no longer a young woman and perhaps she'd never been a strong one. To Esme's ears, this was an argument she would lose eventually by virtue of her daughter's constant attrition as opposed to her own free will. For the first time in her life,

Esme considered herself lucky not to have a daughter. 'And anyway, it wasn't even ten pounds...'

'It doesn't matter how much it was, Mum, the fact is, he's worse than useless, I mean, you're still doing his washing for heaven's sake and all he wants is that house.'

'*That house* is my home.'

'We'll have to sell it. He can't think he can go on living there without paying so much as a penny's rent.'

'I can't sell my house – where would we go?'

'Well, you'll be sensible; you'll move to a nice retirement village, they cost practically nothing so long as you give them your pension and...'

'What about Peter; you can't mean to send him to an old folks' home as well?'

'He's forty-two bloody years old with a wife and family, Mum. Do you really think he's not capable of finding somewhere to live?'

'He can't afford it, you have no idea how much he's paying to keep those kiddies every week.'

'If he was that fond of them perhaps he shouldn't have—' Her words were cut off.

'Diana!' her mother snapped. Esme supposed it was as near to a reprimand as you got when you'd spent your life with a tyrant; first with a husband and now maybe the apple hadn't fallen too far from the tree. It seemed inevitable to Esme that this conversation would go round and round, until the poor woman agreed to put her daughter in charge of all her affairs. Suddenly, Esme felt as if she couldn't stand it, the idea of the old woman being harangued to within an inch of her peace of mind, when she was meant to be here on her holidays. She remembered Peter, a quiet, thoughtful child, not a scowler, not like Diana. Esme couldn't stop herself; she had to do something to help.

'Ahem.' Esme cleared her throat loudly. 'Is that you, Mrs Blackman?' She leaned around the side of her dome chair and cocked her head in their general direction.

'Yes. Oh, it's you, Mrs Goldthorp.'

'Esme, please, call me Esme.' She could hear the older woman make her way across the hall. 'Sit with me for a minute, how have you been? It must be three or four years since you were here?'

'It's far too long, almost seven, if you can believe it.' Constance Blackman had always been the unassuming sort of weak-willed woman who seemed to play second fiddle even to herself, but Esme had always liked her. If Esme could have stirred gumption into her tea instead of sugar when Constance had been married to that brute of a husband, she'd have been pouring it in by the kilo.

'Seven years, eh, where do they go?' Esme thought about that. Seven years ago, she'd been driving into the village, singing in the church choir, and a member of a book club with strong opinions on every subject under the sun. 'Do you know, I think they race by much more quickly on purpose as you get older?'

'My husband died, do you remember him?' Mrs Blackman asked.

'Of course.' Esme stopped herself from saying anything she didn't mean. 'And so you're here with your daughter now?'

Diana muttered something by way of an afflicted greeting

from across the hall before going out on the veranda to make a call.

'That's right. Diana. She's very good to come along with me for a little break…' Constance was about to go singing the awful Diana's praises when Esme stopped her.

'Ah, daughters, they *can* be such a blessing, *if* you're lucky with them.' Esme lowered her voice and patted the chair next to her.

'Yes, you're right of course.' Constance sat and leaned towards her, perhaps understanding that their conversation might be something best kept between themselves. She was not a naturally loud speaker anyway, not like Diana who had made a fuss about going outside to make a phone call.

'Now, my friend, Mary, she had two daughters,' Esme said.

'Had?'

'Yes, poor Mary, she died much too soon of course, just eighty-six, but way before her time. Ingrown toenail, of all things, left too long, the infection you see, well; nasty things, you need to watch your feet when you get to our age,' Esme said wisely, then felt more than saw Mrs Blackman glancing towards her own war injury. 'Oh, no this is nothing just a broken ankle, better in no time. Toenails, that's what you need to look out for.'

'And her daughters?'

'Ah, no, both perfectly healthy last I heard.' Esme really didn't mean to sound disappointed. 'But that's the thing, isn't it. They were dear Mary's pride and joy, one so diligent, she'd have built a nest in your ear before you had time to hear she was there. She had her own car and a flat in the city and a job that was too boring for most of us to stick at for life, but she's probably still there, licking stamps and sealing envelopes. And then, the other, the complete opposite – a dreamer, Mary couldn't do enough for the girl and took the greatest pleasure in looking after her. You'd meet Mary in the supermarket and she'd be picking up the coffee that Jane likes, or the only marmalade Jane can stomach, and they seemed to be as happy as two pears in punch in that little house, just at the back of the church.'

'But…'

'Well, when it came to bringing Mary to the bank or the solicitors, neither girl could be faulted for their enthusiasm. Unfortunately, they weren't so good at taking her to the doctor or the chiropodist, were they?'

'Ah, I see,' Mrs Blackman murmured.

'But do you though?' Esme asked.

'Yes, of course, but it's not like that with Diana and Peter… they're both… well, they're just…' It seemed suddenly she ran out of words for what they both were. 'Anyway, I'm well able to get myself to the doctor and anywhere else I might want to go.' She was a little miffed.

'It's not about getting to the chiropodist, though, is it?' Esme sighed; you had to be so careful talking to other women about their children. 'It's about not being constantly badgered into selling your house, or signing over your bank accounts or making your will…'

'Who mentioned my will? Nobody has mentioned me making a will, anyway, that was all done and dusted years ago when my husband was alive, we agreed everything then…'

'But you could change your mind, if you wanted to…'

'Well, I suppose I could, but why on earth would I want to do that?'

'As I see it, that might be your ace card to having a lovely relaxing holiday with your daughter, one that you'll both remember.' She stopped, to let the woman think for a moment, because sometimes, at their age, it was no harm to gather your thoughts before anyone threw any new ideas at you. Then, Esme groaned as she tried to lean forward. 'I think that somewhere around here Marta has left the guest book, can you see it?'

'Yes, it's right here on the table.'

'Would you mind doing me a little favour?' Esme asked.

'Anything, just say what you need…' She stopped. 'It can't be easy to move about when you've been in the wars?'

'Oh, don't feel too sorry for me, my leg will heal, it's more inconvenient than anything else, but my eyes aren't what they used to be, I'm afraid.' Well, that was the understatement of the day. 'Could you open the page for today, and tell me what it says?'

Esme smiled as sweetly as she could manage, it was damned uncomfortable here, when she sat in the same position for too long, but she would rather die before she would ask a guest for help in holding her leg free while she mooched about to get a more restful position in the chair.

'Ah,' Constance said. She flicked the pages over and stopped when she came to what Esme had wanted her to see.

'Can you see it?'

'Yes, I see it.' She held it a little away from her eyes and began to read the words haltingly. '*A good will is far more valuable to you when you're alive than when you're dead.*'

'Sometimes, it's no harm to use a hammer rather than a carrot to get your message across. You don't have to actually hit the person over the head with it; just don't be afraid to dangle it in front of their noses, if you need to.'

'I see.' Constance Blackman sounded as if a weight had been lifted from her shoulders. 'Of course, you're right, I'm quite happy to have Peter stay with me for as long as he likes, I enjoy the company to be honest. But I can see perfectly well that he should make some small contribution to the housekeeping too.'

'And Diana?'

'She's a good girl, but she's her father's daughter.'

'Well, isn't it time you took that in hand?'

'Do you know, you're right, I think it is and I actually feel as if I might be able for it at this stage.' She placed the book back on the table and leaned back into her dome chair next to Esme.

'It could be the making of you,' Esme said sweetly.

'I might even enjoy it,' Constance whispered.

'Sometimes, we need to remind ourselves that just because we are old, doesn't mean we have to give up.' And it was the truth, Esme had always known it, perhaps she needed to remind herself of it occasionally also. 'And you know as well as I do that there is nothing like a storm to make you appreciate a good day, or even a grey one.'

'Thank you, Esme.' Constance's voice, although still hardly above a whisper, had a lighter sound to it than before.

'Between ourselves, it was beginning to feel as if I had just exchanged one bossy person in my life for another.'

'That's a kind way of putting it.' Esme smiled. 'But you're old enough to be your own boss now.'

'You're absolutely right.' Constance squeezed her hand and headed back towards Diana who had walked into the hall, sighing dramatically at having to wait for her mother.

Esme heard Constance's voice grow sharper and more assured. 'Now, Diana, I want no more nonsense about what I do with my own money or my house. If I hear another word from you, I'm going to call up my solicitor and leave the lot to the cat refuge.'

She sounded a lot more sure than Esme had a feeling she was, but still, Esme smiled and rubbed her hand along the soft blanket Marta had placed across her knees earlier. At least she'd made some small difference to one of her guests. Perhaps she wasn't completely useless after all. She pulled herself slightly up in her chair, sniffing importantly, feeling just a little less insignificant than she had since this blasted plaster went on.

*

'Coffee?' Marta bustled in about an hour later.

'Ugh, sludge,' Esme said, but she took the cup and sipped it anyway. Marta always made very strong coffee. She insisted Irish people were barbaric when it came to what was ultimately hot water and a spoon of instant. 'This Joel Lawson bloke, what's he like?'

'You mean, are you right?' Marta was smiling; Esme could hear it in her voice. 'I'm sure he is every ounce the gentleman, Mrs Goldthorp.' She tried her best to do a southern belle accent, which sounded comical on top of her throaty Spanish voice.

'Frankly my dear...' Esme joined in, remembering how he'd spoken on the phone and she'd instantly imagined him as a Clark Gable type. Of course, she'd gone blank on the actor's name and only remembered his most famous role. 'It'll be interesting to see if I'm right, though.'

She most often was; over the last few years she'd surprised herself with just how close she'd got in matching up telephone voices with people's personalities and sometimes their physical appearances too. She'd be disappointed if Joel Lawson turned out to be grumpy, gropey, five foot nothing, sarcastic and bald.

'You mean if he has a moustache?'

'Don't be silly. No. I mean, he's an older man, well fifties, late forties anyway, but I suspect he might be quite dashing, a little dangerous perhaps, a charmer.'

Actually, she'd be a little disappointed if he didn't have a moustache, did men wear them any more? Esme wasn't sure.

'Ah, I see,' Marta said, but her voice was flat. Perhaps being married to a very bad man had made her forget what it was to admire other men at this point. Esme knew lots of women who did, but there were plenty like herself who took an interest in everyone who crossed their paths, the good, the bad, the ugly and most particularly the dashing. Esme firmly believed that being interested was what had kept her young at heart.

'Anyway, I'm sure I'll meet him as he's passing through.'

A quiver of guilt ran through Esme. It really wasn't fair to let Marta take on responsibility for the guest house like this, there was so much work for just one person. There must be someone who could come in and give a hand with breakfasts and laundry, she reminded Marta again.

*

Esme fell asleep for a little while as the evening drew in, her mind swirling about with a mixture of memories and worries. She dreamed of her mother, at the end. It was frightening really and the older Esme got, the more she realised it. Meredith McEvoy had been such a force of life, from the way she moved to the way she talked, she had been her mother's daughter. She'd been much younger than Esme was now when she died, hardly sixty-seven. They'd celebrated her birthday just the week before. She'd been almost blind for a decade at that point, of course she'd been completely in denial. For the last few years of her life, Meredith McEvoy had set breakfast trays, made pots of tea and counted out sugar lumps while Esme whizzed about the guest house, making sure sheets were changed, breakfasts were cooked and guests were happy.

People often wondered about two women sharing a house. Mother and daughter. They assumed there would be battles, but the truth was, Meredith was too wise to ever get embroiled in her daughter's affairs. She was just happy to have Esme and Colm staying with her. They'd come back out of desperation. For the second time in her life, Esme had been pitched into a pit of depression after the stillbirth of their baby. For too long, it felt as if she might have lost anything that would ever be worth having in the world. Worse, in the dead of night, she wondered if it wasn't all her own doing – payback for past deeds.

But it's funny how life can look after you, and slowly, the Willows began to matter more and more to her. It became her life, even if she'd never have imagined that could be the case all those years ago.

Maybe it was because it had never been her plan, but rather the decision to stay had been made gradually out of Esme's own desire to spend her days in the grand old Victorian house, overlooking the Atlantic and serving up a traditional *céad míle fáilte* to the thousands of guests they'd welcomed to stay over the years.

The trick to living harmoniously together was that neither of them interfered with the other. When Esme noticed the first signs of her mother's frailty, she wordlessly picked up the slack, she worked around her and encouraged her mother to be every bit as much a part of the Willows as she'd always been. There was implicit agreement, tacit respect.

It was Meredith who had shown Esme what it was to appreciate the good in others and it was Meredith who had started the tradition of imagining what the people who were coming to stay were like before they arrived. It had been a game between them, much as it was a game between Esme and Marta now.

Meredith had also started to write a note to uplift them or make them think in each daily page of the guest book.

These days, it was down to Marta to fill in each entry, very many copied out from the year before. A wise thought for every day and she did it meticulously at the start of every year. It had become something of a ritual in the wintry first days of January – they would sit together while Marta read and wrote – and Esme smiled as memories washed over her of all the times those words had made a difference to herself and others.

Esme had stored the original guest books, which dated back to during the war, safely in her room. Years ago, when her eyesight was better, she would take them down occasionally and run her finger along the names, imagining what each guest had been like, because she was certain each person listed there had brought something of themselves to the house. Meredith had believed everyone who stayed had left some small grain of love behind and that was what kept the Willows such a happy place. Sometimes, Esme thought she heard the laughter of two hundred years ring through the empty rooms, reverberating off the walls, rattling the old pipes and brushing against the drapes, and it made her smile to believe that she would never be truly alone.

Esme always understood, this house had saved her life. And she trusted that it could save others too, although she had no reason to suppose that any of her guests particularly needed saving.

*

'You are okay, Esme?' Marta asked, returning from dusting the upstairs hallways.

'I'm fine, just remembering.'

'Yes. You will have so much time for that here,' Marta

said, 'maybe too much time to be good for you. I can bring up magazines if you want...' She stopped short, while a leaden silence stretched out between them. Even still, there were times when she forgot. 'Perhaps not.' She brushed away a stray dark rib that had escaped the tight bun she scraped her hair into each morning. 'I will clear away your cup and bring you some fresh water. Yes?'

'You'll drive yourself into the ground if you keep up fussing over me, when really I'm sure you have plenty to be getting on with.' Esme couldn't help feeling guilty that Marta already had enough to do with running the guest house on her own, the last thing she needed was to be waiting hand and foot on Esme.

'It is really not a problem. I finished tidying the bedrooms and I thought maybe I could sit here and we could chat for a while.' Marta was smiling. At least there was help now – even if the girls from the village weren't exactly experienced, they took a little pressure off Marta.

'For now, we will have afternoon tea,' she said before bustling towards the kitchen. She was back again quickly with a tray perfectly laid and Esme had a feeling she had prepared it earlier; all she'd needed to add was hot water to the tea pot. 'Did I ever mention that my grandfather was blind?' Marta said as she placed a cup on the small table next to Esme.

'I'm sorry, was it...?' There was so much she didn't know about Marta, even though she was probably the closest person to her in the world, although neither would easily admit it.

'Oh, it was a very long time ago. In the war... he was...

my grandmother said he was lucky, it could have been much worse.'

'I suppose that's one way of looking at it.' Esme smiled. 'I think your grandmother might have had an Irish streak to her sense of humour.'

'My grandmother was very strong, very set in her ways, but she had a big heart.' Marta started to laugh. 'I think you would have liked her, but she was very much a woman of the Basque Country –' then she seemed to think for a moment '– but yes, there were similarities to the Irish ways, I suppose.'

Although Marta rarely spoke about her life before she came to Ballycove, Esme had stitched together from snippets over the years that she had been a happy child growing up with her parents and grandparents. She'd married young, to a wealthy man she thought would be good to her, but he had quickly shown himself to be an overbearing bully. They hadn't been married very long when he hit her for the first time and, after that, it soon became a regular feature in her life. Leaving the Basque Country was probably the hardest thing she'd done, but when her mother died, there was every reason to leave. She truly believed that her husband could kill her one day in a violent rage and so she'd walked out with little more than enough money to pay for her bus fare to Paris and from there she'd managed to make her way west. There was no missing the fact that she was carrying a great sadness, regardless of how she managed to cover it over with cups of tea and gruff kindness.

'She taught me how to make coffee properly, real coffee from the Basque...' Marta said and Esme knew that, for once, her thoughts of home had made her smile.

12

Cora

Cora lasted until Wednesday and then knew she could put it off no longer. She had to go back to Cherrywood Crescent, just to make sure Michael was all right. They hadn't spent time apart since she'd been in the maternity ward having Connor. Michael was useless on his own – did he even know where the tea bags were kept to get his breakfast ready, never mind getting his lunch ready?

Was she actually leaving him? No. Of course she wasn't, they'd been married for thirty years, you didn't just walk away from that after an argument over dinner. It was ridiculous.

If they did separate, what on earth would she say to Connor? What would she say to the neighbours, to people who'd known them only as a couple for years?

Oh, God, she didn't want to run into Michael, but some perverse need in her was pushing her back to check on the house – to check on Michael too, if she was honest.

She looked at her watch. There was plenty of time, but still she felt a sickening stirring up in her stomach, as if some new dread was rising up in her as she turned into the Crescent. But she was here now, so there was nothing else for it, the least she could do was take the envelopes that were poking out of the postbox and place them on the hall table. She could be back at the Willows again before Michael even turned his car onto the motorway forty miles away.

'Hey?' Tanya called before Cora could make it from the car to the house. She had hoped to avoid the neighbours, but there was no avoiding Tanya. 'What have you been up to?'

'Nothing, why?'

'Don't look so guilty, I'm not checking up on you, just I noticed your car was gone last night and you never go anywhere!' She rolled her eyes. 'Sorry, but you know what I mean, usually, for summer holidays, you're always knocking about the Crescent, doing your good deeds.'

'Hardly.'

'Don't be so modest, we both know I won't be caught doing a good deed unless there's a hunk involved somewhere.' Tanya threw her head back and laughed and Cora marvelled at the fact that they were both the same age. Whereas Cora trimmed her fringe between hairdressing appointments to cover the frown on her forehead and the laughter lines about her eyes, she noticed that Tanya's skin was as smooth as an eighteen-year-old's. It really was quite astounding. 'So?'

'Huh? Oh, me? I'm just having a little break, I'm staying in a guest house out in Ballycove, just to…' Cora stopped, she really didn't want to have to have a conversation about the state of her marriage with Tanya. 'Unwind.'

'Good for you, it's about time you had a bit of pampering. Make sure you get the works when you're there.'

'Ha-ha.' Cora had a vague memory of Tanya going to some sort of spa years earlier and returning after two weeks with a Turkish masseur and an engagement ring that hadn't lasted much longer than an Irish summer. 'I'll make sure to enjoy it.' And when she thought about it now, apart from all the tears and the emptiness in her real life, it was nice to get away from Cherrywood Crescent and the prying eyes and twitching blinds of the neighbourhood-watch fanatics.

'Well, don't go for too long or someone might come along and snatch up that husband of yours.' Tanya threw her head back and cackled loudly again; and Cora thought that nothing was less likely.

'I'll take my chances.' Cora smiled, because a little part of her wondered if Michael would notice another woman, especially since it felt as if he hadn't noticed Cora in years. Tanya was rattling on about the latest gossip on the Crescent, young Billy Flannery had wrapped his company car around a lamppost on his way home from work the previous evening. Everyone assumed he'd stopped off in the pub on the way home. Cora stood there and let the gossip wash over her, thinking instead that, one day soon, Tanya might be talking about her and Michael and the fact that they were splitting up. That thought made her mouth so dry she almost lost her breath and she began to cough until she was almost breathless with the overwhelming sadness and fear of what suddenly felt like the inevitable end of her marriage.

Although she'd spent most of her married life here and nothing had changed in the short time since she'd surprised herself and walked out the door, there was an uneasiness that seemed to breathe from the walls of the house from the moment she stepped into the hallway. It was crazy, she'd only left two days ago, but it was as if she'd walked into some parallel universe. Everything was the very same, and yet, all was changed completely in some indiscernible way. The living room was exactly as she found it every other morning. Michael's newspaper had been thrown down at his feet and the remote control snuggled next to his cushion on the chair. Even his used teacup with only the sodden remains of his dunked digestive biscuits stood on the floor next to the armchair where Michael had probably spent the evening as usual.

Automatically, she found herself bending to pick up the cup, reaching to draw the curtains back, and then she stopped. The familiar aroma of her home catching her up; it felt colder than she would have expected, but then that was probably just her imagination. At this time of year, she didn't put the heating on and the fire wouldn't be lit for another few months, unless the weather took a drastic dip. Somehow, Cora resisted the urge to pick up the used cup, place the newspaper in the recycling and put the remote control on the coffee table. Instead she stood back and surveyed the room. It had, with the fresh perspective of having been away, taken on a pathetic and worn-out feel.

It was depressing. Standing there, in the middle of the kitchen, Cora wanted to fold over into herself and cry like a baby. Her home, her lovely, if a little shabby, home that she'd poured a lifetime of energy into felt as if it had been completely abandoned. It was as though the place had begun to fade without her. Everything, from the pot plants on the window ledge to the calendar on the wall, just seemed to be a little more tragic than she remembered. And it wasn't that she didn't feel a rush of love for those little things she had acquired over the years. As she stood here, she knew, with certainty, that if she really left Michael and moved into a place of her own, she would want some of these things with her. Not big expensive things, no, Michael could definitely keep the television and the Swiss carriage clock they'd been given as a wedding gift from his parents. She would want to bring the dishes that she'd painstakingly collected over the first ten years of their marriage. That collection marked something close to a labour of love. Each week, she'd marched into the local hardware store and picked up another treasured piece; some weeks, if her housekeeping stretched to it, she'd picked up two, so by the end she had a full set of Galway pottery plates, dishes, cups and saucers that she'd never actually used.

She walked to the old dresser that she'd found in a house clearing sale. She'd spent weeks stripping and cleaning it, so it was back to its solid pine bones. Of course, to be on trend now, it would have to be painted over again in some shade of duck egg, but she loved it still, exactly as it was. Everything was there, just as she'd left it. She ran her finger along the smooth rim of a breakfast dish. The feel of its coolness made her shiver. Was this what it had all come to? She turned on her heels, as if scalded by the thought. She needed to pick up some more clothes. She raced upstairs and began to pack.

Outside she heard the familiar sound of Michael's van pull up. She checked her watch; he was early. Normally, he didn't arrive home for another two hours. She wondered if something had happened. She stood almost to attention, her heart unreasonably hammering in her chest, waiting for him to push through the small door that connected the utility room with the garage. It felt as if it was taking him an age, but when he opened the door into the kitchen, she realised, maybe he too had to steel himself before seeing her, having spotted her car in the drive when he'd arrived home.

'Hello,' he said a little formally and he stood there gazing at her, as if she was an apparition who had appeared in the wrong location. 'So, you're back?'

'No, not back, I was just...' What was she just? Checking to see if he was surviving without her? Well, it appeared he was.

'Ah, Cora, haven't you made your point?' he sighed, glancing around the kitchen. Suddenly, he looked dismal and Cora felt her heart sink with overwhelming pity when she regarded him from this new emotional distance, then he cleared his throat, as if he was about to speak to a stranger. 'It's your house too; you have every right to be here. Were you...'

He appeared to be completely dishevelled and uncared for, his skin dried out from too much sun, covered over with a grey shadow of beard that he hadn't gotten round to shaving that morning. His clothes, normally covered in fresh sawdust, looked as if they hadn't been washed in a week and his big toe peeked out through socks so thin she could almost guess the denier. Where on earth had he come across those? He must have been rooting about in the recycling pile. He looked pathetic and Cora felt her heart break a little more than it had before.

'It's a bit of a mess, sorry…' he said.

'As you say, it's your house too, no need to apologise.' She smiled a little uncomfortably to cover the yawning spasm of grief at where life had so abruptly taken them. 'You've managed, then?'

'Oh, yeah, right, well, you know, it's hardly rocket science and I've well…' He stopped, obviously aware that somehow, somewhere, he'd managed to put his foot in it. 'In saying that, I could die of scurvy if you stayed away any longer.' He tried to grin, but it was obvious that he was feeling the pressure of their awkwardness too.

'You finished early today?' she said to change a subject that wasn't going anywhere she wanted to follow.

'Yeah, well, I'm not much use today. I've driven more nails in my fingers than into the joists, so I just cut out early, try again tomorrow.'

'I'm sorry.'

'Yeah, well.' He shrugged, leaving an uncomfortable silence to linger between them. 'So you've had a little think and you're back to—'

'I haven't made any decisions at all.' She cut him off.

'Oh,' he mumbled and turned away from her, but not before she caught the shock and hurt in his eyes. Perhaps he'd thought she was back for good. 'Cup of tea?' he said awkwardly.

Cora couldn't remember the last time anyone had made tea or anything else for her in this house.

'Okay.'

Did he even know she had given up sugar for Lent five years earlier? She watched as he padded about the kitchen, checking in drawers for things that he should have known weren't there. She was right about the sugar; she watched him ladling in two large spoonfuls before he looked at her hopefully as if to check if she'd like some more.

'I gave it up years ago, Michael.'

'Eh?' And he looked down to the offending spoon in his hand. 'Oh, that's right, so you did,' he said, pouring the tea down the sink and starting again. 'Sorry,' he mumbled, but the most depressing thing of all was, she had a feeling he had no idea what it was she needed him to be sorry about.

Cora found herself surveying the kitchen from this unfamiliar emotional perspective. They hadn't sat here in ages, just the two of them, probably not since Connor was a nipper and tucked in bed at night while they had dinner before flopping in front of the telly, exhausted after a long day. Wasn't that it though? Wasn't that just another symptom of why she couldn't take it any more? Part of her had always believed that someday they'd have dinner here, with her lovely tableware and candles and a crisp white linen tablecloth. She had imagined them on long summer evenings sitting here as a couple, lingering late into the evening with the patio door opened out onto the decking (yes, that same decking that Michael had never managed to build for them). She'd had rose-tinted visions of them entertaining friends here one day in the future, of drinking wine and laughing at jokes that resonated with some memory they'd made together years before. None of that had happened. They didn't have mutual friends; worse, it seemed there were no memories she could think of that either she or Michael could reminisce over together and laugh about until the early hours.

She knew, as she stood here watching him shamble about their kitchen, she should tell him all of this, but she wasn't sure she had the energy to explain, she wasn't sure he'd even understand. Would he even want to hear it? At this point, she didn't think he would. His voice brought her back to the present moment.

'Ah, Cora.' He hung his head and examined his huge hands as if he hadn't noticed them before. 'Look, I'm sorry, for everything. I'm not able for this, you know, I'm just not built for this sort of drama. All right if you want to find yourself, but can't you do it like any other woman your age, take up tennis or drawing or pottery? You don't have to go gallivanting off to the other side of the county.'

'Is that as far as you've managed to think things through? That all of this, my leaving, is nothing more than midlife hysterics? My hormones or the menopause or empty nest syndrome? Is that really the best you can come up with, Michael?' She looked at him now, she was raging, she wanted to cry with temper and disappointment, but she was damned if he was going to see that. 'Look, if that's what you think this is about, we're never going to move forward, we just can't, don't you see that?'

'But…' He waited, opening and closing his mouth, waiting for words to come when he had no idea what to say. Cora got up, grabbed her bag from the worktop and stalked to the door. 'Cora, love…' He sounded so very far away. 'Please, don't go, not like this, I'm sorry.'

She turned to look at him, sitting there, pathetic and alone, and she knew he really was sorry, except he had no idea what he had to be sorry for and, until they took a good long look at themselves, there was no point in plastering over cracks that would only dig deeper into the foundations of whatever happiness they once had.

'Yes, Michael, of course you are. You're sorry for saying something that might upset me, but you don't get it and maybe you never will,' she said sadly, her voice as leaden as her heart, and then she knew, she couldn't do this. She couldn't come back here, not now, not yet. Maybe not ever?

'What do we tell people? What will I say?' He was trying to process things, slowly putting together the pieces that would need to be reassembled if their lives were to diverge at this point.

'People?' She didn't say that he never made time to talk to the neighbours beyond a hurried hello or goodbye as he walked from the house to his van at either end of the working day. 'Nothing. We're just taking time out, they probably won't even realise I'm not here.' It wasn't strictly true, but she couldn't deal with this now. 'I've told Tanya that I'm taking a little break in Ballycove.' Cora tried to close down the top of the bag she had so hurriedly packed, but it was no good, it was like trying to stuff an elephant into a teacup.

'Huh, Tanya,' he snorted. 'Now I see what's going on. Tanya has been saying things to you, that's it, isn't it? Well, life isn't all that rosy on her side of the fence either, you know. We can't all be on permanent holidays going about the place wearing sunglasses the size of dinner plates even in the depths of winter.'

Cora looked at him, for a moment, but she didn't speak. No good could come of having a conversation like this, they were both too emotional.

'Please Cora, please, you can't do this,' he begged.

'Yes, Michael, that's the only thing I can do now.'

'But you can't just leave, what do you mean to do? Live in a hotel for the rest of your days? You can't just up and go after all the years we've been together, we have a family, we've made vows to each other.'

'We did make vows, to cherish and love each other until death do us part.' She hadn't forgotten her vows. 'And we still have a family, we're still married. I just need some space, I think we both do.'

'I don't need space and I don't need you telling me that I need it either.' He harrumphed, a strange echo that managed to sound much louder and odder than perhaps he'd meant it to.

'Okay, fine, well *I* need space, I need space from us.'

'And what about Connor and Lydia? Or have you even thought about them in this great escape plan of yours?'

'Seriously, Michael? Connor is twenty-eight, he hardly thinks of us from one end of the day to the other.' She had thought about Connor, of course she had thought about him. There was no point telling Michael that the idea of them as a family might have been the only thing holding them together for too long.

'We're still parents, or have you decided you need space from that too?'

'That's not fair,' she snapped.

'I'm sorry, you're right, I'm just…' He wiped away a tear from his cheek, but it was too late, he'd started to sob now, great big uncontrollable sobs that he had no idea how to handle.

'We can tell him if you want, we shouldn't lie, but for now, it might be better not to say anything at all, just give ourselves time to work things out between us, what do you think?'

'I won't lie to anyone.' He sniffed.

'Nor would I, but upsetting him now, when he is just happily married, well, it seems unnecessarily cruel, don't you think?'

'I suppose,' he murmured.

'Okay, so that's settled. Unless there's some reason he needs to know right now, we just keep this between ourselves. I'm going to stay put in Ballycove for the next few days and then...'

'And then?' He looked pathetic, as if just waiting for some small scrap of hope from her next words.

'And then, we'll see.'

'It seems you have your mind all made up,' he said and she looked out the window towards the garden beyond because she couldn't bear to see the devastation crumple up his features even more. 'Right, so that's that then,' he said finally, clearing his throat.

'It's just breathing space, Michael, that's all.'

Was that all? The firm bang of the front door behind her felt like a panicky note of daunting accusation as she stood on her own doorstep. She really wasn't quite as sure of things as he might believe her to be.

She made the journey back to Ballycove in a state of shock. She was on automatic pilot, not noticing the houses or the roads she passed by, she could have been driving on the moon for all she noticed.

13

Niamh

Everything about the journey to Ballycove – from the orange sun in the sky before her, to the sea glistening beneath the road and the bursting hedgerows – was dazzling in intensity. It felt as if the vibrancy of the place had been tuned to maximum. A far cry from the overcast greyness she'd left behind her in Dublin. The roads were quiet, as though they'd been cleared just to make her drive more pleasurable. Niamh had stopped for a fifteen-minute break to take in the fresh air at Lough Owel and to enjoy the feeling of having escaped Dublin, skiving off work while her colleagues were still tied to their desks, and, maybe too, to luxuriate in the notion of being free of things she hadn't realised were keeping her a prisoner.

The Willows looked exactly as it did on the website – perhaps a little shabbier than chic, but Niamh needed to be somewhere that just felt homely. This place was perfect.

'Hello?' she called out when she reached the little table that doubled as a reception desk.

'Hello?' A thin voice emerged from one of the dome chairs behind her.

'Oh, hi.' Niamh walked round to look at the woman properly.

'Esme.' The old woman smiled and held her hand out in Niamh's general direction. 'You must be Niamh?'

'That's right and you are Mrs Goldthorp?' And for a moment, Niamh studied the woman and thought she suited this place. There was an air of something homely but stately about her, in the way she held herself, in spite of her raised leg. 'And you run the guest house?'

'Indeed, well, this year, thanks to my banjaxed leg, I'm afraid I've been demoted to being the one-woman welcoming committee. Mind you, perhaps it's time for me to let someone else do the running about now. I have been here a very long time.' Esme laughed. 'Do you want to sit down; I'm afraid Marta is looking after the place virtually single-handedly at the moment so it might take her a minute to arrive at the front desk. Here, sign in while you're waiting.' She held out a large guest book. 'Can you see a quote just along the top of today's page?' she asked, leaning forward slightly.

'Why, yes, it's in Irish. I'm not sure how good my Irish is at this stage.' She read out the neat handwriting at the top of the page. 'Let's see, is it – *Easy to swim with the tide, but swimming against it can bring greater rewards*?' Such a simple sentence and yet it resonated with Niamh, even if she wasn't exactly sure what it meant – for her, at least.

'Ah, of course, one of my favourites.' Esme smiled with satisfaction. And Niamh wondered if the old girl was completely dotty, or if she was far more tuned in to life than maybe Niamh was.

The quote was still ringing in Niamh's ears when she

flopped down on the soft double bed in her room later that night. After she had unpacked, she'd gone exploring, just a round of the village and a little while sitting on one of the benches overlooking the beach.

She yawned loudly; surprised that she was looking forward to sinking into the crisp sheets. Even though the room was old-fashioned, a medley of faded chintz, a cast-iron fireplace and a writing desk that stood about four inches lower than most modern office desks, there was the faintest hint of lavender on the air wafting up from the garden below.

Just as she was about to turn off the bedside light, she caught sight of the tablet she had meant to take, but she was too comfortable and sleepy now to leave this cocoon. She would take it first thing in the morning. Yes, she yawned again. She would definitely take it then.

Thursday

14

Phyllis

Everything was so familiar and for a moment the awareness of it caught in Phyllis Courtney's chest – she shouldn't have come here. It was too much. She should have made some excuse, stayed put and buried her head in the sand for just a little longer.

But she needed to do something and, when she'd mentioned the idea of coming to stay at the Willows to Rob, he'd jumped at it, as if she'd offered him the last seats on a lifeboat making its way from the *Titanic* for both him and Josh. It meant taking Josh out of primary school for a few days, which made it an even bigger adventure for her grandson.

Now she had arrived, she realised it was a mistake. Perhaps it wasn't the place to tell her son that she believed his father was all too quickly being taken from her by the terrible disease that took his grandfather Paedar Courtney years before.

'I'm just so glad you could come,' Esme said, gripping her shoulders with a force that took Phyllis by surprise.

Another surprise was seeing her old friend confined to a dome chair in the hallway of the guest house, with a rug across her knees and a smouldering fire in the grate. She had known about the fall, of course, but somehow, seeing her like this, it brought home to Phyllis that her friend was old now, they both were. Sometimes, when she looked at Kurt, this gradual passing of time struck her in the same immediate and shocking way. She tried to shake the familiar ache from her shoulders; after all, they were lucky to have each other after all this time.

'Are you sure it's all right that we're here? You look...' There was no point lying. Far too much had passed between Phyllis and Esme for anything less than the truth at this point. '... Worn out. I hope this place isn't becoming too much for you?'

'I probably look a lot worse than I feel. And I feel a million times better now that my oldest friend in the world is here.'

'Oh, Esme.' Kurt leaned in and kissed her on the cheek. 'I'd be very careful who you're calling old around here.'

'Ara, go on with you Kurt, Phyllis knows exactly what I mean.'

'Of course I do.' Phyllis patted Esme's hand, glad that in all these years nothing had changed between the three of them. It was strange, but at moments like these, it always felt as if Colm might come through the door at any moment with an armful of wood for the fire.

'So, were you dancing or fighting this time?' Kurt asked, glancing at Esme's raised ankle.

'A little bit of both, perhaps.' Esme smiled and Phyllis wondered if she thought he was making small talk, or if she realised that how she ended up fracturing her leg had probably completely slipped out of Kurt's mind. 'But it doesn't matter now, because you're both here and, even better, I believe Josh and Rob are on their way?'

'You're so good to squeeze us all in at such short notice,' Phyllis said, looking around. But the place hadn't the feel it once had, when it had been so full of guests it seemed as if the seams of the old house might burst. It was funny, but the last few years they'd always visited towards the end of the season, just as everyone was finishing up their summer holidays; Phyllis hadn't thought before about the fact that the guest house wasn't as busy as it had been in the past.

'There was no squeezing needed at all, the rooms were free and even if they weren't we'd have made space somewhere in the house.' Esme did look so happy just to have them here, to Phyllis it felt almost unfair that she had come to run away from problems that there was no running from.

If she was honest with herself, this was probably the last place she could hide from her worries. Her friendship with Esme spanned almost seventy years, since they were two young girls living in the city, they knew each other too well not to notice if something was weighing the other down.

'I'm so looking forward to having a child running through the corridors again,' Esme said wistfully, and Phyllis thought once more of that time long ago when Esme had been pregnant but it wasn't meant to be. After all these years, Phyllis still felt a stab of regret for so much water under the bridge that it was hard to know where the river of sadness began and guilt ended.

'Be careful what you wish for, he's a real handful,' Kurt

said, though he worshipped Josh, they all did. 'He'll be steaming through here at all hours trailing every stray dog in the place behind him if you let him away with it.'

'You forget how much joy they can be…' Esme clapped her hands. She simply adored children.

'And how much hard work too,' Phyllis said because it was what she'd always done, tried to take the shine off having a family when it was something Esme had missed out on. 'He's really looking forward to coming here. He's been talking about it non-stop since Rob told him.'

'And of course, Rob sees it as a sort of passing on of his own childhood memories – he still talks about here and how much he loved those summer holidays as a child.' Kurt chuckled.

There were so many of their memories as a family wrapped up in this place, each year Phyllis had remembered the years before. This time, she was just acutely aware of how quickly time was slipping by. Would this be the last time she and Kurt would make this trek to the west of Ireland and stay here in this beautiful guest house by the sea? She felt the years slipping from her, like grains of sand through her fingers. She didn't even try to count it up this time round. She had a fleeting memory of Rob when he was Josh's age, racing through the front hall with treasures gleaned from beachcombing and his nose kissed with freckles that appeared every summer. Dear Josh. He was such a joy for all of them. Of course, he'd never remember his mother. Paula had died just hours after he was born; he was, in every way, a miracle baby. He was the saving of Rob.

It was funny, but these last few months, the more Phyllis

thought about her son, the more she realised it was time he began to think about moving on with his life. Rob was still young enough to begin again, he could have more children, he'd been a fantastic husband when Paula was alive.

Rob needed this break too as a chance to breathe, but the truth was, Phyllis knew, they all needed to drink in the magic of the sea air and maybe, if the weather was even halfway decent, dip into the reviving cold Atlantic waters. She shivered now, but it had nothing to do with the cold. Rather, it was the certain knowledge that she couldn't pretend everything was just fine for much longer.

15

Esme

Marta was running late. Esme may not have been able to see the watch on her wrist, but she knew from the heat of the sun folding across the blanket on her knees that evening was stretching in and Marta should be home by now. On the one hand, she'd been so delighted to see Marta agree to join the local quilting group, hadn't she all but pushed her out the door for their annual outing for afternoon tea in the Railway Hotel in the next town over? The only reason Marta had gone was because Esme had reassured her that the girl who'd promised to turn up from the village was probably on her way already.

The girl hadn't shown up. Pah! Esme should have known better. She knew the family, the mother had flitted from job to job all her life and the father hadn't bothered with work for as long as anyone could remember. The apple, as they say, often doesn't fall too far from the tree.

The phone vibrating on her knees pulled Esme from her thoughts.

'Hello...' she said tentatively, because she wasn't expecting a call from anyone today.

'Oh, Esme, thank goodness,' Marta said and there was no missing the anxiousness in her voice. 'The blasted bus has broken down and now we are here, on the side of the road, waiting for another one to pick us up, and who do I see but that daft girl, Chloe, who was meant to be looking after you, walking along the road as bold as brass, draped around her boyfriend as if she couldn't stand up on her own.'

'I'm fine, really, Marta, don't worry.'

'Did she even ring to tell you she wouldn't be there?' Marta didn't wait for an answer, because maybe she knew as well as Esme did that the two girls Louis had sent up from the shop were gluggers – they only arrived in to work when it suited them and, so far, it didn't seem to suit them all that very often at all. 'And the worst thing is, we will not be home for hours yet and all I can think of is your dinner and if you are all right and...' She was almost out of breath.

'I'm fine, really, Marta, don't get into such a panic. I'm really fine.'

'But you'll need to...' Marta lowered her voice. 'Go to the toilet and have some dinner and change your position in the chair and I was so worried, but there was no signal and now my phone battery has almost died and...' It was so unlike Marta, she sounded completely at sea.

'Stop now. Don't be silly. I'm tucked up here as cosy and content as can be,' Esme purred; she just wished that Marta hadn't reminded her about using the bathroom, because suddenly, she really needed to go. 'I'm absolutely fine and I'm not on my own, there are plenty of people here.'

'Yes, yes, of course, there's Cora, she said she was going to read in her room for the afternoon, she can help, you will call her, if you need to…' She stopped for a moment as if picking her words. 'You must call her, Esme, if you need something, you promised the doctor you wouldn't try to stand on that leg…'

'I have a broken ankle, Marta, I'm not completely stupid.' Honestly, sometimes, Marta treated her as if she was a child or, worse, some sort of helpless ninny. This was what her life had come to, sitting here in one of the dome chairs each day, while Marta ran the Willows around her and Esme just chatted to guests and picked up phone calls as they came.

'You *will* call her, if you need anything.' There was still an old extension system between the rooms that could be speed dialled on the portable phone which usually sat at reception but which had become Esme's responsibility since the accident.

'I'll call her,' Esme said, but she was losing patience now and perhaps they both knew she had no intention of calling anyone. She'd rather sit here with her legs crossed for a week than ask a guest to bring her to the bathroom. Of course, there was Phyllis, but Esme had a feeling that Phyllis had enough on her plate. Even if her oldest friend had not yet put her worries into words, Esme was quite certain there was more to this holiday than just taking in the sea air. She hung up before Marta could make any more unwelcome suggestions.

It took less than four minutes for Cora Doyle to arrive in the hall next to Esme. Bloody, interfering Marta.

'She shouldn't have called you.' Esme felt as if she couldn't apologise enough, how embarrassing to have to call on a paying guest to help her.

'Well, she did and I'm glad she did. Now, what first, will I make us both a cup of tea, or would you like to freshen up in your room while I put the kettle on? You must be stiff as a board sitting there for this length.'

'I'm fine, really...' Esme said, but she wasn't. Perhaps, if she just moved to the wheelchair, it might make a difference and she wouldn't need to do anything more than sit in a different position for a while.

'I'm sure you are, but I'm here now.' Cora pulled the wheelchair out from behind the ancient screen where Marta had parked it out of sight. 'I could bring you for a walk, if you'd like.'

'Certainly not. I don't want the whole village seeing me being wheeled about the place like an old woman.'

'Of course.' But there was an amused lilt to her voice and even Esme had to laugh when she thought about how silly she was being.

'Sorry. Thank you,' she said, remembering her manners. 'Maybe another time, when I'm a little more...'

'No problem. It must be beyond miserable being stuck in that chair all day.' Cora managed to transfer Esme from the dome chair to the wheelchair without so much as a puff from either of them. 'Now, I'm going to bring you to the bathroom first, I'm not sure how mobile you are, but I looked after a lady who lived a few doors down from us in Cherrywood Crescent, so you're in safe hands, don't worry.'

'You really shouldn't be doing this...'

In spite of the fact that it made Esme want to crumple

up with mortification that a guest would have to so much as make her a cup of coffee, never mind wheel her to the bathroom, Cora made light of it and, somehow, her kindness didn't feel like pity.

Once she was sorted, Cora set her up in her dome chair again, her leg resting on the ottoman, and they chatted happily over tea and Marta's homemade fruit scones. All in all, it was turning out to be a pleasant afternoon. Obviously, Esme would have liked to learn a little more about Cora, but the woman had the infuriating knack of being much too good company to be drawn out on anything much more than her teaching assistant's job, which she loved, and her son's wedding, which sounded like the most wonderful day ever.

Esme, on the other hand, had all but told Cora her whole life story – well, the edited highlights at any rate. She enjoyed talking about her dearest Colm. She couldn't remember the last time she'd told anyone about him, she'd never really been able to talk to Marta about him. He was the complete opposite of the man Marta had married and run away from all those years ago.

'It sounds as if you had a very happy marriage,' Cora said and Esme thought she caught something almost wistful in her voice.

'I think we had. I mean, after we lost the babies, I thought nothing would ever be the same again and I suppose it wasn't, there was always a sense of loss that I carried about with me. But with this place and the people who have come here every summer, somehow, it felt with each year that the emptiness in my heart filled over a little more. Does that sound ridiculous?'

'Not at all. It actually sounds beautiful,' Cora said.

'Oh, look at me.' Esme wiped a tear from her eye. 'You've made me cry.'

'I'm sorry.'

'No, don't be. It's remembering things, sometimes I miss those times so much. I miss being young and vital and racing about and those days when the Willows was full of people and it seemed like nothing could go wrong. The way I remember it, the heating never broke down then and the windows never rattled.' She sighed, because it was true, the ever-increasing number of creaks, rattles and groans that now marked out the fact that things needed to be upgraded or repaired had never seemed to so much as murmur back then. 'It's true what they say, you know, about youth.'

'It's wasted on the young?'

'Yes. It's like happiness and contentment, we don't realise how precious it is, until it's gone,' Esme said and she wondered for a moment if perhaps Cora hadn't wiped away a tear too.

'I envy you.' Cora's voice was so quiet, it was almost a whisper.

'You envy me?' Esme thought nothing could be so ludicrous. She was an old woman, sitting here with a broken leg, in a house that needed a lot of work on it if it was to continue to remain open to guests, and really, if she was honest, mostly she believed that the happiest moments of her life were far behind her. 'Oh, dear, life can't be so bad for you that you envy a half-crocked old biddy like me...' She laughed as she reached out and managed to catch Cora's hand.

'Oh, don't take any notice of me.' She sniffed. 'I'm just feeling sorry for myself now, thinking of you and Colm sitting on the veranda and the fact that you knew, you really knew how much he loved you all along.'

'That's why you're here?' It was only a nudge, but Esme had a feeling it might be enough to open the floodgates. It was obvious that Cora needed to talk to someone and Esme might be an old woman, but she had the time to listen and maybe, with the help of all the years she'd spent here, maybe she could offer her some sort of advice. Maybe.

'Yes. I think my marriage is over. To be honest, it *is* why I came here, to get time to think.' Cora sighed and Esme felt a cloud of guilt for not having tuned into this earlier. She'd been so happy chatting away about the past; she hadn't sensed that Cora had real and pressing concerns in the present.

'A problem shared.' Esme knew this particular saying to be far more valuable than people often realised.

'I'm so sorry, the last thing you need is guests bringing their troubles to your door.' Cora rummaged in her pockets and pulled out a tissue, as if she knew there would be tears.

'Isn't that what we're here for, the Willows and Ballycove – well, if you can't find some comfort here, then I don't know where you'd find it in the whole world and I'm far too old to think the world owes me the favour of orbiting about my feelings.' They both laughed at this, but Esme knew that when marriages went wrong, there wasn't anything to laugh about. 'And if you were in danger of any sort from your husband, I would much prefer that you stay here and take as long as you need to figure out what comes next.'

'Oh, no, Michael would never hurt me, not like that,' Cora said quickly, batting away the very idea of it, which came as a relief to Esme, because you never knew what went on in other people's marriages.

'Well, so long as you know that the Willows will be a safe haven for as long as you need it to sort yourself out.'

'It's not that I need to get away from him because he's cruel or anything like that. It's just, I feel as if... it's as if my marriage has died of neglect. It's been a sort of slow and dragged-out death and it's just been a gradual emptying out of both of us. I suppose people change, maybe I've changed and sometimes, I feel that Michael hasn't.'

'It's not always a bad thing, if a man stays the same, so long as he's a good man. There are worse things. My friend, Helen, her husband took to jogging when he retired. Sixty-six years old and he goes out and buys a pair of shorts that were almost obscene.' Esme thought back to those days, poor Helen. 'Honestly, she could hardly show her face at choir for a month. And then he up and died. I mean, not content with mortifying her with displaying the family jewels all over the village, he kicks the bucket just as she's having the house painted. Seriously, is there any worse time for the hearse to park outside your door for a respectful moment than when you're at that craggy stage between power-wash and first coat?' She smiled. 'It's lovely now, of course, she went for goose-wing grey in the end. Very subtle.'

'I can't see Michael taking up jogging any time soon, he's much too busy going to work and coming home to slump in front of the telly. He spends his days making other women's homes beautiful and, when he comes home, he really just wants the quiet life and, if I'm honest, he's a good man.'

'I had a sense that you wouldn't be married to someone who was a brute. He's probably not perfect, but then which of us is?'

'True – he *is* a good man. I'm just not sure he's the best man for me any more.' Cora stopped, glanced down towards Esme's raised leg. 'Honestly, I feel rather guilty now; you have enough to be doing, getting your leg better after your fall. You shouldn't have to put up with some random woman's marriage problems as well.'

'What else have I to do?' Esme laughed. 'You know, when I moved back here again, I only came for a weekend, to get away too, just to think, but...' she shrugged her shoulders. 'That was a very long time ago.'

'Well, I do hope you'll be seeing the back of me before the season is out.' Cora laughed and Esme had a feeling it was a relieved sound, as if she'd been waiting to talk to someone – anyone – about what was troubling her.

'I knew a woman once who ran away for six weeks. Six whole weeks – imagine? We all wondered where on earth could a woman hide for that length of time. Mind you, in her particular case, I always felt it was better not to know. In the end, she only came back for her shoes, but she told me, just between ourselves mind, that when she came back and saw how well her husband had managed without her, well, it made her think twice about running away again.'

'I see,' Cora said, but Esme had a feeling she really didn't see at all and, perhaps, that was half the problem. 'What a queer story.'

'Not so queer, not really. You see, her name was Mae and they hadn't been married very long, just a year or two, actually. They were at that stage where they should have still been mad for each other or up to their ankles in nappies, but how and ever.'

'What went wrong?'

'He got a different job, driving a lorry. She was at home sometimes for days on end and when he arrived home, well he was exhausted and I suppose they got lazy and, before you knew it, she wanted more and all he could say was that he was giving all he had.'

'But of course, he wasn't...' Cora said quickly.

'Perhaps not, but when Mae went away, she didn't go alone. She had her head turned by a smooth-talking waster who promised her more and delivered plenty to begin but was just as quickly off again.'

'I have no intention of finding another man – smooth-talking or otherwise.'

'Neither did she, he found her. But that's beside the point. The real point is, that when she went back that day to find her old walking shoes, rather than the fancy impractical heels she'd taken with her, something happened.'

'What happened?' Cora was leaning forward now.

'Well, she tried on her comfortable old shoes and she realised that maybe there was a lot to be said for being comfortable, as opposed to being...'

'I think I understand now.' And for a moment, they both fell into silence, Cora perhaps in her thoughts and Esme in her memories. The front door banging made Esme start.

'Oh, *gracias a Dios*, you are fine. You are fine.' Marta

pushed through the front door, sounding out of breath as her shoes slapped against the floor even faster than their usual pace.

'I do hope you didn't go racing up that hill on my account,' Esme said shortly. 'You know, I'm more than capable of looking after myself.'

'I never said you weren't.' Marta dropped into a chair and it felt as if a wave of stress and hot air released from her now that she knew Esme was okay.

'Esme was just telling me a story about a friend of hers.'

'Huh. Esme has known more friends with upside-down lives than we have made upside-down puddings.' Marta got up from her chair and headed towards the kitchen.

'You're very wise, you know that?' Cora leaned across and touched Esme's hand.

'I don't know about that.' Esme thought all she'd done was listen really. 'It's been a lovely evening.'

'I enjoyed it too,' Cora said. 'Anytime you want me to make tea and sit here listening to stories about Colm and the Willows, you know where I am.'

She squeezed Esme's hand and Esme thought how nice it was to have someone around who didn't treat her as if she needed to be wrapped up in cotton wool all the time.

Friday

16

Phyllis

It wasn't fine. It hadn't been fine for months. Probably, it hadn't been fine last time they were here the previous August, but she'd blinded herself to the reality of it. Kurt was slipping away from her and she knew she'd have to face that fact sooner rather than later. It was small things, but now, she found herself worrying if he went out to the garden and she lost sight of him from the kitchen window. He'd gone to the library a few weeks earlier and ended up taking over four hours, returning home with an old shopping bag filled with stones. He couldn't remember where he'd been and, at the time, Phyllis just hadn't wanted to think about it either.

She'd have to tell Rob soon.

'Are you coming, Mum?' Rob poked his head into the room. 'We're all ready, Dad is raring to go, he's even bringing the towels for a swim.'

'It's such a lovely day,' Phyllis murmured. She pushed against the nightmare idea of him swimming out of his depth and forgetting to swim back to her. 'Let's not walk all the way down to the cove today though, eh?' At least, nearer to the village, there was a lifeguard on duty and there would be people around if they needed help.

'Sure.' Rob peered at her. 'Are you played out? Aren't you fit for a long walk?'

'I'm grand, but it's early in the season and we don't know what the tide is like and…'

'Oh, once a mother always a mother.' Rob crossed the room and put his arm around her. They had always been close, but Rob's life had been running at a million miles an hour over the last few years. On the other hand, since she retired, it felt to Phyllis as if her time were moving so slowly it was relentless; sometimes she checked her watch a second time to make sure the hours hadn't come to a complete standstill. These days, it seemed as if the only chance her son really got to reconnect with them was this short respite every year. Oh, of course there were Christmas holidays and weekend visits, but with Josh about everyone's focus was on him, so it felt as if Rob just got lost in the slipstream. 'I know you still worry about us, but you really shouldn't, it's about time to start enjoying your retirement and thinking about yourself for a change.'

'Oh darling, I think I'm blessed enough already and what's the whole point of being a mother if it doesn't give me the right to want you to be as happy as you can be.'

'Well, we are, especially now, here with you and Dad, all of us together.' Rob smiled and Phyllis knew his words were genuine and that made her feel even worse, because she would have to tell him about her concerns for his father this weekend.

It was cruel. Phyllis watched as Kurt swam happily in the water, completely oblivious in this moment about what lay ahead of him. Perhaps it was kinder that way, because when she remembered the last few years with Kurt's father, well, they had both agreed they'd rather be dead than finish up like dear old Paedar Courtney. Her father-in-law had been an articulate gentleman right up until he fell off the cliff of his own awareness into the bottomless ravine the doctors called early onset dementia. From there, he veered from being a pathetic wild-eyed shadow of himself to being filled with a rage that had never had a place in the Courtney home before. All too quickly, he was unrecognisable in both a physical sense and in terms of his personality. It was as if he blew out the candles on his sixty-third birthday as Dr Jekyll and transformed into an unrecognisable Mr Hyde.

It was devastating for his family. Kurt's mother, Janet, in particular lost all footing in life as she watched her beloved husband descend so rapidly into an illness that held him in its grim clutches until the inevitable end. Phyllis couldn't bear to think of the same fate awaiting her darling Kurt.

She had decided, if you could possibly decide something so enormous, that she wouldn't be like Janet. She wouldn't fall to pieces, she would be strong. She had to be strong enough for all of them. She simply had to get things sorted while Kurt still had the wherewithal to make his wishes known to them.

'Aren't you coming in, darling?' Kurt was standing before her, his body reddened from the cold salt water slapping against him. 'You'll be sorry if you don't.'

'Of course, you're right, but I'm not sure that I'm brave

enough just yet,' Phyllis said, untying her shoes and rolling up her trousers. She followed Kurt to the water's edge, her soles tingling on the cool damp sand. Then the first bite of icy water against her toes sent a shiver of giddy excitement through her. It was the salty smell of the beach, the catching breeze and the sensation of the waves sucking gently around her feet and, suddenly, it could have been thirty or forty years earlier. She closed her eyes, felt the sun pat her eyelids. If she stood here, just for a little while, she knew the sand would start to move in ridges with the waves, digging her in deeper and, with the incoming tide, the water would rise up her legs quickly, drenching the bottoms of her trousers. But, oh, it was delicious to pretend, for just these few moments, that she was back there again, back in a time when the only worry she had was getting Rob's school bag and uniform ready for a new term at the end of the summer holidays. Bliss.

'Mum.' Rob was at her side, his hand on her back, steadying her. She'd started to sway in the water. 'Are you all right?' His brows were drawn tight in concern.

'Oh, I'm fine, I was just remembering.' Phyllis smiled. Then she slipped her arm through the crook of her son's elbow.

'Come on, they'll be grand there for a little while. Let's walk along the beach, it'll do your corns good.'

'Excuse me!' Phyllis started to laugh, because she still thought corns and bunions were just for little old ladies and that didn't apply to her. 'So, tell me, how are things going with the new job?' She really wanted to ask if he'd met any nice woman who might slip into his life and fill the void

Paula had so abruptly left behind. But that topic was firmly off limits if they wanted to have a harmonious weekend.

'It's… it's great.' He looked down at the water before them, just as he would have years earlier, either searching for shells or crabs or occasionally trying desperately not to meet his mother's eye. But time had moved on and now, maybe he knew Phyllis wouldn't press him for information he didn't want to share. Privately Phyllis felt she was still entitled to worry about her son and her grandson as much as she decided was warranted. 'Ah, I suppose,' he added, 'it's different, you know, to what I expected.'

'I suppose things always are. But does the good outweigh the bad?'

'That's the question. Still politely badgering the defence, eh?'

'Sorry, it's the habit of a lifetime, hard to give it up just because I'm retired from the law.'

'Don't worry.' Rob smiled. 'But yes, I suppose the good is outweighing the bad. I mean, I'm glad to have the extra responsibility. I'm enjoying the new challenge and, of course, the salary increase is nice too…' He had just bought a new car, nothing flashy, but something he'd never have done if he'd just stayed at his old job.

'But?'

'Hmm, but, it's just not the same, I suppose. I feel as if I've been cut off from people, you know, my colleagues are all…'

'You're their boss now, darling, I'm not sure they will think of you as their colleague any more. You've scored the corner office so you can't expect to stand at the water cooler every morning hearing the dirt on higher-ups, not when you're one of them.'

Actually, Rob was *the* higher-up. He'd been made a partner at the firm of solicitors he'd been working with for over a decade. Of course, as Phyllis saw things, the problem was, work was all he had at this point outside of Josh.

'Are you ever lonely?' she asked.

'No!' He tilted his head back and laughed and then looked across at his mother, meeting her eyes for a long second. 'No, of course not, I'm far too busy to be lonely.' He shook his head as if the idea was completely ridiculous.

'Of course,' Phyllis said, standing for a moment to look at the sun glinting on the water before them. 'What a silly question, sometimes, I don't know what comes into my head.'

'It's still beautiful here,' Rob murmured, drinking in the view before them. 'You know, for all my foreign holidays in my twenties, there's nowhere that can compare to Ballycove.'

'I agree, there's nowhere like it,' Phyllis said. It was calming, standing here, just the sound of the tide pulling up around their feet and the gulls diving in and out of the white breakers in the distance.

They stood there for a while and Phyllis luxuriated in the peace of it all, just being here with her son's arm linked through hers, for a few moments enjoying what it was to be carefree – even if her worries were only being pushed aside for a short while.

They walked back again with the sun in their eyes, Joshua skipping over the waves and splashing down with delight as each one swept past. Kurt was just a little further out, cutting through the water like a man half his age. From here, Phyllis thought, you'd never imagine he was the same man who spent most nights wandering about the house, confused and upset once the sun went down.

He was leaving the water and walking towards them when he stumbled across Josh's ball. He was only yards away and she could see quite clearly the change in his posture, it was subtle, but she'd seen it often enough over the last few months. Oh no. He bent down, picked up the ball and examined it, as if it was some rare artefact and he couldn't quite understand what it was or why it had been left there. Suddenly, expecting a game, Josh took off and ran towards him. He looked so small and vulnerable racing along to play with his grandfather. His delighted screams reminded Phyllis of what true, unadulterated joy could be. But then, he stopped, as if he'd just run into some invisible wall and he was frozen on the other side. He spun round to his father, as if to check he was still there, his expression distorted to shock. His sunburned complexion faded to dazed white and his eyes, round with fear, bulged in their little sockets.

And then, when she looked back at Kurt, Phyllis saw what had pulled the child up so abruptly. Kurt was smashing up the ball, pressing it between his two powerful hands, his blank expression chasing away the happiness of earlier, his body hunched in anger, oblivious to the shocked child nearby.

Josh began to wail and Kurt spun around. Dear God no. Please, don't let him do anything to the child. That was Phyllis's first thought. Don't let him do anything to Josh. And she realised that was what she had been afraid of for months. The silent, clawing notion that the anger he directed at inanimate things could one day be directed at her or some stranger who happened to be standing in his path. Now, he was taking off towards Josh and Phyllis felt her heart contract with the most terrible dread.

'Kurt,' Phyllis called to him, but it was no good. She knew he couldn't hear her, he wouldn't listen to her until the demon that had overtaken him was gone again. 'Dear God, no.' She heard the words escape her lips as she broke into a desperate dash towards them. But even from here, she could hear her grandson's fearful cry.

'Dad.' Rob raced off ahead of her.

'It's okay, it will be okay,' the words escaped her but she knew that the very opposite was true. Nothing would ever be okay again.

Then, from the dunes near Josh, a woman emerged and she too was racing towards the unfolding scene. Phyllis thought she might have a heart attack, her breath caught in her chest and a searing ache felt as if it might cut her right through. She watched, helpless, as the woman picked up Josh and stepped away from Kurt. She was holding him in her sights, not backing down, but moving away from him at the same time.

'He has no right to be littering the beach with this rubbish.' Kurt glared at the child, he was as angry as Phyllis had ever seen him. He didn't even recognise his own grandson. 'Honestly, what sort of parents are you, teaching your child to just throw things at unsuspecting people out for a gentle swim. That thing could do more damage than you realise and there's only one place for it and that's the bin.'

The ball was light and flimsy and he had managed to pierce it by sheer dint of pressure, so it was a pathetic concave, flattened to half its original size.

'The boy didn't mean to upset you.' The young woman was holding onto Josh and, even from a distance, Phyllis could see her grandson was hanging on for dear life. 'It's just a misunderstanding.'

The woman swerved towards Phyllis, but her eyes were sympathetic. She could see this for what it was, a pathetic, confused old man who was standing there now, not entirely sure what it was all about. Kurt dropped what remained of the ball now, as if it was a piece of charcoal straight from the fire.

'Come on Dad, it's all right.' Rob half dragged his father away from the scene.

'It's bloody not all right.' Anger flashed up in Kurt again, spinning him away from Rob, so they both almost lost balance.

'I'm sorry, but... it looks as if he will have to get a new ball.' The woman nudged what was left of the ball with her foot. At this Joshua wailed even more inconsolably.

'Granddad burst my ball...' he wailed.

'Granddad...' Kurt repeated slowly, a notch of recognition widening his eyes. Then one large tear gave way and Phyllis watched as her darling husband realised that something had happened. He had no idea what had just gone on and her heart broke for him in spite of how much he'd scared her only a moment earlier.

'Shush, Josh, it's all right,' Phyllis said.

'We'll get you a new ball, a better ball,' Rob soothed and

he glanced at Kurt, who seemed to have crumpled in on himself so he was only three-quarters the height he'd been before. The woman handed Josh back to Rob who took him in his arms and told him he'd be fine.

'Thank you, I don't know what would have happened if you hadn't arrived just then,' Phyllis said to the woman. She stuck out her hand. Their introductions were hasty but, even so, Niamh Brophy struck her as a woman who had something special about her.

'Niamh?' Rob said simply, and her name lingered between them for a moment.

'It's okay, it was nothing,' she said and then she looked towards Kurt. 'I hope you're feeling better now.'

'What on earth were you thinking, Dad?' Rob, already fair-skinned, had lost what little colour he had and now his eyes looked huge, as if somehow the shock of seeing his father behave in a way so out of character had widened out the sockets to anime proportions. Sometimes, he was so much like Josh, it felt as if looking at her grandson was déjà vu.

'I...' But Kurt just stood there; once again it seemed the right words just wouldn't come.

'It's okay, Kurt,' Phyllis said, linking her arm through his. She turned to Rob, doing her level best to keep her voice even. 'We need to have a long conversation about things, but I had hoped we might enjoy our little holiday first.'

Wasn't that why she'd been so delighted that Rob and Josh could join them? Now, whatever vain hope she had harboured of some divine intervention that would prove her wrong about Kurt's health came crashing down around her.

She'd been only fooling herself and that was devastatingly clear now.

'We definitely need to have a conversation...' Rob said as he gathered up their belongings from the beach with Josh still clinging to him. 'And from the looks of things, it's a conversation we should have had a lot sooner.'

17

Cora

She could get used to this, Cora thought, as she sank deeper into the dome chair in the hallway. It was a draughty spot, but once you chose your seat carefully and tucked your legs up on the deep chair, you might as well be sitting in a nest, protected from any rogue summer breeze that made it up and through the door of the guest house. She had borrowed a paperback from a shelf in the dining room. Trashy and cheap, it was filled with action and not too much sentimentality, just what she needed. It was old and well-thumbed, more like something that had spent much of its life being a casual visitor to the charity shop before it found its forever home here at the Willows.

'Hello.' She had begun to fall asleep when Joel's deep voice startled her from the back of her chair. 'Sorry, I didn't mean to make you jump, but I can't find Marta and I was going to go out for a stroll, but my front door key isn't...'

'Ah, Marta's gone to the village and Esme is having a lie down. I'm not sure when she'll be back. You can borrow mine, if you want?' Cora said, trying to straighten up, because down here it felt as if she was somehow on the back foot. Had she drifted off? Oh, please say she wasn't snoring.

'Well, are you sure? I mean, I'm only going for a walk on the beach, but I didn't want to disturb anyone when I returned.'

'Jinx, I was going to go for a walk when Marta came back too.' Damn, she couldn't believe she had really said that – he'd think she was angling to go with him now.

'Well, we could…' He nodded towards the door.

'Oh, no, I've said I'll keep an eye out here in case Esme needs something.'

'You really are intent on stepping into the breach, aren't you?' He was laughing now and she noticed how his eyes crinkled and, suddenly, she found herself laughing too.

'You make me sound very dedicated, when I'm really not. It's hardly work, sitting curled up with a paperback for an hour or two.' She shook her head.

'Tell you what, I can wait until they get back, then we can share your key?'

'I have a better idea,' she said, hopping up and pulling the key from her pocket. It was the least she could do. The last thing he probably really wanted was her gatecrashing his walk and the last thing she needed was to find herself with a crush on a man who was not her husband. 'I'll pop it in the porch and we can both use it.' She left it under the same plant pot that Marta had used that first night she'd arrived.

'Are you sure?'

'Of course,' she said, looking at him now. There was something about him, apart from being insanely handsome, which she assumed meant he had women falling for him at every turn. There was something else, a sort of cool reserve that made it hard to pin him down. There was danger to him, something that sent your pulse racing or at least, Cora thought, something that made her feel alive. Still no wedding ring – although she told herself she really wasn't checking.

'That's very decent, thank you,' he said. 'I'll organise a key with Marta first thing.'

'You're here for a few weeks over the summer, right?' She was trying to make small talk, because it's what you did in guest houses, wasn't it?

'That's right.'

'Doing a job on the church roof?'

'Yes,' he said, and he walked to the window overlooking the veranda. God, trying to get a word out of him was like drawing blood from a stone.

'Good. Good.'

'Good.' He was standing in the doorway and it felt as if they were teetering on an invisible precipice. In some unfathomable way, she felt stuck, as if her feet had been pinned to the floor and she couldn't move. 'Actually.' He looked at his watch. 'It's probably a bit overcast for that walk. I have a decent bottle of red in the car, if there were some wine glasses, perhaps you'd like to have a drink with me… on the veranda?'

'Oh, no, I couldn't really…' Cora said and he just shrugged. And then, she thought, why couldn't she? 'Not when I'm on duty…' She made a mock salute and wondered why on earth she had to make an excuse about everything, surely she could say yes or no without having to make a song and dance about it. 'Maybe another time,' she tried smiling, but it seemed as if he was looking over her head now, as if his attention had shifted, and that was almost a relief, she could be comfortably invisible again.

'Right.'

'Right,' she said and she managed to turn and almost walk straight into the doorframe. 'Oops.' She sidestepped it, feeling her face burn – it was hard to tell these days which was a hot flash and what was her natural tendency to blush. Thank God, this one stopped at her chin, just embarrassment so.

When Cora made it back to the safety of her dome chair, she felt like kicking herself. What was she, a lovestruck teenager?

18

Phyllis

'How long?' Rob stood with his back to the window. This was the moment Phyllis had been dreading. She had been hoping they could delay it a little longer, but the incident on the beach had put paid to that. She had avoided this conversation, but she knew, after what had happened, there was no running away from it any more. The previous night had not been easy either, Kurt had found it hard to settle, but the truth was, it felt as if he hadn't properly slept in almost ten months. That afternoon, while Kurt rested in bed, they decamped to the rather faded but still grand drawing room along the hall. Josh had been easy to placate once he heard there was sausage and chips for dinner.

'It's been going on for a while, hasn't it, Mum?' Rob asked when he sat down on the settee next to Phyllis.

'Not that long, not really.' Phyllis examined her hands. Her wedding rings, still shining, were so much a part of her at this stage she'd hardly taken them off in almost half a century. 'I was going to tell you this weekend.' This was even harder than she'd expected. 'Honestly, I was. I thought, if we could have a few more days together, the way things always were.' She wanted to cry, but she wouldn't, not if she could help it. She took a deep breath. 'And it hasn't been that bad, not really…'

Because they both remembered what Granddad was like. And Phyllis knew, that's what Rob would be thinking of now, would his own father go down the same road?

'Does Esme know?'

'Esme, no, why would I tell Esme?'

'Well, you two have always been as thick as thieves; Dad always said you had more secrets between you than a bishop in the confessional.'

'No. I haven't told Esme.' The truth was, Esme had enough on her plate already what with her broken ankle and the guest house moving closer to ruin every time they came here.

'So, you've been carrying this all by yourself? Oh, Mum.' In the midst of all the conflicting emotions raging through him at this point, Phyllis knew that the idea of her having to shoulder this on her own was the last straw. And there it was. That was the one stumbling block to her soldiering on alone, to taking full responsibility for Kurt, come what may. No matter what her intentions had always been, Rob wouldn't allow it. He would feel as if it was his duty to step in and help. Phyllis knew Kurt would rather die than be a burden – God knows, he'd said it often enough over the years.

'Have you talked to a doctor?' Rob asked. 'You know, having it confirmed, making a plan, you might think you want to put it off, but it could actually be a relief in the long run.' He squeezed his mother's hand comfortingly. 'And who knows, maybe at this stage it can be slowed down, it might not progress as quickly as…'

'Of course it's not going to progress as quickly as Granddad's,' Phyllis snapped. 'Sorry. But that was years ago, a small fortune has been ploughed into research and drug development since then and Granddad was in complete denial.' She shook her head. 'Indeed, Granny wasn't much better, but that won't be me.'

She straightened her spine. 'We *have* been to the doctor…' Phyllis began, but there wasn't much to tell. Of course, Kurt made a song and dance about going; as far as he was concerned, there was nothing wrong with him. He told her she was fussing about him like an old hen, but he did as she asked and the initial results that had come back were pointing in a direction that she still didn't want to fully accept. There were more to come, nothing was confirmed, she had at least that to cling onto. 'We're waiting for a referral to a clinic, it shouldn't take too long.'

'Does he know?' Rob whispered as if there was some chance of Kurt hearing through the thick walls.

'Sometimes, I think he does, yes. I mean… well, you saw him after what happened on the beach. It's the same every time, but whether he'll remember it afterwards is another matter.' That was the cruelty of the disease. Terrible feelings of fear and guilt in the moment, but unless you had someone close to steer you to safety, there was no guarantee you'd face the reality of it, until it was too late to know the difference.

'You know you can't go through this on your own with him,' Rob said. 'I simply won't have it.'

'Oh, darling, there's nothing to go through at the moment. Your father is perfectly fine most of the time, incidents like the one on the beach are actually preventable, when you realise the danger that he might become upset.'

Or at least, that's what she wanted to believe. She wasn't entirely convinced of it, but she was certain she didn't want her son feeling that he had to drop everything just because she couldn't cope.

'Your father has always been very clear about his wishes, you know that.'

Kurt had spent too long looking at his father and the awful toll it took from not just his mother, but from the whole family. He'd been adamant ever since, if he ended up in the same boat, he would not be a burden. The way he saw it was, in the end, his father had little or no idea where he was or who was taking care of him. Kurt didn't fear death like most people, but he dreaded the idea that he might be left a shell of himself for years on end; to his mind, he'd be better off dead.

'But' – Phyllis brightened now, far more than she felt she had any right to – 'all that is a long way off yet, I'm sure. And this holiday isn't about feeling sad or miserable, it's about relaxing and taking time away from our worries.'

'Oh, Mum.' Rob put his arms around Phyllis. 'You really are something else,' and he squeezed her so tightly it felt as if he was trying to somehow keep her from falling apart.

Outside, the sound of the front door banging in the hall made them jump and Rob was at the drawing room door before Phyllis had even managed to fully understand what the sound was.

'Sorry, I didn't mean to startle you.' It was the woman from the beach arriving in the hall.

'No, no, that's okay, I just thought it was… it doesn't matter.' Rob came back into the room again and somehow, in spite of all the sadness that had engulfed them, it felt as if she'd brought with her some ray of hope.

'We're having sausage and chips for tea,' Josh chorused, racing into the room.

'How lovely for you,' the woman said, bending down to him. 'Actually, I have something for you.' She held out a paper bag, making a show of checking that the contents were what she expected, then she pulled a bright orange ball from it and handed it to him. 'Look what I found in the village…'

'For me? Really, for me?' Josh chirruped and he danced about as happy as a demented bee for a few minutes.

'That's so thoughtful of you,' Phyllis said.

'Not at all, when I saw it, I couldn't leave it there.' Niamh straightened up and tucked a stray strand of hair behind her ear.

'Well, if you fancy joining us for sausage and chips later, dinner is on me, to thank you for coming to our rescue.' It was the least they could do and Phyllis had a feeling Niamh Brophy might be a good distraction for all of them.

'Oh, I couldn't really…' she said, backing away from them. 'Not when you're all here on holiday together, I really couldn't impose.'

'Nonsense,' Rob said, moving towards her, and it seemed for a moment as if some unspoken words passed between them. 'That is if you don't have any other plans?'

'Maybe another time, I'd love to tag along.'

'We'd love to have you,' Phyllis said, and meant it. While on the one hand, a stranger among them would mean it was easier to cover over their worries about Kurt, Phyllis wasn't sure she had the energy to pretend that everything was just dandy and make light conversation over dinner. 'Well, maybe another night, are you here for long?'

'I'd like that.' Perhaps Niamh was just what they needed to fracture the worry and unspoken fear that knotted itself around Phyllis's heart now. When she closed the door to go up to her room, Rob seemed thoughtful for a minute, looking at Josh playing with his new toy.

'She's lovely, isn't she?' Phyllis hoped to steer the conversation away from the looming one that threatened to darken everything about Ballycove for her forever.

'We need to make a plan.' Rob walked to the large bay window which looked across the sweeping lawn and out beyond to the seemingly endless vista of sea and sky. His shoulders were still rigid, there was no missing the strain that pulled a small muscle at the side of his neck, but perhaps a little of the tension of earlier had been somehow diffused.

'And we will, but not until we've had your father fully assessed,' Phyllis said. 'Listen to me, coming here for our summer holiday, all I wanted was to let you know that this was happening. I didn't want it to come as a shock down the road if he suddenly became very…' She couldn't put the words on it. 'And for now, it is manageable, he's fine during the day, it's just sometimes he can't settle at night time, but we are very happy and I don't want to sacrifice a moment of whatever time I have left with him just because…' She took a deep breath; she was going to be strong. 'I promise, I will take all the help I need as soon as I need it.' She smiled stubbornly, unwilling to give in.

'That's sundown? One of the girls at work, her mother had something similar, that's what they called it, I think?' Rob asked. There was no point in lying to him.

'Maybe, but let's not go putting labels on things just yet.'

'Oh Mum, why didn't you tell me sooner?' He looked completely miserable. 'Of course, I understand why you didn't, but at least we know now, I can help out, with—'

'No, absolutely not,' Phyllis cut him off with the finality in her voice she'd always used when he was a child and there would be no broaching argument. 'I meant what I said, I want us to go on living as normally as we can for as long as possible.'

'And then?' He slid his hand into Phyllis's and it was almost enough to make her crack.

'And then, we'll see, it'll depend on what Kurt wants to do and what the doctors say we should do for the best for him.' At the end of the corridor there was the unmistakable sound of a bedroom door opening and the familiar shuffle of Kurt making his way towards the drawing room.

'In here, darling,' Phyllis called out.

'Oh, so plotting and planning, are we?' Kurt smiled as he stuck his head around the door. 'I've been thinking, should we pop into the village for dinner later?'

'What a great idea, my treat,' Rob said and it was all Phyllis could do not to burst into tears at the sudden normality of it all.

19

Niamh

There were three missed calls on Niamh's phone. All of them from work and a text from her mother, reminding her that her aunt's birthday was coming up and they should organise lunch. Nothing from Jeremy. Was it surprising? No, Niamh realised, she wasn't surprised at all. Maybe disappointed; after all, as far as he knew, she'd had the termination, she'd taken herself off to the other side of the country, surely he would have some concern for her? There was no mistaking how he felt about the pregnancy. Niamh placed her hand across her abdomen. It didn't feel anything different to what it had been a month earlier, when there had been no thoughts of missed periods or food poisoning or failing contraception. She knew, as far as Jeremy was concerned, there was no baby, just an inconvenience that she had to take care of.

A huge seagull circled the foamy waves around a small fishing boat making its way to the pier in the distance and, for a moment, Niamh let go of the niggling thoughts and worries of the last few days.

What if she was to call him now? She dug out her phone

from her pocket, his was the first name in her favourites list. By comparison, she knew she came well down his list of priorities.

He should know, though, shouldn't he? That she was still pregnant, still carrying his child, there was still a chance that maybe…

The seagull dropped down now, onto the waves. It was too far away to be sure, but he must have managed to secure something worth stopping for – perhaps the fishermen had thrown something his way.

God, she found herself wishing that something might be thrown her way, a sign that when she took that tablet, everything would go back to normal, that she would slip back into being with Jeremy and, somehow, understand why he had left her to take care of this alone, without even so much as a call to make her feel as if he cared for her.

Niamh was out of breath by the time she made it off the beach and back onto the narrow road towards the guest house.

Kurt and Phyllis Courtney were sitting on the veranda watching the same fishing boat as it unloaded its catch on the pier in the distance. They looked so happy together. Kurt was almost a different person, his face serene, everything in his posture wrapped towards the woman he obviously cared so much for. The whole incident with Kurt Courtney on the beach had been shocking, it had thrown her off balance and she'd reacted on the spur of the moment, dived in to save a child who for one terrible second she thought was in danger.

But kids are resilient, and Josh had settled soon after getting into his father's arms as if somehow, the promise of a new ball and the confident soothing words of his dad had quickly washed away his terror. And yet, even after she'd passed him across, Niamh could still clearly remember the sensation of his skinny little arms clinging to her and it felt as if something shifted subtly at her very core.

Somehow, the whole episode had turned her over, halting her in her thoughts as violently and unexpectedly as walking into a glass door. And it was, she realised, a glass door she couldn't quite open, not without taking a hammer to everything she'd believed her life to be up until this point.

Niamh wasn't even sure what it was that had affected her so much. Of course, it wasn't every day she faced down a man who seemed to have lost all possession of his reason. It wasn't that, rather it was the whole idea of the Courtneys. Three generations, holidaying together – their lives were certainly not perfect, she could see that. But what they had, she realised, was continuity. They had hope, someone to carry things on one day and something to look forward to, a lifetime to stretch far beyond their own.

That night, with the tablet she had not yet taken on the mantelpiece of the little Victorian fireplace, Niamh fell into the comfortable double bed. The window at the far end of the room was open and she listened to wave after wave crash against the rocks on the shoreline. It was a warm night, or maybe she was just warm, but she slept in fits, woke in bursts, the reality of actually being pregnant and alone finally hitting her as she lay in a strange room so far from her own home.

Saturday

20

Cora

A loud bang somewhere in the guest house woke Cora early the next morning. Automatically, she reached out across the bed and was instantly disappointed to realise it was not all some terrible dream. She was alone. Michael was at home in Cherrywood Crescent and she was here – in this gorgeous house, but alone. It was strange, but she missed him most terribly in the mornings. Until she'd come here she hadn't realised that waking up next to Michael and listening to the gentle sound of him breathing next to her was something she'd taken for granted. Now, it dawned on her, she had found great comfort in the simple knowledge that he was just next to her. Today, all she could do was bury her head in her pillow and cry softly at how they had let their lives drift so much that she was actually wondering if she could ever go back to Cherrywood Crescent again.

Eventually, it was clear, there was no point lying here any longer, she needed to be busy, she needed to do something to quell the rush of anxious energy that was flowing through her, making her feel as if every nerve ending was resonating at a pitch too high for any peace of mind.

It was too early to be up and about, probably, and it was still chilly, so she grabbed a small blanket from the nearby chair and threw it around her shoulders. In the kitchen, she solved the mystery of the noise that had woken her. A huge old extractor fan had fallen from the wall onto the cooker beneath it.

'This place is falling down around our ears, but Esme can't see it,' Marta said, stopping beside her and shaking her head. 'You know what I mean, she won't admit we need to get a proper builder in here or just shut the guest house down completely.'

'Let me help.' Cora moved the fan out to the small porch beyond. It was a museum piece, just a miracle it had gone on for as long as it had. She didn't say this to Marta, of course, instead she took the sweeping brush and dusted away the debris that had come away from the wall.

'Let's hope we don't have the health inspector in to visit any time soon,' she muttered as she threw open the kitchen window next to the hob. 'We will have to rely on the morning breeze to take out the smell of cooked breakfasts today.'

Cora boiled the kettle, made a cup of black tea and then she left Marta to bustle about the kitchen and settled down to sit on the veranda. At least she could sip her tea and maybe, if she was lucky, be distracted by the early morning, the sea, the sky, the birds – anything that didn't remind her of Cherrywood Crescent and the fact that she should be lying next to Michael and sleeping contentedly at his side.

She wondered how he was, he probably hadn't slept either. He rang her last night, but her battery had died and so, all she had was a message telling her he was off to bed and that he'd ring her in the morning. What on earth had she done?

'Another early riser?' Joel Lawson was stalking up the driveway. He looked as if he'd just been out for a long walk.

'I'm not normally up this early.' Cora looked at her watch; it was just after six o'clock. And with that, it seemed they stirred up the crows and there was an infernal chattering in the tall pines bordering the north-facing side of the garden. 'How did you sleep?'

'As well as I ever do these days.' He shook his head. 'Listen to me, anyone would think I had something to complain about. There was a problem with some of the joists on the job we're doing and I've been awake since the early hours trying to get my head around how we can fix it most easily.' He smiled then. 'I shouldn't even be here at the weekend, but could I be in a more scenic spot to try and sort out any problems?'

'The bracing walks must help.' She smiled at him; he really was insanely good looking standing there with his hair falling across his eyes. There was a broad-shouldered maleness to him and his eyes danced with a sort of mischief that was downright sexy – even at this ungodly hour of the day. Cora looked out at the sea, suddenly embarrassed; she realised she'd been staring at him.

'You'd think so. Perhaps it's just being somewhere new, this place makes me feel as if I'm a kid on holidays.'

'I imagine it has that effect on everyone who comes to stay.' She rubbed her head, feeling the ache of her own unsettled night. If only her life could be so simple that all she had to think of was childhood memories and enjoying walks on the beach without having to make life-changing decisions.

'What about you?' He smiled. Cora had a feeling he was asking her more than just her thoughts on Ballycove, but she really wasn't going to go into why she needed to stay in a guest house to gather her thoughts and plan for her future.

'Lovely and all as it truly is, I think I'd prefer to be in my bed for another couple of hours,' Cora said. 'Fancy a cup of tea?' She raised her cup to him.

'Sure, if it's no trouble.'

'Not at all.' There was no sign of Marta, but the old extractor fan had been moved from the porch when he followed her back round the house and into the kitchen while she made him a mug of tea, no sugar and hardly any milk. Cora couldn't help noticing, it was the opposite of how she made tea for Michael, who liked his tea sweet and not too hot. They ambled back outside again; Cora, unfamiliar with how sound might travel in the house, didn't want to disturb Esme or the Courtneys (who were staying in the ground-floor rooms) with their conversation at such an early hour. They sat for a while looking out across the bay in silence, Cora trying desperately to push the heavy weight of sadness from her shoulders and enjoy the tide turning on the rocks below.

'It's far more beautiful than it looked on the travel site when I booked it a few months ago.' Joel sipped his tea thoughtfully.

'I can't imagine any camera being able to quite capture the beauty of this place or the homeliness of the Willows.'

'I don't think I've ever stayed anywhere quite like this,' he said.

'Where are you usually based then?'

'Me?' He looked out towards the middle distance for a moment, his voice more melancholy than before. 'I'm not sure I even have a base at this point.'

'Well, where's home?'

'I was born in Galway, but my family were on the move from the start. My dad was an engineer – he worked on bridges, all over the world, we trailed him across the five continents and then, for a while, home was Dublin. But... not any more.'

'Ah,' Cora said, as if she understood, but she didn't.

'I have an apartment in Santry, it's close to the airport. I spend most of the time on the road.'

'Always on holidays,' she said, 'or running away?' She hadn't meant to say that, but maybe, it was what she felt she was doing herself. 'Sorry, I didn't mean you...'

'No. No, nothing to be sorry for, you might be closer to the mark than I'd like to admit.' He looked at her now, for a moment, holding her gaze, and then, perhaps the intimacy between them startling him as much as it did her, he asked, 'Are you running away too?'

'I...' She couldn't talk about her marriage with this stranger. She couldn't do that to Michael – she owed him more loyalty than that. 'No. No, not at all, but if I was going to run away, I couldn't imagine running to anywhere more perfect, could you?' she said.

'No. No, at this moment, I couldn't imagine anywhere

nicer to run to either.' And he smiled as he looked out across the breaking waves in the distance.

It threw her. For the rest of the day, Cora felt as if she'd somehow slipped from her normal groove, as she'd sat there with Joel Lawson. Ridiculous, of course, she was being silly. He'd have forgotten all about their chat on the veranda as soon as he got to work and his attention was needed on roof joists and pinnings and whatever else it was engineers worried about when it came to restoring old churches. It wasn't until she was standing there, scraping her hair back into a ponytail, that she realised what it was about him that she liked. It was simple. He listened to her. He was actively interested in what she had to say and it made her feel, for just the shortest time, as if she was special. He was also drop-dead bloody gorgeous. Although, that was neither here nor there.

That afternoon, she pulled her phone out of her pocket to check for missed calls, not that she expected Michael to ring. He never did usually; there seemed no good reason why on earth he would start now. But she checked just in case; the truth was, she wanted him to call her. She wanted him to fight for her, but she had a feeling she was the only one who had put any energy into saving their marriage.

It was a strange thing. She felt a familiar nervous twist in her stomach now. She wanted him to reach out, to say something, to *say the right thing*, but at the same time, the thought of even having to talk to him made her feel as if all her energy was lapping away from her. It was so different to how interested and energised she'd felt earlier chatting to Joel.

The sound of Esme sneezing loudly in the hallway brought her back to reality with a shiver.

'Can I get you anything?' she asked, although the old woman looked as if she was set up for the day. 'Are you in a draught there?' Cora noticed the front door was ajar while Marta was vigorously cleaning the brasses.

'Oh, dear no, I'm well used to draughts in this house. It's not the cold, it's the irises. I do love them, but they sometimes bring on my hay fever. Still, they always remind me of Henry, for some reason.'

'Henry?'

'Yes, dear Henry. He loved the irises. He could sniff out a patch of irises at fifty yards. Of course, they were the finish of him in the end.'

'I'm sorry.'

'Oh, don't be, he had a good innings and he died happy. The naughty boy had dug up a full bed in Mrs Newcomb's front garden. Well, she wasn't having that and she chased him all the way down towards Perry Pass. Of course, he just thought it was sport, it was lucky she didn't have a heart attack. She was not a young woman and her legs had never been the best since she had her knee replacement – the doctors won't admit it but they don't work for everyone, you know. Anyway, in the excitement, Henry raced straight under a passing van and that was that.'

'Oh dear. Was it instant?'

'Actually, it was frozen foods. But anyway, we did what we could and I thought it would be most fitting if we buried him in the garden.'

'Excuse me?' Cora placed her rattling cup and saucer back on the table, she felt as if she might be sick.

'Under the irises. Marta did it,' Esme said, sipping her coffee and scowling.

'Henry was a cocker. And a very naughty one too,' Marta said, giving the brass door handle one final savage polishing before she stalked off towards the kitchen.

'Ah, I see.' Relief flooded through Cora; for an awful moment, she thought they'd been talking about a person, a husband or a child.

'But there you have it,' Esme said gently. 'It doesn't do to go digging in other people's gardens. Our irises were as good as any to dig up and maybe dear Henry wouldn't have had such an abrupt ending if he'd been content with what was inside his own garden wall.'

'I see,' Cora said again, but she couldn't help thinking that they weren't talking about cocker spaniels or irises any more.

21

Niamh

It was a night of broken sleep, yet by the morning, Niamh felt completely rested. She examined herself in the mirror; from the outside, there was no obvious difference. Her clothes still fitted, her hair looked the same and in her own opinion, at least, she neither looked peaky nor glowing. She didn't even feel one bit nauseous today. Perhaps she was going to get off lightly. To be safe, she decided on a walk before she tackled breakfast.

The beach was glorious. She had managed to make it down before any holiday-makers and the sun fell across the sea from high above the village, making it appear as if there were diamond shards sparkling on the water's edge ahead of her. There was a light breeze, just enough to make her feel as if there was some nameless possibility gathering about her as she walked. At the end of the beach she sat for a while on rocks that she figured were probably submerged during winter storms but today were warm with the early morning sun. It was heaven. In fact it had everything she could possibly need at this moment. On her way back to the guest house she stopped off at the Coffee Shack, a small van selling coffee with chairs and tables overlooking the beach. She ordered decaffeinated latte, surprised herself by taking a sip and, even if it didn't taste exactly as it should, it didn't taste too bad either. She nibbled on a water biscuit and sat there for a long while, watching other customers come and go and thinking about nothing and everything.

The only thing she was missing was a call from Jeremy, which was probably a good thing, since it put everything into perspective for her. As far as he was concerned, she'd already terminated her pregnancy. The problem was over, but somehow, the fact that it had happened at all had reared a wedge between them. Niamh surprised herself by realising that she wasn't entirely unhappy about that. Surely, it was better to know now, than for it to come as an unpleasant surprise at some stage when she actually needed him to stand by her. Yes. Better to know that she was alone than to believe she had some support only for it to be pulled out from beneath her when she truly needed it.

God, those heady romantic days at the start of their relationship were a lifetime away now. She had fallen for Jeremy instantly, even if she wasn't prepared to admit it to herself at the time. He'd always worn a wedding ring; she'd always known he was married. She told herself too, that she'd never have done anything about it, but they were in Paris. The trip was meant to culminate in a meeting of senior-ranking civil servants from across the EU but, thanks to unrest in the city, the meeting had been cancelled and they'd found themselves with two free days and nothing to do but wander the streets. Jeremy had booked dinner for them in the cutest Parisian restaurant and, somehow, one thing had led to another and... Those had been the most passionate two days of her life; even now, the memory stirred something deep within her.

The sound of a car, reversing with that annoying beeping sound, rescued her from spending any longer looking back. She was glad of it.

The sun on her skin warmed her in a way that was comforting. Making her decision would be easy. She would go back to her chintzy double room, take the damned pill and reclaim the life she'd worked so hard for. She could figure out what to do about Jeremy later.

'Hey? Do you mind if I sit here?' A woman of about fifty was temporarily blocking the sun.

'Of course, help yourself,' Niamh said, pushing back the chair.

'I've seen you at the guest house, haven't I? I'm Cora.'

'Niamh.' She looked at the woman when she managed to find a shaded spot to shift to on the seat opposite. There was something about her; Niamh felt as if she too was here to figure out something that she couldn't sort out anywhere else. Was it as pressing as Niamh's worry? She found her hand was once again resting against her stomach. No, probably not. The woman smiled across at Niamh now, as if they were both thinking the same thing at the same time, which was completely ridiculous, of course. 'Are you here for long?'

'How long is a piece of string?' Cora laughed. 'Sorry, I'm not sure, I'm just taking a bit of time out.' She looked down at her coffee now, set about stirring in some milk. 'Time to think. What about you?'

'Very much the same, I'm tempted to stay much longer than I should, but I have to go back to work, so...'

'You better cram in all your thinking time very quickly then.' They both laughed. 'God, I wish *I* could figure out my thoughts in a narrow timeframe.' Cora leaned back in her chair and looked out across the waves. In the sand a woman was sitting while two small children set about building a castle. 'Ah, those were the days.'

'Pardon?'

'You know, when I was your age and my son was little and everything seemed to be just as it was meant to be.'

'And they aren't any more?'

'No. It's like everything I knew was right in my life seems to have taken a road away from me and these days I'm surrounded by things I'm not so sure about any more.'

'At least you're left with something?' Niamh thought about Jeremy and she felt a tear race down her cheek.

'Ah, now, have I put my foot in it? I'm so sorry; I didn't mean to upset you.' Cora handed across a sheaf of paper napkins, moved her chair just a little closer, but it felt to Niamh as if there was no stopping the emotion that had bubbled up inside her. She needed a good cry. And so, once she realised she couldn't contain it any longer, she just let the tears flow.

'Oh, dear.' Cora moved in and put her arm around Niamh's shoulder, which only made her bawl more – somehow, the contact of this total stranger brought her complete alienation from Jeremy into stark contrast.

'It's not you, it's me. You're very kind,' Niamh spluttered.

'Do you want to talk about it?' Cora asked. She sounded

as if she had time to listen and she looked like a woman who had the shoulders to carry not just her own worries, but maybe share someone else's for a while too. And so, the whole sorry story of how Niamh had found her way to Ballycove came tumbling out.

'I can't tell you what to do, but I can tell you, you've done the right thing in coming here,' Cora said, they had been here for so long, their coffee had gone cold but it didn't matter, coffee was the least of Niamh's worries at the moment. Cora nodded to the barista and ordered again, although Niamh wasn't sure she could face it.

Of course, no one could tell her what to do, Niamh knew she had to figure out exactly *why* she hadn't taken that pill yet. She couldn't have a baby, not on her own. She didn't think she even wanted one, at this point. And yet... the pill was still there, sitting on the mantelpiece, waiting for her to finally end this thing that had unhinged everything she'd believed about herself and her life to this point.

'You sound so sure.' Niamh felt better already – what was it they said about sharing your problems.

'I am. I have no idea what I'm going to do about my marriage, but I know that I'll figure it out here. Have you spoken to Esme yet?'

'Yes, I met her in the hallway, she's a funny old bird,' Niamh said. 'Is she a little potty, do you think?'

'Do you know, I haven't fully made up my mind, but every time I sit and talk to her, I feel much better afterwards. And it's not that she gives me advice, she just has a way of getting you to talk and think about things a little differently afterwards. Does that sound as crazy as she seems?'

'Not at all, I felt the same way myself after I spoke to her.'

'You should talk to her again, tell her everything. I bet you'll figure it out afterwards.'

'Thanks so much, Cora.' Niamh rested her hand on the other woman's arm. It was hard to believe they'd just met in a coffee shop, it felt as if they'd known each other for a lifetime.

'Thanks yourself, you're a great listener.' Cora smiled. 'Dear me, at this rate, we might as well order dinner.' She laughed because it looked as if the lunchtime crowd were just arriving.

'What *are* you doing for dinner tonight?' Niamh asked. There was no point in the two of them sitting at a table for one in restaurants at opposite ends of the village.

'Nothing planned, but we could eat together some nights if you'd like?' So they arranged a time and Niamh headed back in the direction of the guest house to have a little rest.

*

Esme Goldthorp appeared to be enjoying a delicious snooze when Niamh got back to the Willows and settled herself into a dome chair opposite her. Sleeping, she seemed like a docile old dote, but Niamh had noticed that when awake her eyes darted about, like a young bird's, waiting hungrily for morsels of conversation and company from all around her. She was built for this life – for operating a guest house. Niamh suspected she thrived on the coming and going and investing herself for a short while in the lives of strangers, who to her mind, while they stayed here, were probably akin to distant relatives she was rather fond of.

She must be in her eighties, but she was small and spry and her interest in everyone around her made her seem younger than her years. Niamh imagined that were it not for the broken ankle, she'd probably still be ferrying tea and coffee in and out of the dining room each morning accompanied by chirpy chatter.

'Ah, my dear, you're back from your walk on the beach?' Esme said as she stirred into life.

'How on earth did you know I was sitting here?'

'Why that perfume of course, it's easily recognisable.'

'Oh, of course, how silly of me.'

'To me, it smells expensive, the sort of perfume you wouldn't go out and buy yourself at first, maybe you'd get it as a gift, but then, after that, if the giver remained in favour, you'd never dream of changing it for something less expensive.'

'And if he didn't?' Niamh found herself laughing at the woman's perception. It must be true what they say about one's remaining senses more than making up for one that's lost.

'Well, I think, if he meant something to you once, but for some reason didn't any more, it's the last thing you'd want to wear. There's a name for it, isn't there? A signature scent – well, that could almost feel like a stamp of ownership following you around, when you might prefer to choose your own signature, so to speak.' Esme smiled sweetly as if they really were just talking about perfume.

'I'm surprised there's any scent left at all, to be honest, I've walked to the furthest end of the beach. I'd have thought the wind and spray would have wrapped me up in the scent of

Ballycove at this point. I can already feel them washing away some of my worries.'

'Well, this place can certainly help you to see straighter, but remember, even after washing away your worries, very often, you have to take action when you get back to your real life.' She paused for a moment, cocked her head a little to the side. 'Or maybe not take any action at all? That too might just be the answer to your worries.'

'I feel as if you know far more about me than I've already told you.' For a moment, Niamh had a crazy notion that her conversation with Cora had somehow travelled on the sea breeze right up through the village and in through the front door of the guest house.

'Oh, dear me, not at all. It's just that you remind me of someone I knew years ago.'

'Oh?' Niamh waited a beat; she had a feeling Esme would tell her without any need to prod her further.

'Yes, she was very young of course, much younger than you, I would say. But she came here for a weekend in winter. Back then, I kept the place open all year round; well we did take in commercials back in those days too. Anyway, Lucy, that was her name, booked in on a Friday night. She was all red eyes, hardly had a word to say for herself and obviously here because something had gone very badly wrong. On the Saturday morning she felt very ill, couldn't look at breakfast, cried and cried. Well, I really didn't know what to do about it all and then, we sat on the veranda in the afternoon, just the two of us, and it all came tumbling out. She was pregnant, you see, and the boy, because that was all he was, just a foolish boy, had gone and taken up with someone else.'

'She hadn't told him she was pregnant before she came here?'

'No. She hadn't. She'd just panicked and run to the first place she could ever remember getting away to in her life. Apparently, she'd come here as a child with her own parents. Anyway, we talked for a long part of that first day and she managed to have dinner and fell asleep soundly that night. When she woke the following morning, before any of us knew it, she'd made up her mind to ring him and so, she'd walked down to the village to make the call. He arrived here by lunchtime in a van he'd borrowed and with the look of a boy who'd been shocked to the core.'

'So, he came to sweep her off her feet?' Niamh was glad; it was a happy ending for the girl. Having a baby on your own in Ireland back in the days when this must have happened would not have been a choice you could have made as easily as you could today.

'Not exactly. You see, while he was a bit of a lad, his uncle was the bishop of Kilcarbery and the family had a certain air about them. It was all very well, him running about the place after every woman he could catch, but the family of a bishop couldn't be seen to have a baby on the wrong side of the blanket, if you see what I mean?'

'Of course.' God, she had so much to be thankful for.

'I didn't like the cut of him from the get-go. He was much too good looking, if that's a thing. Perhaps that's not right either, he was good looking, but much too aware of it, if you can understand the difference? Anyway, Lucy was over the moon. She left here with high plans for a quick wedding and dreams of living happily ever after.'

'And did she?'

'Hmm?' Esme had closed her eyes for a moment. 'What's that, dear?'

'Did she live happily ever after?'

'Well of course not. It was very sad actually. She lost the baby. Tripped apparently, but she was black and blue and, to be honest, I'd say she spent more time in the local A&E over the years than the ambulance did. Her prince charming was a brute, you see, and no good looks can make up for that. We kept in touch, over the years, and then she wrote to me and told me that he'd died. His liver gave up in the end. Lucy was finally free.' She smiled then, as if this was the happy ever after ending. 'You know, this country had things backwards for far too long. If she had been able to choose and end her pregnancy, she would have had a much better life for herself and maybe for the boy too.'

'Did she ever have a family?'

'Later, yes, she met a nice man. Well, I think she'd known him before, but you know how these things go. They had a son.'

'So, she did live happily ever after.'

'She did in the end,' Esme said then leaned forward in the dome chair as if to share a tiny nugget. 'Mind you, she told me that after that, she'd almost get sick every time she smelled even the hint of a perfume called Youth Dew. It's a funny old world, isn't it?'

'Hmm.'

'Well, I mean, these days, she could have just gotten on with things, or decided not to, if you know what I mean.'

'Yes, I think I know perfectly what you mean.' And she

did and somehow, although she wasn't sure why, Niamh felt much better. 'Don't you have any wise words for me? Cora said you just might…'

'Did she indeed?' Esme threw back her head and laughed. 'Oh dear, well now did she?' Then she closed her eyes again. 'Go on.' She held out the guest book towards Niamh. 'Open it on a random page, see what it throws up at you.'

'Okay.' It felt almost like a challenge, two of them playing spin the bottle, but without the kissing. Absurdly, Niamh felt a little nervous settling on the page to open. But then she closed her eyes and just flipped it over. January second. 'It says, *There is only the road you choose to take.*'

'Ooh, now, that's a good one, well done you. Those are good words to live by, indeed.'

'Indeed,' Niamh said.

When Niamh made her way back up to her room, she sat for a while in the window seat with the pill packet in her palm. She looked out at the waves on the beach below.

A feeling of nausea crept up in her again, which she put down initially to the pregnancy, but now she wondered if perhaps it was actually her perfume that was making her feel sick. That was strange, because she'd worn the same perfume, Boadicea Victorious, for years. It *had* been a gift from Jeremy, it was his favourite and she thought, until now, it was hers too.

She remembered Esme's words – *was* it a signature scent or a brand? Urgh. The tablet box fell from her hand, as compulsion pushed her into the shower where she scrubbed off any remaining scent. It was expensive, far too expensive to throw it in the bin, but she knew with certainty that she'd never be able to wear it again. And so she took the almost full bottle and placed it in her handbag. Cora had complimented her on it earlier too, perhaps she would like it.

'You look different,' Cora said when they met up on the veranda that evening, holding her hands and inspecting her in much the same way her mother did.

'Washed out, stressed out and worn out?' Niamh laughed.

'No, I was going to say, glowing… but…' Then she cocked her head to one side and she smiled.

'Okay, you got me, I might still be glowing.' As she said it, Niamh realised she'd never taken the pill. She'd been so consumed with ridding herself of any trace of Jeremy, it was still on the floor in her room.

'I'm delighted for you, either way.'

Cora loved the perfume. 'I won't spray it yet, in case it annoys you again.'

'That's good. I'm just glad it's going to a good home.'

And it felt as if with the giving of it, Niamh was divesting herself of another gate to a prison she hadn't realised she'd been living in. Because their table wouldn't be ready until seven thirty, they sat for a while on the veranda, each content to look out across the garden. They watched, engrossed, while swallows with food for their babies dived like arrows into nests hidden in the deep ivy along the wall. The longer they sat, the more Niamh saw; the whole place was a hive of wildlife activity. Between them, the birds put on an engrossing performance as they just went about their daily routine. This was what she was missing in her viewless Dublin flat. Her flat wouldn't work any more. Well, she corrected herself, it wouldn't work if she decided to keep the baby.

'Josh,' a man's voice called from the side of the house. 'Josh, come on son, it's time to go inside.' Then a familiar little boy with a shock of curls and a cheeky grin darted past the veranda. 'Josh.'

It was Rob Courtney's voice. Niamh recognised it immediately; he rounded the corner, completely frazzled. He was so intent on his search that he hadn't spotted the two women sitting behind him, nor could he find the little boy who had disappeared into a thick wall of rhododendrons.

'Hi,' Niamh said, surprising Rob, so he spun round to see who had been watching them. She got up and walked to the edge of the garden and whispered, 'I would try the rhododendrons if I were you.'

'Oh, thank you.' Relief flooded his face and he raced across the garden, diving into the thick foliage and quickly emerging with the child squealing with excited laughter. 'How on earth I'm going to settle him down to a night's sleep after this is anyone's guess.' He stopped beside Niamh.

'Isn't that what holidays are all about when you're a kid?' She smiled, envying him for a moment as the child wriggled about and then flung his arms about his father's neck, snuggling in as if he would never let go.

'I suppose, but it's been a long day for him and...'

'Oh, I remember what that was like. I'm Cora by the way,' Cora said as she joined them.

'Rob,' he replied as he wrangled his son to the ground, 'and in case you hadn't guessed, this is Josh.'

'Very nice to meet you both again.' Niamh ruffled the child's hair and Josh promptly turned and grinned at her. He was as adorable as he had been that first day on the beach.

'It is, but if we don't get a move on, we'll be late for dinner,' Cora said.

'Yes. Yes, of course,' Rob said, standing aside to let them make their way down the drive. 'Enjoy your dinner,' he called after them and then he turned back towards the house to try and settle his son down for a night's sleep.

'Well, that was interesting.' Cora laughed.

'What?' Niamh looked at her.

'Oh, come on, Niamh, you're pregnant, not stupid – there was enough electricity between you two to power up the whole village.'

'You're crazy, imagining that,' Niamh shot back. 'Anyway, even if there was some small spark, I'm hardly in a place where I can afford to think about making my life any more complicated.'

'Time and uncomplicated circumstances wait for no woman. Life is for grabbing it as it comes along, believe me, I know that much for sure.' Cora linked her arm companionably and they set off on the narrow little downhill road towards the restaurant.

Sunday

22

Phyllis

The following morning, bright and early, as Phyllis sat on the pier watching Kurt cast off his fishing rod, she let her thoughts wander, a luxury she rarely allowed herself these days. But it was early morning and they'd both slept well and been up a good hour before Josh usually woke. She hoped Rob might have a lie-in too; he needed the rest more than any of them at this stage.

In the distance, she watched as a couple made their way back along the beach. They must have left at the crack of dawn. Phyllis thought they were striking, still at that stage where they were besotted with each other, although neither of them were exactly spring chickens. As they came closer, she recognised the woman. Cora. She was staying at the guest house too. Perhaps they were on a second honeymoon.

She and Kurt had never needed a second honeymoon. Their first one was wedding breakfast, registry office and honeymoon all rolled into one. She was lucky she hadn't killed her parents with the disgrace and mortification of their daughter racing off to elope with a fella that they considered at best beneath her and at worst – well, there were words they used back then that thankfully had fallen out of fashion in the meantime.

'Come on,' Kurt said at her side now. He could still read her like a book.

'I was remembering, when we got married.'

'When we ran off together, you mean.' He smiled and she loved the way his eyes creased up now even more than ever with the morning sun beating down on them.

'There was no other way,' she said simply. It was the smallest wedding, just the two of them with Esme and Colm as witnesses; it was all they'd needed.

'I wouldn't change a thing,' he said. She'd often wondered if he'd have found someone else. Perhaps he'd have ended up with a vicar's daughter and taught at the local school and been content with his lot. 'There was never going to be anyone else, you know, not for me,' he said simply.

'Not for me either.' She rested her head against his shoulder, breathing in the scent of soap from his morning shower. Already, his skin felt warm beneath his shirt, as if he was anticipating the balmy day before it even arrived. 'They'd have tried to talk me into marrying one of the local farmers. He'd have been well-to-do no doubt.'

'But he wouldn't have wanted you practising the law when there was tea to be made and children to be reared.'

'No. Indeed.' And Phyllis had enjoyed her career. She'd started out with the intention of being a teacher, but somehow the radical ideals of equality and justice had made their way under her skin in her first year at university, so she'd changed track and qualified as a solicitor, much to her mother's despair.

'You did well. You have nothing to regret, well, unless you regret our moonlight flit to Gretna Green?' He was making fun of her.

'Never,' she said and she leaned back from him to look into his eyes. 'I'll never regret marrying you, Kurt, you are the love of my life.'

'Come here,' he said, pulling her into his chest and wrapping his arm around her, holding her close. 'And you are the love of mine,' he murmured and she knew that they were both on the brink of great sadness, although they were cocooned in the sort of love that most people only got to dream about.

A huge wave crashing against the pier sprayed them with freezing water and even if it made them splutter it also made them laugh. They shrieked and jumped back, suddenly both aware of the danger of standing too close to the edge without keeping an eye on the sea below. They were still laughing when the couple walked towards them. She was surprised that they were not holding hands, they'd seemed so intimate as they'd walked along the beach opposite, but then, it was a bit away and her eyesight was not as strong as it had been when she was younger.

'Hello, caught you out, I see,' the man said as he handed Kurt the towel from the wall behind them.

'We should have been watching instead of remembering,' Kurt said.

'You're both staying at the Willows too?' the man asked.

'Yes, with our son and grandson. We've come most years

for our summer holidays. Are you new here?' Phyllis asked after they made their introductions.

'No,' Cora said. 'I stayed here years ago with my husband and my son when he was small. I suppose, one day soon, Connor will be thinking of bringing his own son or daughter here.' She laughed.

'Wait until you have grandchildren,' Kurt ribbed Joel against his elbow. 'They'll be delighted to come along then so you can do a spot of babysitting.'

'Oh, no. We're not…' Cora laughed and moved a little away from Joel. 'We just met on the beach. This place – I can't keep my eyes closed once the sun breaks through the windows.'

Joel nodded. 'I'm the same. I'm not even on holidays, I'm here to oversee some work on the local church roof.'

'Are you a builder?' Kurt, a lifelong DIY enthusiast, loved nothing better than to pick the brains of every carpenter, plumber and electrician he met.

'No, I'm afraid not, nothing so robust. I'm an engineer.'

'Oh lovely, that must be very interesting, to get to put your stamp on something that's here long after we're all gone,' Kurt said.

'I never thought about it like that, but I suppose. After a while, it's just a job like any other, mainly, these days, it's jobs like this, where you're trying to save other people work.' Joel looked at his watch. 'Speaking of which, it's probably time I was actually getting back, I have some calls to make, lovely and all as it is to be strolling on the beach this morning.' He set off, back up towards the guest house.

They stood for a while, the three of them, looking out

across the incoming tide as it raced towards the beach opposite. It was lovely here, calming, and Phyllis thought it had never looked more spectacular.

'You know, we always said we'd come here for the winter?' Kurt turned to her.

'I don't think the guest house opens during the winter,' Cora said.

'That's such a pity, I remember it is breathtaking here when the sea is raging and the locals have the place to themselves,' Kurt said and Phyllis decided then that she was going to talk to Esme and ask if they could come to stay one more time this year, later than everyone else. That would be something to look forward to, maybe not just for her and Karl, but for Esme too.

23

Niamh

'Ah, is that you, Niamh?' Esme was sitting in the domed chair when Niamh came down to go for an early morning walk.

'Good morning, Esme. How are you today?'

'Oh, I'm very well, I can feel the sun across my legs from the window on the stairs. In my imagination it's still very beautiful. I always thought it dappled the morning sun with the gayness of a child taking a line for a walk and just filling in colours at random and somehow with perfect harmony.'

'It *is* beautiful.'

'Really?' There were tears in the old woman's eyes and, suddenly, Niamh felt a tug at her heart for what it must be to be old and helpless and at the mercy of other people to tell you about the beauty you were missing out on in the world. 'I like to think I can hear and smell the colours sometimes, does that sound a little dotty?' Esme smiled.

'Not at all.' And it didn't, because over the last few days, Niamh had experienced such an explosion in all her senses nothing sounded less crazy to her.

'You've changed your perfume.' The old woman breathed in the air about her as if to confirm it to herself. 'And your footsteps sound lighter, are the worries you brought to the Willows sorting themselves out for you a little bit?'

'How did you know?' Niamh had dropped into the chair opposite. It was too early for anyone else to be up and about.

'Oh, it's just a feeling, one of the few compensations for being stuck here listening to the world pass me by.' Esme was rubbing her palm slowly over the cover of the guest book on her knees. 'It's a funny thing, but, every other year, I was so busy, making breakfasts and sorting out where people were going to fit in, I think I might have almost missed the true essence of what this place should be all about.'

'I'm sure that's not true. I'm sure this place has always felt as if it's a welcoming refuge as well as a fantastic place to spend your holidays.'

'Guests come for very different reasons. I can see that now. I came here once myself, you know, after I lost my baby.' She sounded as if her thoughts had travelled to a very long time ago. 'It was a terrible time. I suppose, these days, you'd call it the baby blues and just get prescribed some tablet and then, before you know it, you'd be back to normal or as near to it as you can ever be after you lose a child, but...'

'Different times, eh?' Niamh thought about the tablet waiting in her room. A very different type of medicine.

'Yes, different times, except we're still the same, aren't we?'

'How is that?' Niamh leaned forward in her seat, realising she'd been sitting rigidly as if on that same tightrope she'd been on for far too long. Now, she took a deep breath, because she knew, she was on the verge of making a decision that could take her out of that holding space forever.

'Well, us – human beings, women! We want to do the right thing for everyone else and it's only really when you get to my age that you begin to see that doing the right thing means starting with yourself, with the sort of life you want to live.'

'So, by suiting myself, I'd be helping everyone else to their best life?'

'I firmly believe it at this stage.' Esme nodded as if to punctuate the idea even more. 'You know…' She stopped and wiped a tear from the corner of her eye. 'I only told you one story, the last time we talked, but I have another, much, much closer to home, if you have time to sit close to me here…'

'Of course, I have time.' But Niamh had a sense that this story might be more unsettling than Esme's other stories.

'This one doesn't have a happy ending or a happy beginning, I'm afraid, but I woke up this morning and I knew I had to tell you.' She took a deep breath, as if about to set out on a long trek into the past. 'It all happened a very long time ago, when things were different to how they are now and a girl was lucky if she had more than one choice to take, if you get my meaning.'

'I think so…'

'It started on the way home, late one night from an after-works drinks night that had stretched on too late and somehow ended up with the office junior being walked home by one of the senior people in the firm. I suppose, her head was turned, there were war stories and you know what it is to have the attention of a powerful man when you really can't think what they might see in you?'

Esme didn't stop because, at this point, it was as if she was talking to herself. 'Anyway, somehow, this girl found herself in a situation where there was an expectation and when she tried to pull away, it wasn't easy, there was too much wrapped up in it, there was drink too, probably too much of it, and maybe that in itself caused some momentary infatuation. Those days, what you'd call consent wasn't something a girl was taught was in her power. The lines between what you wanted or didn't want and what a man expected were blurred, some men thought that a kiss was as good as a nod and if a girl spent the night listening to their stories or maybe sat in awe of them it was an invitation of sorts. A young girl, just up from the country, with a few strong drinks inside her, could easily find the boundaries she'd always lived by blurred when she felt out of her depth. And a man experienced in getting his own way, well, in this case, was fast to exploit that.'

'He raped her?'

'I suppose he did.' Esme shook her head. 'God, even now, all these years later, the lines are blurred, because it wasn't a violent attack with someone jumping out from a dark side street, but it was… how would you say it now, not consensual. There was a balance of power and even if he didn't know it – well, he abused it.'

'I'm so sorry.' Niamh wanted to rush forward and throw her arms around Esme, suddenly glimpsing the vulnerable young girl she must have been all those years ago.

'It's a long time ago now.' Esme's voice was hoarse and her lips curled up as if there was some wisdom from such a terrible thing. 'Anyway, the upshot was, I got pregnant.'

'But you had a choice?'

'I had a good friend. She's still a good friend; she made arrangements for me to travel to England. We saw a woman there who carried out abortions. Perhaps I could have found a proper clinic but I was in shock. After it was all over, I ended up with an infection that wiped me out and who knows…' Her words drifted off. 'At the time, I felt as if dying was better than living with the shame, it was a time when all sense had been turned on its head.'

'Things are different now,' Niamh said. God she was lucky. 'It's all above board, there are more risks crossing the road than there are…'

'Oh, don't get me wrong, I always counted myself lucky. I'd lay down my life for my friend because she saved me when she could have ended up in jail just for helping me. I owe her so much, I mean, if I'd had to go through with that pregnancy, who knows where we'd have ended up.'

'You're still friends?'

'Always, to the very end.' Esme smiled. 'Although, we've never spoken of that trip to England since.' She shook her head. 'Actually, I've never spoken about it to anyone. The thing is, I never regretted it, even later, when I couldn't go full term and have a baby of my own. I mean, the grief of not having a child nearly killed me and I couldn't tell anyone why that was, but…'

'Did your husband know?'

'No one else knew, apart from Phyllis and I.' Esme smiled

now, it was all so long ago. 'The thing is, I'm not sure if the abortion had anything to do with me not being able to have children, but even in my darkest hours, I always knew it had been the right thing to do.'

'Thank you for telling me.' Niamh reached out and touched Esme's hand.

'Oh, dear, I'm not even sure why I'm telling you, but I knew I had to, because... well, maybe it was time I told someone.' She smiled. 'It's an awfully long time to keep something like that hidden and now...'

'There's no shame, only on the man who did that to you. You should always remember that,' Niamh said softly, stroking Esme's hand, hoping that maybe she would get some strength from it.

'Listen, will you open the guest book and read what it says for today for me?'

'Of course.' Niamh took the book, although she wasn't entirely sure she wanted to read what it said. In so many ways it was easier to just keep on the same path she'd always been on – trying to be the best daughter, employee, mistress – being the happiest version of herself suddenly seemed to be the most frightening challenge she could imagine. But what if it was easy? What if she could suit herself and do what she wanted? What would she choose then?

'*To live is the rarest thing in the world. Most people exist, that is all.*' Niamh almost whispered the quote.

'Oscar Wilde said that. I think it might mean something today,' Esme said and then she ran her hand across the tops of her legs which were lit by the dappled sun shining through the grassy panes at the bottom of the stained-glass window above them. 'You know, I might be wrong, but I think that's green.'

'That's amazing, you're right.'

'Maybe I can see more than I think.' Esme smiled and put her finger at the side of her nose. 'Listen to me, it's all changed since my time, but you have a choice now, you can go either way. Just be sure you go the way you want to, not because you feel some sort of desire to do the right thing for the wrong reasons.'

'That's so...' Niamh felt a ball of emotion that defied naming as either love or sadness rise up in her. She placed the book back on Esme's knees. 'I think I need a walk in the fresh air,' she said and what she didn't need to add was that she needed to firm up in her mind that the decision she'd been afraid to make before was almost made.

*

The seafront was just beginning to come to life as Niamh walked along it. Outside the Coffee Shack, the man who'd served her the previous day was setting out tables and chairs and, already, another was standing looking across the waves and sipping a cup of coffee from the van. The tide had yet to turn and for now it was lapping up as close to the perimeter wall as Niamh had seen it since she arrived. Unlike any day for as long as she could remember, she felt swollen up with hope, as if there was something to look forward to, something real, something life-changing, and she knew, as she looked out towards the fishing boats bobbing on the horizon, that at this moment her life was turning on an axis she'd almost written off as being impossible.

She was going to have a baby. She was choosing her own happiness over some silly idea of what was right or what was fair to Jeremy. This was her chance, it might be her only chance, and even if she was certain there would be more babies in the future, she knew in her heart that she wanted this child. Thanks to Esme, Cora and the guest house, she was sure that what was fair to Jeremy was going to be completely unfair to her and getting rid of this baby would be the biggest mistake she could ever make. Yes. She was going to have a baby.

A slight chill swept up through her when she thought about the fact that if she'd gone through with the termination already, Jeremy still would not have called her. She would be completely and utterly alone, carrying with her the knowledge that she might have just thrown away her one and only shot at motherhood. She took a deep breath and felt a wave of relief flood through her.

She'd made her decision. She wanted to call her parents, tell them the good news, but she knew first she would have to call Jeremy. She looked at her watch. He would be at home now, just where he should be. He wouldn't like the idea of her going ahead with it, he would probably sulk and argue with her, but there wasn't very much she could do about that, apart from hang up the phone and ask him to give her back the key to her front door.

Suddenly she was filled with a thrilling new thought. There was a whole new life opening up in front of her. She would need a house, a small house, but a house with a garden and a tree to hang a swing on. She would be part of a tribe that talked about baby yoga and PTAs and met up for coffees and worried about something other than the end of year department financials. Her mother especially would be over the moon. She'd make mewling noises about Jeremy, until Niamh explained the lie of the land, but she would be relieved they'd have nothing to do with him. Her mother had never liked Jeremy, even though she tried hard to pretend otherwise – it looked as if she'd been right in her opinion of him all along.

'Well, you look fantastic,' Cora said when Niamh arrived back at the guest house. 'Have you eaten anything yet?' She looked concerned.

'I had a gorgeous milky latte at the Coffee Shack.' It felt like such a treat to sit outside and watch the world go by.

'You must be settling into it. Perhaps it's just this place, helping you to relax a little.' Cora laughed and maybe she already knew that Niamh's mind had been made up. 'Tasted different, but not entirely sickening?'

'Yes,' Niamh laughed.

'Yes, that was how I felt once I sort of calmed down, it didn't improve the taste, but at least it stopped making me sick.' She made a face as if it was all too recent. 'So, you've done some thinking?' She already knew.

'I have. I'm going to keep her, I mean, it.' Niamh smiled. 'I'm going to keep the baby and...'

'And the father?'

'I'll tell him, of course. I mean, he's going to know anyway, we bump into each other at work all the time, so there's no real getting away from him, unless I look for another job.'

'You can't do that.' Cora was adamant.

'No. I have no intention of finding another job, but maybe

Jeremy will, he's always been very ambitious, maybe this will be the push he needs to send him to Brussels full time.' And she really believed that. Not that he'd waited around for her exactly, but there had never been a good enough reason to leave before.

*

Niamh rang Jeremy later that morning. The few days away had restored her in a way that she'd never imagined they might. Far from being broken and empty, she would return to Dublin in a few days, brimming with plans and looking forward to an exciting future that promised far more than just career success and exotic holidays and being Jeremy's mistress.

'Ah, I was just about to ring you,' he said, answering her call before it had a chance to go to voicemail. She'd timed it for when he was on his way to the golf club to meet up with his weekly four-ball. It was the one time when he wasn't at work she could be sure of getting him alone. 'How are you feeling? I just couldn't get away and I felt so badly, because…'

'Okay.' Niamh stopped him, because suddenly she heard his excuses for what they were, the sad reminder that she would never be on the top of his list, while he had remained firmly on the top of hers for far too long. 'Jeremy, I'm just going to say this quickly, because I know you're in the car and you won't be able to talk once you get to the club.' He didn't even try to interrupt her. 'I didn't go through with it.'

'You what?' His voice sounded more like an echo of himself from a great distance away. 'What do you mean, you didn't go through with it? The termination? The...' He still hadn't referred to the child she was carrying as a baby, as their baby; well, it turned out, it was too late now. It was her baby.

'Exactly. I didn't go through with it.'

'But we agreed, you said you'd made an appointment, I assumed it was...'

'So, you remembered?'

'I've told you, I was sorry, it was impossible at home. The kids were just all over the place and...' Silence. Maybe the enormity of their situation driving home to him. 'Do you want me to be there with you, is that what this is all about?' He stopped, perhaps turning over the possibility of finding the time to hold her hand and watch while she took care of this inconvenient problem. 'Maybe we could do a weekend away, book into somewhere nice, make it about something more than just...'

'No, Jeremy, you don't seem to understand. I'm having this baby.'

There was silence on the other side of the phone; for the first time in his life, Jeremy was lost for words. She could almost hear him considering what was the safest thing to say next.

'I'm not going to get rid of it. I'm going to have the baby on my terms and...'

'But you have to see, I can't just.' She imagined him, dragging his figners through his hair as he always did when he was stressed, afraid in case he set alight some terrible fire that would quickly burn out of his control.

'I'm not asking you to do anything, Jeremy. You and I are

finished. This is your child, biologically speaking, but that's as far as your input goes. Of course, we'll have to talk about maintenance at some point, but I'm not looking for any sort of emotional support from you. I want you to drive over to my flat this morning, take away any of your belongings that are lying about and drop my key through the letter box when you're finished. This thing that we've had, this charade of a relationship, has gone on long enough. I'm ending it here and now and I don't want to hear another word about it.'

'But Niamh darling, you don't mean that's it, we're finished? You can't just decide that you're going to have my child and then stomp about the office as if everything was just normal.' He stopped. 'Don't you see, nothing about this is normal. I mean, you shouldn't even be pregnant...'

'Well, I am, and I'm delighted about it now. So, if you want to keep everything on a nice even keel, you'll do what I ask.'

'But how will you manage? You're on your own, I mean, have you really thought this through?'

'Yes, Jeremy, I've thought it through and I've never been surer of anything in my life.' Even as she said it, looking out across the ocean at the breakers far out in the distance, she knew this was her destiny and she was crazy excited to get going and start this new adventure.

'You can't just make a decision like this; it affects more than just you,' he snapped and suddenly she heard that familiar controlling edge to his voice.

'I absolutely can make my decision and I just have.' She kept her voice level and calm. 'It's like this, Jeremy, you can either do as I ask or you can make this a lot more difficult than it needs to be.'

'Is that a threat?'

'Of course it's not a threat,' she sighed, but at the same time she held the phone away; she had hoped it wouldn't be like this. 'Friends don't threaten each other, Jeremy, and even if you and I were never going to end up getting married to each other, I thought at the very least we would always be friends.'

'Humph,' he managed and she wondered if he had pulled in at the golf club or if he was on some side road listening to her.

'So, I want to have my child and, just as there has been no place for me in your family, there will be no place for you in mine. We probably should have ended things ages ago, but this seems like the right time. I want a clean break; when I go back to work, we are starting fresh. From here on, we are just colleagues and if there's any attempt to sabotage me at work or in any other area, I will come out fighting, Jeremy, and you really do not want that.' Now, that was a threat and it was one she was more than happy to deliver on.

'Fine. You've obviously made up your mind.' He wanted to say more. She could feel it as much in his silence as in the tone of his voice. The truth was, she'd ambushed him with this information, but that had been as much about her own survival as it was about anything else. She imagined him, driving into the golf club, pretending that everything was just perfect, but screwing up his game and probably being angry at both of them for messing everything up.

But then, it dawned on Niamh, as if in some blinding flash

– hadn't it always been like that? Jeremy pretending that his life was perfect when in fact it had been anything but. Yes, on the face of things he had the picture-perfect family, but he also had a mistress tucked away and a job he'd buried himself into that was in many ways as much a prison to him as it was a career he loved. He was, she realised now, as she sat looking out across the ocean, her hand cradling her stomach, as trapped as she had been, only with that one phone call she had broken free.

She would sell her flat; buy a modest two-bedroom cottage, somewhere nice, but not flashy. It would be outside the city, probably near her parents. She would have enough change to keep her home for a long stretch of maternity leave on top of the paid weeks she was due as a matter of course. When she got back to her flat, she would open all the windows, air the place of the last remnants of Jeremy and, the following evening after work, she would call round to her mother and tell her the good news.

She felt happy and light. There was so much to look forward to. She had a few more days before she headed back to her life in Dublin and she planned to enjoy this unexpected happy break in this beautiful place.

24

Esme

Esme sat in the declining evening sunlight. She could feel its warmth stretch out across her leg, imagined it picking out particles of dust on the air around the hallway. The Boyds – a young family from Portlaoise – had just stormed past her like a mini tornado of clamorous kids and drained parents. They brought with them the saltiness of the sea, the cool breeze of the evening and an air of dissatisfaction that told Esme they'd stayed too long on the beach and now they needed dinner and bed, and neither would be delivered quickly enough to give them any real satisfaction. Perhaps Esme was in the same boat. She pulled her cardigan up around her shoulders, she wasn't cold, but she needed a little extra comfort. Had she stayed here too long? Worn out her usefulness? It certainly felt that way with a useless leg and eyes that didn't work properly.

'A penny for them.' Cora Doyle sat down in the chair opposite her. 'Ah,' she said and Esme imagined her smiling. 'I certainly don't miss having to sort out my Connor at the end of a too long day.'

'Not one of the greatest joys of parenting, I'd imagine.' Esme managed a smile, but it was half-hearted. 'Still, it's funny, but looking back, fifty years ago, I'd have given anything to have bad-tempered children, just so long as I had the chance to become a mother.'

'I'm so sorry.'

'Ara sure, it's water under the bridge and perhaps...' Esme was old enough and wise enough to know that while having children changed a woman, not having them had changed her too. Was she better for it in some way? She hoped so. 'That was a very long time ago.'

'Still.' Cora reached out, tucked the blanket around Esme's leg in an action that was somehow far more comforting than just making her comfortable. 'You've ended up with a lot of people who think the world of you. I'm not sure those of us with families are going to have the sort of dedicated care from our children that Marta lavishes on you.'

'I've been very lucky.'

'Maybe, but I think you've attracted good people to you because you're kind and you have a generous spirit. You have probably helped more people than you know over the years, with your wise words.'

'Hah!' Esme snorted. 'My wise words?'

'Yes, you always seem to know the right thing to say.'

'Oh, dear.' Esme sighed. 'Do you really want to know the truth of the guest book?'

Esme closed her eyes, remembered a time very, very long ago. She'd been at her lowest ebb. Her third pregnancy had ended in stillbirth, it had been so close. A baby girl, Eve, although, she'd never had a name, not really. Things were different back then. The hospitals were run as much by the nuns as by the doctors and as far as they were concerned babies weren't babies unless they were baptised. It's funny, it was only later that she felt angry about how things were.

'I was in a bad way, very low. The local doctor all but confirmed that I'd never be able to have a baby. She arrived at thirty-six weeks, but it was already too late to save her. It all happened so quickly, there wasn't time to get to a hospital and, I suppose, everyone was just relieved that I survived it.'

Although, in hindsight, Esme had often wondered if she really did survive it, or had she just gotten through it, out the other side, but utterly changed at the end, so that woman she was before was lost completely?

'Anyway, my mother was beside herself with worry about me. I wouldn't eat, couldn't move, really. I just wanted to die.'

'Oh Esme.'

'The guest book was my mother's way of getting me back on my feet again. She brought it to me, propped it up on the bed before me and made me write in an uplifting quote for every single day of the year ahead. Somehow, by the time I'd selected and written each one, I felt a little better. Then each day, I'd open up the book and it was as if the words gave me some sort of inner strength. It was silly of course, they were just words I'd chosen myself, but they gave me hope. They brought me back to some sort of life, even if it wasn't the one I'd set my heart on.'

'And you kept up the habit of writing them in and…'

'Oh, I haven't written them in for years. Marta has done that now since my eyesight started to fail, but, in a way, it's even nicer, because I'm never sure what words I'm going to find when I start the day.'

'That's such a lovely story.'

'I suppose it is, in its way, and you're right about Marta, I am very lucky, I know that too.' And she did, but maybe having Marta do everything for her was adding to this melancholy that had drifted over her. After all, she couldn't go on relying on her forever, it wouldn't be fair, but if she didn't have Marta, she knew the alternative that lay ahead of her was every bit as hopeless as how she'd felt all those years ago, when she'd first started to write in the guest book.

'Ah, well now, is that where you're hiding yourself?' Paschal Fenlon's voice almost made Esme jump from the chair.

'I didn't hear you knock,' she said, but of course, the likes of Fenlon slid through doors, it was in his nature to slither in the shadows.

'The door is open, I just thought I'd drop in for a chat,' he said and he perched on the end of the coffee table next to her chair, overwhelming her with his expensive aftershave that she had no way of escaping.

'You really shouldn't consider an open door as an invitation, Paschal, and I'm not sure what it is you think we might have to chat about.'

'Well, I should be...' Cora said, although she sounded unsure if she should leave them to it or stay put as back-up.

'Yes,' Paschal said, although Esme had a feeling he never so much as glanced at Cora.

'No need for you to be going anywhere, Cora. Mr Fenlon

and I don't have anything to talk about.' Esme clamped her mouth shut. Even if she was thinking of her leaking roof in the attic and the fan that had taken a few tiles down in the kitchen earlier, she couldn't bring herself to make things comfortable for him.

'I see you've had a bit of bad luck,' he said, obviously not one to be easily put off, but then she'd known that already. Hadn't he bought up any sea-facing site in the village that had come up for sale over the last year or two – God alone knew where the money was coming from, but Esme had a feeling that maybe the devil himself might have a better idea.

'Just a fall, I'll be up and running again before you know it.'

'Still though, all those stairs. It can't be easy, Mrs Goldthorp, and you have to keep this place running, although, I dare say, business isn't what it once was.'

'Actually, we have a full house.' It was quite a few years since they'd been full to the rafters, but it was busy enough for Esme now.

'Oh well, I'm sure that will change once my new hotel goes up.'

'I do hope you have planning permission,' Esme said, although she knew the likes of Paschal Fenlon would have every T crossed and every I dotted and probably enough paid in bribes to smooth over any difficulties. He had plenty of lackeys on his payroll to make sure things would go seamlessly, once he had stacked up all his playing cards.

'Of course,' he said and she could almost feel him looking around, assessing her lovely home, as if already measuring up for the day when it would be his. 'You still haven't gotten round to fixing that roof, I see,' he crowed, already sounding as if he'd won.

'Actually, my husband is coming to check it out this week,' Cora said from the chair opposite. And Esme clamped closed her lips to stop herself from speaking – although she wanted to throw her arms around Cora in gratitude. Esme had a feeling that, in reality, Cora's husband was the last person Cora would want here at the Willows.

'It'll need a new roof, for sure, they don't come cheap.' Fenlon got up from the table, bent down close to Esme and whispered, 'You need to be careful of some cowboy going up there and making a botch job of it, after all, you're hardly going to be able to go up and inspect the work, are you?' Then he stood back and laughed. 'I wouldn't want you spending good money after bad only to make the blasted thing worse when I have to buy you out,' he said with the inevitability of one who truly believed he would own the place.

'Over my dead body.'

'Maybe, but let's face it, you can't go on forever.' Then he made a clicking noise with his tongue before crawling back to whatever rock he usually hid under.

'Urgh,' Cora said. 'What a thoroughly horrible man.'

'Indeed. He wants the Willows, in case you hadn't guessed and...' Each time he came here, he left Esme feeling as if it was more and more her only option.

'Well, he can want all he likes, it's your home and he's out of luck, isn't he?'

'He's right about the roof though. It needs fixing, maybe even replacing.' Esme sighed. He was right too about the fact that for as long as she was stuck here in this dome chair, there was very little she could do about it.

'Well, holes in roofs are not the end of the world, maybe I *could* ask Michael to take a look…' Cora's voice petered off and they both knew that at this moment in time, the Doyles had far more pressing matters to discuss than Esme's roof; still, it was nice of her to say it. 'After all, it's hardly a feat of epic engineering, is it?'

'Is this the kitchen fan that Marta was talking about earlier?' Rob Courtney walked into the corridor.

'Among a catalogue of other things.' Esme smiled. God, she remembered when Rob was a little boy coming here and she would slip him the occasional iced lolly.

'Well, I don't know about the catalogue of other things, but I'm going to put that fan to rights for you, and Marta has already replaced some of the tiles,' he said, patting Esme's shoulder.

'Oh, you really don't have to go doing that,' Esme said, but she knew that a cracked kitchen tile alone would mark them down if they had a visit from the health inspector. Esme smiled, but she hated being old, she hated being blind and she hated being stuck here when she needed to sort out her guest house.

Monday

25

Cora

It was a gut punch. Literally, well, not literally, but it might as well have been. Cora felt it as if someone had taken their fist and rammed it into her stomach. She stood for a moment on the pavement outside the small shop that sold a limited range of builders' supplies – O'Heirs, next door to the pharmacist she had used since her own children were young. She was back in Knockroe with Niamh to pick up, of all things an antihistamine that was safe to take during pregnancy. Hah! She'd just been thinking that at this hour of the day the last person she'd run into was Michael – because Michael was always at work at this hour of the day. And O'Heirs? It was the kind of place she dropped into more frequently than Michael. Michael never came here. It was the sort of shop where DIY enthusiasts picked up construction belts they'd never really use, paint to patch a corner or silicone sealer to fix a crack. Real handymen wouldn't pay the exorbitant prices here, instead they'd go to the huge yard on the outskirts of town where there were discounts most normal people couldn't understand, calculated on square metres and cubic centimetres.

Cora just stood there, trying to make sense of the shadows she was seeing inside the shop window. She was staring with her mouth slightly open at two people, so familiar and yet, here, so oddly strange.

It was Michael. Her Michael and Tanya Farrelly. Stupidly, she found herself checking her watch, because the reasoning part of her brain knew it couldn't be him. He *should* be at work now. He should be sawing joists, nailing down floors or, maybe, reading his red-top with a mug of tea in his hand.

And Tanya *man-eating* Farrelly?

What on earth were they up to? Cora couldn't be sure how long she stood there, taking in the unreal scene before her. They looked as if they were choosing paint, Michael holding up colour cards, Tanya leaning against him, placing another card next to his, gazing (yes, actually gazing!) up at Cora's husband.

Cora wanted to march right in, maybe she would have, but her legs had turned to jelly, her head swam with the very notion of it.

'Hey?' Niamh was at her side. 'What's wrong, you look like you've seen a ghost?' But all Cora could do was point, before taking off in the opposite direction to where she'd parked the car.

'Hang on.' Niamh was racing along beside her, but Cora was walking like a woman possessed. Eventually, Niamh put her hand on Cora's arm. 'What's happened?'

'I...' Cora couldn't put the words together. They were

halfway down the street, she was standing there, her mouth opening and closing, her husband picking out paint colours with the biggest flirt in Cherrywood Crescent, and all she could do was stand there like a goldfish.

Then, out of the side of her eye, she caught sight of them, Tanya in her leopard-print trench coat, tottering on heels that were at least eight inches, her hair a halo of blonde bouffant. Michael was walking along behind her. And in the haze of her volcanic emotions, Cora thought he looked like a stray duckling imprinting onto an insatiable wolf, even if she was dressed up like a lamb. They had obviously picked up paint. Michael was carrying two cans and what looked like a bag of brushes and maybe a tray and roller. He was swaying with the weight, but Tanya was walking ahead, as if on a mission. They were walking in the opposite direction, which was something to be thankful for at least.

'It's Michael,' Cora managed, still gaping at the pair of them, 'my Michael and I think he's having an affair.' She pointed a shaking finger in the direction of the two figures making their way towards the end of the road.

'Come on.' Niamh dragged her into the nearest coffee shop. 'Let's just duck in here for a while and pull ourselves together.'

There was no way they could walk back to the car without risk of bumping into Michael and Tanya now, diversion seemed like the best tactic, although Cora felt as if she would choke if she put so much as a teacup to her lips.

It was a full fifteen minutes before Cora could even make sense of what Niamh was saying. Everything had become a complete blur, everything except the sickening feeling that was filling up her stomach and her chest, making her legs weak and her head spin.

'I'm sure there's a perfectly reasonable explanation,' Niamh was saying, probably not for the first time, but it didn't make any difference because Cora knew Tanya well enough to know that with Tanya, there was never an innocent explanation, whatever about reasonable.

In the time they'd been next-door neighbours, Tanya had made her way through two husbands, three fiancés and too many casual flings to count. When other people went on holidays and brought back a tatty memento, Tanya brought back the waiter or the tour guide. And every single time, it was true love. From the oldest at seventy to the youngest at almost half her age, she confided to Cora, she always thought he was *the one*. Of course, the other women on Cherrywood Crescent steered themselves and their husbands well clear of her.

Cora sighed. It turned out they were right to give her a wide berth. Tanya who had a reputation for liking other women's husbands just a little too much. Tanya who had broken up marriages and families and then cast off the lover she'd lured away. That same Tanya was out purchasing paint with Cora's husband in broad daylight on the main street of the small town that had been their home town forever.

'What on earth is Michael thinking?' she managed to whisper eventually.

'It's probably not what it looks like, really.' Niamh sounded so sure, but Niamh didn't know Tanya.

'The answer is, he's not thinking, not with his brains anyway.' God, Cora had been such a fool, avoiding his calls, running away like that; she might as well have handed Tanya the key to her castle and told her to help herself to anything she wanted.

'You could always ask him?' Niamh leaned forward, but she had no idea. Cora could hardly articulate her own thoughts now, never mind formulate a sentence, much less actually confront Michael and Tanya.

'Hah!' Maybe, she knew, if her marriage was worth saving, confronting them would be the last thing she could do.

'Seriously,' Niamh said.

'Oh God.' A wave of nausea swept over Cora. 'What have I done?'

She couldn't just walk away either, she couldn't just pretend this wasn't happening. But on the other hand, she hadn't the strength to march down that street after them and she was nowhere near ready to go back to Cherrywood Crescent and have it out with them.

'You don't have to do anything yet.' Niamh was holding her hand. Cora only just noticed it now. She was holding her hand and the sheer innocence and honesty of it made Cora want to bawl her eyes out, right here in the middle of the packed café.

'I want to go back to the Willows.' Cora looked at her watch, as if seeing the time would make things any better. They might as well have been sitting here for a week or a month and really, she wasn't sure if she'd know the difference.

'Come on, they're bound to be well gone now.' Niamh picked up the parcel she'd bought. A few toiletries and some herbal spray the pharmacist promised would help to ease morning sickness. Honestly, Cora couldn't remember walking back to the car through the mist of tears that stood persistently in her eyes, how she drove back to Ballycove without killing them both was a miracle, the likes of which she'd never understand.

26

Esme

Later Esme would observe that Marjory Portly moved as if her shape suited her name. Esme heard her schlepping about the hallway for a few minutes before she rang the bell to officially let them know she was there.

'Marta won't hear you.' Esme poked her head around the dome chair, hoping her voice didn't startle the woman who wore sweet-smelling perfume but brought with her an air of fatigue made obvious by loud sighs and deep breaths.

'Oh.' The woman walked round to stand in front of Esme. 'Well, I'm going to have to speak to someone who works here, even if it's not the owner,' she said crisply, as if she'd put away her fatigue in favour of a more professional persona.

'Well, I'm the owner, if I can be any help to you at all?' Esme smiled.

'Ah.' The woman fumbled with her card and held it out towards Esme, realising a little too late that Esme was blind. 'Sorry. I'm Marjory Portly, I have a card, I'm from Public Health – I'm here to carry out a safety inspection.'

'Oh, I didn't realise we were due one.' Esme smiled again.

She was used to dealing with people coming to check over that things were as they should be. Health inspectors had been visiting the guest house for over twenty-five years and there had never been a problem. 'Usually, you let us know, but you're always welcome. Would you like to show yourself around, take a look at the kitchen, through there?'

Esme pointed in the general direction behind the Victorian table that served as a reception desk. It was only as she did so that she remembered the fan that had fallen off the wall the previous day and the fact that if it wasn't for darling Rob Courtney, it might still be languishing in the back porch alongside half a dozen smashed tiles from the wall behind the cooker. She could only pray now that everything had stayed put in the meantime.

'Marta will be down in a little while, she's doing out the rooms, we have some new guests arriving this afternoon,' Esme said.. The McNallys, a couple who had kept to themselves for three days and hardly said boo to a goose, had checked out earlier that morning.

'Of course, I can speak to you both when I've gone through my list,' the woman said, lumbering towards the kitchen as if she were a battleship under siege and looking for a port.

It was longer than Esme cared to remember since she had prayed with the fervour she managed as the woman carried out her inspection and considerably longer since she'd felt this awful sense of dread that this time, for the first time ever, the guest house might not be up to scratch.

Perhaps Paschal Fenlon was right. What could she do with the place now? She hadn't enough money to completely overhaul the Willows so it could be up to the standard of some fancy new-build hotel. And if she could talk the bank manager into lending her the money, which was unlikely, considering her age, they'd need to extend the season to pay the loan back; she liked that they closed for half the year. She enjoyed the winter months here with Marta, catching her breath and pottering about and then looking forward to starting all over again. Esme closed her eyes, interspersing her prayers with depressing thoughts of having to sell her lovely home to Paschal Fenlon, hoping that the prayers might win out in the end, or at least satisfy the woman currently checklisting her kitchen to the satisfaction of health and safety best practice.

Marjory Portly may have walked slowly and huffed and puffed a great deal, but she was quick about her work and she emerged from the kitchen within half an hour, having already checked their fridges, dishes, skirting boards, scourers, pots and pans and also, Esme suspected, behind and beneath a great number of surfaces her colleagues would prefer to ignore if possible. She read her checklist to Esme as if it were a great novel with each point ending in a clear 'Check.'

'So, you are happy the Willows is up to standard?' Esme asked.

'It's as if you knew I was coming,' Marjory said and she flopped into the chair opposite.

'No, you definitely had the element of surprise.' Esme smiled.

'Surprised me too, I can tell you, I only found out I was coming here this morning.'

'Well, we had to replace some tiles that came down

yesterday, but we had no idea that anyone would be looking at them,' Esme said. It was better to be honest, she didn't have to rub her fingers across them to know that the grout was hardly dry at this point.

'Yes. There is something I can help with?' Marta scampered down the stairs.

'Ah Marta.' Esme did the introductions and coffee and biscuits were organised from the kitchen while Esme listened to some of Marjory's stories about the worst places she'd visited over the years. 'It's funny, because normally, they let us know when you're coming.'

'On the annual visits, yes, but not if there's been a complaint,' Marjory said as she munched happily on one of Marta's homemade Florentine biscuits.

'There has been a complaint?' Marta said and Esme imagined her normally straight back galvanising even straighter, until she was sitting rod-like on the chair opposite.

'Yes, I'm afraid so. Honestly, I expected to come to ambulances parked outside the door and a major public health emergency on our hands. That's why I didn't hang around, you can't afford to, when it's public health, can you?' Marjory said a little self-importantly and Esme had a feeling that here was a woman who took the responsibility of her job seriously. It was a good thing too. 'Although, now I've seen how well the place is run, I can't imagine that it was from a guest.' She leaned forward and picked some crumbs from the plate. 'That's why they sent me. We tend to swap around for complaints, so Roger, the inspector who usually comes here, is doing my patch today.'

'Ah Roger.' Esme smiled. Roger Wessel was a sweet man,

who generally stood at the kitchen door almost apologising for having to check that food was stored properly and temperatures were within safe guidelines.

'I really can't imagine why anyone would suggest we might be a health hazard.' Esme couldn't help but feel a little wounded.

'Can't you, really?' There was a harshness in Marta's voice that was unfamiliar. 'It's that awful excuse for a man, Fenlon. I know it in my bones, this is exactly the sort of low thing he would do.'

'Of course, who else.' Esme knew Marta was right, as sure as God made little green apples, Paschal Fenlon had to be the one who complained about them. She had turned him down only yesterday for, it had to be said, the umpteenth time. She quickly explained to Marjory who he was.

'Can we find out who made the complaint?' she asked Marjory now. 'Not that it matters, there isn't much we can do about it anyway, except come through with shining colours.'

'Well, you've done that at least,' Marjory said. 'I can't tell you who made the complaint, but if you're right and it's some sort of bullying tactic, then I will say that you weren't the only business the person complained about. We got a whole batch of them in together and they are all prime locations, small businesses…' She stopped for a moment considering. 'Yes, this is exactly the sort of place a property developer might well have his eye on, now that I come to think of it,' she said.

They sat in silence for a few minutes, each digesting the idea that someone would be nasty enough to set out to cause such trouble for a little guest house perched on the edge of the sea.

'Well, I should be off now.' Marjory gathered up her tick sheets and bags with a little huff and puff as she went. 'Good luck,' she called as she headed out the door towards her next call, and Esme couldn't help but feel the woman thought they might need it.

*

Esme imagined she could hear the sheets flapping on the clothes line in the sea breeze. Marta must have left the side door open when she was racing from one task to the next. She imagined it now, the garden resplendent in the evening sun, the borders a profusion of colour and scent, roses, rhododendrons and camellias in full bloom. How many hours had she spent out there, coaxing growth out of young plants, adding in seedlings and watering diligently on evenings when the day had been too hot to dare to quench their thirst? A chill breeze brushed over her, making her sneeze like a kitten, and she realised that even that sounded weak and limited.

'Hay fever?' Phyllis asked diplomatically before placing a tissue in her hands. 'It's chilly here, isn't it? Oh, no wonder, someone's left the door open.' She walked across and closed it with a soft click.

'Thank you, I was enjoying the fresh air, but it *can* get chilly after a while. Do you know, I remember every single inch of that garden as if I'd just planted each and every flower in it?'

'They'd call it very mindful now, planting things, they

say the earth has properties that somehow make you feel more...' Phyllis stopped, perhaps realising that it was not the soil Esme missed. 'I'm so sorry Esme, it's awful for you being stuck here when I know how much you'd enjoy being outside...'

'It's the doing of things I miss more than anything. It sounds daft, but just making my own bed...' It was that, and it was even getting in and out of it independently that she longed to do by herself now.

'I know you won't want to hear this, but you're lucky, at least you can stay in your own home, you're surrounded by people who are coming and going, you can talk to people, you know where you are...' There was a catch in her old friend's voice and Esme didn't need to see her to know that tears were close to her eyes.

'You're right, of course you are. Don't take any notice of me, I'm just a silly old woman, sitting here and feeling sorry for myself.' She laughed, a slightly hollow sound, but she knew it was the truth.

'There's nothing silly about you, Esme. There never was.'

'Oh, I don't know, compared to you, it feels as if my life has been very small, looking after this place and...' It was the truth. Phyllis Courtney had been a circuit court judge and she'd had a family, a life full of people and accomplishments. 'Compared to you, well, I just about learned to type and do shorthand, neither very well, if I'm honest and then...'

Looking back, it seemed to Esme as if her whole world had fallen off the edge of a cliff with the loss of her babies. The Willows may have saved her, but only just.

'And where has it all gotten me?' Phyllis said drily. 'I'm

old now but, unlike you, I'm almost irrelevant. If it wasn't for the fact that Kurt needs me, what else have I got?' Was that true for her? Esme hadn't imagined that was how the world would look from Phyllis's vantage point. 'I'm holding onto Kurt because I love him, but we don't have forever.'

'Oh, Phyllis, what a thing to say.' Esme knew exactly what Phyllis didn't want to put into words. Even if her eyes weren't working, she could hear it in the way Kurt moved and the way he spoke; or rather, she could hear it in the way he halted mid-sentence, as if the word he was looking for had just been stolen from him when he wasn't looking.

'You already know, don't you?'

'I thought, last year, when you came down that maybe...'

'Last year?'

'Yes. Kurt came into the kitchen one evening looking for Colm. For a moment, I wasn't sure what to say, it sort of startled me, and then, as if he'd never asked, he started to chat away about the salmon he'd caught that day and how wonderful it would have been if only Josh was old enough to join him on the pier.'

'Oh, Esme.' In those words, it felt as if so many worlds were tied together and then, the story of how Kurt was rapidly spinning away from her into a world of his own came flooding out. Dementia – it was such a cruel disease.

'I should have said something, but at the time, well, I think I was in shock, you know. For the briefest of moments, it almost felt as if Kurt brought with him the possibility that Colm might still be here. Does that sound completely crazy?' Esme said, thinking back to a year ago.

'No.' Phyllis sighed and leant back in the chair opposite.

For a while, they sat there, both of them lost in their own thoughts. 'Esme, what on earth am I going to do?'

'It's going to be okay,' Esme said gently, although she had no idea what on earth her dear friend *would* do. 'I mean, once you accept that things are changing, it won't be easy, but I can't think of another person in the whole world who is as strong as you, Phyllie, I really can't.'

'I don't feel strong, all I want to do is run as far away as possible and take Kurt with me, so we might hide from how the future seems to be panning out before us.'

'You'll have help.'

'Of course, there'll be help.' Phyllis Courtney had never been one to take any sort of help. 'I mean, the GP has said they'll send in home help who'll take Kurt out of bed and make sure that I get a break, but that's not what I mean.'

'Ah.' Esme knew what Phyllis meant now. It was one of those conversations they'd had years before, buried like so many other things between them, because it was far too terrible to contemplate. Kurt didn't want to end up like his father, but with dementia, there would be no choice, unless he took matters into his own hands before it was too late. Esme shivered, because her next thought was: or unless Phyllis was charged with the task of helping him to end things before they became unbearable.

'You do realise it isn't going to be all down to you or up to you?' Esme's voice was low. She wasn't trying to upset Phyllis, but even here, in the darkness, with just the weight of guilt that seemed to hang in every word that Phyllis said and more often didn't say, she couldn't miss it.

'Oh God.' Phyllis started to cry. 'What's happening to

me, Esme? I've always been so sure of everything, so sure of myself. I've been the cornerstone for everything, all the way through our lives. When storms hit, I was the one who kept the show going.' She sniffed, it must be hard for a woman like Phyllis to realise that she was not invincible.

'I suppose, when the time comes, you'll know what to do, for the best,' Esme said, and although there was nothing wise about her words, she heard Phyllis exhale, as if some weight had been lifted from her.

'You're right, of course you're right. I'll know what to do when the time comes. The question is, really, if I'll be strong enough to do it.'

'You will be, of course you will. The fact is, Phyllis, we're not just getting older, we're getting wiser too. Do you remember old Nellie Touhill? She used to clean the guest house years ago for me. She'd arrive in every morning, smile on her face as wide as the bay, not a care in the world?'

'Of course I remember poor Nellie, she found Rob's teddy when we were all sure it had been swept away by the tide.'

'Aye, she was always the one to manage to pull the impossible from her sleeve.'

'She was a very sweet woman. Is she still in the village?'

'She was the sweetest, kindest soul you could ever hope to meet. She took care of her parents and her sickly brother until the day they died, dedicated her whole life to them and then, suddenly, I suppose, there was nothing to work for and maybe, in her mind, nothing to live for. Old Nellie died about ten years ago. In the end, her liver failed her. The poor woman became a raging alcoholic, but none of us had an idea. She made her own wine and gin from sloes, nettles, even potatoes. If there was a root or a berry that could be made into alcohol Nellie had a grip on it or, it might be closer to the truth to say, it had a grip on her.'

'But why on earth…' Of course, Phyllis knew there was no good reason why one person could take a drink and leave it at that and the next couldn't so much as smell one but would need to finish the bottle.

'Sure, if we knew the answer to that, wouldn't the country be a far better place today?'

'That's so sad,' Phyllis said. 'Poor Nellie.'

'At the time, the whole village was cut up about it. You see, most of us were so busy getting on with life, we never thought about the one person who ran about looking after everyone else.'

'I have a feeling you're telling me this for a reason.' There was a smile tinting Phyllis's words.

'Oh, I don't know that there has to be a reason for every story, but I suppose, if I was in the business of giving advice instead of bed and breakfast, then I'd be saying that you need to get a bit of something going outside of yourself and Kurt, because even if you both live to be a hundred and sixty years old apiece…'

'I'm not sure I'd want to live that long,' Phyllis said, but of course, if it meant she could hold onto Kurt, she'd be here forever.

'That might be very wise indeed.'

'Could I ask you something?'

'Ask away…'

'This place, you know the way you close for winter…'

'Oh, we have good reason for closing up for the colder

months, you've never felt the cold like we have it here when the north-westerlies are hammering against our windows and doors. Perhaps I'm getting older, but I suspect it has more to do with the age of the Willows, it seems to get colder here every year.' Esme laughed.

'I've never minded the wind or the rain, but I wondered if we could stay, just for a day or two, when the storms arrive? I think it could be a magical memory for Kurt and maybe for me too…'

'Phyllis Courtney, after all these years, surely you know, whether the house is opened or closed, you will always be welcome here, you don't even need to ask. In fact, I'd love you to come back as my personal guest when we're closed up. I won't be guaranteeing that you mightn't have to help me make dinner in the evening, but if you're up for that, I think we could have a grand old time, just the four of us here together.' They sat there for a while in companionable silence, with the heat of the fire gently overcoming the cold that had taken up temporary residence until the front door had been firmly shut.

'You're wrong, you know.' Phyllis grasped Esme's hand.

'Really?'

'Yes, about living a small life. Don't you see, you've done far more than any of us? You've given people hope when they've come here and needed it the most. You've given me some sort of bearing and direction today, and at a time when my professional career is over, you're still going, you're still helping people, even when you can hardly move without it causing you pain, you're still of service to others.'

'Oh, but all I do is sit here all day long.' And yet, Esme felt a smile creep up at the corner of her lips. Maybe she did help people more than she knew.

'You have done so much for people – even if you don't know it. There have been times over the last few months when I felt as if I couldn't put one foot in front of the other ever again and, today, I feel as if maybe there is something to look forward to.' Phyllis was whispering now, urgently, needing her to know.

'Look, it won't always be like this,' Esme said. 'When you get answers and you know for certain where you stand with Kurt, when you make a plan, when life settles into something more normal, please do come and visit me again. Both of you, if Kurt is able, or on your own, if you'd like a little break when the guest house is closed. We can sit out on the veranda and drink tea and put the world to rights?'

'I'd love that, I really would,' Phyllis said now and Esme wondered if this would be the last season of the guest house. Regardless of what the health inspector said, there was still a roof to be repaired and just thinking about winter approaching made her shiver. Perhaps, a week in winter was the perfect punctuation mark if she had to close the doors for good.

27

Cora

'Sit with me,' Esme called when Cora eventually emerged from her room that evening. She was still red-eyed, still shellshocked. 'Well, did you both have a lovely time over in Knockroe?'

'Oh, Esme.' Cora couldn't help it, the whole sorry story came tumbling out. Mercifully, there wasn't a sinner about and she told the old woman everything, wiping snotty tears from her face as she finished up by telling her about seeing Michael and Tanya that afternoon.

'But you don't know, not for certain, do you?' Esme said, and something in her voice calmed Cora, almost like a warm balm folding around the shivering, unhappy core of her. 'I mean, he is a carpenter, isn't he? Perhaps she's asked him to do some job in her house and...'

'Well yes, but...' Cora wanted to believe anything other than the worst, which was what had firmly lodged itself in her mind now. 'I mean, even seeing them there, choosing paint colours together, they just looked so... together.' This was what annoyed her most. Had Tanya managed to talk him into painting her house, while their own house hadn't seen a lick of paint in years and it had come to the point that Cora didn't even mention it any more?

'You really don't think that there's more to it than that, do you?'

'Honestly, I don't know.' Cora dried her eyes again, her skin felt as if she'd spent all day in the Sahara, as if she'd dried out every single pore to the point that it was so parched it might actually crack from all the crying.

'Well, then in that case, it doesn't really matter what he does, does it?'

'How do you mean?' And all Cora could think was, how on earth could Esme be so calm about the fact that her husband of thirty years might be cheating on her?

'Now don't go getting all defensive, just hear me out.' She shook her head and smiled and Cora thought she'd never seen such kindness in eyes that could see so little and yet seemed to see everything worth looking at. 'I had a friend once, Maureen Givens, she married young, much too young to know what she wanted, let alone realise that the man she married would some day have corns, a bald patch and a paunch big enough to deliver twins, if only they could be conceived by a lifelong dedication to Arthur Guinness.'

'We married young,' Cora said a little wistfully. It felt like another twist of the knife. Somehow, having seen Michael and Tanya together, their simple wedding all those years ago was a far more rose-tinted memory compared to the last few years when all she wanted was that man she'd fallen in love with to actually notice she was still there in the room with him.

'Oh, we were all young once,' Esme said a little harshly.

'I was just...'

'You're both different people now and that's how it was with my friend, Maureen. By the time their kids were reared, Maureen was still a relatively young woman, but her husband seemed like an old man and Maureen wanted adventure. All she could talk about was seeing the world and finding herself, well, I mean any fool knows that if you can't find yourself exactly where you are, you're not going to trip over yourself in a student hostel somewhere in the far reaches of the Australian outback, are you?'

'I suppose,' Cora managed to squeeze in just the two words as Esme caught her breath.

'Anyway, she made it all the way to Gatwick. She packed her bags, not too many, because Maureen had every intention of seeing sun, sand, sea and adventure. She told me before she went that she burned her Marigolds in the stove after she'd zipped shut her travel bag the night before.' Esme shook her head. 'Her family were devastated...'

'About the Marigolds?' Marta put in between them, leaving a glass of milk and a half a dozen white tablets of various shapes and sizes on a saucer before Esme.

'Don't be so smart, it doesn't suit you,' Esme snapped.

'Of course they were, their mother had taken off to the far corner of the earth and...' Cora prodded.

'No, not that, she had a mobile phone with her. Of course, these are modern times, she was a modern woman, they were happy she was having her adventure.'

'So?' It felt as if they were going round in circles.

'Well, she hadn't managed to make the transfer from

Gatwick to Stansted before the whole village was talking about the fact that Selina Kelly had all but moved in with her husband and poor Maureen hardly had her passport stamped.'

'Men. Urgh,' Marta said and Cora had a feeling that she'd said it often over the years.

'So, she came back with her tail between her legs?' Cora said, feeling somehow crushed by the choice before her.

'She certainly did not.'

'But you said she'd only gotten to Gatwick when…'

'She'd gotten to Gatwick when she heard the news and probably she was upset, but then, at that point she'd bought her ticket and what was there to come back for anyway?'

'Well, her marriage and her…' Cora mumbled, because at the end of the day, marriage vows were marriage vows and even if your husband forgot he made them, that wasn't an automatic free pass for you.

'Too late, she'd already burned her Marigolds.' Marta laughed, sitting for once on the edge of the chair opposite.

'Yes, but…' Esme made a face in Marta's general direction; it was obvious they'd been over similar ground before. 'It doesn't do to be too cynical.' She turned towards Cora again. 'No, even though Maureen would never admit it, I know she'd have cried buckets on that long-haul flight, probably she spent quite a few weeks there, fighting with herself not to book an early return flight, but she didn't.'

'And her husband?'

'The thing about Selina was that while she looked good and made plenty of herself with magic knickers and war paint, she was just like the rest of us. Living every single day with a man who had little interest beyond what time dinner was put on the table, she let herself go. It was gradual, slow at first, but by the time Maureen arrived back from her adventure Selina looked every one of her years.'

'So, Maureen and her husband got back together?' This didn't seem like a very happy ending either to Cora, but maybe she was too old at this stage to believe in fairy tales.

'Dear Lord no.' Esme threw her head back and laughed. 'Maureen had become the woman she'd always believed she could be. Travelling and facing the world alone was the making of her. She only came back for a visit; she stayed here with me and that's when she confided that Tony had texted her every single day she'd been away.'

'Did Selina know?' But maybe it didn't matter, because already Cora was beginning to feel sorry for the woman – how on earth had that happened? At this moment, she couldn't imagine ever feeling one bit of sympathy for Tanya.

'Who knows? Perhaps she did, but she couldn't back out at that point, could she? She was stuck with Tony for better or for worse, she'd pinned her sails to his mast and the whole village knew, she'd been purring like the cat that got the cream at the start of it all.' Esme reached forward and popped two yellow tablets on her tongue; she washed them down efficiently with a sip of milk. 'The thing is, in a way, they all got what they deserved. Maureen found work on a cruise ship, she spent a few years travelling the world and eventually settled down quite content with herself in one of those holiday resorts in Spain.'

'Was she happy?'

'I don't know, but she told me she hadn't any regrets.'

FAITH HOGAN

Esme smiled and the sentence hung between them for a while. 'When it was obvious that she wasn't ever coming home, Tony really took to the drink. Most days he hardly knew one side of the street from the other and he was dead before his time. Selina was devastated, I think, but it's hard to know. She took up with someone else soon after, of course, it didn't last any length. The last I heard, she was living in Donegal helping with the meals on wheels.'

'Humph, probably eyeing up the most eligible pensioners for her swan song,' Marta said, picking a short silver hair from the arm of the chair.

'I'm not sure what to take from that,' Cora said, but she certainly didn't feel any worse than she had earlier.

'I'm not sure either, but...'

'I'll tell you what, it's better to live a life without regrets than to be forever tied to a man, just because he's a man, that's what you need to take from it,' Marta said.

'But...'

'Do you want to know what I think?' Esme asked, but she didn't wait for an answer. 'I think we have to do what we think is right for us. If Maureen had stayed where she was, nothing would have changed for her; she'd have lived a life forever in the shadows of providing for a husband who didn't really give a fig. By going he realised that he'd had gold all along and, even if she didn't admit it, I think she enjoyed the fact that, each day, he sat down and poured his heart out to her in those messages. I don't know how long they lasted, but I have a feeling that they made up for things a bit. It was almost as if those years hadn't been wasted.'

She stopped for a moment, took a long deep breath. 'I suppose, the thing you have to think about is what you want, not what you think you have to settle for. Don't mind this Tanya one or anything else. You have to figure out what will make you happy. Once you do that, everything will come right in the end, even if it's not exactly what you thought it might be all those years ago when you were probably too young to know what you wanted anyway.'

'Oh, Esme.' It was all Cora could manage, because even Marta was wiping away the tears now.

*

Joel was waiting for Cora with an expensive-looking bottle of red wine when she arrived back at the Willows after an exhausting walk across the beach. She'd needed to tire herself out completely, if that was possible, otherwise, she feared another night spent lying in bed agonising over the state of her marriage and maybe the fact that she only had herself to blame for sending Michael straight into the arms of Tanya Farrelly. She didn't know what she felt any more, that was the truth of it. On one side, she knew, she couldn't go on with how things were, but she had hoped that taking time out might improve matters, not make them a thousand times worse. As far as deciding what would make her happy – she wasn't sure if she could ever truly be happy again, not like she'd been when Connor was little, and it felt as if her whole world had meaning just because he was at the centre of it.

Cora was glad of the chance to put off going to bed for another while and, although it was late, she found glasses in the breakfast room and she and Joel sat companionably on wheezing wicker chairs on the veranda; talking only occasionally about the setting sun and the porpoises playing in the distance. They watched as pleasure boats docked for the night and villagers made their way back from dog walks on the road that wound past the guest house.

'It's beautiful here,' he murmured. 'God, I can't remember when I last felt so…'

'At peace? I know, there's something like magic about this place.' Cora managed to smile because it felt as if the yawning beauty of the place was filling her soul to capacity and there was no room for the pain or misery that seemed to have taken lodgings there for far too long. 'Sorry. We've begun to finish each other's sentences,' she said.

'Like an old married couple,' Joel joked.

'No, just like very good friends,' she corrected him quickly. She was sure he hadn't meant anything by it. Still, it was better to be clear about where they stood, even if at this point she wasn't sure exactly where her feet fitted any more or indeed which direction they should be facing.

They'd come to the end of the bottle, perhaps a little too fast, although they'd been sitting here for hours. It couldn't be hours, could it? Her mind had enjoyed the break from wondering what Michael and Tanya might be up to back in Cherrywood Crescent.

Next to her, Joel had obviously spotted her wedding ring and made a point of looking away when she turned it over on her finger. He hadn't asked if she was still married, perhaps he'd assumed she was a widow. It wasn't a secret and yet she made light of her time here to him, as if it was just a holiday.

She told him about Connor's wedding and his lovely wife Lydia. She told him about her job in a school in the next town over and then, when it was almost dark, he talked about his ex-wife. Alison, a woman who had been as tied up in his business as she was in his heart, until he realised that she was good for neither. She had quickly moved on. When Joel talked about it, it sounded as if it all happened a long time ago. Cora told him about Michael.

'Michael isn't one for leaving his own corner,' she said.

'So, you're just going to stay in different houses for the summer and then…'

'Well yes.' A tightening nerve in her jaw might have given away the tension of lying, but she owed Michael the loyalty of not discussing their marriage with someone who was almost a complete stranger, even if it felt as if she'd known him for years. 'I can't remember when I've felt so…' she paused, then added, 'I had hoped we'd do the Camino Way, but I think I'm having a much nicer time here.'

'I always wanted to do the Camino Way.'

'Oh well.' She couldn't look at him. She was trying hard not to keep score of all the ways she wished Michael was more like Joel.

'I don't think I'd let you out of my sight for five minutes, never mind a whole summer.' He laughed and so did she, because it didn't sound as if he was coming onto her in some way, even though a little part of her wondered what would happen if he did. God, that made her suddenly shudder. She left down her glass. Too much wine. It was time to stop before she lost sight of herself and everything else that counted in her life.

'He might be glad of the peace and quiet.' Cora laughed and hoped it sounded lighter than she felt.

'Well, he's cock-eyed crazy if that's the case,' Joel said, then lowered his voice to something that surprised them both a little. 'What I mean is, you're very good company. I think I'd enjoy spending time with you, even if we were looking out over the biggest dump in the place instead of this fabulous view.'

And then, Cora yawned, because maybe she was tired, more honestly it was because she was afraid of that frisson of electricity that had been building up between them for the last few evenings. She should at least admit it was there, to herself. The thing she didn't want to think about was that it had been there from the moment she met him.

She took a deep breath; it was time to call it a night before things led somewhere she hadn't intended to go. The last thing she wanted to do was make things even worse than they already were.

That night, as Cora lay in her bed, she was acutely conscious that, somewhere in the big old house, Joel Lawson was undressing and slipping between cotton sheets for the night too. Perhaps it was better than wondering where Michael was sleeping tonight, or worse, if he was sleeping with Tanya. Pushing all of these thoughts from her mind, she closed her eyes and eventually drifted off to the sound of the tide turning in the distance.

28

Niamh

It wasn't an epiphany. Niamh couldn't say what *it* was exactly, but gradually, over the course of the last few days, well, maybe since she'd first found out she was pregnant, the news had settled on her. Admittedly, it had been shocking at first.

She smiled now. Thinking of that first day to herself – it had been like a bombshell landing on her lap, complete and utter panic at the idea of what might lie ahead of her.

Niamh had thought coming to Ballycove was about taking that tablet, ending this pregnancy before it really had a chance to begin, but now she wondered if coming here had been her way of taking time out of her real life, to take stock and maybe examine where she was going exactly. Walking along the beach, on days when she knew her colleagues were hard at work, had somehow given her time to think in a way she'd never taken time to do so before.

No one had judged her. Not at the clinic, that day she'd shown up, a shadow of her usual confident self. Here in

Ballycove, she'd made friends with Cora, spilled her heart and fears out to the woman and all she'd done was console her – there'd been no pressure to choose either way.

But, if she was honest, it was everything about this place that had clinched it.

She'd woken gently, to the sound of the sea whispering through the open window. In the garden below, she heard the sounds of father and son, playing football in the garden. Josh Courtney was, to her mind at least, the sweetest little boy. He had just the right amount of naughtiness mixed with angelic sweetness so you couldn't be cross with him for any length of time.

Yesterday, she had made up her mind, Niamh knew what she was going to do. Last night, she walked over to the mantelpiece, took down the pill that was waiting there and flushed it down the toilet. Then she picked up her mobile and rang her parents.

'Oh, darling, I can't believe it!' her mother squealed. There was no mention of Jeremy, perhaps her mother hoped he wasn't the father. 'When are you due... Have you had a scan... Are you going to find out if it's a boy or a girl or... Oh, my, what if it's twins...'

'Hold your horses,' her father chimed in from the background, but his voice, usually so calm and unflappable sounded excited and she knew, he would adore the idea of a grandchild.

'Thanks Daddy, let me catch my breath, I've only just told you that I'm pregnant,' Niamh laughed. But she couldn't help getting carried away on the idea of this alternative, brighter future that had suddenly begun to unfold before her. Her mother talked for a long time about the idea of being a grandmother and Niamh only just realised how much it meant to her and, maybe, what she'd have made her do without, if this hadn't happened by accident. 'Mum, you haven't asked me about Jeremy,' she said because he was the next person she'd have to talk to.

'Well, I didn't like to... I mean, is he... happy about the news?' God help her poor mother, she was doing her best to say the right thing, but they both knew that whichever way Jeremy went, it would mean a broken family one way or another.

'I'm not giving him a choice. He knows about the baby, but he has his own family, I don't expect him to be part of mine.'

'Ah.' Her mother's most tactful response, it was a failsafe.

'So, I've told him, I'm going it alone.' Just telling him was enough for now. Niamh hadn't given any great thought to things like maintenance or access or anything else much, beyond looking forward to the exciting future unfurling before her.

'Oh, my dear Niamh, you're never, ever going to be alone, especially not in this,' her mother said and it made Niamh feel even a million times better than she already did.

It was as she walking along the beach later that evening that her mobile rang. Jeremy would be driving home from work now and, she knew, her voice when she spoke would fill up his Lexus.

'Hey,' he said but there was a distinct lack of enthusiasm in his voice.

'Long day?' she couldn't help asking, even though,

truthfully, she knew it was no longer her concern what his days were like, good, bad, long, short or otherwise.

'Hmm.' He sounded distracted. 'How's your holiday going?'

'We both know it's not a holiday, Jeremy.'

'Sorry. You know what I mean. How are you?'

'I'm fine. I've spent the last few days walking on the most scenic beach in Ireland and I'm still pregnant, in case you're interested.' There was no better way to put it. Well, telling him she was actually looking forward to having her baby might be rubbing his nose in it a little too much.

'Look, Niamh, I know you're upset and you're probably not thinking this through but…'

'I'm not a bit upset, Jeremy, and you're right, I have some more thinking to do but I've made my decision…'

'Niamh, if this is just about you wanting me to hold your hand and pretend that we're love's young dream?' His voice sounded so cruel – how had she not noticed that before?

'No. Not at all Jeremy.' He had just made this so much easier. 'Actually, you're the last one I'd want holding my hand now. We're finished, I've already told you this, I can't make it any clearer than that.'

'But what about…?' In the background, she could hear a ticking sound, and assumed he was pulling in to the side on the motorway.

'The baby?' she said for him.

'Yes. The…' It seemed he couldn't even call the bundle of cells she was carrying by what it actually was, the beginning of a new life, her new family. 'You can't just decide something like that, not on your own, I do have some rights, you know.'

'Yes. And if you'd like to come and see us in the maternity ward, you can bring in some flowers and maybe some champagne for me, but that's as near as any rights you're going to have.' She wanted to slam down the phone, end this call and continue on her lovely peaceful walk, but the truth was, she was shaking inside, shivering as if the whole Atlantic had covered her with freezing spray.

'Look, Niamh, you can't have thought this through. You can't just decide you're going to have a baby. How will you manage? On your own? You don't expect me to...'

'I've never expected anything from you and maybe that was half the problem with us. But I've had my eyes opened for me in the last few days. When I know what I want you to do, I'll let you know.' She had to say this, because really, no matter how happy she felt about being pregnant now, it was a long road. This child was still part of Jeremy and he did have to take some responsibility for his actions. 'And, Jeremy, by the way, I can manage perfectly on my own. Thank you.'

Of course, she knew he wasn't actually worried about her either way. All Jeremy was worried about, all he ever cared about was how this would affect his life.

'I really feel...'

'I don't care what you feel, Jeremy.' She ended the call, with a tinge of regret that, after all their years together, Jeremy had turned out to be such an absolute disappointment of a man.

Tuesday

29

Phyllis

Phyllis tried to move as quietly as she could around the bedroom while Kurt slept. She glanced at him now over her shoulder, one eye on the mirror as she coloured her eyebrows in with dark brown pencil. He was fast asleep, snoring loudly. She found the rhythm of it soothing, found herself smiling as she watched him; these days the sound of his deepest sleep was comforting beyond any measure she could apply. He'd never snored at the beginning of their marriage, but these last few months, it seemed that when he eventually settled into sleep in the early hours of the morning, he drifted to somewhere so deeply cut off from wakefulness, it stole away even the familiar pattern of his breathing along with his old zest for starting the day before anyone else.

Phyllis was tired, but there was no sleeping for her now. She leaned a little closer to the mirror. She had long stopped inspecting her face for new lines at this point; perhaps she was growing comfortable with the fact that she had settled into old age with as much of her former self as she could.

She had always subscribed to the notion that if she looked after her skin with an expensive night cream and a robust sunblock, that would be enough to see her through the ageing process better than the generations before at least. She cocked her head to the side, she didn't look too bad for a woman in her eighties. She laughed at herself now, a deprecating sound, because she'd never been a vain woman. She'd always been much too busy with her job and her life to have very much time left over to be consumed with her looks.

Perhaps it was being all so aware of the changes taking place before her eyes on a daily basis in her husband. That thought pulled her up short, fixing her with a familiar wave of grim grief that felt as if it arrested every other emotion in her, such was its intensity.

Kurt, stirring in his sleep behind her, shook her from those maudlin feelings she knew from experience could suck away at her whole day.

She couldn't afford to be anything less than positive today. Today was *the* day. The day when they would have confirmed what she already knew (even if she wasn't prepared to admit it). She'd had a text the previous day, checking if they could call into the surgery, but instead, she'd organised a phone call. Their GP, a bright young woman called Meera, had taken over from Victor McKenzie a year ago. It was funny, Kurt had been reluctant to see the new doctor, putting up all sort of arguments, when they both knew it was all about her being a woman and, more than that, a woman wearing a head covering who wasn't even as old as half his age.

Phyllis on her part was glad of the change. She had a lot more faith in the thorough approach of the straight-talking woman than she'd had in the lazy, easy manner of her predecessor.

Eleven o'clock. In her head, Phyllis knew, Meera wouldn't call before that, she knew that Kurt would be sleeping and she was the sort of woman who would time things so she wouldn't cut into the precious quiet morning time that had increasingly become Phyllis's only opportunity to stop and think.

Eleven o'clock. The words rumbled in her brain. Just in case, she picked up her phone, tucked it into her pocket and slipped out of the bedroom, leaving her husband blissfully unaware they were moving closer to having answers neither of them wanted to hear.

In the dining room, it seemed at first glance that every table had already been taken. Phyllis had picked up the morning paper from the table in front of Esme, who told her she'd been up and ready for hours already. She was her usual cheery self, as if a broken ankle and a summer spent relegated to a dome chair wasn't a crushing blow. Yes, Phyllis thought, I could do with taking a leaf out of Esme's book when it comes to braving things out today.

From the furthest corner, she spotted Niamh, the girl who had come to Josh's rescue on the beach. She was sitting alone at a round table for two. At just that moment, she raised her head, smiled at Phyllis and waved her over.

'Sit here,' she said. 'I'll be finishing up soon anyway and I'm sure we can gather up another chair or two if your family arrive.'

'Oh, no. It'll just be me for now,' Phyllis said, pulling out the chair and sitting down gratefully. 'You managed to get the best seat in the house.'

'I did.' Niamh smiled and gazed out across the gardens, which rolled away from the window and down towards a tableau of various willow trees. Many years ago, as Esme had explained more times than Phyllis could count, the house had been given its name after some distant relation of her grandfather had brought back a dozen varieties of willow trees from the United States, to be joined later by other varieties from Eastern Europe.

'Apparently,' Phyllis told Niamh now, 'they are one of the few trees that cross-propagate, so, the willows here are like no other willows in the world.'

'That's amazing,' Niamh said and perhaps, like Phyllis when she'd learned about them, she was admiring the trees now with new eyes. 'I had wondered about the name of the place, especially when there are so many other trees and shrubs and the view – I mean, most guest houses would have gone for something run of the mill, like "Sea View" or something equally uninspired.' She smiled. 'I think I love this place even more now.'

'Yes, it's pretty special.' Phyllis told Niamh about the many holidays they'd had over the years here and then, as the coffee arrived and one of the young girls who was helping out this year placed her breakfast on the table before her, she found herself telling Niamh about her family. 'We were all so cut up when Rob's wife, Paula, died.'

'I'm so sorry, I never realised, she must have been very young... I can't imagine how you'd get over that,' Niamh said, and although the words were simple, Phyllis felt as if somehow they were heartfelt. 'It must have been very hard for Rob and now, as the years will pass, it's going to be hard on Josh too.'

'I know, I've hoped for a long time that Rob would meet someone, you know. Not to take Paula's place. No one could ever do that, but someone he could depend on, to share things with, because he has a great capacity for joy in spite of everything he's been through.'

'I'm sure they must be queuing up for him,' Niamh smiled.

'They might well be, but he just hasn't managed to meet… *the one*.' It was a pity, but then Phyllis had a feeling he hadn't been exactly searching for someone.

'Oh, well, I'm sure when the time is right.' Niamh topped up her coffee and looked out towards the garden. And there was something in the calm set of her that prodded a realisation in Phyllis. She would be perfect for Rob, if only she was available or looking for someone.

'What about you? Are you married?' Phyllis asked, breaking into her thoughts.

'No, I'm afraid I'm a little like your son, I haven't found the one yet either!' She laughed, but there was something hollow in the sound of it.

'I'm sorry, I shouldn't pry,' Phyllis said, immediately regretting the fact that she sounded like one of those old women who had nothing else to do but mind everyone else's business.

'Don't be. It's probably just a raw nerve.' Niamh looked at her now. She was straightforward, deception and secrets would not sit easily with her, Phyllis decided. She'd developed a sixth sense for liars many years ago when she sat on the bench. 'I've just ended my relationship with a man who...'

'Oh, I really have put my foot in it.' Phyllis wished she could twist the seconds backwards and not have opened up this conversation to begin with. The last thing she'd wanted was to make Niamh uncomfortable.

'Please, don't feel bad. It wasn't a good relationship to begin with and maybe, if it wasn't for... well, there's always something good to be found in just about anything, isn't there, if you think about it hard enough or wait around long enough?' Her smile was sweet, as if within the sadness of loss perhaps she had found something more profoundly meaningful than she'd ever expected to find. 'He was...' She stopped, looked out at the garden again.

'Married?' Phyllis said, because suddenly it was so strikingly obvious. Otherwise, Niamh would have been married years ago, settled into family life, probably still with a demanding job on the side, she was the kind of woman who would need to keep her mind occupied in many directions. There was a good brain there – emotional intelligence, it was something else Phyllis had developed a bit of a natural detector for.

'It's shocking, isn't it?' Niamh stopped, toyed with the teaspoon, as if she might add some sugar to her coffee, but Phyllis noticed that she hadn't actually drunk any yet. 'I mean, sometimes, I can't actually believe it myself. I'm not even sure how it happened, how I became one of *those* women who has an affair with someone else's husband.'

'It happens,' Phyllis said. She wasn't going to sit in judgement of anyone at this point. 'In my opinion, for what it's worth, you've probably suffered enough, there's no point in beating yourself up any further with notions of guilt or shame or anything else. It's time to reclaim what's left of your life and your time.'

'I did spend a lot of time feeling all those things and sitting around waiting to be fitted in to other people's plans,' Niamh said a little sadly, but then she turned to Phyllis and smiled, she lowered her voice, just a fraction, not that anyone was listening. There was far too much noise going on at one of the other tables where put-upon parents were doing their best to placate a child who had no interest in breakfast and wanted only to go to the beach. 'I'm pregnant.' Her expression was transformed. 'I mean, only just and I probably shouldn't be telling anyone, because you know they say…'

'Oh, don't mind those old wives tales, a baby is always good news!' Phyllis said, and she felt a little guilty for that niggling feeling of dashed hopes as far as a romance between Niamh and Rob. 'But how will it all work, with…?'

'I'm not really sure. I mean, I've told him – Jeremy – that I'm going it alone. I'm having this baby and we are going to be a family. Jeremy has his own family, I don't love him any more, I'm not sure that I was ever anything more than *in love* with him, if that makes sense.'

'A baby is a big responsibility on your own. I mean, not only financially, but as much and all as you will love the child, a baby is hard work.'

'I know, but it's what I want more than anything.'

'Well, then, congratulations. I'm thrilled for you, I'm sure you're going to make a wonderful mother.' And Phyllis looked at her again and somehow managed to like her even more than before, although she hardly knew her. It was such a pity that she and Rob couldn't have maybe made something of the time here to get to know each other. It was terrible timing; Phyllis knew Niamh would have far too much going on to have room for anyone in her life for quite some time to come. And, in Phyllis's opinion, the last thing Rob needed was more responsibility on top of what he already had.

*

Phyllis knew, a fraction of a second before the phone rang, that Dr Meera was about to call them. She knew it because her heart felt as if it ricocheted about in her chest and her rib cage tightened in a little, just enough to make her catch her breath.

Kurt was sitting on the bed, tying his laces. They were going to meet Rob and Josh at the village play park. Their tennis rackets lay across the bed. Kurt had high hopes that they might manage a quick game while Phyllis pushed Josh on the swings.

She dropped down beside him now, almost making him lose his balance, then she reached out and took his hand, holding the phone in front of him, so he could see who was calling. He steadied himself for a moment, then said: 'Go on, answer it, we might as well get it over with.'

'Meera.' Phyllis swiped up the call button, so the screen was filled with the GP sitting at her desk in the consulting room they'd visited just a few weeks earlier.

'Hello Phyllis,' the doctor said, squinting into the phone. 'Are you both enjoying your holiday?' She sat back a little again as if she'd managed to focus in on them and was settling down for a chat, rather than giving them the results of Kurt's recent tests.

'Yes, we've been lucky with the weather, it's just lovely here.'

'Actually, we're just on our way out for a game of tennis,' Kurt piped up next to her and he squeezed Phyllis's hand a little tighter as if to reassure her that this phone call would change nothing. If only that was the case, she thought.

'Are the results back?' Phyllis asked, but of course, there would be no call if they weren't in. The surgery was always busy. Meera didn't have time to ring up for a casual chat with every other patient on her books.

'That's why I'm ringing. You'll remember, we carried out a number of tests here in the surgery?'

'How could I forget? All those blood tests, lots of prodding and poking, I was lucky to have a drop of blood left in me.' Kurt laughed, but there was a note of triumph in his voice that he remembered.

'That's right, Kurt. Those samples were sent off for analysis to rule out any other medical causes for how you've been feeling.' Meera stopped for a moment. 'Those have come back and the good news is that you are in good physical health. Nothing untoward has shown up in your results, no markers we need to follow up on.'

And yet, Phyllis thought back to that day in the surgery when Meera had run the simple AMTS and Kurt had scored just six, which she'd read later was a borderline marker.

'And, the memory clinic?' Phyllis asked, because she'd spent a full day with Kurt answering questions about everything and anything in an attempt for them to gauge how well his short- and medium-term memory was working. He'd had to answer questions on all sorts of things, based mainly around the fact that Phyllis had been told to keep a diary of things for a few weeks beforehand. She had felt almost like a traitor handing over her notes, while at the same time knowing that these were the people in whom she had to place her trust if they were to save Kurt from the same fate as his father.

'Yes. They have sent on their results also.' Meera stopped for a moment, looked down at her notes. 'I can send you a copy of this file, but I needed to go through it first. Would you like me to read it to you or…?'

'Just tell us what they say, doctor. We can go through the nuts and bolts of it over our own kitchen table with a cup of tea when we get home.' There was an edge to Kurt's voice that betrayed the worry he was trying so hard to hide.

'I'm sorry to say that your results are indicating a number of high scores on their memory-loss scales. The consultant has suggested we book you in for an MRI as soon as possible and he's sending on a follow-up appointment for you.'

It was all words. Just words and they were floating past Phyllis, with only a few managing to land on her awareness, because she'd already known and this was just unwanted confirmation. Had she been hoping against all hope that it would be different?

'It's okay, my darling.' Kurt moved his arm up and around her shoulders, he was hugging her close now, because she couldn't talk, she couldn't listen, she could hardly breathe. It took a few minutes for her to gather herself enough so she could straighten her spine, wipe the tears from her eyes and look at Meera again, sitting there with her eyes full of pity for them.

'It's okay, I'm fine,' Phyllis lied, clearing her throat and somehow managing to draw up her lips into something that might pass for neutrality – there was no point trying to fool anyone that she was smiling.

'You'll need time, for it to settle on you. For both of you, to come to terms with the road ahead of you,' Meera said.

'What's next?' Kurt asked meekly.

'Next, we organise an MRI. With your health insurance, that should come back fairly quickly. That'll show us where and how much damage is done. Once we have that, the geriatric consultant – he's Mr Duffy and I can't tell you how brilliant he is – he will look at how best to go forward from here on.'

'What actually happens though?' Phyllis asked and she was surprised at how steady her voice sounded.

'He'll look at prescribing medication. That will be a mixture of drugs to slow down any further damage to the brain cells and some behaviour medication to help with the physical symptoms.'

'Hah! I've never felt better, look.' Kurt reached forward, picked up his old tennis racket. 'And I bet I'd beat most fellas half my age on the court,' he said jovially.

'I have no doubt you would, Kurt,' Meera laughed, 'but think how much better you'll be if you're getting a full eight hours' sleep a night and your appetite is back to normal.'

'Fair enough,' Kurt said, and he laid the racket against the side of the bed.

'Look, it'll be at least a week before you get another appointment. The best thing you can do now is enjoy the rest of your holidays.' Meera smiled at them and Phyllis decided she was very glad that they had such a lovely GP.

'We can definitely manage that, can't we darling?' Kurt was looking into Phyllis's eyes for confirmation.

'We certainly can,' Phyllis said and, when they hung up the phone, she decided there would be no more maudlin thoughts today, just counting her blessings for every minute they had left to them.

30

Cora

'Can't you just come home this evening, tell them that you...?' Michael was pleading. 'I mean, it's not as if you're needed there, not like here...'

'That's not the point, Michael,' Cora murmured. The gulf between them was far greater now than it had been before and he had rung her at the worst possible time. She was sitting in the hallway, opposite Esme. How could she have a normal conversation with him when all she could think about was the sight of himself and Tanya that day in Knockroe?

'Look, this silliness... it has to stop, we're still married to each other and whatever chance we have of fixing things, we're not going to do it if you're thirty miles away.'

'I need time,' Cora said and she placed her hand on Esme's knee, whispering that she'd take the call in her room. She raced up the stairs two at a time. Brushing past Niamh on the landing, she made a face, as if to let her know that she couldn't talk now, but perhaps they'd meet up later.

'Look, Cora, I don't know what you're playing at, but

I don't think I can sit for a whole night in that swanky restaurant and lie to our son. I can't just pretend everything is all right, when it's not.' And that was it, Cora thought. Michael hated going to restaurants, well, he basically hated anything that was outside his normal routine.

'So, you'd prefer to ruin his holiday and take all the joy out of their mini honeymoon, just because we can't act like adults and put on a brave face to support our son?' It was below the belt, but it was the truth. She lowered her voice. 'Michael, honestly, I don't think I can face the house or Cherrywood Crescent yet.' If she walked into that kitchen, with the stains of a lifetime written across the walls and the chips of their marriage etched into the doorjambs, she felt as if she might just completely crumble.

'If you'll just come back, it won't be like it was. I'm going to make sure of that,' he said, grappling for anything that might convince her.

'But it will, don't you see?' It wasn't even about the wonky kitchen cabinet doors or the number of times over the years she'd asked him to paint the kitchen or fix the broken step on the stairs. It wasn't about mowing the lawn every Saturday morning or the fact that they'd never gotten round to laying the patio, even though the bricks had been lined up at the side of the house for over a decade. It was more the fact that, now, she saw those things as symptomatic of the state her marriage had become. And worse, a little voice inside her head niggled at her, reminding her that he had obviously made time to think about the state of Tanya Farrelly's walls and probably a lot more than that too, if Tanya played true to form.

'Please, Cora, please, I'm not even asking that we put this behind us, but surely we can sit down and talk.'

The problem was, she couldn't talk to him. She hadn't the words now.

'We'll be talking soon enough when we meet up with Connor and Lydia.' She banged down the phone. Oh God. She didn't know what she wanted from him at this point. And, the worst part of that was, with Joel Lawson around, it was only adding to her confusion.

She sat on the edge of the bed and tried to straighten out her thoughts, but in the end she felt only sadness and anger. Sadness at the waste of it all and anger at the fact she'd thrown away all these years on a man who really didn't understand her at all, but was only too happy to try and understand the woman next door.

Cora stomped out of the guest house. How dare Michael ring her up and pretend that he was the injured party when she now knew quite well that he'd probably just been biding his time for her to go so he could shack up with the next-door neighbour. And then another thought came to her – why did he want her back? Had Tanya tired of him already? Or was it just that he missed home-cooked meals and not having to worry about clean laundry, because, certainly, Tanya wouldn't be taking on responsibility for any of that.

It felt as if he hadn't noticed Cora for years and she'd hardly closed the door behind her before he was parading up and down the town with Tanya. Probably she had him redecorating the whole house for her now he was what she would consider fair game.

How could he fall for Tanya bloody Farrelly? Anybody

but that man-eating opportunist. And to think, Cora had actually considered Tanya her friend. It wasn't that the other women on the cul-de-sac hadn't warned her often enough, but it was just inconceivable that Michael would ever fall for Tanya's too-obvious charms. It was, she thought now, flying in the face of all that was natural in the world. After all, hadn't he been the one who suggested they were too old to have a sex life? Hah! Tanya Farrelly would chew him up and spit him out before her breakfast and her freshly painted walls would be a long-standing memorial to his stupidity and his gross disloyalty to Cora.

What was she saying? If Michael had gone off with Tanya, who had she to blame but herself? He was still an attractive man. Even if Cora didn't normally notice it, she'd noticed it well enough when she saw him standing there chatting to Tanya. This was entirely her own doing. Wasn't it Cora who had marched out the door, holier than thou, because he wasn't quite up to scratch? Well, it looked like he'd been up to scratch for Tanya.

And how would that work exactly? Or did she really want to know, probably not. Tanya couldn't cook a sausage to save her life, never mind a casserole. Michael would bloody starve to death if he was expecting service as usual in Tanya's house. Cora couldn't imagine anything more culinary in Tanya's kitchen than coconut oil and avocados which Tanya recommended for extra shiny hair between stylist appointments.

Cora felt like going over to Cherrywood Crescent right now, and telling the pair of them that she knew exactly what was going on.

Damn Tanya Farrelly and damn Michael too. Cora turned on her heels and headed for her car, livid and distraught all at once. She sat there for a minute, then stuck the key in the ignition with a sense of purpose at odds with every fibre in her. She had driven to the gate before her anger began to turn to something much more about herself than about anyone else. Automatically, she flicked the indicator on to take the road towards the town centre.

She was almost out of Ballycove before she made her mind up where she was going to exactly. She had an outfit to buy for this dinner at the Railway Hotel with Connor and Lydia and, the way she felt, she was bloody well going to book an appointment at the hairdresser's and the beautician's, only not at The Pink Door – where Tanya worked. She'd book something in one of the other places in town, somewhere expensive, for the whole works – she could afford it. She needed it, and God knew but it was long overdue.

It was after five by the time Cora arrived back in Ballycove. She'd spent a bomb and it hadn't made her one bit happier. Who on earth said retail therapy actually cured anything? She was just wrecked tired with a lot less cash in her bank account. Somehow, she had ended up with two dresses, a pair of high-heeled sandals she wasn't confident she could even walk in and a clutch that would carry little more than a credit card, her car keys and a tube of lip gloss. Thank goodness she'd had sense before she talked herself into a statement necklace, those things weighed a tonne and, even if they did perfectly match her shoes, she'd have felt awkward and false wearing something that just wasn't her. Though at this moment, she wasn't sure who she was exactly, would she ever be completely sure again?

*

Cora had just opened the bottle of wine and was sitting on the veranda when Joel's car slid into the drive. It was a beautiful evening, perfect really, with a pink sky, the promise of a full moon and waves still breaking white in the distance.

'Would you like a glass?' she asked, because goodness knew, she'd drunk enough of his since they'd been here. Tonight, she needed a drink. It had been an emotional day. How other women saw shopping as therapy, she'd never know, but then, her expedition had been all about revenge and maybe a little about jealousy too. Joel sat lazily on the bench next to her and she could feel the warm day and his hard work radiate against her forearm when they brushed too close.

'So, what do people do around here for fun at the weekends?' he asked out of the blue.

'I'm not sure, probably go to the pub, or maybe the cinema in the next town over. Or I suppose there's the pick of restaurants open this time of year if you fancied eating out.' She looked at him then. 'Why? I thought you were planning on going back to Dublin at the weekends to catch up on stuff in your office?' There was no reason why he couldn't stay, as far as Cora knew Esme had kept his room free for him for the season.

'Usually, but I can work from here too, most of it is just admin anyway. They're doing a huge construction job not far from my apartment and, to be honest, it's not exactly relaxing there at the moment and I can't see it improving any time soon.'

'But what about...' She stopped, she'd never asked him about who might be in Dublin. Just because there was no wife didn't mean there wasn't a girlfriend.

'Oh, don't worry, no one is going to notice if I don't go back for a month, never mind a weekend.' He shook his head and laughed. 'It's not like Ballycove where neighbours come knocking if you don't take in your milk for two days.'

'I'm sure that has its blessings too.'

'Maybe, when you're younger, but you know, these days, I'm not so sure.' For a moment, she wondered if he was saying something more than just reflecting on a place to live.

'I think, it's only as we get older that we see the value of having neighbours and people around us, people who care and matter to us.'

'You're lucky, maybe you learned that in time,' he said and there was a tinge of sadness in his eyes as he looked at her, as if he'd let something slip away from him that he had no chance of pulling back.

'I don't know about that. I've lived a very small life, always in the same place, I didn't get to choose who'd be around forever, any more than anyone does.'

But of course, maybe she was doing that now, weeding out what she didn't want any more – was that what she was doing with Michael? Did she really not want him now?

Joel looked at her. 'So, if I was to stay around this weekend, would you come down to the village with me on Saturday, just for a drink?' It was casual, not a date, she was sure of that, but at the same time, she knew, even if there was nothing in it, that wasn't how Michael would see things.

'It's funny, I very rarely go anywhere, but this weekend my son and daughter in-law have invited us out for a meal at the Railway Hotel, over in Knockroe.' She felt as if she was letting Joel down, somehow, which of course was ludicrous. 'But, I'll be here most of the weekend anyway and I'm always happy to sit on the veranda...' she said, trying in her own way to soften the blow – which of course, wasn't a blow, because she was absolutely certain he had not been asking her out on a date.

'Well, that's nice, an opportunity to get all dressed up. I've heard about the Railway Hotel, it sounds swanky.' He was making fun of her now.

'I'll have you know I can get as dolled up as the best of them, I don't spend all my time wearing T-shirts and jeans.' She laughed now, enjoying his company.

'Sorry,' he stopped, 'I'm sure you'll look absolutely beautiful.' And for a moment, it felt as if every single sound in the universe had ground to a sudden halt. 'I mean...'

'Don't worry.' Cora reached forward and topped up their glasses, but her hands were shaking because suddenly it felt as if the ground beneath had tipped over slightly and, in some strange way, she felt as if it might never quite tip back to where it was before. 'I know what you mean, I'm not going to turn up looking like I'm after walking five miles along the breezy beach.'

And she sat back down into what felt like a strangely fuelled atmosphere.

The conversation played around in her head for a long

time afterwards. Later, alone in her room, she couldn't help but unpick it. Had Joel Lawson been asking her on a date? Had he made an overture to her that neither of them quite understood or intended? And mostly, the thought that kept flooding through her in waves of guilty emotion: she had enjoyed the sensation that sitting next to him in that slightly charged silence had ignited in her. That night, as she lay in bed, it felt as if she was still giddy with the kind of excitement that she couldn't remember feeling in years and it was delicious, even if she knew it was dangerous. But maybe, that's what she had been craving, a little danger, a little excitement, a little adventure.

*

A summer storm blew in heavy over the Atlantic early the following morning, waking Cora before the light peeked through the curtains. She lay there for a long time, thinking of Michael and the mess they'd made of everything. Every so often, thoughts of Joel came colliding with the overwhelming sense of regret and stirred up something far more complicated in her mind.

Once she was up and going for the day, it was easier to convince herself that Joel had meant nothing more than a friendly drink in the village. Of course it was just a casual conversation and somehow she'd let her imagination run away with her and tied it up with all these silly infatuated thoughts that belonged inside the head of some silly girl, not a middle-aged, married woman.

'Penny for them?' Joel was standing at the dining room door.

'Oh, you startled me.' She swung round, sending the sugar from the bowl she was holding in a spray across the dining room. She had just been returning it from the hall where Esme had finished her mid-morning coffee.

'Sorry,' he said, bending down at the same time as her to tidy up the mess. Their heads brushed together, too close, and she stopped, felt him halt too and his breath, soft and warm against her cheek. Her heart, hammering in her chest, was so loud it felt as if it could be heard at the far end of the beach. It was too obvious, too easy to lean in and wait to be kissed, and she had a feeling that was exactly what would come next. Cora jumped up before something happened that she couldn't take back.

'I'll get a brush and pan,' she said, racing to the kitchen, out of breath because of what might have happened in her imagination. Oh, God, she thought, what have I done?

31

Esme

'You can't park there.' The man sounded as if his uniform was two sizes too small for him and he was the sort who should never have been given a uniform to begin with.

Everything about being back here for her appointment set Esme's nerves on end. It was just a check-up, Marta had said, sensing Esme's unease.

It wouldn't have been hard to pick up on it. Esme had woken up in bad form with everything and everybody, as if someone had marched into her room overnight and stolen away with her symmetry, so now, it felt as if everything about her was off balance. Marta wasn't much better, but she was trying to coax Esme along, if only for an easier life for herself.

'And where do you suggest I park?' Marta spat at the man. 'On that sign, it says, "Set down".'

'It says "Set down *only*".'

'So, I am to abandon an old woman on the doorstep and just leave her there?' Marta grumbled and Esme cleared her throat loudly. She did not like to be referred to as an old woman and Marta should know better.

'Right, right.' The man went to open the passenger door. 'If you unload her here and then you can drive to the car park.'

'I am not a delivery of turnips to be left on the doorstep.' Esme bristled.

'Well, no, but you're blocking up every car that passes through here,' the man said and it sounded as if he said the same thing a hundred times every single day.

'Fine,' Marta said, because at this stage, even though Esme couldn't see them, she had a feeling they were holding up a good number of cars behind them already. She sat, uncomfortably, in the passenger seat while Marta and the man set about getting her wheelchair from the back of the car and manoeuvring it so it was at just the right angle for her to transfer safely. Eventually, it seemed someone else took the man's attention and so, mercifully, Esme and Marta were left to get her organised in peace.

Inside the hospital wasn't a lot better. Marta pushed her chair up next to a vending machine, so she was facing the grey light that flooded through the wall of glass in the foyer. In spite of spitting rain outside, the natural light was still a blessing, compared to screeching artificial brightness at the back of the foyer.

'Don't be too long.' Esme bit her lip. She hated that she sounded so pathetic to her own ears, but here, surrounded by strangers she couldn't see and stranded in this bloody chair, she felt completely vulnerable.

'I'll be as quick as I can be,' Marta promised. 'Don't run off on me.' It was meant to be a joke, but neither of them was much in the mood to summon any smiles.

There was no way of gauging how long Marta was gone for, but from her memory, Esme knew that the hospital car park was quite a distance on foot. She also remembered that most days it was chock-a-block and it wouldn't be unusual at this time of the day to have to wait in line until a parking spot became available. The first few minutes ticked by slowly and Esme tried hard to dig up some happy thoughts so her mind could wander, but the noise levels here were too loud to either tune in or out of the conversations around her. Her hands clenched tighter around the arms of her chair and she longed to be back in Ballycove. Occasionally, a loud voice booming over everything else would make her jump, the door swinging about admitting or disgorging would cause a cold stir of disappointment, and the shadows of people milling around her all combined to make her feel as if she was on the edge of everything, even herself.

It really did take an age for Marta to return. Esme began to wonder if perhaps something had happened to her friend, perhaps there'd been an accident. Maybe she'd been caught under the wheels of a speeding ambulance or one of those awful barrier gates had crashed down on top of the roof of the car and Marta was crushed beneath. Did that actually ever happen? It could, Esme was quite sure it could. God, by the time Marta arrived back, huffing and puffing from her run up the endless steps, two at a time, which were meant to be a shortcut from the car park, Esme had almost planned out her funeral.

'Are you okay? I am so sorry, there was no parking. How can a hospital have no car parking space available?' Marta sounded even more cross now than she had with the parking porter earlier. 'Come on, or you will be late for your appointment.' She released the brakes on the chair and began to push Esme towards the consulting room, following arrows on the floor that Esme could no longer see.

For all that, Esme felt at the end they might as well have just made a phone call appointment and saved themselves the trip all the way over to Knockroe. Some youngsters, hardly old enough to have finished school, never mind medical school, took a look at her leg, compared old X-rays to new ones and told her to come back in two weeks' time. There was no mention of taking her first steps, no mention of getting rid of the horrible heavy cast and not so much as a dickie bird of when she'd be back to normal.

'You can't expect miracles. These things take time.' Marta was matter-of-fact, trying hard to ignore the tears that rested on the edges of Esme's clouded eyes.

'I wasn't expecting miracles, just a little hope,' Esme said as she arrived in what she guessed was the foyer once more. 'Can I stay somewhere else while you're bringing the car round, it's…' she shuddered. She couldn't face another half an hour sitting here, not knowing quite what was going on around her, not knowing if someone was right beside her and at the same time feeling all pitying eyes on her, without being able to challenge them with a thwarting stare in return.

'Oh, Esme, I will be as quick as I can…' Marta said hurriedly and she pushed the chair back against a wall, so Esme was at least out of the main flow of traffic. 'It won't take so long this time; I'll be back before you know it.' And then she was rushing off to get the car and Esme was left sitting in the foyer once more.

This time, perhaps it was the anticlimax of an appointment that she hadn't really been looking forward to anyway, or maybe it was just that she was a little down in herself, but she felt a great big ball of self-pity rise up in her. She wanted to cry, but instead she held her breath, swallowing down the burning feeling that had risen from her gut to her throat, quashing down the depressing knowledge that she was old, vulnerable and all but useless if she didn't have Marta to help her now. She hated being old. She hated being blind and, most of all, she hated being in this wheelchair.

'Sorry, dearie, we'll have to move you along from there.' A gruff voice was at her chair, unlocking it and swinging her without warning out into the main thoroughfare of the foyer.

'No. Stop, you can't just...' but her voice was faint, she knew, too low to be heard above the din and racket behind them.

'Only for a minute, dearie, and then I'll have you back again. Have to make way for a stretcher,' the man was saying. She might as well have been a bag of cabbage; he wasn't listening to her, just weaving her in and out of other people, so now the brightness of earlier had dimmed right down. To her limited vision it seemed as if he might have pushed her into a windowless room somewhere in the hospital bowels. As he swung her into whatever he thought was a safe position for her, she shivered, tried to pull her jacket closer about her shoulders, it was cold here.

'Won't be long, don't go anywhere now.' He laughed, as if she hadn't heard that joke before. And then he was gone and Esme knew she was completely alone. The bustle of the foyer was hardly even an echo in the distance. Where on earth was she?

'Hello,' she called out, but her voice sounded old and weak and she knew no one would hear her, there was no one here. She started to cry, great big fat tears rolling down her cheeks, balls of vulnerable despair building up inside of her, as if she would never know again what it was not to be feeble. When you were old, this place only exposed you for what you really were – frail, dependent, miserable.

'Help,' she tried again. Someone would have to come and get her, although the brute who had pushed her in here seemed an unlikely rescuer. 'Help me, please, someone.'

And she knew she sounded like those dotty old birds who spent all day in hospital beds, asking for someone to take them home, when, even at home, it seemed they had lost their place. Their value reduced by the very fact they had spent up their time and they were clearly thrown on the scrap heap, except they hadn't quite put two and two together yet. Panic began to slither up her spine, a dry sensation that crept out and into every single cell, so she began to shiver, but not with cold any more. This was something else. She caught her breath, her heart thumping against her chest. Was she going to have some sort of breakdown, a seizure brought on by complete and total panic? And so she gave herself up completely to those huge big, walloping, body-shaking tears, the likes of which she hadn't produced since she was a small child. It was all racing away from her. What on earth was going to become of her?

'You all right there?' The voice came from her left – young and probably a male, but it was hard to tell, because it trembled between boy and girl.

'Yes, yes, I'm fine,' Esme stuttered, trying desperately to calm down her breathing, so she didn't look like a complete ninny. Her voice sounded brittle. She wiped her cheeks roughly.

'It's just you don't look fine.' The boy had moved closer. 'Can I get you a cup of tea from the shop? Or maybe...' He trailed off.

'That's really kind of you, but...' Oh dear, his kindness was only making her feel worse and now, although it felt as if she'd cried herself out, she hiccupped, her breath catching in her throat.

'Would you like a mint then?' he asked, shoving something in front of her, perhaps not fully realising she couldn't see.

'No. Thank you.' She tried to turn in her chair, but it was no good, she was stuck there, nowhere to go, no way to get there. 'I'm really fine.'

'How did you hurt your leg?' he asked, obviously oblivious to her complete humiliation and the fact that she was so mortified she could hardly drag her eyes from the floor.

'Playing football, how do you think?'

'That's funny,' he said, unwrapping whatever sweets he had; they smelled like gumdrops, not mints. 'Here,' he said, dropping one into her lap. 'I wouldn't mind having a broken leg like that. I could get all my mates to sign the cast. I might even get a footballer to sign it, that would be cool, wouldn't it?'

'Would it?'

'Yeah, course it would.' He cleared his throat. 'Will I sign yours? It's just, it looks like you have no mates when you don't have any...'

'No, I think I'll manage, thank you.'

'Fine. Be like that,' he said and she felt him turning away from her. It was only then that something caught her up.

'Maybe you could wheel me back down to the main foyer?'

'Sure, it's only round the corner,' he said and she imagined him shrugging his shoulders. He yanked the chair from behind, but the brakes were still on. 'Bugger,' he said as she tried to direct him. Esme held her breath for the return journey, half expecting her leg to be crashed into every doorjamb and corner on the way. But, to her relief, they managed to get back to the noisy foyer unscathed.

'You need to find me a spot, opposite the large windows, against the wall, if you can,' she said, because otherwise it would take Marta even longer to find her and the last thing Esme wanted was to stay here for one minute more than she needed to.

'So, why are you here?' she asked, although part of her didn't want to know, not really, because she had an idea it would make her feel even more pathetic than before. But he had plonked himself down in the seat next to her and it would be churlish not to engage in some polite conversation.

'Oh, me, I'm in for treatment, no cool plaster for me. But I do get time off school, though of course I'm always too sick for a day or two afterwards to actually enjoy it.' He kicked an imaginary scuff at the end of his shoe.

'What sort of treatment?'

'Chemo, of course, what do you think, I wear my hair like this for fun.' He sighed as if he was explaining something to someone very, very stupid.

'I'm sorry. I didn't see, I'm blind, you see,' she said it easily and it struck her, it wasn't something she'd ever had to tell anyone before.

'Cooler than cancer, I suppose, but poxy luck for both of us, eh?' He stopped chewing for a minute, as if considering her, maybe knowing that she wouldn't ask, but she wanted to know, even though she didn't want to know. 'Tumour on my brain, the doctors said it was almost gone, but it came back again.'

'That's bad luck, I'm sorry,' she said and she really was, because suddenly, she wondered at his bravery compared to her own. 'Actually, I wouldn't mind one of those sweets now, if you could put it in my hand, please.'

And so it was that by the time Marta returned, Esme was sitting in the foyer chewing a gumdrop and, despite everything, she found herself smiling more widely than she'd done in quite some time.

'I hate this bloody place,' Marta said under her breath as they made it through the doors fifteen minutes later.

'Me too,' Esme said, but she wondered if maybe there were some diamonds in the rough of it all.

'Hey, what's that on your cast?' Marta asked as she folded

a rug over Esme's knees once she had tucked her into the passenger seat.

'Oh, that, it's an autograph.'

'Hmm,' Marta said and Esme knew she was shaking her head and maybe even smiling as she started up the engine to bring them home.

*

Maybe it was her visit to the hospital and the feeling that for a short while she was as inconsequential and powerless as a leaf falling in the autumn, but Esme couldn't shake a deeply penetrating insight from her bones. Perhaps, for the first time, her true vulnerability had been exposed to her. Without Marta there at her side, Esme was to a large extent utterly helpless at this moment.

'Nothing happened, you were fine,' Marta said to her as she hurried her along getting her up and ready the following day when Esme tried to explain. 'The only thing that will come of you having a long face is that you will scare the visitors – you don't want that now, do you?'

'Pah!' Esme was sorry she'd mentioned it at all.

'The last thing anyone wants when they go on holiday is to be reminded of any daily worries. They come here to escape that, you always said so yourself.'

'I can assure you,' Esme said crisply. 'No one will have the foggiest idea that I am anything other than delighted to see them coming through the door of the guest house. That's how it's always been and it's how it will continue to be.'

Except, as she sat there that day, she couldn't shake the

feeling that she was no longer a young, able-bodied woman. She was old, she was broken and, if all things had been even, she would have just soldiered on but at that moment she was tired and crushed by the fact that each day she sat there she imagined she heard a new creak or rattle added onto the symphony of sounds in the old house.

The crash when it came didn't make her jump so much as almost propelled her from her seat and nearly ended up with her capsizing over, if it hadn't been for Marta putting a firm hand on her chair to keep her steady.

'Dear God, what was that?' Esme almost didn't want to know.

'I will check. I am sure it is nothing to worry ourselves about too much.' But even Esme knew that Marta was blessing herself as she rushed towards the front door. It took a few minutes for her to return and, when she did, she had Joel Lawson at her side.

'Four slates,' he said ominously. 'They crashed down onto the driveway.'

'Oh, no.' It was like an unbuttoning of the armour Esme had been so desperately trying to hold in place. It felt as if the house was finally giving up and her reserves of bravery deserted her. She was aware that her hand was shaking, a small nerve somewhere in her body giving away the terror that four roof tiles were the ominous start of the end. What now?

'It could have been a lot worse; they might just as easily have ended up embedded in a car roof or, worse, someone's head.' If Joel Lawson was trying to make her feel better, it really wasn't working.

'So, it's true what that awful Fenlon man said.' Marta's voice was heavy, as if her words carried the weight of the entire roof on them.

'What was that?' Joel Lawson asked, but to Esme, his voice was little more than an echo, as her mind filled up with what seemed to stretch inevitably before her – selling up, shutting down a lifetime of memories. How could she do that? Oh God, it felt like someone had opened a trap door under her soul and her heart pounded with terror in her chest.

'He said this place was only fit for demolition. I know he thinks the kindest thing to do would be to raze it to the ground and start again. He makes me feel that it is a death trap waiting to kill someone.' Esme only said the words that had been rattling around her head, as if they were a terrible prayer she'd learned off by heart at some point.

'Oh, I don't know about that. I mean, I've seen places a lot worse than this brought back to splendid life.'

'Probably, but by people who have pockets that are deeper than the continental shelf no doubt.' Esme dabbed the tissue she was holding to her eyes. She was too emotional for tears, but it was an automatic movement, something to stop her hands from shaking.

'Esme, please, don't go upsetting yourself.' Marta's hand hovered above her shoulder.

'I'm sorry. I just can't bear the thoughts of losing this place. I'm too old to start over, all my memories are here. I can't just walk away, it's not as easy as that.'

'Why on earth would you walk away?' Joel sat down opposite her now. 'Even the newest of houses can have loose slates. You need someone to go up there and take a look at them for you before you go writing the whole house off because of a few broken slates. It's probably just a patch-up job, anyway.'

'Oh, I'm afraid it's going to be a lot more than that.' Esme couldn't shake off the gloom that had, if she was honest, been penetrating the outer reaches of her world since she'd fallen off that bloody table.

'Now, seriously, you're getting yourself all worked up just because of some jackeen coming in here and talking about something he hasn't even properly looked at,' Joel said.

'He wants to buy the place,' Marta said.

'Ah well, in that case, of course he's going to want to point out all the problems.' Joel Lawson shook his head. 'Look, it's an old building, but the church is older and you don't want to see that torn down, do you?'

'Well no, but…' Esme wanted to believe him, but who on earth was going to come out and look at the roof for her? Every builder in the country was up to their eyes in far more lucrative work than she could offer.

'No, of course not. You don't tear down a thing of beauty and replace it with some modern box that won't have half the personality and none of the history attached to it.'

'He is right, Esme,' Marta said.

'Thank you,' Esme managed. 'You are the voice of reason.' Or at least she hoped he was, after all he was an engineer. Of course, she knew Joel Lawson only took on jobs that cost hundreds of thousands of euros – that the church roof wasn't going to be a cut-price job. It would take years for the entire village to pay off the debt of having it replaced and, even if Esme could get a bank loan to cover replacing the roof, there weren't enough years left ahead of her to even pay off a fraction of what it would cost.

Wednesday

32

Cora

Connor's voice when he rang was like a ninja attack on Cora's conscience and her equilibrium, so afterwards she felt as if she'd been thrown off balance. *Of course, of course, it would be perfect,* she reassured him and then, the second she hung up the call, she dialled Michael.

'We've said we'll go.' If there was anything she could do to get out of this dinner, she'd grab at the chance to miss it and yet, it seemed she wasn't prepared to let Michael back out easily. Funny, but for so many years, she'd wished that for her birthday or her anniversary he would surprise her with dinner out. Now, when they were going to the swankiest restaurant around, she really felt as if she'd rather curl up under a duvet and hide out until it was all over.

'Will we...' Michael didn't continue, because maybe neither of them had the courage to explain to anyone exactly what was going on between them at the moment.

'No. Let's just leave things as they are for now,' she said firmly before hanging up the phone and feeling that familiar pang of loneliness she felt every time she talked to Michael these days. She still hadn't figured out if it was some residual emotion from when they'd lived together in what felt like an unending silence or if, perhaps, she actually missed him. Now, when they spoke, he really did feel like a stranger. Perhaps this was how people felt about pets they'd surrendered to the local ISPCA? Having loved them dearly, parting was a wrench after much soul-searching, but somehow they were no longer yours, even though, in the depths of you, it felt as if they always would be.

To make matters more confusing, Michael was beginning to say the right things. Checking how she felt and asking her to come back to Cherrywood Crescent – that was what she'd craved for so long, wasn't it? Probably she'd spent too much time around Marta, but she almost wanted to check if it was because he needed his laundry done and his dinner cooked. He'd begged her to meet up, just to talk things over, he said. He'd promised all sorts of things from foreign holidays every year to painting the house from the skirting boards to the roof. Cora reminded him he'd been promising to paint the house for twenty years and, anyway, she hadn't moved out because the paint was faded or the doorframes were chipped. God, she'd have given anything for him to have offered to paint the house six months ago, or even to just suggest a walk on the beach together, while a holiday would have sent her into happy delirium. But now? After seeing him with Tanya, it all meant nothing, because the only thing worse than him not saying these things was that she wasn't sure she could believe him.

*

Cora listened as the local church chimed out nine hours across the village, landing as an echoing jangle on the veranda of the guest house where she'd been sitting long enough to begin to feel the cold bite into her skin. When the drive lit up with the arrival of Joel's Mercedes, she knew she should go inside and get a cardigan from her room, but it was too lovely to leave this spot, with the sun orange and fading across the sea in the distance.

'Hey.' Joel sprinted up the steps to the veranda although he was laden down with what looked like a pile of drawings and a satchel fit to burst with folders that threatened to escape at any moment. 'Glad I caught you.'

He looked at her for a moment, his gaze lingering on her eyes. From among the bags, he took out what looked like takeout.

'Since you won't come to dinner with me,' Joel smiled, 'I thought maybe I could bring dinner to you.' It was late, the sun was hanging low enough in the sky to cast long shadows across the garden. She had to admit, she was hungry.

'You shouldn't have,' she said, but as he set down everything on the veranda and the aroma of spicy Indian food began to permeate the air, her stomach rumbled. She was starving. She hadn't eaten since breakfast.

'It's hardly cordon bleu and I was getting something for myself, I could hardly leave you here starving.' He laughed as her stomach growled again.

'Shall we eat on the veranda?' she asked. There was a table in the corner, she could clear it off and enjoy the last of the day's sun on the beach below. 'Goodness, you've bought enough to feed an army.' She laughed as he continued to take foil containers out of the bag.

'I didn't mean to, but there was a sharing starter and main course and since I wasn't sure what you liked...'

'For the record, I like anything that doesn't involve me having to prepare it.'

She laughed again as they carried out the plates and cutlery to use for their meal. Esme wouldn't mind, but Cora would wash everything and put it away afterwards; habit of a lifetime. She couldn't bear the idea of making even more work for Marta.

'Ta da,' he said, producing two cans of soft drinks. 'Sorry, it's not Bollinger, but I have to keep a clear head.'

'Never a bad thing.' The drink was refreshing, cold and fizzy, just what she needed at the end of a long sunny day. 'How is the church roof coming along?' she asked, not just to be polite but because it was interesting.

'Better than I expected,' he said, passing along a prawn dish that looked delicious. 'I just have to finalise these plans and then the hard work is done, for a little while at least. Actually...' He looked at her now.

'What?'

'Would you like to take a look at them with me? It's just variations really, but you could be my second set of eyes?'

'I'd love to.' Michael never asked for her opinion – hah, she thought now, why would he? Wasn't he getting Tanya's opinion these days?

'I'd say you have a good eye.' He was watching her and even if she was still back in Cherrywood Crescent in her mind, thinking of both Michael and Tanya poring over paint colours for Tanya's house, it was nice to feel appreciated. 'This is lovely,' Joel said.

'It is,' she agreed, taking a deep breath and sinking back into the chair. There was so much food, but really, she was tired and her thoughts were racing in too many directions to eat much more.

'I think it's being here with you that's...' He had moved closer now, was leaning towards her as if expecting something to happen.

'I can't...' she said, sitting up and breaking the spell.

'Don't you ever get lonely?' He picked up some rice and chicken and popped it into his mouth, chewing thoughtfully as he watched her.

'Doesn't everyone?' she said too quickly.

'Do they?'

'I don't know, I assume they do, at some point.' Maybe it was her turn now. She hadn't been lonely, properly lonely, for years, not since her father died and she'd stood at his grave on her own so many evenings when she should probably have been out enjoying herself, meeting people, getting on with life. 'I was never lonely when Connor was at home, I mean, I didn't even think about being lonely then...' Her words drifted.

'I feel as if I've been lonely forever,' he said, staring out into the vastness of the Atlantic. 'Even when I was married, it felt as if I was drifting – is that a terrible thing to say?' He cleared his throat.

'I'm sorry,' she started, but she wasn't sure what else to say. 'I mean... perhaps you just haven't found *the one*.' She stopped, because this was dangerous ground and she knew it when he raised his eyebrows at her. 'Don't make fun of me, you know what I mean, maybe *the one* isn't a wife or a girlfriend, maybe it's just a good friend or a dog, or a…'

She was blushing, trying hard to dig herself out of a hole that was only getting deeper, not because of what she was saying, but rather because the tension between them seemed to have overflowed and there was no pretending it wasn't there now.

'It's not your fault.' He smiled at her, then he bit his lip for a moment, reminding her of Connor suddenly, in that way he would chew over a problem he couldn't figure out on his bottom lip before he asked for help. 'It's just, since I came here and met you… I haven't felt lonely, not even once.'

'It's a very special place,' she murmured. A small part of her wondered if being on your own was any lonelier than sharing a house with someone who felt as if they were a million miles away. When she said this, he looked at her for a long moment.

'Yeah, I suppose, that's not a great place to be either.' He stretched his legs out before him, taking just a moment to think of something he didn't want to say. 'Look at us, feeling sorry for ourselves when we're surrounded by this.'

He waved his hand around and he was right. In this very moment, Cora did not feel lonely, she still felt a little disappointed at where her life seemed to be ending up, but the loneliness had crept away from her in the seconds that moved more slowly here on the veranda with Joel.

'Maybe,' he said, breaking into her thoughts, 'it's possible that up until this point was just Act One for both of us.'

'How do you mean?' she asked, conscious that he had moved closer to her again.

'I mean, we don't have to settle for where our lives have ended up, surely we can choose again?'

'You make it sound so simple.' She laughed.

'It could be,' he said, leaning in and kissing her lightly on her lips. It made her gasp, although thankfully she didn't make a sound, but for a moment she was frozen and then her lips became traitors to her, because they began to move too. He was teasing her, with soft brushes across her lips, making her want more of him, to taste him, to feel his arms around her. Cora couldn't be sure how long they sat like that, just kissing, but then she became aware that something had changed, like a lowering of the temperature, although she was far from cold.

She pulled away from Joel, just as his hand was moving down her blouse, opening the top button. There was someone on the drive. She hadn't heard a car park up, but someone was standing there, in the shadows, watching them.

And then she heard the sound of footsteps, making a retreat, back down the driveway, and she held her breath for a moment, because she knew who those steps belonged to.

Michael.

She imagined his car reverse from the end of the driveway, through the gates and off onto the main road again, back to Cherrywood Crescent. Back to the life she'd left and now, she wondered, even if she wanted it, was there any way back to that world again?

*

Cora had kissed Joel back. That was what shocked her as much as anything. Well that and the fact that she was pretty sure the scuttling sound on the driveway meant someone had seen them. At the time, she'd been convinced it was Michael. Guilty conscience, perhaps, but since he had not bothered to follow her out to Ballycove before, she had no good reason to believe he would make his way there at that late hour when, under normal circumstances, she would have been tucked up in bed. In fact, apart from that day when she'd collected her belongings, there had only been phone calls between them since she left. (He didn't know that she'd seen him with Tanya and if hadn't been for Niamh being there too, Cora was fairly sure she'd have convinced herself it was her mind playing tricks on her.) He had put on a good show of saying he wanted her back, but actions spoke louder than words and wasn't that the whole problem with her marriage to begin with. She tried to tell herself that the noise on the driveway had been nothing and nobody, just her overactive, *overguilty*, imagination.

The kiss itself had been surprising, unlocking something deep in her that she hadn't felt in a very long time. But still it wasn't right.

'I'm sorry, Joel. I can't...' she'd said as she managed to pull herself away from him.

'But you want this as much as I do, I know you do...' He looked hurt.

'Maybe, on some level, but I'm married to Michael and that still counts for something.'

'Come on... you're here, he's over thirty miles away?'

'We have to sort things out, that's for sure, but even if we never get back together, I can't do this while there's still a chance for my marriage.'

And that was it. Michael was not perfect. It all might mean very little to him, but when all was said and done, you don't just throw away thirty years of marriage, do you? By the following morning, she could hardly bear to look at herself in the mirror. Tears streamed from her eyes and all she wanted to do was scrub away this feeling that she'd let them both down with her stupidity. The truth was, she'd never so much as flirted with another man since she'd met Michael. It just wasn't in her DNA.

Later, as she sat on a huge rock at the end of the beach, she looked out towards the sea and wondered if perhaps that was half the problem. Maybe if she'd been one of those women who enjoyed the attention of other men, Michael might have had to work harder and maybe their marriage wouldn't have withered away to little more than a perfunctory kiss on the cheek for birthdays and special occasions.

She was thankful beyond reason when Esme mentioned that Joel had gone to a meeting in Dublin first thing in the morning. At least that would give them a little space; maybe when he came back, they could put last night behind them and be friends again. She breathed a deep, depressed sigh. There was no question about it. They were living in different worlds and, regardless of what happened between her and Michael, she simply couldn't entertain any thoughts of starting up something with Joel Lawson.

Thursday

33

Esme

Esme was quite sure Joel Lawson must be very tall, not so much from the shadow he cast across the hall, because she never actually saw him against the light to tell, but he had the voice of a tall man. It was just as well, because Esme had never been very keen on short men. Short dogs and short men, she'd trust neither, even if she'd never admit that to anyone apart from Marta. Marta's husband had been short; she hadn't actually said so, but Esme was convinced of that.

Yes, Esme liked tall men, they made her feel safe, as if by their very height they would ward off any threat. She wondered now if Cora Doyle felt the same way. Was Michael Doyle a short man? Was he the sort of man who liked to take a bad day out on the people closest to him? Cora certainly seemed to be hitting it off with Joel Lawson. They had sat out most evenings for the past week on the veranda, long after Esme went to bed. Sometimes, she imagined she could hear their laughter on the breeze at her window, but maybe that was just wishful thinking, her hope of a happy ever after for Cora.

'You're back,' she greeted Joel although she wasn't sure he'd even noticed her. She'd caught his aftershave on the temperate evening air first. A sharp male cologne that was expensive, but not overbearing. It smelled more of soap or crisp linen rather than the average musky sweet scents she thought of as aftershave. He was unmistakable, he brought with him a distinctly male presence, it sat on the air around him as if to announce his languorous stride that Esme imagined cutting through the foyer into fewer steps than anyone else staying in the guest house this summer. She was tucked into her dome chair facing the crackling fire, all but invisible to anyone walking through the hallway.

'Yes, another day's work done,' he said, poking his head around her chair, so he was looking down at her. 'I never spotted you there.' He stopped for a moment. 'Can I get you anything?'

'No, no. I'm quite content,' Esme said and then she smiled. 'I'm catching the evening rays, it's funny how with each passing minute I think I can feel the sun sinking in the sky.' She traced her hands across the rug that Marta had spread out over her legs, feeling the dappled folds of warmth where she imagined the sun slicing through the windows across the hall.

'You don't need the sun for it to be beautiful here,' he said softly and she knew he was moving away from her.

'You know, some of the villagers go swimming down there all the time. Even in the depths of winter.' She wanted to hold onto him a little longer, get a sense of this man who seemed to be stealing Cora Doyle's heart away if the laughter on the veranda each evening was anything to go by.

'Well, fair play to them, I'm not sure it would be my cup of tea.'

'You've probably heard about our Ladies' Midnight Swimming Club?'

'Ahh...'

'Well, of course, it mightn't be your thing, but for the last few years now, all the women of the village head down and swim in the nip for the local hospice.'

'That's decent of them.' He chuckled.

'Is it?' Esme wasn't entirely convinced. 'Dora Flatly is eighty-nine and she's still enough woman for three of us. Let me tell you, I'd worry about the effects on the local fish. The sight of Dora in all her glory might be enough to send out the message that we have whales in the bay. A lot of families here depend on the fishing, don't you know?'

'Well, as you say, it's at night time,' Joel said. 'Didn't I hear somewhere that most fish are blind anyway?'

'Are they? Well, that's something, I suppose... perhaps there are blessings to count after all,' she said before she leaned back in her chair to ponder on the next great question that occurred to her. She cleared her throat and pulled her sleeves down towards her cuffs. It *was* chilly here in spite of the sun outside, although she wouldn't admit that to Marta in a fit or the woman would be tossing more fuel on the fire and she had done more than enough already to make Esme comfortable. 'You know, you've really given me something to think about there... and not just about the fish, let me tell you.'

'Glad to be of service.' He was making fun of her now.

'The church roof is coming along well, I hear. I hope you

know, it was a huge worry for the whole parish, we love our little church, it might not be the Basilica, but to us…' She had spent so much of her life there, between singing in the choir and occasionally helping out with the flowers.

'It's going to be perfect, better than it was to start. The builders are doing a fine job and we're using the very best of materials. The way they are going at it sometimes, I think they want it to outlast the sea.' He laughed at this, but Esme was happy to hear it.

'But you have more work to do here?'

'I'm not sure they actually need me all that badly, but there's unfinished business…'

'Ah.' She didn't say the name, but she had a feeling it had less to do with the church roof and more to do with Cora Doyle. 'You know, she's married,' Esme murmured and it felt for a moment as if time itself had stopped ticking. She waited a beat, she could backpedal, pretend she really was a little dotty.

'Not very happily, though, or she wouldn't be here?' He dropped into the seat and now she had a feeling he was lying back, crossing one leg over the other, as if he might enjoy talking to her for a while longer.

'I don't know about that, but I do know that, when it comes to these things, someone always gets hurt.' She had a feeling that even if Cora Doyle's head could be turned, she wouldn't leave the west of Ireland as easily as she might be tempted away from her husband. Joel Lawson may be enjoying his summer by the sea, but he was undoubtedly a city boy.

'Maybe I'm willing to risk my heart on it.' And there it

was, Esme could hear steeliness to his voice, he had gambled before and won. It was the quality that would have marked him out so his business was successful; he was a man who got what he wanted if he decided it was for him.

'Maybe, but you'd need to be quite sure, because thirty years of marriage is a lot to ask her to turn her back on. They have a son, she has a home, a job, a life here, you need to be very, very sure before she uproots everything for what might just be a summer of madness.'

'You think I'm playing with her?' He sounded as if nothing could be less likely.

'I'm sorry, I don't mean to pry, it's just, marriages can be funny, sometimes people simply forget how to be together – if that makes sense.' She sighed, leaned forward a little towards him. 'A friend of mine had all but given up on hers. Oh, this was years ago, back in the days when marriages just didn't end. You got what you got and you stuck with it to the bitter finishing line. And she would have kept on going, even if the silence of the union was killing her as slowly and surely as the passing of time.'

'What happened?' he asked.

'She met someone else, there was such a scandal in the village. He'd come to Ballycove to recover after a car accident, but soon they were running into each other at every turn and then one day she told him about her marriage and...'

'Well, we haven't talked about Cora's marriage,' he said as if that changed everything. 'Actually, we don't talk about much at all.'

'Indeed,' Esme said. She wasn't worried about how Joel Lawson's heart might fare in all of this, but she was suddenly more worried about Cora. 'We found my friend at the pier, washed up after almost a week at sea.'

'I'm so sorry,' he said and he sounded as if he was.

'It was the guilt, you see, although they hadn't actually done anything wrong, not really, but she couldn't live with herself. Perhaps a part of her believed that her only shot of happiness was with this man who had made her feel as if she wasn't invisible any more. She told me, just before the tragedy, that for the first time in years, she actually felt as if she was alive.'

'But surely that was a good thing?' Joel Lawson sounded as if he was cast adrift in unfamiliar waters, completely out of his depth. 'I mean, that she had a shot at happiness.'

'Maybe she forgot that the only one who had the real power to make her happy was herself?' Esme said quietly. 'I'm sure she had moments with him, where it felt as if... well, as if she was truly alive, but I think being happy is an altogether different thing, if that makes sense?'

'It probably does, but...' He stopped, maybe realising this wasn't a conversation he'd ever meant to have with a dotty old lady with a dodgy leg.

'Are you on the Facebook at all?' Esme leaned forward slightly.

'Facebook, well, I probably am, I mean, everyone was, at some point, weren't they?'

'Were they?' she said faintly. 'Perhaps they were, but now, it seems to be all old dears like me, tuning in to see what's happening with the local church choir or keeping up with family on the other side of the world and people we thought we lost along the way.'

'Oh, I'm sure you haven't lost…'

'The thing is, we all lose people.' She smiled sweetly. 'I mean, my friend Helen was telling me about a couple who had gone their separate ways, forty years apart. He'd gone to work in Australia, probably thought far-off fields were greener, and she'd married and had a family, grandchildren probably, before she looked him up again.'

Esme shook her head. 'By then of course, she was a widow, you see? I'm not even sure if her marriage was happy or not, but she never forgot her first love, you never do, not really, do you? Anyway, forty years later, there they are tying the knot, love's young dream and all that water under the bridge forgotten about, because they only remembered the best bits, the further they'd come away from each other.'

'Oh, I don't know, my first love was physics and I went off it pretty quickly when I was doing my post-graduate degree, let me tell you. I don't suppose I'll ever be mad about it again.' He laughed, but she was not going to be put off.

'Hmm. Well, my first love was Walter Hutch. He was six foot tall and he had the most startling blue eyes, I can still remember them. He asked me to the pictures and I let him hold my hand all the way through.'

'Ahh,' he said, but she had a sense that he was growing uncomfortable, perhaps he knew where she was going with it.

'The thing is, I'm not going to look him up on Facebook, like that other woman did. Poor Walter died in 1966 – drowned on his father's fishing boat. It was very tragic, at the time.'

'I'm so sorry.'

'Oh, no, we weren't together then, he'd turned into a right boyo, well, it was on the cards, those eyes were far too gamey to be good.' She smiled, thinking fondly of him. 'I suppose that we can't all be like that woman on the Facebook, but a lot of women are. They think they want something different, but in the end we always finish up with the same thing, because there is no escaping who we truly are, is there? After all is said and done, it's up to us how happy we're going to be in life, isn't it?'

'So, you think that Cora would always be looking over her shoulder? Thinking of her husband?'

'I think it's a lot of history to turn your back on, especially when you have a family together. She hasn't left him; she's only come here to think. If he was beating her black and blue every night, or likely to gamble the house away from under her, well then I'd say get your armour shined up and rev up your steed, she would absolutely love and deserve to be rescued. But I don't think that's how she feels.'

'I'll tell you what.' Joel leaned in close and she could feel him smiling at her, because of course, she was little more than a silly old woman. 'What if we just see how things work out? I promise not to cause any trouble, but we'll let Cora decide for herself, how's that?'

'It sounds fair enough to me.' Esme heard him get up from his seat and reached out to hold onto him for a moment longer. 'I'm not just thinking about her, you know; I'm thinking about you too. I wouldn't want you to suffer either, not if it can be helped.' She meant it, most sincerely; he was a nice enough man from what she could gauge. 'You probably think I'm a terrible busybody, sticking my nose in where it's not wanted, but...'

'You're a lovely, kind woman, and I don't for one minute think you are a busybody. I think you really care and that's very precious – it's a long time since anyone put themselves out to save me from heartbreak.' He bent down and kissed her lightly on the top of her head. 'It's just a pity I can't ask *you* on a date...'

'Oh, but you could.' She was joking with him now. 'Except, I do have a lot of admirers, you might have to join a very long queue.'

And then they were both laughing and she knew that she'd done her best to keep everyone as happy as she could. The rest was up to them.

34

Phyllis

Phyllis had almost forgotten what it was to have a child who begged to stay in the icy water long after any adult would have been happy to dry themselves off and retreat to somewhere warm with tea or coffee or something stronger. Josh was still jumping about in the waves, while Rob had earlier been relegated to standing on the edge of the water, his eyes trained on his son. She could hear him in the distance, calling out just five minutes more and then they could... and his voice faded off because perhaps they all knew that, at Josh's age, there wasn't very much that could compete with bombing full body into waves and searching in the clear water for fast-moving crawlies to inspect.

Phyllis closed her eyes. Next to her, sitting on the blanket with his back against the rocks, Kurt was absorbed in the newspaper. She stretched back a little, checking if he was still awake.

When she looked up again, she spotted Niamh. Her silhouette was unmistakable in the distance, that shock of wild red hair, untameable in the light summer breeze. Phyllis sighed. Such a pity. She and Rob would have made such a handsome pair. She could hear their laughter carried on the air. God, she could hardly remember the last time she'd heard Rob laugh like that. It sent a pang of sadness through her, so real it felt as if it stabbed against her heart. Bad timing. Terrible timing, really. The last thing Rob needed was the responsibility of another man's child and Niamh had enough on her plate with a new baby without having the drama of joining a family in the throes of coming to terms with what lay ahead of them with Kurt.

'She's a nice girl,' Kurt said, as if reading her thoughts.

'She really is.'

'But you're not sure about her.'

'No, no, she's lovely, truly. And you know, I'd love to see Rob meet someone but...'

'He could do worse.' Kurt looked over the top of his glasses and she knew it was an invitation to tell him exactly why she wasn't as enthusiastic as she might be.

'She's pregnant.'

'Is she?' he asked as if it was no more serious a thing to consider than if she had blue eyes or brown.

'With someone else's baby,' Phyllis said.

'These are modern times.' He smiled, but it was a line she'd often used to explain why she'd made a judgement that seemed to fly against all they'd believed when they were young.

'It makes everything very complicated though, don't you think?'

'Does it?' Kurt lowered the paper. He looked down along the beach again for a moment; reassessing the three of them anew. 'I don't know, I think there are worse things, more complicated things that people overcome. I mean, when is love not complicated?'

'Maybe you're right,' Phyllis said and it felt as if a huge worry was lifted off her.

'Anyway, it won't be down to us, will it?'

'No, I suppose not.' And she remembered the boy that her mother had high hopes she'd marry all those years ago. He was a good Catholic boy, a boy who was going to inherit a large family farm and probably end up giving her a dozen children who would all have his aversion to books and his love of the pub. She'd had a lucky escape, even if her mother hadn't talked to her for six months after she'd run off to marry Kurt. Sometimes, mothers didn't know best.

'Granddad, Granddad, look.' Josh had come racing up the beach clutching a huge whelk shell as if he'd just found gold.

'Oh, my, you know what you can do with that...' Kurt was saying as he put it to the child's ear and Josh stood wide-eyed and listening hard to hear the echo of the ocean.

'I've just invited Niamh to join us for dinner,' Rob said when they had ambled back to where Phyllis and Kurt had been sitting.

'How lovely,' Phyllis said.

'I really can't impose myself on you,' Niamh said. 'After all, you've only got a few days left here together, you'll want to spend it as a family.'

'Absolutely not, you must come with us, the more the merrier.' Kurt stood up to put his arm around Rob's shoulders. 'My wife has explained how you've already come to my rescue, it's time we said thank you with a meal at the very least.'

God, Phyllis thought, how much she loved Kurt, especially when she caught glimpses of that kind man she'd fallen head over heels for all those years ago.

'We'd love to have you along.' Phyllis smiled and she looked at Rob, who she suspected might be falling in love with this woman he knew so little about, but he was his mother's son and she knew he would find a way towards his own happiness, regardless of what obstacles lay in his path. And for that, she was very glad indeed.

35

Esme

If her visit to the hospital had taught Esme anything, beyond the fact that she had absolutely no right to feel sorry for herself, it was that Marta had become more than a friend or a woman who ran the guest house for her now that she couldn't run it herself as she once had. Their relationship had, over the course of the time she'd been here, been turned on its head – whereas once, she had offered a refuge to Marta, now Marta was the reason she could have sanctuary in her own home. More than that, she had become family, even if they weren't related.

It was like espionage. Esme had to ask Cora Doyle to drop in to Stephen Leather's office. That was the problem with being blind, it was impossible to make a phone call without being sure there was no one listening to every word behind your back. Of course, Stephen retired years ago, but Maya Lattimer had joined the firm and Esme had always been fond of the Lattimer girls. Her mother had played in the garden as a child and Esme had been firm friends with her grandmother and her aunts. Maya was invited for afternoon tea, which Marta had been given strict instructions was to be served in the small parlour off the main sitting room.

'The parlour?' Marta sighed.

'Yes, there are things we need to talk about.' Esme couldn't explain, because to do so would mean an additional strain of responsibility on Marta's shoulders and that was the very last thing she wanted.

Maya was punctual and, even if Esme hadn't properly seen her in over a decade, she knew the girl had not changed one bit. She'd always been striking, but more than that she was whip-smart and unaffected, too. She'd been the village kid who seemed to be good at everything when she was growing up. She sang like an angel in the church choir and captained the local girls' football team.

'Well, this is lovely,' she said, kissing Esme lightly on her cheek, and her voice seemed to smile even as she spoke.

'Well, it *is* private and I needed to talk to you without anyone overhearing. I'm not sure what it's like here, it probably needs a good dusting. I can't remember the last time anyone sat in here.' That wasn't entirely true. In the coldest of winter months, this is where Esme and Marta sat on evenings when the larger rooms were far too big to heat. Here there was a small cast-iron fireplace and heavy drapes on the window. It was next to the kitchen and sealed off from any draughts by virtue of the fact it was furthest from the front door and hidden from the back. 'I hope it's not too cramped.'

'It's perfect,' Maya said and she set about pouring their tea and piling treats on their plates. 'I'm going to be stuffed after this; you will be in such big trouble with my mother. She's planning on a healthy salad for dinner.' Maya laughed. She had brought along a box filled with fresh lettuce, tomatoes, spring onions and strawberries from her mother's kitchen garden. 'So, tell me, what's it all about?' she said once they'd settled in and started into their tea.

'It's my will.'

'Ah, I see…'

'No, I'm not sure you do. You see, I've never made a will before, which is a bit silly considering, well, I'm hardly in the first flush of youth.'

'It's not silly at all, everyone gets round to it when they are ready. Some people just take a little longer than others, but it's a good thing to do, to feel that everything will be settled properly, when you're gone.'

'Have you made a will?' Esme asked, but of course, Maya was hardly twenty-five.

'I have, actually.' She laughed. It was a lovely tinkling sound – if Esme was to describe it she might even say it was sparkling. 'Of course, I don't have a lovely guest house to leave behind me, but I think a will is about more than just material things. For me it was about getting things straight, you know, in the event that…'

'Oh?' Esme couldn't imagine what a young woman like Maya would want to have straightened out.

'You seem surprised! I was thinking about things like organ donation and how I wanted a humanist celebration of my life, rather than some dour church affair.'

'Ah, yes, that makes a lot of sense.' Esme smiled. 'Actually, I like that idea, I might even borrow it.'

'Feel free.' Maya laughed.

'The real thing I wanted to settle though is this place. Do you know, I don't have a single close relative left to my name?' Esme shook her head.

'Oh, in that case, you really do need to put something in place; otherwise, the tax collector will be rubbing his hands together when the time comes.'

'Exactly,' Esme said. It wasn't even this that had made her contact Maya though. It was more the idea that she'd become so dependent on Marta. Marta hadn't so much offered to take care of Esme as insisted. She'd worked like a slave and she would never expect or take anything in return, and Esme was reluctant to offer it, for fear of creating some kind of tacit responsibility on her. The last thing she wanted was Marta feeling she *had* to be there, because Esme couldn't manage without her, even if, they both knew, that was the case already. 'I want to leave everything I own to Marta. I want to set it all out in my will, but I want it kept between us, I don't want her to feel...'

'I understand.' Maya had the good grace not to mention the words 'beholden' or 'obliged' or 'indebted'. 'I can draw up something, maybe pop in at the same time next week, would that suit you?'

'That sounds just perfect,' Esme said and she raised her cup slightly as if to toast the plan and she sighed, as if she had just slipped one of the last pieces into a jigsaw that had taken a lifetime to complete.

Friday

36

Phyllis

Sitting here, Phyllis Courtney could almost convince herself everything was going to work out well in the end. It was a wonderful evening. Almost like old times. If she closed her eyes and opened them really quickly, she might have been able to pretend that her family was just as it had always been. Kurt opposite her, tucking into a medium well-done steak, appeared to have no worries or fears about the future. Opposite her, Rob chatted away to Niamh as if they'd known each other forever. It felt as if the Courtney family hadn't a care in the world and Phyllis sat there, sipping a slightly warm glass of house white and willing it to go on forever.

The restaurant was just a small, family-run, cosy affair, where the owners pretended to remember them from previous visits, although they weren't fooling Phyllis. Still, they made a show of giving them their favourite table – it was early in the season and the Courtneys played their part by pretending not to notice that the menu hadn't changed in years and neither had the décor. None of that mattered, they'd come here for the view of the sea and the lighthouse in the distance, and the memories of years earlier far more than anything else.

Kurt squeezed her hand, reminding her that the most important memories were the ones they were making right now.

'You know how much I love you,' he whispered to her, 'always have, always will,' and his breath on her cheek made her heart stop for a moment, as if something really momentous had passed between them without her fully realising it.

'Oh, darling.' She smiled at him, if only they could freeze-frame this time forever.

She had so much to be thankful for. They'd made the best memories here, particularly over the last few years. It had become a place where time was wound back and the worries that niggled them for the rest of the year were forgotten.

'I'm thinking of selling my flat,' Niamh announced as they waited for dessert.

'It's a good time to sell.' Rob smiled. 'Terrible time to buy somewhere new though.'

'I know, and I love my flat too, but it's time for me to buy a house. I want a garden and a sense of community around me.'

'A good house is an investment in any economy,' Kurt said.

'We do a lot of conveyance work and it's never been busier, but you still see the occasional gem come on the market,' Rob said. 'I can help you out with the paperwork, if you'd like.'

'That's so kind of you.' Niamh laughed. 'But I have to find the property first.'

Phyllis had a feeling she was the only one here who knew there was more to Niamh upsizing than a desire to plant begonias and join a residents' association.

After the desserts arrived, they fell into contented silence and, all too soon, it was time to go back to the guest house for the night. Phyllis couldn't remember ever wishing so acutely they could stretch a holiday out for just a little longer.

'I might just toddle off to the little boys' room before we go,' Kurt said and he kissed Phyllis's forehead and gazed into her eyes for just a moment.

'And I'm going to pay that bill,' Rob said.

'Thank you, darling,' Phyllis said to Rob, but she was deep in conversation with Niamh about all the holidays they'd had in Ballycove over the years and how it was the perfect place to bring a young family. As they sat there, she noticed the restaurant had become quite busy, with couples and families filling up the tables around them. It was early yet, they could manage a walk along the beach if they fancied it on the way home.

'Where's Dad?' Rob asked after sorting out the bill and chatting to the restaurant owners.

'He went to the bathroom.' Phyllis checked her watch. 'Oh no, that must have been ten minutes ago, maybe longer.' Panic began to rise up in her and she watched as Rob darted through the door to the toilets to find Kurt.

'He's not there,' he said when he returned a moment later. His voice was measured, trying not to panic them too much.

'But?' Niamh was pulling her shawl about her shoulders.

'There's a back door, left wide open. He must have been confused and headed out there instead of coming back into the restaurant,' Rob said, turning away from them. 'I'm going to head out there now, it's a narrow lane that runs all the way to the end of the main street. I'll meet you round the front in a few minutes.'

'Come on, Gran.' Josh began to drag Phyllis back towards the Willows, while Rob raced out the back door in hopes of tracing his father's steps. Niamh agreed to take the opposite direction down to the bottom of the village, in search of Kurt. Phyllis prayed that Kurt had wound up at the guest house after his confusion cleared. She walked quickly, her eyes darting to every corner of the road ahead of her, down driveways and into gardens – she couldn't help it, it felt as if he could be anywhere. At this moment, all she wanted was to find him.

At least, Phyllis thought, the village ran to little more than a couple of streets, a market square and a back alley. She frantically walked the length of one before turning back again; hope knotting along her spine that Niamh and Rob would emerge at the end of the street with Kurt at their sides.

'Gran.' Josh's voice at her side reminded her she was holding his hand so tightly that it was uncomfortable. He pulled loose and ran ahead and, as she watched him turn in the large gates to the Willows, Phyllis pulled up short. *You know how much I love you. Always have, always will.* Kurt's words from earlier cut through her like a knife. Had he been saying goodbye? It had been there in the back of her mind for some time now, that idea that he wouldn't wait for the disease to come and get him. He'd never asked her to help him end it all and she had been grateful for that, but... Oh, God. Not like this. She prayed. Not yet. Not like this.

The guest house, when she pushed open the front door, felt unwholesomely normal. There was that familiar mixture of lavender, wood polish and fire smoke, low lights picking out the dome chairs that they had spent many hours sitting in before blazing fires or watching through the doors at falling sunsets. It was the sound of it that unnerved Phyllis most; a muffled symphony of hissing, rattling and Esme's soft snores from before the dying fire. She rushed through the foyer and pushed open the door of their room, but it was exactly as they'd left it earlier that day. Josh was jumping up and down on his bed in the room opposite, but Phyllis hadn't the energy to stop him never mind wheedle him into his pyjamas.

'Phyllis.' Esme sounded drowsy, as if she had just woken with the commotion. She craned her neck around to look at her. 'Is something wrong?'

'I...' Phyllis moved towards her friend. 'It's Kurt, one minute he was there and the next...' She felt her voice quiver. It was getting darker outside. Suddenly, her chest felt as if it was closing up tight. Panic nipped at her nerve endings, so it caught up her words as if she'd been running too hard to catch her breath.

'It's okay, we'll ask Marta to help you search for him, if you'd like,' Esme said and she picked a little brass bell from the table before her and started to ring it vigorously.

'He's not here. He's... we were in the village for dinner and he just disappeared.' Phyllis's eyes slid down towards Josh, who had raced out to her side. He grabbed her hand

and held it tightly. She had to remain calm for him, even if her mind chased shadows towards the beach below with a terrifying fear that they were already too late. It was growing darker and on the way back she couldn't help but notice that the tide was on its way in.

'Have you checked the beach? Do you think he might be...?'

'I can't think...' Phyllis could feel her reserves breaking, as if nothing around her made sense any more. What would she do if anything happened to Kurt? She took a deep, steadying breath. 'I don't know, Rob and Niamh, the woman who is staying here too, are looking for him in the village but if he's wandered down to the beach...' Phyllis shuddered. 'He could forget where he is and it's worse at night time. He's probably completely confused.' She stopped. 'He's going to be really scared now.' She couldn't bear to think of him wandering and afraid in a place he didn't know well or, worse, that he'd decided to take matters into his own hands.

'Let's turn on all the lights and sit on the veranda and keep a look-out, okay?'

'What's happening?' Marta arrived into the hallway.

'Kurt is missing,' Esme said.

'It's okay,' a voice said. A tall man came in from outside; he had been hovering on the edge of their conversation for a minute. 'I'm going to go and search for him along the beach. He's probably not there, but just in case, before it gets completely dark.' His voice was so calm it reassured Phyllis, even though part of her knew there was every reason to worry. 'Cora, you'll come too, won't you?' Esme's bell had roused everyone in the house.

'Of course, I'll help, we can split up,' Cora said and then she looked at Phyllis. 'You'll be all right here with Esme to keep an eye out in case he comes home on his own?'

'Of course, you're very kind, you know, to help like this...'

'Don't be daft, of course we're going to make sure that he is all right.'

Marta reached around the front door and switched on the porch lights, so with a flick of a switch it felt as if the house might be a beacon to welcome Kurt home.

With that the little search party pulled out onto the road towards the village in the huge Mercedes that had been parked at the top of the drive, and it seemed to Phyllis that everything got just a little darker.

Two hours crawled by while Phyllis tried to rattle off prayers she thought she'd forgotten years earlier. She all but wore a track from the dome chairs at the fireplace to the old double swing on the veranda. Esme did her best to break up the tension by prattling on about how often people went missing and were found safe and sound in the most unlikely places. By the time Joel Lawson's car pulled back into the driveway, Phyllis believed Kurt to be dead. She had imagined him, walking along the pier and losing his footing, or worse, knowing what was ahead of him and deciding he wasn't going to sit and wait for the inevitable to choke the last dregs of vitality from him. And she realised, as she sat on that veranda, a place she'd taken so much for granted on her previous visits, that Kurt taking his own life was by far the more likely outcome of tonight. She really didn't believe he was so far gone that he would be in any danger other than what he might realise he could cause himself.

Once she'd recognised what she'd known already, it almost felt as if her breathing steadied. The stars over her head shone a little brighter; if her dear Kurt had taken that decision, she would be heartbroken, but she would find in it something to be grateful for too – the fact that he had somehow won.

The car lights illuminating the gladioli stirred her from these dark imaginings. She realised she hadn't even heard the engine thunder along the quiet roads. It pulled up at the front of the house, a long expensive vehicle which at first she didn't recognise, until Niamh emerged from the back seat nearest to the house and then, while Phyllis still held her breath, she watched as Kurt unfurled himself and stood a little lower than was his full height on the driveway. She ran towards him, knowing immediately that he was lost to her, taken to that place where he was a stranger, confused and fearful of even the most familiar things around him.

'It's okay Kurt, it's me, you're safe now,' Phyllis murmured over and over as she clung to his damp jacket. He smelled of the sea and as if he'd fallen down in rubbish somewhere but it didn't matter. He was here, with her, and he was safe. As they climbed up the steps to the guest house, to close out the door on the longest possible day, a small voice in Phyllis's head wondered if perhaps choosing his own ending might not indeed have been the kindest outcome of all.

*

It was always the same. After an unsettled night, Kurt could sleep into the following week if she didn't waken him. He would be tired for most of the day. It was terrible what you could grow to expect to be normal. There was no sleeping for Phyllis but, determined to make the most of things, she enjoyed breakfast early and set off for a short walk before Rob or anyone else surfaced. She headed towards the pier – not a direction she had walked all that often on her own over the years, compared to the long sandy beach. But she enjoyed the flurry of activity as the local fishermen went about their business with a busy dance of seagulls flocking above them in the hope of picking up some small morsel of unwanted catch. She sat for a short while, thinking about the previous evening. Somehow, she could convince herself here, in the early morning sunshine, that maybe they'd made a bit of a mountain out of a molehill.

Eventually, as she spotted a few walkers on the beach in the distance, she realised she would have to go back. She was only partly aware that the idea of returning to what had become the responsibility of her life weighed down upon her in a way it never had before.

The Willows was much busier when she returned, with guests about to book out. She met Niamh carrying her case to her car. Rob had already said his goodbyes and they'd agreed he would take on the legal work when she eventually found that house.

'You should ring him up to come and look over some of the properties with you.' Phyllis smiled at Niamh. If she had learned anything last night, it was that time was far too precious to waste; whatever complications there may be ahead if Rob got involved with Niamh, they would be complications of the very best kind. Phyllis had a feeling it might do both of them good. Perhaps Niamh needed someone in her life as much as Rob did, even if she was every bit as much and more in denial about it. Phyllis wondered fleetingly, was it very old-fashioned to suppose that everyone wanted the same sort of happy ever after she'd wished for?

Josh met her at the porch door. 'Gran, Gran, you'll never guess…' He was as excited as ever.

'No, tell me what?'

'We're going to meet Niamh when we get back home and…' He stopped, building up to the climax of his exciting news. 'And she's going to come with us to the zoo. She said they've got real penguins there…'

'Well, that is terrific news,' Phyllis said, scooping the child up in her arms. Oh, how she loved him and what wonderful news that maybe Rob was finally beginning to see that there might be more to life than just going to work each day and caring for his son. 'Where's your dad now?' she asked, but Josh had already slid down and was dragging her towards the breakfast room, telling her he was having more sausages for breakfast and wasn't this the BEST holiday ever?

Rob looked far more relaxed than Phyllis felt. He was sitting with coffee and the morning paper as if he hadn't a care in the world. He poured a cup for Phyllis and smiled at her and she wondered for a moment if his good humour was more about seeing Niamh just a while earlier than it was about seeing his old mother. She couldn't help but notice a small stain of lipstick on his cheek.

Yes, sitting there with the sun sparkling on the old-fashioned silverware, everything could almost be perfect.

'Is Dad still sleeping?' Rob asked as she finished her coffee.

'Oh God, your father, I completely forgot.' She got up and

raced towards their room. It was almost ten o'clock. How on earth had that happened? But he would still be asleep probably, out cold to a world that was slowly ravelling away from him.

She pushed open the door gently. She liked to waken him slowly, not giving him a start, but rather, she would sit on the side of the bed and whisper to him that it was time to get up, if he wanted to get a good start on the day.

Except, when she pulled aside the curtains this morning and turned to sit on the side of the bed, it was obvious he'd already gotten an early start on the day. The bed was empty.

'Kurt,' she called about the room, but it wasn't that large; she knew he wasn't here.

She walked down the corridor, trying to keep the panic she felt at bay. She wouldn't raise the alarm just yet. Instead, she arrived in the entrance hall with a plan, but his familiar voice from behind one of the dome chairs pulled her up. She stood stock-still, listening to how much the familiarity of his tone cut through the newly acquired weakness of it.

'So, you see, Esme, something *must* have happened...' he was saying.

'But you're here now, aren't you?' Esme reminded him.

'That's true...' he agreed.

'You can't really worry about what happened yesterday. No one was hurt, all you can do is plan for tomorrow. Can you do that, do you think? Make a plan that will take some of this terrible worry from your shoulders?'

'It's not my shoulders that I'm worried about so much...' He made a sound, as if to laugh, but really, it was too close to the bone for it to be funny. 'My father went the same way, but he dragged it out. I'm not sure if he had a choice that he'd have wanted it that way...'

'You have to think about your family too.' Esme's voice had risen, perhaps realising that Kurt wasn't talking about some sort of treatment.

'Of course, I'd only want to do the thing that would cause them the least pain.'

'You should really take a look in my book...' Esme said and Phyllis had a feeling that her oldest friend was smiling.

'Your book? Ah, the guest book? Okay, but I think we've already signed in.' Although he didn't sound a hundred per cent sure. Was that what it would be like for him from here on, never quite sure of anything?

'No, no, don't be silly, I don't want you to sign it. I want you to read it.' Esme passed over the large book from one dome chair to the other. 'Now, open up the last day of your holidays, the day you should be signing out. Is there something at the top of the page? A note, perhaps? Can you see it?' She was prodding him, probably because she couldn't see his features; she wasn't sure if he was still with her or not.

'Yes, yes, I found it.' His voice sounded different, stronger, as if he'd just stepped back to a time when there was no doubt about anything. That was the Kurt that Phyllis had fallen in love with all those years ago – he'd been a man to depend on, the one person she knew would always be her rock. It wasn't lost on her that, now, she needed to be his.

'What does it say? Will you read it for me?'

'It's...' His voice faltered. 'It says... *Every day is a new day, just as it went before does not mean it has to go the same today, you can choose your own path or follow the footsteps worn out before you.*' The words seemed to sit on the still air for a long time. 'So, you think...'

'It doesn't matter what I think, Kurt, I think what matters is what you want the rest of your time with your family to be.'

'You know all I want is to find a way of holding onto what I have for as long as I can.' He sniffed, as if there might be a tear in his eye, and Phyllis, unseen at his back, felt her heart break a little more. 'Perhaps I am lucky, at least I can shape how I want the time left to me, I can do that, and it's a lot more than my father had...' He was thinking out loud now, but there was an expanding lustre in his tone.

'It sounds like the start of a plan, at any rate.' Esme reached out and touched his arm. 'My old book doesn't have all the answers, but maybe it can point you in the direction of making the decisions that are right for you and Phyllis.'

'I think it already has...' he said and Phyllis wiped a tear from her eye, because for the first time since she had realised that something was wrong, she began to feel as if there might be some small ray of hope.

Saturday

37

Cora

The Railway Hotel was as splendid as Cora had ever seen it. She and Michael agreed to meet half an hour before Connor and Lydia arrived down for dinner. He was waiting for her in the lounge with a glass of beer and an inscrutable expression.

'How have you been?' she asked, suddenly too absurdly nervous to take in anything much more than the fact that he looked better than he had in years, well, apart from looking tired. Had he lost weight? Surely not, it was only two weeks, but he looked different, perhaps she was just seeing him from a new perspective. He offered to get her a drink and she was relieved to sit down and tuck her treacherous high heels underneath her.

'Busy, you know.' He gave what was almost a half-smile and she wondered if perhaps Tanya had been keeping him occupied. 'You look...'

He stopped. He was not used to giving her compliments, but he didn't need to tell her she looked well, his expression when she'd walked through the door was enough to let her know she had surprised him. He'd probably have a stroke if he realised just how much she'd spent on her clothes, hair and make-up for the night. It didn't matter, she felt confident – apart from the killer heels. She'd even go so far as to say she felt beautiful.

'Beautiful,' he finished after a moment and when she met his eyes it felt as if something between them had changed in that heartbeat.

'Thank you.' She smiled but her insides were churning with a giddy attraction he seemed to have ignited in her with just one word. She sipped her glass of wine, cleared her throat. Whatever was happening here, one night, one compliment, one word, was not enough to make everything right. 'You look good too.' It was the truth.

'I made an effort. I think I'm finally beginning to understand.'

'Well, that's not what we're here for this evening.' She cut him short, because here, with Connor and Lydia, was not the time to sort out their marriage problems. Tonight was about celebrating their son's marriage, not retrieving their own. 'You haven't said anything?'

She was checking if he'd told Connor, but Michael shook his head. She sighed now, looked about the lounge suddenly aware there was so much they needed to talk about. It came at her as a flash – the certainty that she'd been running away from it. They should have sat down and tried to sort things out already, but all she'd done was put miles between them.

'This place is doing all right.' Michael followed her gaze around the lounge. It was early but already every other table was taken; the bar nicely sprinkled with customers.

All people like themselves, middle-aged couples and small family groups, out for a night, celebrating being alive, being in love, just being together with good food and a few drinks. 'I suppose it's what people do, most weekends...' His voice petered off.

'I didn't want to be out painting the town red every weekend, Michael, this is not about that.'

'I know, but... maybe you were right. Being here, it's not too bad... it might have done us good. Given us something to mark out things by.' He looked at her now, reached out for her hand, but she snatched it away. 'I'm so sorry, all those birthdays and anniversaries, I should have made an effort. We should have just come here or anywhere just to be together. I really wish we had now.'

He looked across the bar, his eyes sad for a moment, but then, as if he'd nudged himself into sensibleness again, he went on, 'Anyway, no point looking back, we're here now, we might as well make the best of it, just in case...'

He let his words hang, but she knew there was nothing in them to make her feel bad. He was thinking exactly what she was thinking: if this was their one night out and they ended up permanently going their separate ways at the end of the summer, then they should enjoy any time they had left together.

'Thank you, Michael.' She meant it, because she realised that she couldn't have borne it if he'd shown up here looking wretched, being miserable, digging up the sympathy votes from Connor and Lydia. Instead, he'd spruced himself up, so he looked bloody good, and he was wearing a determination in his eyes that she knew meant he wouldn't let her down.

'Oh Cora.' Lydia was standing at the table, air kissing them both. 'I hardly recognised you both, you look so...'

She was taking both of them in and, true enough, they had probably scrubbed up better for this evening than they had for the wedding, but then, they had a whole other agenda going on here. Connor too seemed taken aback by his father's linen jacket and smart jeans.

'It's like you've finally emerged into this century, Dad,' he laughed. 'You look... you both look so... young,' he said as he opened the menu and pushed his glasses up his nose.

The meal was just perfect – it was easy to see why the Railway Hotel had such a fabulous reputation. The staff made a fuss of them and the manager arrived down with a bottle of champagne to celebrate the return of his old friends. He made a point of sitting next to Cora and chatting to her especially, but then, she supposed, she had made most of the wedding arrangements.

'You better look out, Dad,' Connor said after he left, 'I think he has his eye on Mum.'

They all laughed, but Cora had a feeling Michael did not laugh as heartily as the rest. She felt a gnawing guilt when she remembered that kiss on the veranda with Joel. She shivered, shook herself out; hadn't Tanya Farrelly already begun to sink her teeth into Michael? It didn't look as if he had been trying too hard to fend her off the day she spotted them in town. That alone made her feel, if not better then at least a little less guilty.

Later, after their desserts, they moved from the restaurant back into the lounge and sat next to the open doors which billowed their soft voile curtains gently on the evening breeze.

In spite of the fact that Cora and Michael were basically sitting here and lying to their son and daughter-in-law, Cora managed to sink into a relatively relaxed state, undoubtedly helped along by the champagne, but also because Michael was being such good company. It was as if he'd experienced a great epiphany and with the new wardrobe the sales assistant had thrown in an interesting and engaging personality as a bonus. For a few moments, she found herself observing their little group from the outside and she realised this was what she'd always dreamed of. Those days she'd imagined lay ahead of her at some future date had actually arrived. They were sitting together, chatting and laughing, having eaten dinner with the windows open and beautiful white nets billowing in the evening breeze nearby. It may not be in their own kitchen, but maybe it was even better here, because she hadn't had to do the cooking and she had never gone out and bought those perfect white curtains to begin with anyway.

That thought resonated with her at some deeper level than she expected. She looked across at Michael now, realising that perhaps he was not the only one to blame for where they'd ended up. If he had been slow to compliment her or make her feel as if their relationship still had any magic left, she too should own up to the fact she had let things slip over the years. She'd spent thirty years completely consumed with her family – which of course was part of the deal when you were a mother. But, sitting here, thinking back, she realised that maybe she should have pushed out a half an hour occasionally and spent time investing in her relationship with her husband.

She remembered back to the early days, when Connor

was small and she'd toddle upstairs and read a nursery book to him before falling asleep in his bed, while Michael went about microwaving his dinner and eating alone in front of the TV. Even at weekends, when they all sat down together, she had made a lot more of Connor's cute little sentences than she had made time to listen to her husband.

She regarded Michael now, his hands big and strong on the arms of his chair. He had worked so hard, first so they could afford the deposit on their house and then later to pay off the mortgage as quickly as they could so they could start pouring money into a fund for college for Connor. He had chosen to work his annual summer holidays each year on extra jobs, just so she didn't have to go out to work and leave Connor at the crèche. And then, when Connor didn't need her all the time and she'd taken up the job as a classroom assistant, to give him his due, Michael had been quietly happy for her.

Maybe he was right, maybe all she was suffering was empty nest syndrome. Maybe they'd have gone on happily for years if Connor still needed her as he had done in the early years.

'You're a million miles away.' Michael reached out and touched her arm now.

'No. No. Not really, I'm thinking about those curtains and how well something like that would have suited our kitchen,' she smiled at him. It didn't mean that they were getting back together, but it was exactly what was on her mind – and then some!

*

'We need to talk,' Michael said once they were sitting in the shared taxi.

'Not tonight, let's not talk about it all tonight, it's been such a lovely evening.' They were speeding too fast towards Cherrywood Crescent. It was the sensible thing, to share a taxi, and it was on the way to Ballycove.

'It has,' he said and he shifted his gaze from her to the passing street lights. Cora realised, just as they pulled in outside their house, that she would have loved to stretch the evening even further out.

'Will you come in? There's something I want you to see, maybe have a brandy to finish off the night?' He was looking at her now, hopefully, and she knew that she should just stay in the taxi and travel directly back to the guest house. But still.

'Okay, just for half an hour.' They paid the taxi and took his number so he could collect her again after his next run and drop her out to Ballycove. Michael led the way up towards the front door, his gait jaunty, almost self-conscious, it seemed to Cora.

'Oh my God,' she gasped. Inside was not what Cora had expected. Since she'd been here last, Michael had completely stripped out the hallway and painted it a soft grey that looked like downy cotton covering the walls, so rich and soft she was tempted to caress it with her palm. The original parquet floor that they'd covered over with carpet more than twenty years ago had been stripped back and polished so it shone brilliantly. Every, or almost every, family photograph from the living room, kitchen and hallway had been reframed in soft white matching frames and mounts. They filled the wall along the stairs, which were carpeted in a sea green matting that looked and smelled as if it had just been tacked into place on each step only five minutes earlier. 'How on earth did you do all this in just...'

'I had a little help, all those favours I'd done over the years for people,' he smiled sadly, because they both knew that those favours had cost them summer holidays and weekends when other families were spending time together. 'Well, I called them in,' he said and then he lowered his voice, sending a shiver of something unfamiliar through her, 'for you.'

'Michael, it's...' She felt a tear fall from her eye as she took in every single memory captured in those photographs. She'd hung them originally in mismatched frames and sometimes homemade mounts.

'You haven't seen the half of it yet.' He was smiling now, grinning from ear to ear, and she wondered when was the last time he had an opportunity to show off his work to her. He pushed the door through to the kitchen, which had been transformed from the mess it was the last time she was here. He'd even tidied it.

'No, I can't take the credit for that,' he said and she noticed his colour rise when she commented on the near empty worktops and sink free from dirty dishes. Was he actually blushing?

'Ah, Tanya?' she said a little sadly, although no one was less likely than their glamorous neighbour to be up to her elbows in sudsy water.

'Tanya?' He laughed. 'Are you serious? Tanya wouldn't know one end of the dishwasher from the other. No, for tonight, just for tonight mind, I got a mate of mine to organise contract cleaners to come in and give the place a full once-over. They arrived at two this afternoon, probably only left five minutes ago.'

And then there was that laugh again and she watched as his eyes crinkled up and she filled with a sadness because it was far too long since she'd made him laugh or even shared a laugh with him.

'Brandy?' He reached up to her baking cupboard and pulled down an unopened bottle that she remembered buying at Christmas, just in case.

'Why not?' She walked over to the kitchen table and looked out on the garden, expecting to find it covered in weeds. She pulled back the patio doors, walked out and drank in the aroma of freshly cut grass. 'You've mowed the lawn?' she said a little begrudgingly, because he had managed to get lovely straight lines up and down it and it was as short as a putting green. When Cora did it, honestly, it looked like an outbreak of crop circles, worked out around any permanent features she didn't have to move.

'Yeah, well, it was probably just about my turn.' He handed her one of the brandy balloons that had been left sitting in the sideboard in the living room for the last thirty years. There was a set of six of them, old-fashioned thin glass that almost felt too delicate to use, so she'd stored them away and forgotten they were there. Another swell of sadness welled up in her; had she really put off using these for some day and when had she expected some day to come?

'Will we sit in the garden or here?'

'Let's sit here and look out at the garden,' she said, because it was just perfect here, far more perfect than she'd ever imagined it could be.

'You'll have to see the sitting room before you go, of course,' he said, pulling out a kitchen chair for her.

'You've tackled the sitting room too?'

'Well, yes, you've been saying for years we needed to spruce the place up a bit, and goodness knows, I've had enough time on my hands these last few days, so...'

But he was talking to himself, because Cora was already up and admiring his handiwork before he could finish.

'Oh, my...' she couldn't speak. He'd carried the same colours through to here also, pulled up the carpet, and St Theresa only knew how, but he'd managed to make the parquet floor look a million dollars. It shone like glass beneath her feet. She started to cry. She was overwhelmed with how much he'd done, but of course, she had a feeling that this wasn't done for her. She could see Tanya Farrelly's stamp all over this room. There was no way Michael would have thrown out his ancient old recliner in favour of this natty new look that might have been catapulted from *The Jetsons*, not even if Cora had nagged him for another twenty years.

'What is it? I've done this all for you, I thought it might show you how much I love you and it was my way of saying sorry. I thought you'd like it?' He was beside her now, not sure what to do to make things right. 'I really didn't mean to upset you... Is it the furniture? Or the curtains? I'm so sorry,

I just cleared everything out, I had hoped it would be like a new start for us… You know, start as you mean to go on and all that… and…'

She turned to him and he looked odd, a peculiar amalgamation of the man she'd known for most of her life and this strange new person who'd transformed their home, almost transformed himself just to make things right. But for who?

'Is this for me or for Tanya?' she had to know.

'What? What do you mean, is it for Tanya?' The words came out like a huge balloon inflating. 'Why on earth would I do all this for the next-door neighbour?'

'I'm not stupid Michael, I saw you in town together and this –' she pointed at the mustard velvet two-seater '– you didn't choose this or think about getting all those photographs changed into new frames.'

'No, of course I didn't. That's the problem, I wouldn't have thought of any of it, if you hadn't made me stop and look at myself, and yes, Tanya came in and helped me choose things here.' He stopped, examined his new trainers. 'Well, she helped me pick out basically everything, but that was all she did. There was never anything more to it than that… there never would be, not for me,' he said and there were tears in his eyes also. 'You might have fancied a change, but I never did. Not once, in all the years I've known you. I've loved only you and I'm so sorry if I didn't say it often enough, or show it, but now… I'm showing you now, if it's not too late.'

'Oh, Michael.' Cora shook her head, she wasn't sure if it was too late. After all, she'd been the one to walk out, she'd been the one to kiss someone else. It was finally time. She needed to be honest at least with herself. Maybe she'd been half to blame for where they'd ended up too. She walked back towards the kitchen, suddenly aware of the complete and utter silence that surrounded them. Michael followed her, took up both their drinks and placed one in her hand. He looked at the clock, and they both knew that the taxi driver would be turning into the drive pretty soon. She sighed, deeply. She knew what she wanted, she'd always known, she wanted only Michael – faults and all, she'd loved him for too long to just walk away from him.

'The thing is, Michael, maybe it wasn't all your fault.' She walked over to the window. It was still bare, still waiting for her to hang up those net curtains that would billow in the summer evening air. 'Maybe I lost sight of you as much as you did of me.'

'It doesn't mean we can't find each other again. I'll do anything, Cora, anything to make things right.' He was begging her now.

'You've done so much already.' She had to tell him about that kiss. There was no going forward until she did. 'If we're going to move forward, it'll be down to both of us making more of an effort, and I see now that it doesn't just happen.' She smiled, thinking of the net curtains she'd never bought, never hung. Marriages, like dreams, didn't just happen; you had to do some work to get there. 'Out at the guest house, a few nights ago... I...' She stopped, trying to find the words. Michael had moved close to her now but, before she kissed him, she had to tell him about Joel Lawson.

'I already know.' He pulled her close to him and the unexpected intimacy of being swept up by this man who had suddenly become a stranger to her on so many levels took her breath away. 'But I'm kissing you now, so let's just forget about everything else.'

August

38

Niamh

Perhaps it was just being pregnant, or maybe it was the fact Niamh kept noticing things she hadn't noticed before, but being back in her flat after her break at the Willows somehow didn't feel as if she'd come home, not really.

Jeremy had cleared out his belongings with surprising efficiency. There wasn't so much as a rib of his hair to be found in the flat. Not only did he take his toothbrush, his books and all those spare things that seemed to have lived there for the past few years, but it almost felt as if the place had been gone through by industrial cleaners. Had he actually bleached and scrubbed himself out of her life as thoroughly as he could in an effort to expunge any trace of himself, beyond the one she was carrying inside her?

There had always, she could admit to herself now, been a cold streak to him. They had come together more on the basis of strong physical attraction than any great meeting of minds or emotions. When he stayed over, they talked more about work than any other topic, mostly they just slept together and then Jeremy always had to rush off.

She'd been such a fool. She had swallowed all that garbage about things being on her own terms, not having to live like generations before her and having the freedom to choose, when all she'd done was fractionalise her own happiness for something that had never gone beyond the physical. How on earth had she not seen it before? Probably that was why it lasted as long as it did.

She sipped some of the cold water that seemed to be the only drink she could face today. She held the glass out towards the light, she loved those glasses, she'd picked them up years ago in the Dandelion Market for half nothing. Second-hand, but she had a feeling they'd only been taken out of the box and hardly used; even if they were old, they'd been safely stored. She smiled, tracing a droplet of condensation up the side of the glass before placing it on her tongue. God, she'd had a lucky escape. She was glad to have cut her ties with Jeremy. Strangely, with the breaking away from him, it felt as if her life had suddenly taken on a new direction.

As if to agree with her, the doorbell sounded out in the hallway. She jumped and glanced at her watch. They were early. She pulled her cardigan from the back of the sofa; the weather promised to be good, but she didn't want to take any chances on getting a chill.

'Hey.' Rob was standing with the passenger door held open for her. He leaned across and kissed her, lightly on the lips. It felt as if there was so much promise between them, but they were taking things slowly. After all, it wasn't as if the future was going to be without complications. She'd learned her lesson with Jeremy, this time she was being completely up front with what she wanted and what she could give. She was having a baby and she was only letting people into her life who were happy for her. Rob and Josh were as excited about the baby as she was; there was no room for games any more.

'Niamh, Niamh, you'll never guess what?' Josh was already wound up and red-faced at the prospect of a day at the zoo. He was obsessed with penguins and it was just one more endearing quality – she was certain, most boys his age would want lions, tigers and bears.

'I probably won't, you'd better tell me.' She looked across at Rob, who was smiling.

'Just one guess, go on, just one…'

'Okay, they've opened a new unicorn pen at the zoo?' she asked with as serious an expression as she could manage.

'No! Don't be silly, there are no such things as unicorns.' He started to laugh. 'Tell her Dad, they can't have unicorns, because they are magical. Even if there were any, we wouldn't be able to *see* them, would we?'

'No, Josh, you're right there,' Rob said, joining a snaking queue of traffic heading in the same direction as they were. It looked as if they weren't the only ones to decide to visit the Phoenix Park today. 'We won't be seeing any unicorns today.'

'So what's the big news?' Niamh teased Josh now. 'You better tell me before I burst with curiosity.' She laughed because Josh looked like *he* might explode if he didn't get to tell her exactly what it was.

'We're going to see your new house.' It came out in a rush and he looked as if with it he managed to catch his breath.

'We are?' she laughed, because there was no new house. Although she had only just begun to search, already she had a feeling that the cute house with a garden she'd thought would be hers might be a pipe dream.

'Tell her Daddy, tell her.' Josh was rocking over and back on his booster seat now. It was probably just her delicate constitution but Niamh thought she felt the car sway with the movement, and actually, it almost made her stomach heave.

'Go on then…' She looked across at Rob who was smiling with his eyes fixed on the road. There was something in the determined set of his mouth, as if he was trying not to give anything away, but when he glanced across at her, she could see he was almost as excited as Josh.

'Well, don't get your hopes up now, but one of our clients whose father passed away a year ago mentioned that they might be putting his house up for sale. It's probably going to need a bit of work, it hasn't been lived in for a few years, but the location is perfect and it sounded as if it might be just what you're looking for.'

'Daddy says there's a huge swing in the back garden and I can have a go on it today, but when the baby comes, I will be in charge of pushing her.' Josh swished his hand over and back. 'Gently, I can only push her very gently.'

'What if the baby is a boy?' Niamh was laughing again, too happy to care what the baby was, so long as it was healthy.

'Oh, cool, a boy baby would be even better, he can be in goal.'

'Well, Josh, a girl could be in goal too…' Rob said.

'Okay. Well, I get to swing on it today anyway,' which seemed to be the winning point in the conversation as far as Josh was concerned.

They drove for another half hour. Traffic was against them, but being a little further out from the city would suit Niamh just fine. She noticed too that the further they went, the nearer they were getting to where Rob and Josh lived.

'Now, it's just a bungalow at the end of a cul-de-sac, it's not Buckingham Palace.' A small nerve twitched in Rob's cheek, something Niamh had already learned was a sign he was nervous about something.

'You're so sweet,' she murmured.

'I'm just trying to get you sorted.'

'I know and I really appreciate it. Even if it's not the house for me, it's nice that you…' She stopped. It was just a house. But it was so much more than Jeremy had ever done for her and she smiled across at him now. 'Well, it's just nice,' she settled on before turning back and winking at Josh.

Rob was right. The bungalow would need some TLC. It hadn't been lived in for about three years, if the unopened post on the kitchen table was anything to go by. It was dated and faded and had all the hallmarks of an inelegantly built bungalow from the decade that taste forgot, but, the moment Niamh saw the place, she knew she had to have it.

For all its flaws, it was just a ten-minute walk from her parents' house and even closer to Rob and Josh's place. There were three tiny bedrooms, a sitting room, a kitchen and a large room that might have been a garage once, but the previous owner had turned it into a workshop.

'Apparently, he was a bit of a wood carver in his spare

time,' Rob said. There was plenty of evidence of the hobby scattered throughout the house, from cup coasters to a rustic clock that wouldn't have looked out of place hanging in a hunting lodge in the depths of Texas. 'But you know, in time, you could knock through here, make the whole back of the house into a kitchen-cum-family-room, windows all along to make the most of the garden.'

He was still talking, but Niamh had walked out into the garden. Josh had already explored the house and it held little interest for him, but the garden, well that was a whole other thing.

'Look at me, Niamh, look at how high I can go.' He was energetically to-ing and fro-ing from the old rope swing hanging from a huge willow tree at the very end of the garden, red-faced and happy.

'Isn't that like the trees at the back of the guest house in Ballycove?' Rob was at her side now.

'Yes. It's a willow and…' Niamh smiled up at him. 'I think it's a sign.'

'You like it?'

'I love it,' she said and she felt so happy she thought she might burst. 'I love it so much, I want to buy it right now and get moving on making it into a home for me and the baby.'

'I hope you'll be open to having guests over,' Rob said.

'Oh, Rob, nothing would make me happier.'

'Look, look what I've found.' Josh came racing towards them, with a tiny frog he had found near the border fence.

'Actually, maybe I'm just a little happier now,' she said, bending down to examine the frog, but really, just wanting to share in Josh's excitement before he crashed off into his next adventure.

'Well, here's to making each other happy every single day,' Rob said and he took her in his arms and kissed her and she knew that this was the first step to having her own family. At last, and it was all thanks to that little guest house in Ballycove.

39

Esme

The letter had arrived that morning, apparently.

'I was too busy until now to read it,' Marta said briskly, rubbing at some stain that had dared to settle into the top of the ottoman. 'It is from home.'

'Home?' Esme managed and she concentrated hard on keeping her expression neutral, but it was not proving easy. Esme couldn't remember even one occasion when anyone had contacted Marta from Spain. Mostly, it felt as if that part of Marta's life had never really happened, or if it did, it was so far away and so long ago that it was little more than an opaque shadow, hardly even real any more.

'Who is it from?' she asked carefully, because she knew there'd been a time when the one thing Marta feared more than anything else was the idea that her husband might find her and follow her here.

'It is not from him,' Marta said as if reading her thoughts.

'But it is about him. It is a letter from his sister-in-law. Isabel is married to my brother-in-law, Jóse Luis.'

She stopped for a moment as if wondering what to say next.

'So, she tracked you down and wrote to you?'

'She wrote to tell me that he is dead.'

'Who, your brother-in-law?'

'No, of course not, what difference does it make to me either way if Jóse Luis is alive or dead?' She stopped and Esme could only imagine that the apple hadn't fallen too far from the tree and perhaps one brother was as bad as the other.

'No, Ángel died earlier this year, it took them months to find me to tell me and Isabel wasn't even sure if this is the right address for me.' Marta sniffed, but then shivered, so Esme would know that she was certainly not about to shed any crocodile tears over a man who had almost killed her once.

'But she did?' Esme prompted. 'Track you down?'

'Yes, she managed to finally talk the local funeral director into giving her the address.'

'The funeral director?'

'I have put flowers on my parents' grave a few times each year, for their birthdays, their anniversary, you know, those times when if I'd been there, I would have cut flowers and placed them there myself.' There was heaviness about her voice now and it was one of those rare occasions when Esme could hear all her decades weigh on her shoulders heavily. She always thought of Marta as being a young woman, she forgot that time was passing for both of them.

'So, you could go back there now, back to the Basque Country that you loved so much, now that he's...' It seemed blunt to say dead, but really, Marta couldn't have gone back before because he was alive… 'Gone?'

'I suppose I can.' Marta settled back into her chair and Esme felt a small stab of guilt. It had been a long time since Marta had sat down and actually sunk into a chair, or at least it seemed that way to Esme. 'But for now, well…'

'Please, don't feel you have to stay just because of the guest house or me, it's so long since you were home, you must feel a great loneliness for it sometimes.'

Esme was saying the words, but she felt as if her insides were somersaulting. What on earth would she do without Marta here? How would she manage? Of course, she could get staff in to run the house, she could even get home help in to care for herself until she got her feet under her again, but she had a feeling it wouldn't be very long until some busybody social worker came knocking on her door and did their best to bully her into some sort of nursing home. It would be for her own good, of course, or at least that is what they would believe. All of that, though, Esme knew, was nothing next to the fact that she would miss Marta dearly if she wasn't here. Not that she'd ever said it, but Marta was as close to family as she had now. She stirred in her chair, but she couldn't get comfortable.

'Oof,' she groaned; it was a long time to spend sitting in one place day in and day out.

'Here, let me.' Marta was pulling out cushions from behind her, rearranging them, lifting her up a little further in the chair again. 'That's better, isn't it?'

'You really don't have to; I can do all this for myself.'

'I know that, Esme.' Marta settled down in the chair

opposite again, unfolded the letter and sat silently for a while. 'Maybe I will go back, you know, to see my parents' grave, to see the village, just to see the blueness of the skies again.'

'You should.' Esme felt a little part of her wither and die inside.

'But not yet.'

'Well, don't feel that you have to hang about for me, because I'll have you know...' Esme started again. She couldn't have Marta putting her life on hold for someone who wasn't even related to her.

'I don't,' Marta said crossly. 'Sometimes, you are a very silly old woman, Esme.'

'I'm not old and I'm not silly,' Esme snapped.

'You are being both now. I will go back, but not yet, not until the time is right.' And with that, she was up and rubbing her duster along the top of the coffee table. 'Now, I will make us both dinner and no more of this silly talk.'

Esme sank back into her dome chair again. It seemed that she couldn't pull herself up, her head, her shoulders, even her chin had slumped down into themselves. She moped there for what felt like a long time, plunging into a dark mood that she had no idea how to pull herself out of. This was exactly what she'd always worried about at the back of her mind. This was everything that was wrong with getting old, with needing other people, with being blind, with being laid up with a broken leg. She thought of the kid in the hospital, of his brittle cheeriness – why couldn't she have a measure of that about her? Why couldn't she dig it up from somewhere within her?

40

Phyllis

The last four days had been truly the darkest days Phyllis Courtney had ever lived through. They had been more difficult even than at the start of Kurt's illness when she had been completely alone and doing her best to hide the truth of it from everyone else, including and most especially from Kurt.

It had begun on Tuesday. It was a bleak day anyway, the sky had turned to dark pewter and the Irish Sea had pushed in a summer storm worse than Phyllis could ever remember in the month of August. The phone woke her in the early hours of the morning. A young girl, a guard it turned out, who sounded as if she was hardly old enough to take the bus across town on her own, let alone be left responsible for her Kurt.

'I am sorry, but your husband is here...' It was the middle of the night, well actually the early hours of the morning, and Phyllis had woken with the uneasy feeling that she had nodded off for five minutes in front of the telly, only to suddenly realise that she'd slept for five hours.

'Kurt? Kurt is there?' Still stupidly half asleep, she felt about the sofa for her reading glasses, as if they might help her to make sense of the voice on the phone. The television had switched from the documentary she'd been watching to those long-playing advertisements that masqueraded as entertainment. Phyllis pointed the remote control at the vaguely familiar woman trying to sell her insomniac audience gold jewellery that was not really gold. She muted her with a deliberateness that had little connection to the control she felt over anything else in life at this moment. 'Kurt is there... Where exactly?'

'Rathgar Garda Station.'

'Dear God, that's miles away.' Icy sweat veiled across her skin and she shivered, although the room was not cold. 'Sorry, I didn't mean... it's just how on earth did he get to Rathgar, we live in...'

'Dundrum,' the guard said. 'I know, your husband told us, but you also had it sewn onto his jacket, which is a brilliant help, by the way.'

'Oh, I don't understand, how on earth did he manage to get to Rathgar?' But actually, Phyllis couldn't understand how she'd fallen so deeply asleep that she hadn't heard him leave the house, she hadn't heard the door open and close, she hadn't missed him for five hours. Five hours. Anything could have happened to him. 'I fell asleep, I never fall asleep.'

'Caring for someone like your husband, if you're on your own, is going to wear you down, everyone has to sleep at some point,' the woman said at the other end of the phone; she sounded as if she was talking from experience. 'Anyway, the main thing is, he's safe and sound here. We can drop him back to you, or you can come and collect him.'

'Of course, I'll come, you've done enough already and, anyway, it might be even more unsettling for Kurt, arriving here in the middle of the night in a garda car.'

'Whatever you think is best. But if you're tired, we can use an unmarked car, have him with you in half an hour, give you time to sort yourself out before he gets there.'

'Well, it would be quicker, I suppose.' Because by the time she splashed some water on her face and drove all the way over to Rathgar and then managed to get him into the car for the journey home, it would be a good hour before they were settling in for what remained of the night. 'Thank you,' she said, although she felt more relief than gratitude.

Of course, Kurt had left the front door wide open when he'd made his escape. They were lucky he was alive, but Phyllis shivered when she thought about the fact that only two weeks earlier the house across the road had been burgled in the small hours. The man who lived there, ten years older than Kurt, had been badly beaten by the thugs who were just intent on taking every valuable they could lay their hands on. They'd let themselves in an unlocked, slightly ajar bathroom window – and there she'd been fast asleep with the front door wide open.

Phyllis shivered. She had thought that when Kurt had begun his new medication, he would at the very least be able to sleep at night. What if he never managed to sleep? How on earth would she manage to keep him safe? Fear twisted a knot in her stomach, so it felt as if even her breath was restricted by an invisible force she would never be free of, until her darling Kurt was so ill he couldn't leave his room. And then, of course, she was washed over with the sort of guilt that just tumbled every other thought and hope from her. God, she hated this disease.

As it turned out, Kurt had been wandering about the car park in the local shopping centre when he was spotted on CCTV. He hadn't managed to get to Rathgar on his own, but he'd been picked up by a patrol car and brought there for his own safety, until they could figure out where he'd come from.

It had taken the police four hours to track Phyllis down. Kurt had given them a dozen different telephone numbers, all of them incorrect, and he couldn't tell them where he lived, only that his wife would be very worried about him, which seemed to cause him even more agitation than the fact he was missing in the first place.

At least, when he did get home, against all the odds, he was calm and, after hugging her as if he'd been away on a mini-break, he yawned and toddled off to bed for the night. He slept soundly, as if he hadn't a care in the world. Phyllis on the other hand felt as if her whole world was caving in on her and she knew that they had now crossed into territory where she would need more help, if she was going to keep him safe.

*

It took Phyllis two days to find the words to tell Rob about what had happened. She needed him to hear exactly what she wanted to say, not just fly into a panic and worry about how they were coping. He'd be keen to take on a whole lot more responsibility than she wanted to lay on his doorstep. She needed, as they say, to get her ducks in a row.

'I can't believe you didn't ring me when you realised he was missing.'

'Oh, darling, he was never actually missing, not as far as I was concerned. I just fell asleep, it's really much more my fault that it was your father's. And he was hardly outside the door when he was in the safe hands of the gardaí.'

She laughed, a tinkling sound that didn't give away the hollow feeling that had taken up residence in her stomach since it happened.

'Mum, you're not getting the chance to rest properly, I can see it in your eyes. You haven't had a good night's sleep since we stayed at the guest house, you look positively ragged.'

'Well, thank you for that.' She pushed against his arm jokingly. She'd given up worrying about the dark circles under her eyes; there were more important things to think about now.

'Look, just one night a week, an occasional weekend. If we get someone to come in and stay with him, so you can go to bed at least, you can't go on like this... surely you can see that.' He reached out and took her hand. 'Please, Mum, I'm begging you, for both your sakes. It's...'

'You're right.' She held her hands up, because he *was* right. Phyllis had never felt so worn out in her life. And it wasn't just about her. It was all very well heroically keeping the show on the road, but if the other night had taught her anything, it was that she couldn't keep Kurt safe unless she had some help. 'That's what I wanted to talk to you about, I've already been tracking something down.'

'Oh, thank God.' Rob breathed a sigh of obvious relief. 'Tell me you've found someone who'll move in with you, or at least stay a few nights to let you have a decent sleep.'

'Actually, it was Meera who sorted us out,' she said, still not sure how her GP had managed to move things so quickly, although it helped that they had good insurance, one of the things that Kurt had always insisted on. Just in case. 'Meera has managed to get Kurt two nights' respite every two weeks in a very nice retirement home. They specialise in dementia care and probably, long term, they are suggesting it's better if he gets familiar with somewhere now, so if the time comes when he has to...' She didn't want to think about it too much, it was enough to know that maybe one day they'd have to take that route. 'She gave me a number for a private care group, too. They're sending in a carer two nights a week, it's expensive, but again, our insurance will go a long way in covering the costs, so...'

'Oh, Mum, I can't tell you how relieved I am.' But Rob looked at her now, as if suddenly he realised what she'd done. 'You wouldn't have told me about Dad going missing until you had it all sorted out, would you?'

'Oh, don't be cross with me, I had to make sure that we could suit ourselves and Kurt is very happy with what we've organised.' She smiled at him now.

'I wouldn't have marched him into a nursing home, you know?' Rob shook his head.

'I know that, darling, I know, but I didn't want you to feel you had to come over here and watch over us either.' And that was it, really. Already, she could see, life was beginning to expand for her son. He was making room in it not just for

Niamh, but he was talking about the new baby too. There was no way she was going to put any extra pressure on him, not now it finally looked as if he was moving forward with his life.

'Okay, okay, fair enough.' He smiled and looked out at the garden where Kurt and Josh were busy pottering about the vegetable patch, both of them on their knees with trowels, hands covered in clay, chatting happily as if they hadn't a care in the world. 'Since everything seems to be ticking over so well here, I wonder... I was going to maybe do a barbecue next weekend, have a few people round.'

'How lovely, of course, we'd love to come, anyone there we haven't already met?' She couldn't remember the last time Rob had organised any kind of party or gathering and she had a feeling there might be an agenda behind this one.

'Well, actually, I'm inviting Niamh and her family round too, I thought it might be a nice chance for us all to get to know each other...'

'Oh, Rob, I'm so pleased...' she said and she really, really was.

September

The season's end

41

Esme

Esme couldn't help fussing over the tea tray. Well, it was just nice to be able to move around and pick over things again, even if Marta kept going on about using her walking aid so as not to put too much pressure on her leg. And, it wasn't every day they had afternoon tea. Cora had organised it earlier in the week, just as she'd promised when she left to go back to her own life. Esme wasn't sure which she was looking forward to more, catching up with Cora or finally getting the measure of Michael Doyle.

'This place hasn't changed a bit since we stayed here years ago,' Michael said and Esme could feel his eyes dancing around the hall.

'It probably hasn't much, except like me everything is a bit older, the doors creak more loudly and if I don't manage to do something about that roof, I'm not so sure how much longer we'll be able to use the top-floor rooms.'

That was the truth; even if Esme did a good job hiding it from herself these days, there was no hiding it from a man who spent his life working in the building trade.

'Oh, from the looks of it, there's not that much to do to get it patched up. A few days with decent weather and I could have that secured for the winter as good as Fort Knox. If I ran some insulation up there too, you wouldn't know yourselves when the cold weather comes.'

'Could you do that? Would you be able to take on a job like that, wouldn't it be very...' It would be expensive, but there was money in the kitty from the summer season. They could definitely stretch to a patch-up job and, even if it was expensive, there wasn't much of a choice. So far, the only one who had looked at it had told her it was only good for demolition, but then, Paschal Fenlon had high hopes to build a dozen holiday homes on the site.

'I'd be delighted to take it on for you. How about we say, weather permitting, the first weekend you're closed up? There'll be a bit of a mess, but if we have all hands on deck, we'll get through it quickly. I'll organise all the materials and do the job myself, in return for two nights' bed and breakfast – I think Cora would love that.'

'Really?' Esme was afraid in case she'd misheard him. 'You'd do that, you'd come in here and fix the roof and...?'

'It's the very least I can do. I have a lot to thank you both for. From what Cora tells me about when she stayed here, you steered us back together with your wise words and kindness. Even if I fixed every creaking door and leaking window for you, I'd still be in your debt, Esme.'

'I was right about you.' Esme smiled.

'Oh?'

'Yes, I had a feeling you were a good egg. I'm so glad things have worked out for you both.' She missed having

Cora here. She'd always been there at the right moment to get her extra sugar for her coffee when Marta wasn't watching. 'I hope you get the new start you both deserve.'

'Let me tell you, it won't be for the want of trying. We're already planning our summer holidays next year,' Michael said.

'Finally doing the Camino Way, then?'

'Well, maybe not next year, but we are going to go away somewhere for a week or two, just the two of us, and maybe, if you'll have us, we'll stay here for a long weekend near the end of the season?' He laughed. 'Maybe next year I'll tackle another job or two for you, if you're willing to put up with us again?'

'Of course we'll have you, in fact we'll give you our best room and I'll even invite you to dinner.' It was a funny thing, but only a few weeks ago, Esme had wondered if there would be another season – what with the age of the house and Fenlon telling her it was only fit for demolition. Now she felt stronger, she knew, she might not go on forever, but the same didn't apply to the Willows, if Marta wanted to keep it going after she was gone.

'Now, there's an offer we can't refuse,' Michael said. She heard him move forward in his chair. 'This place is really very special. You and Marta – the way Cora talked about you both, she made it sound almost magical.'

'Really? I'm not sure I've done very much this year; it's mostly down to Marta. All I've been doing for the whole summer is sitting here…' It really had been the most unusual season. Sitting here, listening to it all happening around her, welcoming people and saying goodbye – in hindsight, it had actually been quite enjoyable.

'You know...' he said and then he cleared his throat, as if what he was going to say next was important, 'you've looked after Cora and, if it wasn't for this place, she might as easily have ended up going over to our son in London.'

'Wherever she went, I'm sure she would have come back to you. Some people are meant to be together.' Although, Esme had wondered for a while if Joel Lawson had had his way, he might have turned Cora's head forever, but there was no need for Michael to know that now.

'I'm not so sure I deserved her when she left me at first. I mean, I wasn't a bad husband, but we didn't have much fun, I can see that now.'

'Well, I'm sure there are better times ahead.'

'I'm going to make damn sure there are and part of that will be coming out to Ballycove sometimes for a long walk on the beach and maybe we'll drop up to you and say hello.'

'I'd love that, so would Marta. She'll make us coffee and complain that we Irish haven't the first clue about anything.'

'I can hear you – I am right here,' Marta called from beyond the door.

'Oh, don't worry, I know you are.' Esme shook her head and a devilish grin played about her lips. 'Honestly, just because I'm almost blind, I'm not deaf or stupid.'

'No, but you're very stubborn.' Marta laughed.

'Right, that's it,' Cora said, placing a cake stand on the table. 'We have sandwiches, Victoria sponge and some treats I picked up in the cake shop on my way.'

Next to her, Marta placed the tea set down with a rattle of saucers and spoons. 'What are you two whispering about?'

'Well, I was just going to ask Esme if she wouldn't mind...' Michael paused as if he wasn't sure if he should continue.

'Go on, tell me, I won't bite.'

'It's silly really, I was out here one night and the garden smelled just beautiful. I'm thinking I might overhaul our old plot at home – when I do, could I get some cuttings...?'

'Of course, take all you want.' And a little part of Esme felt as if in some way it was like extending the guest house. 'I would love it if you did – you'll have to take some willow. Later in the year, when I'm properly up on my feet again, I'll sort out pots for you. You could have your own slice of the guest house right outside your door.'

'That's exactly what I thought.' And then Michael leaned forward and began to set up cups and saucers for each of them and Esme felt as if, somehow, she had just witnessed a very special happy ending.

*

There was little more than a hen's kick between the sound of Cora and Michael's car leaving and the arrival of what Esme knew to be the sleek purr of Joel Lawson's engine. It had been weeks since he'd returned to Dublin, and, from what she could gather, this would be his final stay in Ballycove. The church roof was all but complete; all that remained was an inspection and signing off of some paperwork for the insurance company.

Esme was glad he and Cora had missed each other, but

when he arrived into the hallway she called him over to sit with her for a while.

'I have fresh coffee – just grab a cup from the dining room,' she whispered conspiratorially. 'You've done a fine job. Everyone in the village is full of praise at how well the church looks,' she said as he sank into the chair opposite her.

'Well, in that case, my work here really is done,' he laughed, 'it's time to let the painters get on with it.' They sat in silence for a while, Esme wondering if he knew that Cora and Michael were happily reunited.

'Have you heard of Movember?' Better to beat about the bush for a while, she decided. It didn't matter if he thought she was completely dotty, in many ways, she enjoyed the idea of it.

'Movember?'

'Yes, you know, it's November but with an M,' she said, as though speaking to a simpleton.

'Yes. Of course. It's been around for a while now. I think it's to raise money for some charity or other.'

'Isn't that funny?' She giggled and then she leaned forward, as if to collude with him. 'Tell me, would you do it?'

'Would I do what?'

'Shave it off, of course.'

'Shave off what?' He sounded as if he had no idea what she was talking about.

'Your moustache.' She sighed; honestly, you'd have thought he'd be able to keep up.

'But I don't have a moustache.'

'You don't?' That was disappointing. She'd pictured him

as dark, broad-shouldered, moustached and, above all, rakish.

'No. Never have.'

'Oh dear, well, that really is a shame.' She leaned back in her chair again and she thought she heard him breathe a sigh of relief, until she smiled and said, 'Perhaps you should consider one. I really feel that a moustache might be the making of you.'

And they both laughed at that.

42

Phyllis

The phone call from Esme was exactly what Phyllis needed.

'Come to Ballycove, just for a few days even. It would do us both good.'

'I can't be marching in on top of you just when you're about to close up for the season.' Although Phyllis had suggested it herself originally, but that had been when she'd hoped Kurt would come too. Now she knew it would be her first trip to Ballycove alone.

'Don't be silly, I'd love to see you. I'm just getting my foot under me again; it'll be as good as a holiday for both of us.'

It seemed Esme had everything organised. There was no denying she'd need a little help; she was managing with a walking aid at this stage and in a week's time the house would be empty of guests. Apparently then Cora's husband was going to do a major job on the roof and insulate the whole attic space for her – Esme was as excited as a child at the prospect of having the place torn up and put back together again. Years ago, Phyllis and Kurt had gone to stay there once in autumn and it had been lovely. Perhaps she'd be doing Esme a favour by going to stay with her for a few days. Yes, it would do them both good, she decided.

'If you're sure.' Phyllis took a long deep breath. Even thinking about going back to Ballycove felt as if it was unknotting some of the tension that strained along her spine too deeply these days. Kurt would be staying over in the respite home, he was delighted she was getting the chance of a mini-break, although she had to remind him about fifty times that she would be going. The fresh sea air might be exactly what she needed to wash away some of the worry and guilt of knowing that he was drifting from her and she was helpless to pull him back.

'I'd love it.' She heard her own voice wistful and grateful. Yes. The guest house was exactly where she needed to be now.

43

Niamh

Niamh rested her hand on her slightly protruding baby bump. It had become automatic at this stage, touching her tummy, stopping for a moment to consider all she had to look forward to. Sometimes, she couldn't quite believe how quickly her life had transformed from where it had been just a few months earlier. It felt as if her world had split into before and after her visit to Ballycove. If she hadn't gone there, she probably would have terminated her pregnancy. God, it still made her hands sweat just thinking of it, it had been such a close call, but then how could she have ever known she could be this content?

Facing Jeremy at work in the first weeks after she broke things off was every bit as hard as she had expected, but somehow, it became easier. She didn't love him, not after all that had happened. It turned out she'd been wrong about him. He *had* been the man her mother believed him to be all along. Age and great wisdom had meant that her mother would never breathe a word of those thoughts out loud, but

Niamh knew it and she loved her mother even more for not saying, *I could have told you so.*

The funny thing about deciding to go ahead with the pregnancy and ending her relationship with Jeremy was that it seemed to open up a crack in her world and somehow it had allowed a whole new host of people into her life. There was Cora Doyle for one. They spoke every other week now. Cora had taken on her pregnancy as if Niamh was her own daughter and there was a constant stream of messages on her phone with suggestions for supplements, baby store deals and articles about how to look after yourself when you're pregnant.

'I'll be so spoiled if I keep following your advice,' she had joked with Cora more than once.

'Not at all, or no more than you deserve at any rate.' Cora was adamant, they were meeting up again before the birth, she had even offered to come and stay afterwards for a while to give Niamh a chance to catch her breath.

It seemed these days Niamh was inundated with offers of help. Suddenly, she knew what it was to be surrounded by people who loved her, not on their terms, when they could fit her around their own family, like Jeremy had, but on her terms. It felt as if Cora, Rob, Josh and Phyllis were all squeezing in and filling up any space that might be left over, so Niamh was far from alone in being a lone parent; if anything it felt as if an entire village was behind her. Even Esme was crocheting booties, gloves and hats – enough to fill a whole maternity ward, according to Cora.

'Hey, wakey, wakey!' Rob called as he held out the end of a tape measure before her. 'Kitchens don't just measure themselves, you know.' He was laughing, those gorgeous eyes dancing with the sort of good humour that Niamh had only recently realised Jeremy had never possessed.

'I was actually planning,' Niamh joked back, but of course, they both knew she was daydreaming. She was imagining what the bungalow would be like when the baby arrived and light flooded in across where her breakfast table was going to stand in the centre of the soon-to-be-extended kitchen.

'Sure you were.' Rob shook his head and tucked a pencil behind his ear. She suspected he was the kind of man who would slip easily into marriage and spending the weekend doing DIY jobs about the house. Out in the garden, he had already put up a bird table – it was unfortunate that the birds were not yet enamoured by Josh thundering past to the swing at the end, but they would get used to it. The garden was long and private and facing east, there would be room to sit outside and place a paddling pool at the far end when the summer months trapped whatever heat they could. For now, Josh was enjoying the swing, but Niamh planned to make it into the sort of garden where they could have long lazy lunches and children could play or just hang out and shoot the breeze when they got a little older.

'Well, don't get too carried away yet, wait until we see how good we are at assembling kitchens before we go starting on anything more ambitious.' Rob took the pencil from behind his ear and jotted down the measurements neatly.

'I'm so...' Happy, Niamh wanted to say, but a little part of her was afraid to tempt fate. They were going to pick out her new kitchen today. It felt as if most of the house was being kitted out from IKEA but she was short on time. The sale of her own flat had already gone through and she'd have to move out within the next week or so. They ran the tape measure around the kitchen twice, just to be sure.

'Me too.' Rob pulled her close, kissing her forehead lightly before holding her at arm's length for a moment and looking into her eyes. 'It's going to be great, just perfect,' he said and she knew he was right. She loved the cottage; it was everything she'd hoped for and she'd managed to get it at the right price.

Far more than just taking on the conveyance work and helping her to get the place straightened out, Rob had become so much more than just a friend. Sometimes, she wondered at the fact that she had settled for someone like Jeremy for so long, when there was a man like Rob waiting in the wings, if only she'd known it. It seemed every weekend there was something to do, somewhere to go and, sometimes, there was just the two of them, in her little flat while Josh spent time at his granny's, and Niamh and Rob fell quietly, madly in love with each other.

And then there were Phyllis and Kurt. Niamh knew she was lucky to have met Rob's father when she did; each time now they visited, she could see him sink a little further away from them. He was rapidly being devoured by a disease they were trying hard to slow down with every medical intervention available. Although she managed to do a fairly decent job of covering over how much she worried about him with Rob, Phyllis occasionally let her guard down with Niamh and so they'd taken to having lunch together now and again. Phyllis was good company, she was vital and alive and Niamh enjoyed every time they met up, because although they did talk about Kurt, they also talked about a million other things under the sun.

'Going to Ballycove will do you the world of good,' she told Phyllis when they met for lunch.

'Apart from...' It was obvious to everyone that Phyllis was struggling not to feel guilty for trying to carry on as normal, while her husband got used to staying in a respite room every fortnight. 'I'm really looking forward to it. It'll be a bit like it was back when it was just Esme and me in our little flat, before either of us fell in love or got married or got old!' She made a face and then smiled. 'It'll be good for both of us, to catch up and have something to...'

'To look forward to?'

'Does that sound terrible?'

'Oh, Phyllis, of course not, you need to have things to look forward to and so does Esme.' It was the truth. Niamh thought her heart would break when she imagined what it must be like to have your whole life pulled from under you the way Phyllis and Kurt had.

'I just feel so guilty, you know...' And there it was, Phyllis's husband of fifty years was slipping away from everything he knew and she still had a good life stretching out ahead of her. These last few weeks, he'd become an old man, a really old man, the sort who could easily wither away into someone unrecognisable. Phyllis had confided in Niamh that sometimes she thought death would have been easier to cope with. Whatever notions she'd had that they could stretch out their time together were well and truly dying in the water now.

'You're just grieving, that's normal. You have nothing to

feel guilty about; it's just the way things have turned out. He wants you to be happy, don't let him down now. He told Rob, he knew in his heart this is how things were always going to turn out for him and he has come to terms with it. He's worked so hard to make sure everything is taken care of; it would be such a waste if you were to just wallow in enough misery for you both.'

The fact was, the doctors had said Kurt could live for years, but they all knew he'd become quite frail so quickly there wasn't that much time left, for which he would have been glad; he'd never wanted to be a burden.

'Of course, you're right. And we have this new baby to look forward to.' Phyllis reached out and placed her hand across Niamh's expanding belly. It was the strangest thing but her baby had brought so many people into her life and it felt as if everyone was looking forward to the birth almost as much as Niamh.

The day she had attended her first scan was probably the *best* day ever. Everything had just gone so perfectly, she couldn't have planned it better. Her mother had offered to bring her to the appointment, not to go in with her, but when Niamh said she'd be welcome to, she thought her mother might burst with pride.

Afterwards, they'd sat in the car for over half an hour just gazing at the black and white strips, blurry combinations of shadows and light, but there, Niamh convinced herself, was her daughter and she had never seen anything so perfectly beautiful before.

44

Cora

Cora and Michael walked out of the travel agents like a pair who'd just won the lottery. It felt that way to Cora, at least. In two weeks' time it would be her thirty-first wedding anniversary and all right, perhaps it was a close shave, but they were going to celebrate it together.

Michael told her if he had one regret it was that he hadn't pushed the boat out for their thirtieth. She could see it made him squirm now, even thinking about the fact that their pearl wedding anniversary had come and gone and he hadn't even so much as bought a card for Cora, never mind a string of pearls or a pair of earrings. Esme told them it was never too late and so this year he'd picked up a gift he said hoped would backdate to the previous year and this year's gift was a holiday for just the two of them. They had a lot of making up for time lost to do and, even if he had never been much of a one for travelling, she had a feeling he was really looking forward to this holiday as much as she was. Truly, Esme was right – it was never too late to start again.

In the weeks since Cora had come back to Cherrywood

Crescent, she felt as if their lives had completely transformed. They'd never been busier, but it suited them, between long walks together and mucking in to put a few things right in the Willows, they'd both lost weight. Tanya even asked Cora if she'd joined a gym. It was, Cora knew, Tanya's idea of a compliment. She was undoubtedly one of those women who thought you could never be too glamorous or too thin.

And yet, Cora realised that, in spite of what all the other women on Cherrywood Crescent had warned her of, Tanya had not made a move on Michael; if anything, she'd done her level best to get them back together.

'I really missed you.' Tanya threw her arms around Cora when she realised she was back for good. And Cora knew she meant it. It turned out they were not just neighbours, they actually were friends. They might not pop into each other's houses or watch the soap operas together, but Tanya was the one looking out for her when the other women on Cherrywood Crescent were probably just gossiping behind her back. Tanya, the woman who couldn't boil an egg, had come into her home and insisted that everything be made as perfect as it could be for her.

'Good God, I was so afraid you wouldn't like it, but I knew, someone had to take the place in hand, you've been far too soft on Michael over the years.' She smiled. 'Are you sure you like the sofa?'

'Oh my God, Tanya, I love everything about it.' And maybe Tanya was right, maybe Cora had been a bit soft for far too long. Maybe the best thing she'd ever done was to put herself first and run away to Ballycove. 'It was above and beyond though. I mean, even the photographs, how much time did that take? Gathering them all up and then deciding how to hang them?' Because there was no way Michael would have done that in a million years, he just wouldn't have seen the point of it.

'Never mind that, it was worth it.' Tanya waved her away with talons that were a striking shade of electric blue today, perfectly matching her earrings. 'Honestly, I'd have rehung the entire Tate Gallery just to make sure you came back, the other women would completely ignore me on the Crescent if you weren't here, Cora.'

If how Cora saw Tanya changed, it was nothing compared to how things had changed in her relationship with Michael. These days her once cooking-phobic husband had all but taken over the kitchen. And it wasn't just scrambled eggs on toast either; just the other evening, he'd whipped out his phone to look up recipes. Whereas before he couldn't take his eyes off the television, these days she couldn't remember the last time they'd switched on the TV.

It was as if everything between them had been turned on its head somehow and even Cora felt as if she'd changed. Sometimes she caught him looking at her when he thought she wasn't aware of it. He'd ask her what she was thinking of; perhaps he was wondering if she was thinking about Joel Lawson, maybe regretting that she hadn't chosen him instead. They didn't speak about that night. But maybe it was the reason why Michael worked so hard to make sure no one would come along and turn her head again.

'Cora.' Michael's voice at the back door woke her from her thoughts. 'I picked up two lovely steaks in the butcher's if you fancy them for dinner tonight.' He was putting shopping into the fridge and cupboards when she walked into the kitchen.

'Great,' she said, taking down the chopping board to slice an onion.

'Oh, no.' He was standing behind her back, his arms wrapped around her. 'No, no. I'll cook. What if we eat in the garden, maybe you could bring a glass of wine outside and relax?' His voice was whispering in her ear and she felt that familiar stirring of love for him within her.

'We don't really need to eat just yet, do we?' she asked, still in his arms and turning to face him. 'I mean, it's just the two of us, surely we could…' She reached up and kissed him, long, slow and lingering, so there was no doubt of what she would much prefer to do before she sat in the garden and ate dinner.

'Oh, Cora.' His voice a moan as much as a whisper. 'I love you so much.'

'And I love you too,' she said, leading him up the stairs to show him exactly how much she still loved him and, it turned out, that was a great deal more than even she had realised at the start of the summer.

45

Esme

It was the same every year, even this year: once they'd closed the Willows for the season, Marta and Esme sank into a routine of their own making. With each passing day now, Esme felt as if she was getting stronger. She could navigate her way carefully around the ground floor of the house, although Marta was driving her cuckoo with constantly reminding her to use her walking aid. Because there were no guests and therefore no breakfasts to make or beds to change, Marta moved a lot more slowly now. She no longer whooshed through Esme's room, throwing back the curtains, depositing tea at her elbow before the crows had a chance to open their eyes in the tall willows outside. Instead, she tapped gently on the door, sometimes after nine o'clock, and they had a leisurely breakfast, with Esme having the time to dress and tidy herself up, going at her own pace.

'We are getting there,' Marta said one morning as she placed the tea pot on the table before them.

'We are. Not long now.' Esme was due back at the hospital

later in the day and she had high hopes that they would suggest stairs were her next challenge.

'All in good time.' Marta sniffed. She'd warned Esme often enough about running before she could walk. Pah, Esme thought every time, that would be a fine thing.

'You know, once we get the all-clear, there's no reason why you can't go and visit your village again.' Esme decided to broach the subject that had weighed on her mind for the last couple of weeks.

'Yes, of course, and I've told you often, all in good time.' Marta was scraping the porridge from the bottom of the saucepan, emptying it into both their bowls.

'I really don't want you to put it off for too long.' Esme began again, because the more she'd thought about it, the more she knew that the right thing to do was to send Marta away and hope she came back again.

'Look, let's be sensible.' Marta blew out a long, exasperated breath. 'You are eighty-two years old, Esme. You are recovering from a broken leg...'

'Yes, but I want you to know, that shouldn't hold you back.'

'But of course it's holding me back.' Marta banged down her spoon with a temper that rarely extended to anything beyond stains she couldn't remove from a hand towel or weather that refused to clear up for her daily walk. 'How do you propose we get you up sixty steps into an airplane when you haven't even walked up the stairs in your own home?'

'Me?' Esme must have said, her voice was strangled with emotion though and it sounded more like a croak, as if she was clearing her throat. 'I hadn't thought, I mean, I hadn't expected that you would want me to...' Esme began to cry, but her tears were a mixture of so many warm, happy emotions that she could hardly say much more.

'Oh, Esme, stop this crying now, it's not your fault that you've...'

'Oh, Marta, darling, don't you see, I'm not upset, I'm just so happy that you want me to come along with you.'

'Well, of course you'd come along with me. You didn't think I'd go without you?' she sighed again, a dramatic sound that Esme imagined coincided with much shaking of her head. 'What would be the point in going on my own, when I've told you so much about the Basque Country? I want you to come along, to meet my neighbours, to see where I lived and...'

'To drink your horrible coffee.' Esme made a show of shivering and wrinkling her nose.

'Yes, that too, although, you know what they say...'

'No.'

'It is impossible to teach an old dog new tricks.' Marta leaned forward and poured tea for both of them. 'We will have coffee, proper coffee later in the day,' she said, but Esme could hear the smile in her voice and she thought once more of how much she'd grown to love this woman. She was warmed to her core to know that one day, when she was resting up in Shanganagh cemetery next to Colm and the rest of her family, Marta would have this place. She would know how much she'd always meant to Esme, even if neither of them had been very good at saying it over the years.

'Well, how is it going?' Cora asked when she dropped over for afternoon tea later. Michael had begun mending the roof the previous week and he had promised to secure the rattling windows and maybe, if he had time, begin to draught proof some of the doors before winter took hold of the village.

'Honestly, it's like a concentration camp.' Esme sighed. 'Marta has me doing every exercise twice as often as I need to, you'd think I was training to do a marathon at the end of it all.'

'I heard that.' Marta placed a tray with coffee for three on the table before them.

'You were meant to, I didn't exactly whisper,' Esme said, but her tone betrayed great fondness in her voice far more than her words. 'And you, is it good to get back to normal? How is school?'

'It's different to before,' Cora said. 'It's different.'

'Isn't that what you wanted?' Marta poured her a cup.

'Well, yes, I suppose it is.' Cora thought about it for a minute. 'I wouldn't go back to how things were before, if that's what you're asking.'

'I knew a woman once...' Esme ran her finger across her upper lip, as if trying to remember the woman's name.

'Here we go,' Marta said, leaning forward and placing Esme's hand next to her piping hot coffee cup, so she touched it briefly with her finger.

'It's a story worth telling,' Esme muttered.

'Tell me, go on, I want to hear.' Cora reached out a hand and touched Esme's arm.

'You see.' Esme's voice had grown stronger, or at least, it felt that way, as if she'd resurrected some part of herself that had been drifting away at the start of the summer. What she had to say *was* important, maybe it had taken being stuck here in that dome chair for the whole summer to realise it. Marta just smiled, glad that her vitality was returning.

'Her name was Violet Standish. She had grown up in the big house – you know the sort, while we were having bread and butter sandwiches with a sprinkle of sugar for a treat, they were tucking into Victoria sponge.' Esme smiled at the memory. 'Anyway, the Standish family fell on hard times and everything was sold. Violet ended up living with her sister in a small house in the village and she spent most of her life counting her pennies and very thankful to have what she had. Then, just as we were ringing in the year 2000, word travelled about the village that the Standish family had come into a legacy. It was out of nowhere apparently, some long-forgotten relative had made their fortune in America. The inheritance ran to millions of dollars, or so they said. Of course, by this point, poor Violet was eighty-five if she was a day. She'd forgotten how to spend money. She'd been so busy cutting her cloth to suit her measure that she'd lost track of how to make life more comfortable if she spent it on little things, like Victoria sponge or central heating for her cottage or even a decent coat to wear to church on a Sunday.'

'I think Cora probably has a decent coat and…' Marta murmured and rolled her eyes good-naturedly.

'Oh, I know that, but what I'm saying is, she's come into a turn of good times. Cora's legacy is that instead of winning her fortune back, she's won a second chance at happiness in her marriage.'

'Yes but…' Cora began and stopped when Esme shook her head.

'You haven't let me finish.' Esme sipped her coffee, placed the cup thoughtfully down on the saucer, her fingers carefully fanned about the sides to make sure it was all steady. 'Poor Violet Standish, when she died, it turned out she had millions in the bank and hardly any food in her fridge. She had an open fire in the kitchen and no fuel in her shed and she was wearing layers of threadbare cardigans to keep warm, when she could have had the whole place kitted out twenty times over and bought a wardrobe full of furs and cashmere if she'd fancied it.'

'So, you're saying to enjoy my good fortune?'

'I'm saying you deserve it, make peace with the fact that your life is what you'd hoped it might be. I'm saying that it does no good to be like Violet Standish and continue to live as if your luck hasn't changed. I think you should more than enjoy it, I think you should bask in it.'

'Okay, that sounds like very good advice to me,' Marta said, throwing her hands up in the air and then racing off towards the clothes line as a light mist began to stretch across the garden from the sea below.

'Hmm, I suppose, it'll just take some time to get used to how things have changed between us.'

'I'm sure it'll all settle down before you know it.'

'Maybe. But maybe the problem wasn't completely with Michael either and that is niggling at me too. It's hard to explain.'

'Well, start with something small.' It was always best, it was what Esme always did, with her little stories.

'It's the curtains,' Cora started.

'The curtains? What on earth have the curtains got to do with anything?' Esme smiled but her eyes narrowed as if they might see more than was her ration these days.

'You see, I always had this dream that one day, when Connor was gone off into the world and it was just the two of us, we'd sit down to dinner each evening and chat and laugh and look out into the garden and I'd be... happy.'

'And aren't you doing that?'

'Well, yes, but... Oh, don't take any notice of me, I'm just being silly.'

'It's not silly if it's how you feel.'

'Okay, well, in my mind's eye, the kitchen probably didn't look half as good as it does now, Michael and I would have lots to talk about, there'd be a spark of attraction between us and, on the window, I would have beautiful billowing white curtains.'

'So?'

'Well, all the while I was busy criticising Michael for not making an effort, but the fact is, Esme, I was perfectly well able to paint my own kitchen if I'd been bothered and...' She rolled her eyes and whispered the next few words, because it was actually mortifying that she was admitting to this. 'At the very least, I should have gone out and bought the curtains, hung the bloody things and maybe made an effort too.'

'Ah, I see...' Esme reached over and took Cora's hand. 'Is that all that's worrying you? A touch of guilt because Michael has made such a huge effort?'

'I suppose it is.'

'Well, you've got two choices. You can either tell Michael, confess that you were maybe a little bit responsible for the fact that your marriage almost died right there between the pair of you, or you can sit back and let him continue to spoil you rotten.'

'What would you do?'

'Me? I wouldn't worry too much about it.' Esme stopped then and smiled, an unfathomable expression on her face. 'Actually, maybe I do know what I'd do...'

She got up and reached behind her, feeling her way along the shelf at her back until she found what she was looking for. She opened the guest book to an empty page where no guests were booked in for that day.

'There you go...' she said, 'well, then read it out for me.'

'I...' Cora was laughing too hard to say the words out loud, but when she eventually caught her breath they both began to laugh at the old saying. '*A good word never broke a tooth.*'

'That's good advice, indeed,' Marta said. Esme just smiled, because she was much too wise to say another word.

October

Epilogue

A bonfire. Esme loved bonfires, especially in the dark months. She wasn't sure who had organised it, but she told the young man who arrived earlier in the week that he was welcome to the old chairs that were stacked at the back of the shed. They were eaten with woodworm and what better end for them than to give heat and pleasure to the village on a cold winter's night.

'You can't be serious?' Marta huffed.

'Oh but I am.'

Esme had called Paschal Fenlon the previous afternoon. She needed to talk to him and wondered if he wouldn't like to bring them both to the bonfire. After all, she reasoned, he had a fine car and he still seemed set on having the Willows if her new friend Marjory was to be believed. Apparently, he had all but submitted planning permission to the council with his plans for the site.

Esme smiled when she heard the front doorbell ring. At this time of year, with the guest house closed up for the season, he could no longer just amble about the place at his leisure.

'Ah, Paschal, how lovely. I'm really looking forward to this, so is Marta.'

'Humph.' Marta grunted. She wasn't in the humour for small talk, especially with the likes of Paschal Fenlon.

They had booked their tickets to fly from Dublin to Spain in January. In fairness Marta had booked them, on the computer of all things. Even the passports had been managed without Esme having to leave the house. If Marta was a bit grumpy, Esme thought on this occasion that maybe she deserved a free pass.

Paschal bundled the two ladies into his big ugly jeep. It was surprisingly plush, Esme noted, although the overpowering aroma of air freshener almost took her breath away. It was just a short drive to the bonfire and then Paschal gallantly escorted her to where her friends from the choir had set aside some chairs for them – a little back from the fire, but near enough to feel the warmth of it when it was lit and close enough so Esme could hear the excited chatter of the village children nearby.

It was a magical evening, her first real outing since the summer, because she couldn't bear the idea of anyone seeing her in a wheelchair or using the walking aid the physio had insisted on. She had standards, after all.

'So, what now?' Paschal was at her elbow as soon as the flames began to die down and the noise from the nearby crowds turned from childish excitement to the voices of adults, patrolling the fire to make sure it wasn't abused by any silly youngsters bent on making dangerous fun.

'Oh, back to the Willows, I suppose.' Esme looked at Marta who was even less likely to go anywhere but home than she was. 'And I thought, maybe we could have a chat about the place on our way.' She smiled, keeping her voice as light as if she had wonderful news that would absolutely make his day.

'Great,' he rubbed his hands together as if delighted his plan had worked out after all.

'So,' she said, once he sat beside her and turned on the engine. Marta leaned a little forward in the back of the car, Esme could almost feel her holding her breath.

'So, indeed? You've got some good news for me?' he drawled as if it had always been a foregone conclusion.

'I have, Paschal, indeed I have.' She smiled sweetly. 'You see, I've managed to get the roof fixed. A lovely man, a husband of one of our guests, has come over and put those slates to rights and he's going to insulate the whole attic for me, which is very kind.'

'I... I don't understand,' Paschal said softly.

'Oh, don't you?' she asked. 'No? It's just I knew how worried you were about us, up there, in our big old house with a roof that might come in on top of us and...'

'Eh?'

'Well, I mean, that is why you contacted the health inspector's office, isn't it?' Esme had been biding her time to confront him and it was worth waiting for this moment just to enjoy the shocked disappointment in his voice.

'I never...'

'Oh, but you did, I know you did. And do you realise, it was probably the best thing you could have done, because it made me see sense.'

'Sense?' he said, and she knew he wasn't sure which way he should take that.

'Yes. You see, I'm not only keeping my guest house,

Paschal, I'm making sure that it's going to be in good hands long after I'm gone.'

'So you've dragged me out here tonight to tell me that you're not going to…'

She could hear the anger in his voice, like a child denied a toy that had never been his to begin with.

'Well, you could say that, but you could also say we've had a lovely night and you've had a chance to get to know Marta, the next owner of the Willows, as well as being able to put your mind at rest that the place is in good hands and in sound condition.'

'I…' He was fit to be tied, Esme could hear him, he wanted to shout and bang his fists probably, but they were just pulling into the Willows.

'So, now, we'll say goodnight.' Esme opened her door and waited for a second, while Marta ran round to help her safely into the house. 'And Paschal, now that you know the score, I won't be expecting any more surprise visits from the health inspectors, because it could be seen as harassment and I'm sure that Sergeant O'Mahony wouldn't want to think his old godmother was being upset by a *respectable* businessman, eh?'

The roar of his engine and squeal of his brakes as Esme and Marta made their way back up towards the veranda made her smile because she knew, now she'd finally set him straight, he wouldn't be annoying them any more.

'That was good,' Marta said, but then she stopped for a moment. Esme, what you said about the future of the Willows, I really don't think… I mean, I don't expect you to leave it to me… it's too much.'

'Oh, Marta, darling, it's exactly how things were always meant to be.' She laughed. 'Come on, let's have a nightcap and a good old chat about the exciting times ahead of us.'

And there were exciting times ahead, or at least, Esme knew, plenty more happy days, here at her little guest house by the sea.

Acknowledgements

This has been a wonderful book to write – and when I look back, I will believe I enjoyed every moment, but it wouldn't be the book it is today without the following.

Thank you to my publishers – Aria Fiction – Rachel Faulkner-Willcocks and the dream team that are Aria.

Thank you to Judith Murdoch, my agent.

Thank you to my family – for putting up with me – Tomás, Cristín, Roisín and Seán and especially James.

Thank you, Bernadine and David and Stephen, for the walks that provided welcome distractions!

And a special mention to Christine Cafferkey.

Dermot Barrett – for a lovely morning spent talking about willow trees – and Helen Falconer for making out the wood from the trees of a different sort.

About the Author

FAITH HOGAN lives in the west of Ireland with her husband, four children and a busy chocolate Labrador. She has an Hons Degree in English Literature and Psychology, has worked as a fashion model and in the intellectual disability and mental health sector. *The Guest House By The Sea* is her ninth novel.